GROWN MEN CRY OUT AT NIGHT

KARL WEGENER

KW

FJK-KW

GROWN MEN CRY OUT AT NIGHT

First Printing, 2022

ISBN: 979-8-88757-282-6 (Paperback)
ISBN: 979-8-88757-283-3 (Ebook)

To my wife, Jody. This book wouldn't have been possible without your love and support.

This book is also dedicated to the thousands of slave laborers who lost their lives while building the Valentin Bunker, and to those who survived to tell the story of their ordeal. Although most of your names may have been lost to history, we shall never forget your suffering and sacrifice.

CONTENTS

GLOSSARY OF TERMS AND CULTURAL REFERENCES

Abwehr	The German military intelligence organization.
Adjutant	A military officer who assists the commanding officer with administrative duties.
AG	Abbreviation for Adjutant General, the chief administrative officer within a military organization, similar to a director of human resources in the civilian world.
AWOL	Absent without leave or an unexcused absence in military parlance.
Battle of El Alemein	A battle fought near the western frontier of Egypt between 23 October and 4 November 1942, where the Axis army of Italy and Germany suffered a defeat by the British Eighth Army. The battle marked the turning point in the North African campaign of World War II.

Bierdeckel	The German word for beer coaster. This heavy paper coaster usually bears the logo of the local brewery and it is ubiquitous in all German pubs.
BOQ	Abbreviation for Bachelor Officer's Quarters, which housed single or unaccompanied officers.
CIC	Counter Intelligence Corp. An intelligence agency that operated within the United States Army.
CID	Abbreviation for the Criminal Investigative Division in the U.S. armed forces. CID agents operate similarly to plain clothes detectives in civilian police departments.
Coup de grace	The death blow, usually administered to end the suffering of a soldier mortally wounded in combat.
Croix de Guerre (1939-1945)	A French military decoration to honor men and women who fought against the Axis armies during World War 2.
Die Bremer Stadtmusikanten	The Bremen Town Musicians, a German fairy tale from the Brothers Grimm story.
G2	The military intelligence staff at the division level and above in the U.S. Army.

Gestapo	Abbreviation for Geheime Staatspolizei, the secret police organization of Nazi Germany.
Hauptsturmfurher	A Nazi Party paramilitary rank.
Humber Armored Car	A British light armored vehicle widely used during World War 2. More than 5.400 were manufactured during the war.
Kapo	A prisoner-trustee assigned by German SS troops to oversee forced labor in Nazi-run concentration and slave labor camps. Kapos also enforced camp rules and often meted out punishment. They were hated by other prisoners.
Kaserne	The German word for barracks that is also used when naming garrison locations for U.S. troops in Germany.
Kriegsmarine	The Germany navy from 1935 to 1945.
Landpolitzei	The term for German state police.
Leftenant	The British term for lieutenant, a junior military officer.
Liebchen	The German word for sweetheart. A term of affection.
Marineoberbauamt	The German term for a naval construction project office.

MI6	The British Secret Intelligence Service responsible for covert intelligence collection and operations overseas.
MP	Abbreviation for Military Police.
Oberleutnant	A German army officer rank that translates to senior lieutenant.
Oma	The German word for grandmother.
Opa	The German word for grandfather.
Ratline	A system of escape routes for Nazis and Fascists attempting to flee Europe after World War 2.
Recce or Recon	Reconnaissance. The term recce was first used in 1941 by the British. The Americans tended to use the word recon.
Reichsmark	The currency of Germany from 1924 to mid-1948 when it was replaced by the East German Mark in East Germany and the Deutsch Mark in West Germany.
Schwarzmarkt	The German word for black market.
SOE	Special Operations Executive, a clandestine intelligence service set up by Winston Churchill.
SOP	Standard Operating Procedure.

Spam	Canned meat products manufactured by the U.S. company Hormel.
Stevedore	A longshoreman or dock worker.
"Top"	U.S. Army slang for 1st Sergeant, the "top" sergeant in a company.
TWX	Pronounced Twix, TWX is an abbreviation for teletypewriter exchange. It also refers to the message sent via a teletype.
Verboten	The German word for forbidden.
Waffen SS	The combat arms branch of the Nazi Party's Schutzstaffel (SS) organization.
Webley MK IV-38	Webley MK IV-38 was a .38 caliber pistol used by British officers during World War II.
Wehrmacht	The German army during World War II.
XXX Corps	XXX Corps (pronounced 30 Corps or 30th Corps) was a major British fighting unit during World War II. XXX Corps saw action in North Africa, Sicily, Normandy, the Netherlands, and Northern Germany.

Chapter One

You wouldn't know it by looking at him, but the Pole was only twenty-five years old. Once a vibrant and robust young man, he had lost nearly a third of his body weight in the past six months. His hair, once blond and wavy, had fallen out in patches due to malnutrition, and what hair remained was shorn completely. His scalp was covered in scabs from scratching at the bites by the lice that infested the barracks where he now lived. The lice found a way to thrive in conditions where humans could barely survive.

"Steady, Pavel," he told one of his comrades on the construction crew. "Try to lift with your legs," he said as he rushed over to help the man lift a hundred-pound bag of concrete and carry it to the mixer, where water would be added, turning the dry mix into a slurry that workers would pour to create the walkways, ramps, walls, ceilings, and the other structures within the massive facility they were building.

"Pace yourself, Fyodor," he called out to another worker. "It's early, and we have a long night ahead of us. The work will always be there for us."

As the Pole continued to help mix the concrete, he looked up to see a young German woman enter the bay where he and his crew were working. She was carrying a large black ledger book and was accompanied by an enormous armed guard, a corporal, who looked like a giant standing next to the woman. She had arrived in the bay just as she did every week, and it was his responsibility as a crew commander to give her the report on the number of workers on duty. Tonight the total was seventeen, down three from the normal complement of twenty workers. Two had died during the night, their bodies worn down by the relentless work and the starvation diet. The third was too weak to make the evening formation, and the Pole feared he would be dead by morning. He was amazed the man had lasted as long as he had, since he was at least twice his own age.

"I'll be right back, Pavel," he said. "Just continue to mix, and I'll give you a hand when I return." The Pole dusted off his striped uniform, a futile gesture, as concrete dust managed to permeate every fiber of his uniform and every pore of his body. He straightened himself up and, with as much of a resolute manner as he could muster, he strode over to the platform where the woman was standing, waiting for him to give her the report.

"Good evening, Fraulein," he said with a smile. Every week it was the same, and it had become a game for the Pole. Could he show sufficient courtesy to the woman that would cause her to smile? Every week he tried, but she was not interested in playing his game. She simply stared, looking through him as if he were invisible.

"Number?" she asked curtly.

"Tonight we have only seventeen, Fraulein."

"No talking. It's forbidden," she replied, frowning as she jotted the number into the ledger book in her hands. *Seventeen is not a good number. There must always be twenty,* she thought. The corporal standing watch over her with his rifle at the ready in the port-arms position started to move toward the Pole to intercede, but the woman said, "It's all right, Corporal. It's fine," and the giant man stopped. She turned and started to walk away so she could continue with her duties. She took just two steps, and then something truly astonishing happened. The woman stopped, looked back over her shoulder at the Pole, and said, "And it's Frau, not Fraulein. I'm married, you see." And then she allowed herself to smile, ever so slightly.

Victory, the Pole thought! *I did it. I got her to look at me and see me!*

"Excuse me," he replied. "I hope you do not take offense."

"No, of course not," was her reply. "No offense taken."

Suddenly from the other side of the bay they heard a voice shout, "Halt!"

The two of them looked over to where the shout had come from and saw the Gestapo officer standing twenty feet away. He had observed the conversation between them.

"Stop that man. Hold him," the officer shouted, and two Kapos rushed over. They were prisoners themselves, but they received special privileges for enforcing the myriad rules governing the camp and the construction site.

"Hurry, you must leave. Get back to work," the woman said, fear rising in her voice.

The Pole turned to walk away but was immediately grabbed by the Kapos. *What more could they do to me*, he thought as the Gestapo officer approached. They twisted his arms behind his back, and he winced in pain, but as he stood in the arms of his captors to await his fate, a smile came over his face.

***

In battle, somebody always has to be first, and during the war that distinction more often than not fell to reconnaissance units, the advanced guard, the scouts. In the American Army, these units were organized into battalions. The British organized them into squadrons, but their function was the same. They were the troops that moved quickly in lightly armored vehicles and led the way to make first contact with the enemy.

At the mission briefing the night before, the leaders of a recce squadron from the British 3rd Infantry division were told it would be a cakewalk after the many weeks of heavy fighting they had experienced, but none of them believed that. They were told it was a simple, straightforward operation with a single objective. The squadron was to take and hold what the division's intelligence chief described as a large bunker facility located along the Weser River, just a few kilometers north of the village of Farge.

Intelligence didn't share what, if anything, they knew about the purpose and function of the facility, but they emphasized that it was a high-priority target and they wanted to take control of it as quickly as possible. Intelligence said the facility had been abandoned and there would likely be little to no resistance. That's what the intel types said anyway, but no officer or man in attendance believed that either.

The operation was part of an effort to mop up the last elements of resistance in and around Bremen Germany, a city which now lay in smoldering ruin about fifty kilometers to the south of the bunker. British troops were finally able to enter Bremen on April 26, 1945, after seven days of the heaviest fighting they had experienced as Montgomery's forces drove their way across Germany toward Kiel and Denmark. Today was April 27, and the war in Europe would soon be over, but it would not be over on this day.

The mission plan dictated that once the squadron secured the grounds surrounding the facility, they would wait until Royal Engineers cleared away any mines or booby traps left by the previous occupants. The squadron's infantry soldiers would then move inside the bunker itself to clear out any remaining Germans who might have decided to make a last stand. They were ordered to seize documents and equipment, gather any other tactical intelligence information they could find, take prisoners and watch over them until they could be processed and interrogated, and hold their positions at the facility until relieved by elements of the 20th Armored Infantry Brigade. The 20th would hold the facility until more intel types arrived to gnaw away on the carcass of the bunker until it was picked clean of its secrets.

The squadron consisted of 7 officers and 165 enlisted men, and together they headed out in the predawn darkness towards the target. They were light and not at 100 percent strength, but this was a cakewalk, or so they were told. But although they were at less than 100 percent strength, they still required more than thirty armored vehicles and lorries as they moved at high speed on a hard-surface road that ran along the Weser River just off to their left. The convoy eventually came to a fork in the road, where the squadron split into two groups. One section from the squadron remained on the river road, which continued in a northwesterly direction. This section would eventually take positions on the northern perimeter of the bunker. A narrow canal there led directly into the bunker and served as its northern boundary. The canal connected to the Weser River, which eventually fed into the North Sea, a distance of nearly one hundred kilometers to the north. The squadron section was to prevent anyone or anything from escaping to the north.

The remainder of the squadron took the fork to the right and continued on a loose-surface gravel road that ran to the northeast. It would eventually lead to the south side of the bunker and to what was believed to be its main vehicle entrance. Once in position, the squadron would have the bunker completely surrounded, and its attack could then commence.

Sunrise came quickly on that April morning in Northern Germany. The main body of the squadron was still about three kilometers away when vehicle drivers noticed a large structure on the horizon, arising out from the otherwise flat German plain and illuminated by the early-morning sunlight from the southeast. As they continued their approach, the structure appeared to grow larger and larger until it dominated the landscape. As instructed, the squadron radios and their operators maintained their silence, but inside each vehicle the same conversations took place, the same questions were asked, the same astonished expressions appeared.

"Do you see that?"

"What the hell is that?"

"Blimey, look at the size of that thing!"

And there were many more colorful variations.

As the lead column came to within a kilometer of the bunker, radio silence was broken. Radio sets came alive with the voice of the squadron commander, who said, "Advance guard, move into your positions."

Two Humber armored cars along with three light-armored vehicles and seven armored personnel carriers broke out of the convoy into a tactical formation and sped toward the main entrance. They stopped about one hundred meters from the front gate and waited. The bunker and surrounding grounds were surrounded by a five-meter-high fence topped with concertina wire. The large double gate at the entrance was open. A single rail line lay about fifty meters to the east of the main gate. A second double gate for the rail line was closed, and three rail vans sat inside the wire fence. Standing next to the bunker as they did, the rail vans looked like toys, mismatched and built to the wrong scale when compared to the bunker that towered above them. But they were real. The bunker was that big.

Once again the squadron radio network crackled, this time with the voice of the section leader from the attack squadron moving to the northern side of the facility.

"We're in position now, sir. We see no movement, everything is quiet."

The squadron commander's Humber pulled up alongside the lead vehicle in the advanced guard. The commander popped the turret hatch and poked his head up through the narrow opening. Prematurely gray hair belied the boyish features of the army major, who hailed from the Midlands, not far from Nottingham, and was in command that day. He was careful to expose as little of himself as possible. Recce squadron commanders made good targets of opportunity for enemy snipers. He grabbed the field glasses hanging around his neck, raised them, and scanned the entrance to the facility.

The hatch from the adjacent armored car popped open, and a young sergeant, who also happened to be from Nottingham, stuck out his head and called to the commander, "Bloody hell! What kind of place is this, sir?"

The bunker was indeed something to behold. From his vantage point, the commander judged it to be roughly one hundred meters wide, nearly thirty meters tall, and more than four hundred meters in its full length. He could make out what looked like landscaping near the edge of the structure, small shrubs, grass, and even a small shed-like building, undoubtedly placed there to confuse Allied pilots into thinking it was all a normal part of the local terrain.

"It appears to be a very large bunker, Sergeant. That is about all I know about it at this moment," was the commander's reply.

"Christ, I've never seen anything like it, sir."

"Indeed." He continued to peer through his glasses looking for movement, anything.

"Sergeant, would you kindly see if anyone is home? Give me four or five short bursts on the guard tower to our right. And then lay down suppression fire all across the front of the bunker from the defilade over there on the left of the main gate and toward what appears to be the entrance doors to the bunker." The commander then got on the radio to inform the squadron they were taking a few shots "across the bow" of the bunker, but he instructed the rest of the force to hold their fire until his order.

"Yes, sir! With pleasure, sir!" and the eager young sergeant slid down inside his vehicle. He opened fire with his Bren submachine guns from inside the turret, splintering the guard tower. He then laid down a steady stream of fire directed at the gate and the front of the bunker.

The commander observed from his hatch turret. Nothing. No reaction. The sergeant once again popped his head out.

"It seems that nobody is home, Sergeant." The commander then gave the order over the radio, "All units move forward and secure the perimeter. Hold your positions inside the perimeter until the Royal Engineers give us the 'all clear.'"

The commander continued to observe from the vehicle hatch. His men and vehicles quickly took up positions inside the bunker complex. As he gazed at the dark monolith, he thought back to when he first saw the Great Pyramids at Giza. He was just a young "leftenant" back then, serving in North Africa and facing battle for the first time on his first combat assignment. He was granted a few days leave in Cairo after the second battle of El Alemein and he felt lucky to be alive. As he gazed upon the Great Pyramids that day, he was left with a sense of awe, of wonderment. They were built with a profound purpose. But this! This was different.

The young sergeant called over one last time before moving his vehicle onto the bunker complex.

"What is this place, sir? What went on here?"

The commander looked at his sergeant and said, "They call this place Bunker Valentin, the Valentin Bunker. As for what went on here?" he said, returning his gaze to the black bunker that now had a name. "There was misery. And it was evil, Sergeant. Nothing but pure evil."

Chapter Two

If one color could describe Bremen, Germany, it would be gray, the same color that described every city in Germany in 1946. Clouds of gray dust billowed up, created by the massive amounts of demolition and construction work, detritus from moving the tons of debris caused by the Allied bombing during the war. It mixed with the salt air coming off the North Sea to create a gray-tinged fog that hung in the air for hours each day, then eventually floated down, covering streets, sidewalks, buildings, and vehicles with a coat of fine gray powder. Pedestrians who walked to work or to the shops and markets that reopened around the city kicked up more dust, which in turn covered their shoes and clothing. As pedestrians shuffled along the sidewalks and streets, the cuffs on men's trousers acted like brooms that continually swept the pavement until they became coated with dust that turned their original color to gray.

The end of war brought a persistent and steady cleanup and construction effort, fueled not only by a desire to move on and rebuild, but also by the German obsession with tidiness and orderliness. The sounds from hammers, pickaxes, and shovels could be heard nearly round the clock as construction crews, along with ordinary Germans all across the Allied-controlled portion of Germany, tore down the old and damaged structures to put up new ones. They worked tirelessly to repair roads, water mains and sewer lines. Although scores of workers carted off piles of debris every day in horse-drawn wagons, a mountain of rubble still remained. In Bremen alone, over sixty percent of the city's homes were destroyed, and a year after the war's end, streets were still blocked off, and many bridges over the Weser River that weren't destroyed were severely damaged and still impassable and unusable.

Before the war, Therese Weber could walk from her flat on the Hollerallee in the Altstadt district of town just north of the Weser River to her parents' house in about twenty minutes. They lived in the Neustadt district of Bremen, just on the other side of the river about a mile away as the crow flies. Before the war, it was a pleasant and easy stroll along tree-lined streets lined with brick and stone apartments and houses, leading to the Kaiser bridge across the river. Now, more than a year after the end of the war, the same walk would take her close to an hour. All of the disruption from demolition and reconstruction made Therese's once easy walk much longer, much more circuitous. Unable to cross the Weser at the Kaiser Bridge, which was heavily damaged during the war, she was now required to walk all the way down to the Stephani Bridge and backtrack to her parents' house, a journey that now totaled about three miles.

But at least three times a week, Theresa packed up a large pram, bundled her two children into it, and made the trek with them to visit with her parents. Her children loved spending time with their Oma and Opa, preferring them to their landlady, who looked after young Wilhelm, who was almost five, and Anna Karolina, who was not yet four, while Therese was at work.

Therese's flat, as she called it, was far from ideal, but she was better off than many Germans. About two-thirds of all houses and apartments were destroyed during the war. The apartment where she and her husband had lived before the war was among those destroyed. Therese and her children were left homeless, but with the help of family friends, she was fortunate to secure two small rooms in a large house where she lived with two other families. So their thrice-weekly visits to Oma and Opa gave them a chance to leave their cramped surroundings, where they lived with strangers in a building that was foreign to them, for a place that was familiar and welcoming.

The children's pram had been a gift from Therese's in-laws, the Webers, just before Anna Karolina was born in 1942. It was large even by German standards and even though the children were no longer infants, they still could sit comfortably inside. With its stained hardwood exterior, heavy foam cushions, rubber tires, and chromium-plated handles and trim, it was the kind of pram in which any German parent would have proudly paraded their child through the park on a Sunday afternoon. It was big, heavy, and solidly built. It was unmistakably German.

Her parents' house, which was built before the turn of the century, was damaged, but it was standing and habitable. Water was still running, the toilet still flushed, and electricity, subject to outages, was available. They could cook and prepare meals on her mother's wood-burning stove in the kitchen, although finding wood was definitely a problem, and obtaining enough food to eat given the military government's system for rationing food and control of its means of distribution was a constant challenge.

But Therese had a plan for all of that, a plan she hoped would ensure that her children would survive to see a better day. Therese Weber was a woman of action, a woman who meticulously planned out everything in her life, including her marriage to Hauptsturmfurher Wilhelm Weber, a childhood sweetheart who was an up-and-coming infantry officer serving in the 11th Infantry Division, Waffen SS. The last time Therese saw her husband was in October 1944 when he was able to secure a short leave home to visit and to celebrate their fifth wedding anniversary. Just three days after he returned to his unit, he would die, shot by partisans on the outskirts of Sarajevo at the Vrelo Bosna, the source of the Bosna River. Therese didn't have the luxury of time to grieve or to think about what might have been. Their lives, filled with such promise when she and Wilhelm married in 1939, were forever changed by the war. But now her choice was either to feel sorry for herself or to muster the strength and courage to do something about her circumstances. She had two young children, Wilhelm and Anna Karolina, and two elderly parents who needed her. They were all each other had. Her two brothers died in the war, one during the siege of Leningrad and the other at Kursk. Her sister, who also lost her husband, had been living in Berlin with her two children. Therese hadn't heard from her since early April 1945 when the Red Army laid siege to the city, eventually demolishing the last bastion of Nazism and extracting a dreadful toll on the city's last defenders and remaining inhabitants. Her many attempts to contact her sister had been unsuccessful, so she concluded that her sister and the children had perished. She could always hope that somehow they survived and would miraculously appear on her parents' doorstep, but their chances diminished with each passing day as the Red Army tightened its grip on Berlin and across the Soviet zone of occupation.

For Therese, there was no time to feel sorry for herself or her situation. There was only time for action, and she was determined to focus on what she felt was her duty as an army officer's wife, as a dutiful daughter to her parents, and as the mother to her children. "Hitler led us to ruin. We have to think of ourselves now," she would say, echoing the sentiments of millions of Germans.

She did not mind the extra time it took for her to complete her circuitous route because it always took her past shops that included a butcher, a dairy and green grocer, a bakery, several clothing stores, and specialty stores including a fabric shop, a jewelry store, and a furniture and upholstery business. The shops were up and running, their proprietors determined to rebuild and return to a life of prosperity through sheer force of will.

As Therese walked by the shops that drew her interest on one fine weekday afternoon, she stopped to look into the store windows, and as the various proprietors saw her, they would call out to her.

"Do you think it might rain today, Frau Weber?" was the common question asked by the local butcher, baker, fishmonger, or green grocer.

"Yes, I think there is a good chance if the conditions are right," she would reply.

Or they might ask, "Do you think it will be sunny and warm next weekend?"

"Yes, of course," would be her reply. "I believe the weather is finally turning for the better."

Therese didn't know much about forecasting the weather and didn't much care. In reality, these questions and her responses were part of an elaborate code that she had set up to communicate with her "customers." Therese's plan, which she had been carrying out for nearly nine months now, involved taking advantage of the lucrative black market that thrived in Bremen and throughout the rest of Germany. The code let her customers know when Therese had products available for them and, most importantly for her, whether or not they could afford to pay for them. If they exchanged chit-chat about the possibility of rain, that meant that Therese had alcohol and liquor for sale. If they inquired if the weather would be clear, cloudy, or windy, it meant they wanted to purchase tobacco products, usually American cigarettes with Lucky Strike and Chesterfield the preferred brands, although British Dunhills would do in a pinch.

Payment was never in cash, as the Reichsmark was virtually worthless, and nobody really wanted it. But there was a brisk market for items that could be turned into cash elsewhere. Gold watches, diamond rings, necklaces, earrings, and even furniture items would be exchanged for cigarettes and whiskey—the coin of the black market realm. The word on the street was that you could buy a house in Bremen for fifty cartons of cigarettes.

Therese's business partner in the whole scheme was an enterprising U.S. Army supply sergeant, a friendly, easygoing young man named Lanny Perdue, a staff sergeant from Baton Rouge, Louisiana, who spoke with a thick Cajun accent and managed the *Stars & Stripes* newsstand on Camp Grohn, the main U.S. military base in Bremen. Perdue took an immediate liking to Therese, who, even after giving birth to two children, was still young and very pretty. He had an affinity for young German women. Therese's best friend, Karla Jung, was Perdue's girlfriend, and she worked alongside him at the newsstand. It was Karla who arranged for Therese to meet Perdue and persuaded him to hire her. Therese's slender build, blonde hair, and blue eyes were enough for him to overlook the fact that she barely spoke a word of English when they first met. Nevertheless, he hired her to keep shelves stocked and to ring up the purchases from customers, who were mainly GIs and other Allied soldiers. Therese was hardworking and willing to learn. After a few months of Lanny's daily English lessons, Therese could cuss and throw GI slang around like a native.

"The eagle shits every Friday," she would say in her heavily accented English, while ringing up purchases from the line of GIs eager to spend their money. Eagle day meant it was payday, and it was always the busiest day of the week at the newsstand.

"I see you boys are flush with pocket lettuce today," she would say to no one in particular in the queue of customers, referring to the wads of army script that GIs used for currency. Therese's mastery of army slang always made the GIs laugh, and Perdue got a kick out of it, too. Therese had no shortage of admirers among the newsstand's patrons, which included several high-ranking officers. But she put her foot down whenever a soldier, regardless of rank or position, tried to ask her out or get too close to her. She was all business when it came to her job, and she wasn't interested in words of affection, professions of love, romance, or lifelong happiness. Propositions of nights out on the town or one-night stands were strictly *verboten* in her book. She put her foot down immediately and wasn't afraid to tell a soldier just where he could put his proposal. Perdue was also there to help keep anyone from getting out of line and was happy to do so. He kept a close eye on what he thought were "his girls."

It was an especially busy Friday, and after the newsstand had closed, Perdue sat at his desk, struggling to tally up the daily receipts and balance the newsstand's cash ledger. Arithmetic wasn't a strength for Perdue, who never attended school beyond the eighth grade. As she went about her work restocking shelves and tidying up the store, Therese noticed Perdue cursing under his breath after erasing an item in the ledger, writing a new entry into the column, only to erase it once again after he failed to balance the accounts. Therese casually mentioned that she could manage the store's books, too.

"I can do that," she said after watching him write and then erase a ledger entry more than a half dozen times.

"You can do what? What are you talking about? How would you know what to do?"

"I trained as a bookkeeper. That's what I did. It was my job. I managed the books for a very important construction company during the war." She went on to explain that she was an office manager for a construction project office managed by the Marineoberbauamt Bremen and that she was also the special assistant to the project manager. "I kept track of all of the money that came in and all of the expenses, I managed the construction materials inventory, ordered supplies, paid the bills, took care of the payroll, I managed it all. I even kept track of . . .," and she suddenly stopped herself mid-sentence.

"Kept track of what?" asked Perdue. "What else did you keep track of?"

"Never mind that," she replied, hastily changing the subject back to the task at hand. "Here, let me see that," she said, and she took the ledger from Perdue, looked it over, and went on to show him first-hand what she meant by quickly counting up the day's receipts and expertly tallying them into the ledger and balancing the books. Perdue was thrilled that he'd be able to pass off this work to Therese.

"I'll be damned. Hell, why am I wasting my time doing this? From now on, it'll be your job to count up all the money and balance the books. You sure you can handle this? I can't afford to have you make mistakes. The captain will be all over my ass if you make mistakes."

"I can do this. Don't worry," she replied.

"And you can't tell anybody about this. If anyone asks you who does the books, you say it's me, right?

"Yes, I understand. You're the boss. You manage the books."

"All right, then. Let's give it a try. But no funny business. If you have any problems with this, you come to me, understand?

"Yes, completely."

The next morning when Therese arrived for work at the newsstand, Perdue was already there. As she set about to get the store ready to open, he motioned for her to come over to the counter where he stood behind the cash register and said to her directly, "I have a business proposition for you."

"What business? What kind of business?" she asked skeptically, jumping to the wrong conclusion. Perdue had never made advances toward her before, and she wouldn't stand for it now.

"Calm down, just calm yourself down," he said, sensing that she was taking his offer the wrong way. "It's a chance for you to make a little money on the side," he added, realizing immediately that he was making it worse. "What do you call it? *Schwarzmarkt*! The black market. You call it *Schwarzmarkt*, right?"

"*Ja,*! *Es heißt Schwarzmarkt*. That's what it is called," she said, switching to English.

Perdue went on to explain how a little black market activity on the side would be helpful for both of them. He would purchase liquor, tobacco, groceries, and other hot commodities from the post exchange and commissary. She would exchange them for high-end commodities that he would sell to his buddies. They would split the profits from the sale of the goods, and she could use her share to purchase food, clothing, or anything else she or her family needed. Perdue told her that if she gave him money from her cut, he would even buy her hard-to-find items like sugar, butter, or salt from the base commissary.

"It's not like we're the only ones doing it. Everybody's getting rich, and I'm over here, away from home and my family. I have to think about my future, and so do you. I don't see anything wrong with it. I won't be here forever. I only have another eighteen months and then I'm out of here. After I leave, you'll be in a better place, too. It will help you make sure your kids have something to eat, get a decent meal, have nice things. You know what I mean? So waddya say?"

"Does Karla know about this?"

"You bet I know. I've been working with Lanny since I started here." Therese whirled around as her best friend from childhood emerged from the back room of the newsstand. Karla approached Therese with a big smile on her face, extended her arms, and enveloped Therese with a warm hug.

"She's been working with me from day one," Perdue said laughing. "She's been beggin' me to get you involved. Every day, every night she asks, 'Have you told her yet? Have you asked her yet?' Well, now I told you, and now I'm asking."

Therese stared at Perdue, trying to weigh her options as she considered what to do next. He was right. Everyone was involved in some sort of black market activity because it was the only way ordinary Germans could survive. She had bartered for food and other necessary items before, but this was different. It was not the kind of activity she would have considered before the war. But these were extraordinary times, and the rules she lived by in the past no longer applied. Even her best friend in life was involved, so in the end, it was an easy decision for her to make.

"All right, I'll do it. Just tell me what you want me to do."

Perdue explained how and when he would provide the goods that she could exchange. Perdue was especially keen to exchange items for gold and jewelry, but just last week he sold a handmade mahogany dining set to an artillery officer. He figured that whatever he could get his hands on, he could find a way to sell it.

He and Karla had already decided that Therese would have her own territory, the Neustadt section of Bremen where her parents lived. She knew the neighborhood; she was known there, had a reason to be there, and it would provide perfect cover for her. Therese was sold on the idea. The three of them laughed about what they would do with all of their riches.

"Maybe we'll all go to America and drive around in a big Cadillac," Therese joked.

"I'll be driving a Packard," Karla shrieked.

"When I get back, I'm going to get a big-ass Buick. A convertible," Perdue said, joining in the fun. *God, this is the best duty ever. I'm sure gonna miss this when it's all over,* he thought.

It was Karla who suggested that the group needed a name.

"What shall we call ourselves?" she joked. "We need to have a name for our gang."

Die Bremer Stadtmusikanten, Therese immediately replied. "The Bremen Town Musicians," she said switching back into English. "It's from the Brothers Grimm story."

Perdue didn't get the reference. Karla and Therese just stared at each other for a moment, shaking almost hysterically until they couldn't hold it any longer and burst into howls of laughter.

"But there are only three of us," Karla said, "Who's the fourth animal?

"That's okay, we don't need the ass!" Therese said referring to the donkey, who along with a dog, cat, and rooster, made up the four animals in the Grimm Brothers story.

"Just as long as we have the cock," said Karla, laughing at Perdue.

"Huh, what? What are you two carrying on about?" Perdue still didn't get it.

"It's okay, *Liebchen,* I'll tell you tonight," Karla said as she and Therese continued to giggle and laugh like schoolgirls, something they hadn't been able to do in a very long time.

The Bremen Town Musicians were now in business. Therese was, after all, a woman of action.

Chapter Three

It was shortly after 10:00 on an unseasonably warm Tuesday morning in early April 1946 when James Banbury sat across from the desk of U.S. Army Colonel Edward Richardson, the G2 or chief intelligence officer for the United States Forces, European Theater. Although he wore the uniform of a British Army major, Banbury was, in fact, a member of Britain's Secret Intelligence Service—Military Intelligence Section Six, to be precise, commonly known as MI6.

Banbury sat patiently as Richardson quickly read through a thick sheaf of papers in the classified personnel file he had in front of him. Banbury irritably flicked off a small piece of lint from the sleeve of his jacket. A fastidious man with an aristocratic bearing, he took great pride in wearing his uniform and insisted that everyone in his charge do the same. He sat across from Richardson with a ramrod-stiff posture, striving to appear as tall as possible and maximize his full height of five feet seven inches and not an inch less. He took a moment to remove his wire-rimmed spectacles, noticing a small smudge on the right lens. *Must have inadvertently touched it*, he thought as he wiped the lens clean with the perfectly folded and lightly starched handkerchief that he always kept in his trouser pocket. His service cap rested neatly in his lap, and not a single strand of his jet-black hair, which he combed straight back, was out of place. That would have been out of character for him.

Banbury and Richardson were a study in opposites. Banbury was neat and immaculate. The only thing neat about Richardson was his close-cropped hair. Banbury was thin and reedy, with the build of a long-distance runner. Richardson, on the other hand, was a mountain of a man, resembling an overstuffed, rumpled sofa. He was six feet tall and weighed in at close to three hundred pounds. Richardson's uniform was constantly wrinkled, the buttons of his shirt and jacket strained to contain his girth, his tie was always loose, and the top button of his shirt was always undone at the collar, in contrast to Banbury's neatly pressed uniform, buttoned-up appearance, and perfectly formed Windsor knot.

Neither of them cared very much for the other, but they could be mutually tolerant in small doses. None of that mattered today, however. Banbury knew he had to put aside any differences. He needed to achieve a meeting of the minds with Richardson, and his visit would not be considered successful if it ended in anything less than complete agreement.

Banbury, who served as the British intelligence liaison officer to the Americans, was present that day to make a polite request of Richardson—a "request" in quotes—because the decision had already been made. Richardson was only being consulted on the assumption that he would abide by the decision, or the "request," as long as he could be made to feel that he actually had a say in the matter.

The file that Richardson intensely scrutinized this morning documented the wartime service record of Ludmilla Haas, aka Luba Haas, aka Felicja Nowak, aka more than a half-dozen other cover and code names given to her, a woman purported to be thirty-five, born in the former German city of Danzig, a city now returned to Poland and renamed Gdansk.

Haas, whose father was ethnic German and mother a Polish Jew, was an agent of the SOE, the Special Operations Executive, a clandestine intelligence service set up by Winston Churchill with the job to, among other things, "set fire to the continent." Haas was one of the SOE's most successful agents, man or woman. Just after the German invasion in 1939, she was infiltrated into Poland, where she established and operated pro-British and Allied information and propaganda networks. She went from there to distribute money, supplies, and arms to members of the Polish resistance. She also collected and reported vital intelligence on German troop strength, their composition, movement, and, most importantly, their plans, intentions, and what they did after their plans went awry, as military plans usually do. She was able to escape from Poland after the Germans crushed the Polish uprising, and in the late summer of 1944 she parachuted into France, where she helped to orchestrate a campaign of sabotage, destruction, and terror on the retreating German army as American, British, French, and other Allied forces closed in from the West as the Soviet Red Army advanced from the East. For her efforts, the French awarded her the Croix de Guerre, and the British made her an Officer of the Order of the British Empire, at the time a rare recognition for a man, let alone a woman. Now, it seemed, she was at a crossroads in her life and career.

Richardson slowly closed the file and looked at a letter of introduction that outlined the details of the "request." General Dwight D. Eisenhower, who after the war took over as the chief of staff of the army, signed the "request" himself. While Eisenhower hedged a bit, stating in his letter that Colonel Richardson was the final authority on the matter, he strongly suggested that every effort be made to accommodate the "request," which was to assign Haas to the U.S. Army Counterintelligence Corps Detachment in Bremen, Germany. Luba Haas clearly had friends in high places.

"She's obviously a very impressive woman, with an incredible record of service. But what am I supposed to do with her?"

"Consider it a loan, or a gift," said Banbury. "You're terribly short-handed, and she will be able to pitch in and help. She speaks at least five languages and has more field experience than any one you have. Um, no offense, of course," he said, quickly backtracking. "That was not meant as a criticism of your men, you understand."

"Of course. No offense taken," Richardson replied with more than a bit of sarcasm, working hard to remain diplomatic. He sat in silence for a few minutes, weighing his options as he mulled over the letter and its implications.

"I suppose she comes with a wireless operator so she can report back to y'all on what goes on here." Although he was educated at Harvard and spent his entire adult life and pre-war career as a banker in Boston, the languid drawl from the Tidewater region of Virginia that revealed his true roots always crept back into Richardson's speech when he became flustered or angry.

"Now that would be brilliant! I wish I had thought of it," Banbury cheerily said with a smile, making a sincere but inappropriate and ill-advised attempt at humor.

Richardson wasn't laughing. It wasn't funny at all, but then he fully realized the situation he was in. Eisenhower's letter gave him a little wiggle room, but not much. He shook his head in resignation and hoped he wasn't taking on someone else's problems. He had enough of his own to deal with.

"You're actually doing us an enormous favor," Banbury said, continuing his effort to smooth over the situation with Richardson. "This is a genuine act of cooperation, it's all in the spirit of the special relationship between our two nations and our two organizations. She wants to be in an operational role, and we just don't have anything for her. We can't send her back to Poland, she's too well known. The Russians have already tried to kill her twice, and she wouldn't sit well with the new Polish regime either. She is certainly not a communist and has no use for them."

He waited for a response from Richardson, and when none came, he continued, "Look, I've known her for years. We worked together during her time in Poland and France, and frankly, she's just not cut out for a desk job."

"It's soul crushing for her," he added. "As you read in her file, her husband was tracked to the Farge concentration camp outside of Bremen. That was the camp that provided the workers for the bunker complex. I have another file here that summarizes everything we've uncovered about the bunker facility and the camps that supported it," he said as he handed over another large binder marked "Most Secret" at the top and bottom of its cover.

"Both facilities are now within your area, the Bremen Enclave. We've passed on this file to you with the hope that you'll be able to continue where we left off. Thousands of people died building this bunker, and the people responsible must be held accountable. We're also looking for something else. We believe that certain Gestapo officers who have yet to be captured can identify the individual who compromised our agent networks in Poland. We have some ideas on that subject, and they are contained in the documents I've passed over to you. Haas can definitely help your men quickly come up to speed."

Banbury paused for a moment as Richardson picked up the file and gauged its heft. The secret binder was at least four inches thick.

"It's a little late for that, isn't it?" said Richardson. "I mean, the Russians are clearly in control of Poland now."

Banbury sat without responding.

"What do you have going on in Poland? You still have active cells there, don't you? I'm not surprised, of course."

"I cannot comment on that specifically, Colonel, but I am authorized to brief you on our program if you agree to this request. I'll brief you and your team fully. We're prepared to read you into the program and cooperate fully with you," he stated somberly, hoping Richardson appreciated the significance of his offer.

"At any rate," Banbury continued, "we have several conflicting reports about Haas's husband. We know he was forced to work at the bunker, and we also have a report from a supposed eyewitness that says he was pushed onto a rail van filled with Russian and Polish POWs at the Farge camp. The fact is, we don't know what happened to him. Or any of the other prisoners, for that matter. The camp guards were naval infantry, with a smattering of SS and Gestapo mixed in. They were fleeing a sinking ship, so to speak, and were trying to make their escape and remove any evidence as to what transpired there. The supposed sighting was just days before XXX Corps liberated the facility and the city of Bremen.

"Simply put, Mrs. Haas wants to find him, or at least find out what happened to him, and I think—we think—she deserves some special consideration," Banbury said, choosing his words carefully, "given her extraordinary service during the war. We hope you see it that way too. She is a bit of a fish out of water now. She's just not suited for life in a headquarters environment, it's too restrictive for her . . ., but she really will be an asset to your men. And of course, there is another reason, and while it carries some risk, it also represents a considerable up-side, if you agree to the request, of course."

Then Banbury fell silent. He had nothing more to add and hoped that he had made his case. If he hadn't, he still could pull enough strings to make it all happen, but he hoped it wouldn't have to come to that.

Richardson reflected on Banbury's words and Eisenhower's letter outlining the "request." This must be one special woman, he thought, and wondered where the true soldiers and warriors were supposed to go when a war ended, when they no longer had a place or purpose.

"I know a lot of people like that," he replied. "They're wired differently from most people. And after what they did in the war, I'm not sure they'll ever be the same. Oh, what the hell! I think we can find a spot for her with us in Bremen. We'll help you find whoever compromised your operations, but I want all of the details. If you expect us to take on this assignment, you can't hold anything back, Understand? Every last detail," Richardson said. "I want to make sure my man there will be okay with it."

"Thank you very much, Colonel," Banbury replied. "On behalf of British intelligence, I can tell you that we truly appreciate it. Bloody hell, I am personally very grateful. Mrs. Haas," and once again he stopped himself midsentence. He drew in a deep breath to regain his composure. "On the plus side, it won't cost you anything. She'll continue to remain on our payroll. You just need to find a place for her to sit."

"What about accommodations? Where will she live? Eat?"

"We have already arranged housing at a local hotel—the Hotel Zur Post, I believe it is called. I understand your men have already set up their field office there. She can take her meals at the hotel as well. We've arranged for a subsistence allowance for her, so there is no need for her to dine with your men, even though she loves being one of the boys. She . . .," he paused for a moment to carefully select his words once again, "really isn't suited for headquarters work. I cannot emphasize that enough. She belongs in the field, with the other field types."

"I get it. All right, I just want to run it by my man and get his buy-in."

"Very thoughtful and democratic of you," Banbury said cheerfully.

"Consider it to be in the spirit of cooperation and our special relationship," Richardson countered.

"Fair enough," Banbury said with a wry smile. "Lehman is his name, right? What if he says no?"

Richardson glared at Banbury, but he was impressed that he knew Lehman's name and wondered what else he knew. Lehman had just been reassigned to Bremen less than three months ago.

"Then I'll give him a direct order, he'll salute, and he'll do it. He'll say yes, I guarantee it," Richardson replied, satisfied with his answer. "Now, tell me the real reason you're here."

Chapter Four

Casper Lehman couldn't remember the last time he had had a decent night's sleep. Every night it was the same. Thoughts and visions would swirl in his head as he slept, visions ranging from the mundane to the horrible until they overwhelmed him, and he would cry out with a piercing scream, scaring the bejesus out of anyone who might be nearby. Eventually he would awaken, bathed in a pool of sweat, gasping for air. Loud noises also startled him, causing him to duck and sometimes dive for cover. He had a perpetually upset stomach, for which the doctors prescribed some terrible-tasting milky liquid, and then there were the migraines that started in the back of his neck and head and moved all the way across the top of his scalp, blinding him and causing him to retreat into the darkness where the dream cycle would begin once again. The pills the doctors prescribed didn't help this condition, and he was a mess.

Lehman had been in it since the beginning. When Germany declared war on America in December 1941, he rushed to sign up and fight. An immigrant himself, his family had left Germany just before the Great War and came to America. His father, mother, three older sisters, and young Lehman eventually made their way to Louisville, Kentucky, where they lived in the Germantown section. His father, through hard work, would build a successful landscape architecture business, but the work eventually killed him. He died when Lehman was just ten years old. Lehman's mother died when he was fifteen, and he was left to be raised by his oldest sister, Rose, who along with her husband took over the family business.

Lehman grew up speaking German. His father's family came from the Bremen area and Lehman still had family there. His mother was one of the Volga Germans—she grew up on a farm outside of Saratov Russia and spoke both German and Russian. Lehman picked up that language from her. He had a natural gift for language, learned to speak French fluently in college, and eventually worked his way to a law degree at the University of Louisville.

The army had been tipped off to Lehman's linguistic gifts by a former classmate of his, a man of dubious character, but who came from an old Kentucky family of influence. Lehman jokingly referred to his friend as "Number One," and because of this friendship, Lehman was immediately recruited for the counterintelligence corps.

His law degree didn't hurt either. The early days of Army counterintelligence were dominated by former cops, lawyers, and judges. Lehman became one of the "Ritchie Boys," a group of soldiers named after a secret military base in western Maryland, Camp Ritchie, where they were trained in the darker arts of combat. They learned the techniques of combat interrogation, intelligence collection and analysis, counterintelligence, agent handling and operations, hand-to-hand combat—all the tradecraft necessary to wage a war of subterfuge and deception. All told, there would be some 19,000 of them, and the Ritchie Boys, about a quarter of them German Jews who escaped the rise of Hitler in the late 1920s and early '30s, would comprise an army within an army. They would go on to serve during the war in the U.S. Army Counterintelligence Corps, the CIC.

Lehman was among the first American troops to set foot in Northern Africa, and then he went on to Sicily and Italy. He landed in Normandy at Utah beach in the second wave, serving with the 45th Infantry Division as they made their final push across France and into Germany. He thought he had been through it all and seen every depravity that could be inflicted by man until he was among the first to set foot in the concentration camps at Landsberg and Dachau. That is where he experienced more sights he would never be able to un-see, memories he would never be able to forget.

At the end of the war, when given the chance to demobilize with the rest of his men, he chose to stay on. He could have gone home but decided to remain in Germany after his wife decided at some point during the more than four years he was away fighting that it would be a good time to upgrade her choice of a husband to someone with a closer proximity. He didn't know what he wanted to do or where he wanted to be, so he figured that staying in Germany was as good a place as any to figure that out. He was, after all, born in Germany.

Lehman's friends always called him "Cap," a nickname his sister Rose gave him, and it stuck. The men in the unit he led called him Cap, too. Cap was now a captain, having been recently promoted, and he was the CO of the 323rdCounterintelligence Corps Detachment, a unit that consisted of only thirteen men, nine military personnel and four War Department civilians. Except for Lehman and his first sergeant, Walt Lefkowicz, the rest of his men were on their first deployment overseas, they were all new, inexperienced in how to do their jobs and largely clueless as to what was expected of them. Some of them were too young to have fought in the war when America first joined it, others spent their time stateside, but it had been over a year since the war in Europe ended, and they were all eager to prove themselves. Lehman and his men were now part of an army of occupation, adjusting to the new role and new rules that came about from being the conqueror. Sometimes those rules were being made up as they merrily went along.

This morning was like most mornings, and as Lehman fought to wake himself from his latest nightly episode, he felt huge hands grabbing him firmly by his shoulders, shaking him, and a voice yelling, "Cap! Cap! Wake up!" Lehman forced his eyes to open wide, looked up, and saw Lefkowicz standing over him shouting, "Wake up, Cap! Come on. You're dreaming again. Wake up, dammit!"

Lehman lifted his arms to shield his eyes from the bright glare of the room's overhead lights. He was finally able to take a deep breath and slowly exhale with a long sigh. He looked at the large clock on the wall across the room and saw it was now 0532 hours. Time to get up anyway, he figured.

"You okay, Cap?" Lefkowicz asked with a concerned but "here we go again" look on his face.

"Yeah, yeah, I'm okay, I'm fine."

Lefkowicz slowly released his grip, waiting until he was sure that Lehman had totally awakened before completely letting him go. This wasn't the first time he had come to Lehman's side during the night. They had been through a lot together, but these dreams, nightmares, or whatever that Lehman was experiencing always scared the crap out of him, and he wasn't one to scare easily.

He and Lehman had known each other since before the war. They met in New York City, where Lefkowicz was one of the first Jewish cops to walk a beat for the NYPD. Like Lehman, Lefkowicz was an immigrant; he came to America as a teenager with his family from Wroclaw, Poland. The two met at the counter in a coffee shop in lower Manhattan, where they struck up a conversation that started with "Can you pass the ketchup?" They got together once or twice a week for breakfast and eventually wound up working together. Lehman convinced Lefkowicz that he could put his police skills to better use working for the American National Life & Casualty Insurance Company, where Lehman ran the fraud division. He'd certainly make more money. Lefkowicz became Lehman's lead investigator, using his contacts at the NYPD who supplied him with information that would help them bust a host of colorful characters, including thieves who filed fake stolen property claims, arsonists, and other miscreants who attempted to defraud "The Company," as it was known by those who worked there.

When the war broke out, Lehman and Lefkowicz decided to enlist together. They trained at Camp Ritchie together, they fought, connived, and out-thought captured SS officers and hundreds of POWs they interrogated together. Once, during an interrogation, Lehman donned a makeshift Red Army uniform and posed as a Russian colonel while Lefkowicz interrogated a stubborn SS officer, telling him that if he didn't give them the information he wanted, he'd gladly turn him over to the Russians, pointing to Lehman. Lehman proceeded to berate the officer in perfect Russian, then in German, saying that unless he talked, he'd spend whatever days he had left doing hard labor in a gulag in Siberia and be lost forever.

"You think you Germans are the only ones who know how to work people to death? We'll teach you things in Siberia you could never imagine, and when they are finished with you, they'll bury your rotting corpse in the tundra for eternity. Nobody will ever know what happened to you. You'll simply disappear, forever," Lehman told the terrified officer.

They got the information and then some. The shaken officer told Lehman and Lefkowicz everything they wanted to know, and as a reward, he was shipped off with his tail between his legs like a beaten dog to Camp Rockfield, a German POW camp located near the appropriately named town of Germantown, Wisconsin, a far cry from Vladivostok.

Lehman and Lefkowicz bonded through the sum of their experiences together. As unlikely as it might seem, two immigrants—a Polish Jew from the Bronx and a German and lapsed Catholic from Louisville—became the best of friends, the best friend either of them had ever had.

Coming out of his dream, Lehman was able to prop himself up on the bunk, shook his head, and squinted. He fumbled around looking for his glasses—he couldn't see a thing without them—and eventually found them on the table next to the bunk, put them on, and eventually the room came into focus. He was in the small anteroom next to the detachment duty office where he and Lefkowicz were pulling the all-night watch. Even though their rank and position allowed both of them to skip such duty, they always took their turn. That was the way they had been doing it since they shipped out together, that was the way they had run every CIC unit, and that was the way they would continue to do it until someone told them they had to do it differently.

"What's happening? Did anything come in overnight? Anything important?" Lehman asked, referring to the constant flow of intelligence reports funneled to the unit from headquarters. He swung his legs off the bunk and sat upright, hands on his knees, and slowly rose to stand. He was stiff from a restless few hours of sleep. His uniform was rumpled, and he needed a shave.

"Just the usual," Lefkowicz replied. "The MPs and Landpolitzei arrested a German national trying to exchange black market cigarettes and booze. It was a woman, and they were able to arrest her because of the tip we gave CID. So chalk one up for us. They picked her up late yesterday afternoon, and after CID is done with her, we'll get a crack. Other than that, it's been quiet. There is a train arriving from Helmstedt this morning at 09:30 with 119 people on board including 38 children. Mostly Germans from the East, a few ex-POWs, and there also are supposed to be 23 Poles on board. There are a handful that might be from Lithuania, but we'll have to see when they arrive."

Lehman stood silently, nervously tugging on his left ear, taking in all of the information and forcing himself to wake up. He grabbed the cigarette case from his shirt pocket and looked down at it before opening it. It was gold and had his initials engraved on the outside, a gift from his sister—a graduation present when he became the first person ever in his family to graduate from university. He ran his fingers over his initials, feeling them underneath his fingertips. Finally, he flipped the case open and pulled a cigarette out and put it between his lips. He could taste the bitterness from the tobacco, even without lighting it. But Lehman couldn't see without his glasses, and he couldn't think without lighting up, at least not at this time of day, and he spent the next several minutes fumbling in his trousers looking for his lighter. He also could never remember where he put it, even though he always said to himself, *always put it in your right trouser pocket. That's right. That's where it is.*

His search finally successful, he held his familiar lighter in his hand and turned it over nervously, repeatedly flicking open the top and then shutting it, over and over and over. As he played with the lighter, he flashed back to the moment when it came into his possession.

It was in December 1944, and he had just walked into the division command post near a tiny Belgian town called Bastogne. He was there to brief the commander about some new and disturbing information he and his men had acquired during several POW interrogations. It seemed that the Germans planned to masquerade as GIs in an attempt to infiltrate American lines, and that it was part of a major attack they had planned to launch. Now Lehman had to make sure the division and all of 12th Army prepared for the German attack, which could come any day now.

Lehman often could be found in the Division CP. He was always there briefing the commanding general—or the "old man," as he was called—on the latest intel he and his men had produced. Lehman was a regular fixture there. He knew all of the officers and enlisted men who were assigned there. They were good guys mostly. They were grateful to be assigned to a division command post located miles from the actual front. Anything could happen, of course, but at least none of the headquarters staff was serving on the front lines.

"The old man is running late, Cap," the duty officer named Hutchinson said without even looking up. He was hunched over a typewriter, slowly pecking out a report of some sort. Headquarters staff loved reports.

"How late, Hutch? What I have for him can't wait."

"He should be here in a few minutes. He's with the adjutant going over the replacement personnel reports, or something like that."

"All right, I guess I'll have to wait," Lehman replied as he pulled a cigarette out. "You got a light?"

Hutchinson looked up at Lehman and laughed, "You're always bumming a light. Here, take mine," he said, reaching down into his right trouser pocket for a lighter that he handed over to Lehman. "Here you go. Just keep it."

"Keep it? Are you sure? You don't want it? Aren't you going to need it?"

"Nah, you keep it. I'm trying to quit anyway," he said with a laugh. "If the Krauts don't kill me, cigarettes will. Besides, the old man doesn't like us smoking inside the CP anyway."

Lehman took the lighter and looked at it. It was brand new. "All right, as long as you're sure. Thanks, Hutch. I'll take good care of it. I'll just step outside and grab a quick smoke while I wait for the general."

"You're welcome. I'll give you a shout out when the old man gets back."

Lehman stepped out of the CP tent, and when he struck the lighter, its chimney lit up like a Christmas candle. *Hmm, Hutch must have just filled this up with oil,* he thought. *Good man.*

As he stood outside, he saw the mess tent about fifty yards away and decided to see if he could grab a cup of coffee to go with his cigarette. He began to slowly jog over to the mess and was not more than ten feet from its entrance when he heard the unmistakable shriek of incoming artillery. He immediately hit the ground, and that's when the first shell hit.

All hell broke loose as artillery rained down on the division headquarters encampment. Men rushed out of the mess tent and dove into pre-dug foxholes that were lined with sandbags, but they offered little protection against the incoming shells. Lehman looked up to find better cover, and to his horror saw a smoldering hole where the division command post had stood. Hutchinson and anyone else inside the tent would have been immediately vaporized by the explosion that came from a direct hit.

Now, Lehman once again looked down at the lighter in his hand. It was a Zippo with black crackle finish. Most of the finish had been worn off from use during the two-plus years Lehman possessed the lighter, the silver undercoating now visible. As he looked at it, he felt the pain of survivor's guilt. Hutchinson had gifted the lighter to him just minutes before he would be blown to bits. But Lehman also thought the lighter was a good luck charm. Now, every time he held the lighter, every time he used it, he felt lucky. He felt lucky that he decided to grab a smoke that day in 1944 and that he didn't linger to talk to Hutchinson. He felt especially lucky that he had stepped out of the division CP near the small village of Bastogne on the morning of December 16, 1944, the day that marked the start of the last major German ground offensive of the war, an offensive that would later be known as the Battle of the Bulge. He struck the Zippo once again, and its chimney flared up just like a candle on Christmas morning. *It still works like a charm. A good luck charm*, he thought. He lit the cigarette that dangled from his mouth.

"Have you assigned a team for the screening?" he asked Lefkowicz while taking a long drag off his cigarette, then exhaling and watching the blue smoke curled up toward the ceiling.

"No, I wanted to talk to you about it first."

"Okay. Then let's have Kiefer and Hodak do the screening. Hodak is our best Polish linguist—after you, of course," Lehman said with a smile. "You and I can take turns monitoring the sessions, from our fancy new room. If they identify anyone of interest, we can do a more detailed debriefing. We'll see if those four civilian geniuses that we got can actually do their job. What about IDs and ration cards? Who do we have for that?"

"We can assign the two clerks for that," Lefkowicz replied. "What are their names, Mahler and Wojtas? With the four of them together, they should be able to process the whole lot by midday, assuming the train arrives on time. We'll have a platoon of MPs there to help us keep the lines moving forward and keep everybody nice and orderly. I think it might be a good idea to see if we can get some chow set up for the people, too. God only knows the last time they might have been fed. People are more cooperative on a full stomach."

"Good idea," Lehman said. "Bread, soup, give them something hot."

"I'll take care of it."

Neither man had a chance to say anything else before the relative quiet of the morning was broken by the shrill ring from the phone on the duty desk. The phone was German and rang twice when calls came in, different from what Lehman was used to in the States, and it always startled and annoyed him.

Lefkowicz was closest to the desk, so he reached over, picked up the receiver, and answered, "323d CIC Detachment, First Sergeant Lefkowicz, sir."

He listened for a few seconds and then motioned for Lehman to come over to the phone.

"Yessir, he's right here." He handed the phone to Lehman, covering the mouthpiece with his hand, and said, "It's the G2, Colonel Richardson, and he wants to speak with you."

What the hell? Lehman thought as he took the phone. "This is Captain Lehman, sir."

"Cap, it's Ed Richardson." His voice crackled over the line. The connection was poor, but Lehman recognized Richardson's voice for it was Richardson himself who assigned Lehman to Bremen.

"I know it's early, but I'm glad I caught you. I'm getting ready to hop on a plane to Bremen later today at around 1200 hours. I want to visit you and see how you are doing. There's also something I need to talk to you about, and I want to do it in person. I have new orders for you, a special assignment. Can you clear whatever you were doing today and arrange for transportation to your office? We should arrive not later than 13:30 or so."

"Yessir, of course, sir. I can meet you at the airfield myself with a driver. I'll pick you up in my jeep."

"If you don't mind, kindly arrange for a driver and a staff car. I'm traveling with two other people from British Intelligence, and they'll have a lot of gear with them. We'll go directly from the airfield to Hotel Zur Post. I understand that's where you've set up anyway. We need to get one of them checked in there. That's where she'll be staying."

"She, sir?"

There was a slight pause and Richardson said, "Yes, she. I want you to meet her and make sure you're okay with it."

"Yes, sir. Okay with what, sir?"

"Well, she's going to be assigned to your unit, and I want to go over your orders with you both in the room so you both understand the ground rules. She's a very impressive person, Cap. She's got a lot of experience. You'll understand better when I give you the details. This is a good thing, trust me."

Trust me, Lehman thought. That certainly raised a red flag. During his time in the army, Lehman had seen and experienced many incongruous things. Those incongruities could be explained as "it's just the way the army does things. It's the army way." Last-minute changes to assignments, screwball procedures, strange orders followed by new orders that contradicted the previous orders that came down without explanation were just situations Lehman had come to expect. He probably would have been more worried if everything were neat, tidy, and logical. *Trust me, my ass,* he thought.

"Fine, sir, we'll be there. Is there anything I need to do to prepare or get ready for this?"

"We'll need a secure briefing room or whatever you have that can accommodate us," Richardson replied. "I'll explain everything in person. We can't do this over the phone. It's too sensitive," he said, already violating OPSEC by saying how sensitive and serious the meeting would be. "You clear?"

"Yes, sir, all clear. We'll be waiting for you."

"Good. And Cap, all of this is coming straight from the top. And I mean the very, very top. I'll see you later today. Richardson out."

Well, isn't that great. If anybody is listening in, they now know that something's going down in Bremen this afternoon, thought Lehman. *Wonderful, just wonderful.*

And with that the phone line went dead. Lehman returned the handset into its cradle and pulled out another cigarette from his pocket. He fumbled with his lighter, finally getting it to light, and inhaled slowly and very deeply, blowing smoke rings up into the air.

"Well?" asked Lefkowicz. "What's going on? I take it we're getting visitors."

"Yep, it would seem so. Apparently, we're getting a new guy and that new guy is a woman."

"A woman?" Lefkowicz said incredulously, "How's that gonna work?"

"Richardson said he'd explain everything when he gets here. We have new orders, it seems, and they come from the very top, whatever that means. So, your guess is as good as mine."

"Well, I don't have a clue, but something must be hot enough for the G2 of the whole friggin' theater of operations to fly up here on such short notice."

"Yep, that pretty much sums up the situation," Lehman said. "I'll want you there, so we're just going to have to hope the new guys can handle the screening and hope they don't screw things up too badly. I need you to call the motor pool when they open and arrange for a staff car. Apparently, there's an entourage and our jeep won't cut it. Get a big car, the biggest one they have, and make sure it's all clean and shiny. They're bringing all their gear with them," he said with a laugh.

"Where do you want to meet them?" Lefkowicz asked. "We're not exactly set up for dog-and-pony shows. You have the biggest office, and it's the size of a broom closet."

"Let's use the large debriefing room, the special room," Lehman said, referring to the room's unique properties that only he and Lefkowicz knew about. "Scrounge up a big table and some chairs. Take them from the hotel if you have to. Talk to that manager guy. He's always looking for ways to get more money out of us."

"I'll hit him up first thing."

"Okay, then. I guess I had better shower, shave and put on a clean uniform. They say you only have one chance to make a good first impression."

Lehman grabbed his service cap and started for the door.

"Jesus, why does everything have to happen at once?" Lefkowicz yelled from across the room. "The war's over. It's supposed to be the peacetime army now."

"It's still the army," Lehman said over his shoulder. "It's always one snafu after another, right?"

Lehman stopped in the open doorway and thought for a moment.

"Somehow I don't think this war is totally over for us. It's just a feeling," he said as he walked out and slammed the door behind him.

Chapter Five

Richardson was standing near the wing of the Beechcraft C-45 transport, its silver fuselage glistening in the bright midday sun, and watched the blue RAF staff car approach. As it drove closer and out onto the tarmac, he could see the driver and Banbury sitting in front. He squinted and was able to make out the shape of what appeared to be a woman dressed in an RAF uniform sitting alone in the back seat. The car stopped about twenty feet short of where Richardson stood, and he could see Banbury talking to the driver.

After he finished whatever he had to say, he opened the door, quickly jumped out, and stood alongside the car. After a few seconds, the rear door opened, and a woman emerged. She was slight of build, five feet two or three inches tall, her dark hair pulled up neatly underneath an RAF service cap. Her facial features were delicate. She had dark, almond-shaped eyes, she wore no lipstick or other make-up, and her skin was the color of porcelain. She stood straight, proud, with a look of confidence that bordered on defiance. Richardson couldn't pinpoint what made her so, but she looked uncommonly beautiful, not in a movie star way but in an everywoman way. She walked the line between ordinary and exotic, plain and elegant, accessible yet distant. There was something Richardson couldn't quite put his finger on, but her demeanor and appearance elicited a strong, visceral and animal response that he found irresistible and repellant at the same time.

The woman was wearing an immaculately tailored and perfectly fitted uniform of the Women's Auxiliary Air Force, and Richardson recognized the insignia of rank she wore on the sleeve of her tunic—a flight officer, he noted. He also noticed the decorations and ribbons pinned just above the tunic pocket on her left side. Richardson counted the ribbons, and the ribbon on the top, in the position of highest precedence, indicated she was an Officer of the Order of the British Empire. A George Medal and French Croix de Guerre were among the eight decorations she wore in total. The personnel file he read yesterday listed the award citations documenting her bravery, fearlessness, and resourcefulness under fire during combat. It was one thing to read about her, and now here she was, Ludmilla Haas, standing right in front of him.

As the driver hopped out of the vehicle to fetch the items stored in the boot, Banbury and Haas walked quickly up to Richardson, and each smartly offered the open-handed salute of the British armed forces. Richardson returned the salute, and Banbury spoke.

"Colonel, this is Flight Officer Ludmilla Haas," Banbury said, nodding at Haas. "Flight Officer Haas, this is Colonel Richardson, the head of U.S. Army intelligence operations for the European theater of operations."

"It's a pleasure to meet you, Colonel," Haas said with a Polish accent. Her voice was surprisingly deep, given her small frame, and it had the raspy quality of cigarettes and whiskey. She extended her hand to offer a handshake, which Richardson accepted. Her firm handshake belied her diminutive stature, and Richardson could tell that she was physically strong and fit. Even under her uniform, her body was firm and taut, the product of her rigorous wartime training.

Then he remembered from reading her personnel file that Haas excelled in unarmed combat. Her file contained the training evals from Major Roger de Wesselow, the Coldstream Guards officer who ran the SOE training facility at Wanborough Manor: "She hates guns and shuns their use, but she is extraordinarily skilled with her weapon of choice, a custom-crafted, ivory-handled Shanghai knife that she always carries strapped to her thigh. She is as adept at silent killing as any man I have ever trained."

Once again, it was a conflicting vision that Richardson found simultaneously abhorrent yet alluring and, ultimately, irresistible.

"Welcome, welcome to Frankfort, Flight Officer Haas." Richardson stammered; his cheeks were made warm from more than the midday sun. His Southern accent was coming out again.

"Please call me Luba, Colonel. If that is all right with you." She immediately began to assess Richardson, sizing him up both physically and mentally, a process that was drilled into her years ago and had become second nature to her from practice and out of necessity.

"Luba," he repeated, trying to emulate her pronunciation. "Yes, of course. It's good to meet you, Luba. I understand this is your first time back in Germany since the war began. Is that correct?"

"Yes, Colonel. I would have liked to be in Germany long ago, but never had the opportunity before today," she replied, giving Banbury a cold look.

After six years deployed behind the front lines of the war, this was the first time Luba Haas was able to stand on German soil. She was dropped into Poland in 1939 as one of the first operatives there before the SOE officially accepted women into its ranks. She fought in Poland, then in North Africa and in the Middle East, supporting Churchill's strategy of attacking Germany's soft underbelly until a proper second front could be opened in the West. Haas parachuted into France in advance of the Allied landings on Normandy and helped coordinate French resistance attacks on German lines of communication. After France was liberated, she was recalled to London's SOE headquarters to await further assignment. Given her record, she thought she'd be among the first to airdrop into Germany. That assignment never came.

There was an awkward moment of silence, and then Richardson decided to make small talk.

"I've had the opportunity to review your record. Major Banbury was kind enough to share it with me. Your service has been nothing short of remarkable. We all owe you our gratitude for everything you've done and for the sacrifices you've made."

"Thank you, Colonel," Hass replied. "I'm afraid not everyone would agree with you, but thank you, nonetheless. Like everyone, I was just trying to do my bit and contribute. The war seems such a long time ago.

People are now just trying to put it out of their minds and forget about it, don't you agree? But we all had to do our part, right? We couldn't sit idle. Especially when your country and your very existence were threatened. Unfortunately, life in Poland hasn't improved," she added.

"We've been able to win the war," Richardson replied, "but who wins the peace is yet to be determined. It's going to be even harder, and the damn Russians aren't making it any easier. There is an entirely new kind of conflict brewing now." The trio once again settled into another awkward silence while they watched Banbury's driver gather two large duffel suitcases and what appeared to be a map case and place them alongside the rear of the aircraft. A young Army Air Force sergeant grabbed the items and tossed them up into a rear door to stow them during the flight.

"In addition to the files I've already shared with you," Banbury said, "I'm prepared to pass on everything we know about the Valentin Bunker, the Farge camp, and, of course, about the other topic we discussed." His voice dropped off. He did not want to share too much on an open tarmac. "At any rate, you and your men can decide how you want to tackle the assignment and how best to use Luba—excuse me, Flight Officer Haas," quickly correcting himself in an effort to keep the discussion on formal terms. "I know she has some excellent suggestions as to how to organize the mission. The flight officer is known for having a strong point of view. On many topics," he added, looking at Haas, hoping she would take his cue and hold her tongue.

Richardson just looked at both of them, not quite sure how to react to Banbury's comments. He wasn't used to working with women and certainly didn't know what to do with a woman that had more field experience than most of the men he currently worked with.

"Good. Good," Richardson said nervously. "Well, look, there's no reason to stand here. The flight will take us about an hour and a half, so let's just get aboard and get going." And then he suddenly added, "Luba, I need to have a word with the major for a minute. In private. Why don't you go on ahead and board? We'll be right up," he said, indicating with a sweep of his hand that Haas should proceed up the boarding ramp.

She smiled at Richardson and then gave Banbury a look of suspicion. She clearly didn't like being dismissed and kept out of anything related to the mission.

"Of course," she said through a forced smile. "But may I say one thing before we board, Colonel?"

Banbury looked nervous, wondering what Haas would say, what would come out of her mouth.

"I want to thank you for this opportunity to serve with you and your men." *There, I said it she thought. I can play the game too, James. And you'd better tell me what you talked about. I'm not to be shushed off like some schoolgirl.*

Banbury looked relieved, and then he saw Haas's icy stare. He knew she would not let this go.

In reality, Haas hated small talk and would normally be happy to board the plane and fly in silence. She usually refused to engage in social conventions, including polite conversation, so the fact that she was engaging with Richardson was out of character for her. It wasn't that she was antisocial; she loved people. But when she was on a mission, she was all business, all action. She would review and practice every detail of her mission plan, over and over until they became second nature to her. On missions, she remained cool and aloof. She wasn't there to make conversation or friends, especially when the probability of survival was in the single digits. She saw no reason to get to know someone who would be dead in a matter of hours or days.

Her experience at MI6 headquarters made her hate social interaction even more. She always had free rein in the field, and she made decisions quickly and boldly. She had no use for office politics and the pecking order that existed at headquarters. After cooling her heels in London since the liberation of France, she became frustrated and downright belligerent to her SOE colleagues as she was passed over on multiple occasions for operational assignments in favor of less qualified but more politically savvy male operatives. There also were attempts to tarnish her reputation. The "Eton boys," as she liked to call them, floated rumors that she was an alcoholic who could not control her temper, and that when drunk, she would fly into alcohol-fueled fits of rage. An especially scandalous set of rumors suggested that drink drove her to indiscretions with both men and women. In the end, nothing could ever be proved, but the damage was done. Their attitudes toward her were based on simple resentment. How dare this woman from Poland with an abbreviated secondary education stand in the way of their destiny? Her experience during the war was no substitute for their breeding and public-school education. Whatever she might have accomplished in the past was over. It was time to put her out to pasture like a reliable old mare. In their eyes, she was done.

But Banbury would not give up on the best agent he ever ran. When he realized how difficult it was for her to fit in, he began to coach her on how to make nice with others. They both knew that she might not get another chance to work in the field. *I am not done*, she said to herself over and over. Even old operatives like her could learn new tricks, and she was determined not to mess this up. She had survived the war with her instincts and ability to think on her feet.

"I know you'll make important contributions," Richardson replied with an earnest quality that Haas decided was neither patronizing nor condescending. "Your presence is vital to our mutual success."

Well, that's something at least, she thought. *I'm in the game and no longer sidelined. Now I have to turn it to my advantage.*

"Please go ahead and board, Luba," said Banbury. "We'll join you in just a minute." He hoped he wouldn't have to ask her again.

Haas gave Banbury a look that said *I expect you to tell me everything,* then smiled at Richardson and replied demurely, "Yes, sir, I'll see you aboard," then smartly turned and made her way up.

Richardson waited until Haas was aboard and inside the aircraft before turning to Banbury.

"All right, you're going to play this just like we talked about yesterday, right?

"To the letter, Colonel. To the letter."

"Good, good. Make sure you do that." Richardson had spent the war years behind a desk in Washington as OSS chief Bill Donovan's personal assistant. This was his first time in the field, and it was a strange experience. He felt out of place and out of his element. "I'll bring Lehman into line if need be. Just tell your side of the story. I'll make sure we get what we want." By now, the pilot had started both engines, and their roar prevented any meaningful conversation.

"Shall we board, Colonel?" shouted Banbury.

Richardson simply nodded and bounded quickly up the ramp to the waiting aircraft with Banbury right behind him. The door closed behind them, and the ground crew pulled out the wheel chocks and guided the aircraft off the tarmac and onto the runway. Within just a few minutes, the engines roared even louder, and the aircraft rolled down the runway, picking up speed until it finally lifted up into the cloudless sky.

Banbury's driver made a note of the time as the plane lifted off the ground, and later he would report back to MI6 headquarters that Luba Haas was on her way to Bremen.

Chapter Six

It was just past noon, and Therese had the day off from her job at the newsstand. She had the children bundled up back-to-back in their pram, which, in addition to carrying her children, served another very important purpose. Mainly with the help of Perdue, Therese had designed and built two secret compartments hidden inside the pram. They had pulled up its plush foam cushions and built storage compartments underneath, where the children sat and where they could store and hide a variety of items. Underneath the pram, they added another compartment with a sliding door, hidden by the hardwood exterior. Mothers with children were less likely to attract attention and be searched by the Landpolitzei or at the military police checkpoints still set up around the city. She would flash a smile, admonish her children to be quiet and behave—"Children should be seen and not heard," she —, and was waved through, untouched and unchecked.

This was a typical delivery day, and as Therese slowly made her way through Bremen's Altstadt, her seemingly circuitous route would take her by the businesses and several homes of the customers who were expecting packages from her. They engaged in their coded conversations about the weather, and over the course of the next hour, Therese bartered with her customers as they exchanged watches, gold coins, diamond earrings, two exquisite fire opal rings, as well as a pork roast, two chickens, fresh eggs, milk, flour, and sugar—all of these goods for cigarettes, whiskey, and a special treat, American chocolate.

As Therese and her customers made the exchange, she emptied the pram of the contraband it carried and carefully repacked it with the food and other items she received. They were all safely stored and hidden from view.

The fresh food items were part of Therese's "cut" of the business. Perdue would take the other items, sell them to GIs for military scrip, and after giving Therese her cut of those transactions, he would send the money back to his mother in Baton Rouge for her to put into his bank account. He said he wanted to open a gas station and car repair shop when he returned. Therese in turn would use her cut to buy cigarettes, whiskey, and tinned, preserved food items from Perdue, which, as part of the cycle, allowed her to feed her family. She and her family had never seen or tasted many of the items that they now ate in order to survive.

"What is this?" her father asked her as he looked inside an open jar at the brown, gooey substance within. It smelled like nuts.

"It's something they call peanut butter," she replied. "The Americans love it."

And, of course, there were more mysterious products of unknown provenance.

"And what is this?" asked Therese's mother as she watched her daughter frying what appeared to be meat or some sort of rectangular-shaped sausage that came out of a tin.

"It's something they call Spam," was her reply. "It's like sausage, I think."

"Hmm, smells good," her mother said as she took in the aroma coming off the frying pan. "It looks strange. But it smells delicious!"

When Therese arrived at her parents' house by the early afternoon on Sundays, she would sit down and divide up the spoils of her work with her mother, and the two of them would prepare a proper Sunday dinner, a dinner that would rival any they had prior to the war.

She pushed the heavy pram, laden with goods, up the short walkway to the front door, and her children squealed with delight at the sight of their Oma as she peeked out the door. Therese's mother came out to greet them with a worried look on her face.

"Thank goodness, you're all here. I've been worried about you. You're late."

"Yes, it took a little longer this week."

"There was someone here looking for you," her mother said in a whisper, looking nervously around the neighborhood to see if anyone was watching them. Neighbors always seemed to want to know each other's business. "I didn't like the way he looked, so I sent him away and told him not to bother us. I told him to leave us alone."

"A visitor for me?" Therese replied. "Did he ask for me by name? Who was it? Did he say his name? What did he want? I can't imagine who it might be."

"Let's get you and the children inside. I don't want to talk out here."

Therese pushed the pram into the house, helped the children out, and as her father entered the room, they ran over to him crying out joyfully, "Opa, Opa!" They each grabbed at their grandfather's legs, clamoring to be picked up and held. He bent down, kissed each child on the top of the head, and then stood expectantly as he and his wife watched Therese unpack the pram and placed its bounty on the kitchen table. Their reaction was the same every week.

"Come, children," her father said. "Come into the garden with me, and we'll play outside while your Mama and Oma prepare our dinner."

Therese's father, Karl Josef , was a skilled machinist and worked many years for the same marine construction firm that employed Therese. He was well respected on the job, and he used his influence to help his daughter obtain her job there. It also helped that Therese was a party member and the wife of an Army officer, so her father was more than happy to open doors for her.

Therese took great pride in her work; her dedication gave her a sense of accomplishment, independence, and self-worth. Even after she and Wilhelm married, they agreed that she could continue with her job. It was important work for a large and prestigious enterprise that was helping in the war effort. That was how they explained it to the other officers, and their wives who couldn't understand why Therese wanted to do anything other than take care of her husband and their children and make more babies.

Her father had always been able to provide for his family, but the last six years had taken a toll on him. A veteran who survived the Great War, for him the second war was one too many, and after losing two sons and very probably Therese's sister along with her children, he had enough. He had no more fight left in him. But he was stubborn and prideful, and he now felt a sense of shame that he had to rely on his daughter to put food on the table. He knew that Therese was involved in the black market, but he didn't want to know any of the details. He knew that food and clothing were hard to come by. There weren't enough ration coupons in their books for all of this. But somehow food and clothing appeared each week in his home. He just didn't want to know how. When Therese arrived every Sunday afternoon, he would simply leave the room to let his wife deal with it all.

Therese's mother Johanne was in many ways the exact opposite of her husband. Traditional, cautious and averse to risk, Johanne thought a woman's place was to be at home, taking care of her family. That should be fulfilling enough, and it certainly was enough work. She never understood Therese's independent streak, and she constantly worried about her black-market activities.

"My God, Therese, look at all of this," she said as she made a mental inventory of all the items Therese had laid out on the kitchen table. "What if you get caught? It's so dangerous."

"I won't get caught, Mama. And you and Papa would starve to death if you had to live off your ration book," she said. "We have the same conversation every week. Everyone is doing it because it is the only way we can properly live. So, let's get this all put away and prepare our dinner together. Just like we've always done, all right Mama?"

She gave the very same "Do as I say" look that she learned from her mother, and her mother relented. She knew that it would be no use to argue with Therese about the matter, on this day or on any day. So she simply sighed and shrugged her shoulders and set about to help her daughter put everything away.

Just ten minutes later, they stood side-by-side in the kitchen cooking together just as they did years ago before the war. Guilt be damned— Johanne always looked forward to Sundays and enjoying a meal together as a family. She just wouldn't think about where the food came from. After all, they had to eat, and if they didn't eat this food, someone else would, so why shouldn't it be them?

"Now tell me about this man who showed up," said Therese. "What did he say and what did he want?" Her mother's face immediately turned ashen with worry.

Chapter Seven

Therese's parents were quiet throughout their meal and listened in silence as she went through a litany of complaints about the Americans, the British, the newly formed German government, and how the Social Democrats were ruining the city now that they've been released from the labor camps. She saved some of her harshest words for Lanny Perdue.

"He's probably cheating me out of money, I'm sure of it," she would say every week. "I do all of the hard work, he does nothing. I'm the one putting my ass on the line on the street every week."

"I thought you said it wasn't dangerous. You can always stop," said her mother. "We'll find another way. We'll manage."

Therese's response was to glare at her mother in silence.

Finally, at about four o'clock, Therese was ready to make the return trip to her flat on the Hollerallee. She bundled the children back into the pram, said her goodbyes to her parents, and began the walk back, now pushing a much lighter pram so she was able to walk at a faster pace.

She was not more than a few hundred feet down the street when a tall man stepped out of a narrow alleyway off to the right. She had not seen this man in over a year. Her last memory of him was when he and the guards marched the last prisoners away from the Valentin Bunker where she worked. She could only guess what had become of the prisoners, but she knew that it would not have been a good outcome. Therese recognized the man immediately. No longer wearing the uniform of the SS, he was now dressed in a shabby brown jacket with mismatched blue trousers, and he wore a dark gray felt hat that he pulled down over his forehead in an effort to conceal his face. His jacket and trousers were wrinkled as though he had slept in them, and he had a scraggly beard and needed a haircut. He walked quickly toward her and stopped in front of the pram directly in her path, blocking the way down the sidewalk.

"I need your help. I know what you are doing now, and you have something that I need and want," the man said menacingly. "I need to get out of Bremen, and if you don't help me, I'll report you to the Landpolitzei. I won't take no for an answer, and I've arranged a little demonstration just to let you know I am serious."

He stared at Therese without expression as he waited for a response.

Therese stood there for a moment in stunned silence, not knowing what she should do and wondering what he meant. She considered her options. There was nowhere to run, and even if there were, she wouldn't be able to outrun him pushing the pram with her children in it. But she also knew that it was still daylight and that she would be safe. He wouldn't dare harm her. Or would he?

"Good afternoon, Oberleutnant," she replied, using his military rank. She struggled to remain as calm as possible, even though her heart was pounding. She kept saying over and over to herself, "*Keep calm, don't show him any fear.*" She waited for his reaction and could see that she had caught him off guard. He wasn't quite sure what to do.

"It's Dettmer now. Just Dettmer."

Gestapo Senior Lieutenant Heinz Ullrich Dettmer was the chief of security at the Valentin Bunker. Therese had heard through her contacts that Dettmer's superior officer, Gestapo Lieutenant Colonel Wilhelm Meyer, who oversaw the security of the bunker along with the Neuengamme concentration camp complex, including the Farge camp, had been arrested and tried for war crimes, and now was awaiting sentencing. Dettmer had not been captured and was not as big a fish as his former boss, but he was still a fish, and Therese knew he would be wanted by the Allies.

So here he was, threatening her. *What does he know? What does he think he knows?* She could call his bluff, knowing that in all likelihood he would not want to go to the police. But she didn't want to risk it either. She'd talk to him to find out what he wanted.

"Ah, yes, of course! It is so good to see you, *Herr* Dettmer," she said through a forced smile while emphasizing the word "Herr." "It's been such a long, long time. I hope you've been well. Would you walk with me and the children for a bit? We can talk about the old days, and we can catch up with what you are doing now. I want to hear all about it."

She quickly maneuvered the pram around him, the children looking on in wide-eyed wonder. She motioned for Dettmer to take a place alongside her, and the two of them began to walk together down the street toward the Stephani Bridge, engaged in animated conversation not just about their past but also about their future.

Chapter Eight

Ludmilla Haas was seated at the far end of a table in the large room that had been set up to host the meeting that would serve as her introduction to Lehman. She sat to the right of Richardson, who was at the very end of the table, and she pretended to busy herself by reading a copy of a report, the details of which Banbury would present this morning. She was intimately familiar with all of its contents. She herself had gathered many of the key pieces of intelligence it contained.

Although she had tried her hand at drafting the very report she now held in her hands, as well as many other reports during the months she languished at headquarters, she could never quite master the dispassionate language favored by the old boys in the analysis section who delivered their judgments to an ever-growing group of consumers that ran from mid-level staffers and bureaucrats to military commanders and to an ever-growing number of politicians across the political spectrum. These days, anyone who aspired to move up in government service understood that they needed to belong to that special club, the cognoscenti who gave them access to secrets that only those on the inside could know.

Most of the men who authored this specific report had never worked in the field during the war. They had certainly never been shot at, and truth be told, those who actually saw service on the front, especially those who served within the ranks of the SOE, had fallen out of favor inside MI6 since the end of the war. It was a new game now, and in the collective mind of the new regime, it was a time for new thinking, a new way of viewing the world, and a new way of doing things. For these Young Turks, whose aim was to prevent the next war, conflict was an intellectual exercise, a game to be played, an abstraction. Armies and national boundaries were objects that could be placed and moved around on large maps displayed on enormous tables or on the walls of various situation rooms in which they held court, and their placement varied based on the scenario being played out. Even most of the men at headquarters who actually served during the war and wore the uniform were rear-echelon types, eager to say they did their bit, but in reality they didn't have their own skin in the game. They played the game with other people's money.

From the day she came on to active duty within the SOE, but especially now since being absorbed into the ranks of the Secret Intelligence Service, Haas had a reputation for being hot-tempered—and the fact that she was a woman did not help her—who would fly off the handle at the slightest provocation. She never developed the ability, much less the interest, to hold herself back, to select her words calmly and carefully. She was the master of elegant vituperation and, when all else failed, would hurl invectives and curses at those who crossed her.

For Luba Haas, risk was measured by her level of willingness to sacrifice her own life, which most of the intelligence types at headquarters with whom she worked for the past year and who had never served in combat had no experience with. The war was over now, and for them, risk was measured by doing those things that could advance one's career. And sacrificing career was rarely an acceptable risk. For Haas, everything was an acceptable risk, because she knew what it felt like to be on the business end of a bullet.

When she was in the field, Haas simply never saw the need to hold anything back, and her communiqués conveyed the passion and energy she put into her work. Fools be damned, she would report back what she saw and heard, unedited and unfiltered. She told people what she thought they needed to know, not what they wanted to hear.

"This is our last opportunity," she wrote in a frantic dispatch from Warsaw just before she orchestrated her own escape from the city in the late summer of 1944. She had organized a network of agents and fighters to support the Polish government-in-exile's attempt to recapture Warsaw and assert their own authority as the Germans retreated in the face of the advance of the Red Army.

Her cable went on; "Russians have ceased fighting and advance has stopped. Polish forces have crossed Vistula, but Russians refuse to enter city. Russians ignoring our attempts at radio contact."

Haas knew that without Russian support, the Home Army would not be able to hold the initiative and would fail to retake the city. Most importantly, the Underground would not be able to assert Polish sovereignty on behalf of the government-in-exile based in London. She concluded her cable with a stark prophecy.

"Russians holding out until Polish Communist factions assert control. If this happens, Poland will be lost again."

It was Banbury who was on the receiving end of that cable. He had recruited Haas and had been with her since she trained at Audley End north of London. He also knew that while Haas was passionate and prone to fits of temper—some called her "that excitable woman," others called her a loner and a law unto herself—her understanding of what was actually happening on the ground was always driven by facts and by what she was able to observe. When she coded and transmitted this particular communiqué, Haas definitely knew what was at stake. She had previously reported how communists backed by Russia were infiltrating the greater-Warsaw area.

"Working on airdrop for supplies now. Standby for further instructions" was Banbury's terse, two-sentence reply. He made no mention of whether the Russians had responded to requests for support. Stalin himself ordered a halt to operations and even went so far as to refuse British planes access to nearby Soviet airbases. He wanted the uprising to fail, and even direct appeals for help from Churchill to Roosevelt on the matter went unanswered. Finally, Churchill decided on his own to initiate air drops to aid the beleaguered Home Army. The air drops were an abysmal failure, with every plane in eighteen out of twenty missions shot down. Even the Americans fared no better when they tried. They were able to drop supplies, but those landed in the hands of the Wehrmacht, and, given the lack of arms, ammunition, and men, the Germans eventually crushed the Polish resistance. On Stalin's orders, the Red Army resumed its push westward and captured Warsaw, but now he had his proxies in place to call the shots, and the question of who would eventually control Poland was decided.

For Haas, the defeat was a double blow, and it was also personal. Her husband, Wojchiech Dabrowski, was an idealistic man ten years her junior, one of those fighting with the Home Army, attempting to retake Poland from its German occupiers. The two had met while he was in training at Audley End House in Essex, and after a whirlwind romance, they were married before he parachuted back into Poland to rejoin the fight there.

As the battle to retake Warsaw crumbled, it also became apparent that the Abwehr—German military intelligence—had somehow penetrated the SOE networks. Dozens of SOE agents and radio operators were rounded up, killed, or both. Dabrowski was captured while attempting to reach a church in Mokatow outside of Warsaw, a place friendly to SOE operatives. The church's priest, Fr. Pawel Kaminski, had routinely hidden agents and members of the Polish resistance, along with providing shelter, food, and clothing. Kaminski was murdered, and instead of freedom, the Gestapo and Wehrmacht soldiers were there to meet Dabrowski. Someone had betrayed him.

Haas didn't know if Dabrowski was alive or dead, although she feared it was the latter. She had heard nothing of his whereabouts except for statements by captured camp guards saying all the Farge prisoners were loaded up onto railcars to be sent to the death camp at Mauthausen. One of the guards actually remembered Dabrowski—he recognized him from photographs—and said the last time he remembered seeing him was when Dabrowski and the other prisoners were sent to work for the 7 p.m. shift at the bunker, several months before the camp was liberated. He didn't remember seeing him after that. But Haas knew even this could be a lie or a fabrication of imagination. The guard could have simply been telling his interrogators what they wanted to hear. There was no way to know for sure.

She also knew there was nothing that could be done to save Poland now that the communists were in place, backed by the Red Army. But she could avenge the loss of her husband by tracking down those who betrayed him. That was her *raison d'être,* and it gave her not only a purpose, but also the primal motivation to play the game with all of its confounding rules. She would play along with Banbury, Richardson, Lehman, and anyone else until the time was right. She would smile, be attentive, engage in conversation, and say "yes, of course," or "how right you are" even though she may have to bite her tongue when those words made her sick from uttering them. She would bide her time and keep her powder dry, as the old boys at headquarters liked to say, until the time, place, and opportunity came to exact revenge.

Haas observed Lehman carefully as he stood in the doorway and looked around the room as if he were seeing it for the first time. This was partly true, because just the day before, this room was used to screen refugees or to interrogate former German POWs and other persons of interest. But through ingenuity, resourcefulness, and a little arm twist-ing, Lefkowicz had been able to transform an otherwise drab, utilitarian room into a place that was at least suitable for the very important visitors here today.

It was all part of what Lehman liked to call "setting the stage," where everything in a physical space, down to the furniture, was placed with the purpose of encouraging a person to talk and reveal information. On that stage today, Lehman wanted to play the welcoming host.

Lehman stood in the doorway taking it all in. He surveyed the heavy conference table and matching chairs, noting the ornate carving on the table and chair legs. *That must weigh a ton! How did they get that in here,* he wondered? He was especially amused at the curtains that hung from the two small windows on either side of the room, and the flowers. *Flowers?* he thought, looking across the table at the colorful bouquet neatly arranged in a decorative vase in the middle of the table like a holiday centerpiece. He watched as Banbury set up two easels, the first holding a 1:250,000 -scale topographic map of the greater-Bremen area. The other easel held six aerial reconnaissance photos of a set of facilities he could not recognize. More than a dozen folders filled with what appeared to be photographs were stacked on the table in front of him. They would make his case in the event words failed him.

Lehman glanced over at Lefkowicz, who was busy assisting Banbury. Lefkowicz just shrugged his shoulders and tried not to laugh aloud, but just smiled knowing that his handiwork had been noticed.

Haas tried to read Lehman's body language and the unspoken dialogue going on between him and Lefkowicz. She tried to get a sense of him, just as she would have done during the war, when she had to rely on her instincts to quickly tell her if she would be able to trust a man or woman she was meeting for the first time. She decided that Lehman looked rather plain. He wasn't unpleasant to look at, and he wasn't ugly. He was just ordinary. He certainly would not stand out in a crowd. He was not tall and was slight of build with hazel eyes and light brown hair with a receding hairline. He was the complete opposite of Lefkowicz, who she thought looked like a stevedore with his stocky, fireplug-shaped build and powerful arms. Now there was a man people would likely remember, as he would certainly make an impression upon them. Lefkowicz had memorable features, but Lehman on the other hand had no real defining characteristics, and Haas liked that. She thought that this was a man who could use his ordinariness as a skill. Ordinariness could keep you alive in the situations Haas was most accustomed to. He possessed both the physical features and, judging from her first impression, the demeanor that allowed him to blend into a crowd. The only thing notable about him were the horn-rimmed glasses, no doubt U.S. Army issue, which were askew on his face. Otherwise, Lehman didn't stand out, but he could always be there, and Haas thought that he would have fit in quite nicely into the SOE, assuming he had the other prerequisite skills.

Lehman noticed Haas staring at him from across the room and was about to stare back when he glanced at Richardson sitting at the far end of the table. Richardson looked up and motioned for him to join them, indicating that he should take the seat immediately to his left, directly across from Haas. Lehman walked across the room, took his place, and patiently waited. They all sat in silence. Richardson and Haas closed the thick folder and stopped pretending to read as Banbury indicated to Richardson that he was ready to proceed by clearing his throat. Lefkowicz sat at the other end of the table near the door to the room.

"I want to get started," Richardson said. "We have a lot of ground to cover, and we'll need the rest of the afternoon. Captain Lehman— Cap—I want to thank you and First Sergeant Lefkowicz for setting up this meeting on such short notice." Lefkowicz took this as an invitation to sit closer and moved around the far end of the table to take a seat next to Lehman. *Might as well sit up close*, he thought. They were both ready for the show.

"I want to introduce our guests. This is Major Banbury, who is the British intelligence liaison officer. And this," he said, pointing to Haas, "is Royal Air Force Flight Officer Luba Haas. Don't let her uniform fool you, Cap. She's SOE and served in Africa, Poland, and France."

Richardson paused a moment just to see if there was any reaction. It was now Lehman's turn to observe Haas.

"Yessir, it's good to have you all here," Lehman said, allowing his Southern charm to kick in by looking Haas straight in the eye while nodding his head in both recognition and admiration for her service.

"Are you ready to proceed, James?" Richardson asked.

"Yes, Colonel," Banbury said as he turned away from the easel holding the reconnaissance photos and spoke directly to Lehman.

"The briefing you are about to receive is classified Most Secret, or Top Secret as you Americans say, and the mission we are laying out today will enable you to avenge the deaths of thousands of your comrades."

Lehman stiffened and sat upright in his chair. "*Avenge the deaths of thousands?*" *Who's avenging?* Lehman thought to himself. *What the hell?* Banbury definitely got his attention, and not in a good way.

Chapter Nine

"What we are looking at here," continued Banbury without pause as he pointed to the photographs mounted on the easel, "are aerial reconnaissance photographs taken of two facilities situated approximately forty-five kilometers northwest of where we are sitting this morning. The three photographs on the left are of a labor camp located outside of a small village named Farge. And these three on the right are of a protective bunker that housed a U-boat factory and assembly facility.

It was code-named Valentin by the Germans, and that is how we refer to it today, the Valentin Bunker. Valentin is the largest bunker in Germany and is located near the village of Rekum, approximately six kilometers from the Farge labor camp," he said, pointing out each of the facilities on the topo map.

"Both of these facilities were liberated by elements of XXX Corps a year ago now." Banbury recited a litany of facts and figures about the bunker and the role it played during the war.

"The Germans began construction on Valentin Bunker in the middle of 1943. It was abandoned in late March 1945 just before our troops occupied it. The bunker construction was overseen by Organization Todt, which was responsible for almost all of the large-scale engineering and construction projects within Germany and across their occupied territories. Everything is summarized in this report," he said, dropping a copy of the report onto the table. "I will be leaving this copy for you, along with all of the materials you see before you."

Banbury was able to recount every fact, every known detail available about the two facilities based on a treasure trove of intelligence information gathered from every possible source. The report itself was compiled from intercepted Ultra and tactical radio communications, aerial reconnaissance photos combined with photographs taken on-site when the camp and bunker were liberated. All of the information was corroborated by first-hand accounts from former prisoners and interrogation reports from captured camp guards, the civilian staff, and local villagers, and it painted a grim picture of life inside the Farge camp and the bunker.

"It seems that Albert Speer," he said, referring to Germany's minister of armaments and war production and a close ally of Hitler, "was a huge fan of your Henry Ford. Speer wanted to mass-produce submarines in the same way Ford produced automobiles. He needed a place to build Germany's next-generation submarine, and he wanted to produce them faster, but he knew Germany lacked the requisite facilities to set up proper assembly lines. The existing submarine pens to the north were getting hammered by Allied bombing. The Valentin Bunker was built to rectify that. Speer decided to build the bunker in Rekum because the area was rural and there were fewer military targets nearby to draw the attention of Allied bombers. Yet, because it was situated next to the Weser River, it had easy access to the North Sea. In all, it would have been a perfect place to build and launch submarines."

Banbury went on to explain that if the bunker had become operational, it would have eventually produced more than a dozen submarines each month, submarines that were in a class by themselves and more advanced than any boat currently in service with any navy, Allied or Axis.

"Naval intelligence units from both of our respective service branches have been all over the facility," he added, "Had this facility become operational earlier in the war, it could have—and I emphasize the word 'could'—it could have changed the war's trajectory and outcome. Unlike other submarines that have to surface to attack, the new Class XXII attack submarine that would have been built at the Valentin Bunker could operate completely submerged for longer periods of time. It could," he added ominously, emphasizing what might have been, "have changed the battle for the North Atlantic by disrupting the flow of vital supplies to England."

Haas sat silent as Banbury went on about Valentin, barely paying attention to his words. She had heard all of this before. But as he described the activities that went on at Farge, her attention shifted.

"And this is the Farge labor camp," he said, once again pointing to photographs on the easel and to its location on the topo map. "It was built to house the workers who built Valentin. We do not know in total how many prisoners were held there. There were probably upwards of three thousand men housed at the height of construction. They consisted of political prisoners, communists, anyone thought to be a subversive element to the Reich, or whoever the Nazis thought displayed antisocial behavior. And then there were the prisoners of war. Russians, French, Greeks, and, of course, a large number of Poles," he said as he looked over at Haas.

"Farge was among the thousands of labor camps that existed across Germany," Banbury continued, "and the Nazis used slave laborers in these camps to produce the materiel necessary for the war. They could not have prosecuted the war without slave labor. But because the tide of the war had turned, and probably out of desperation, prisoners at the Farge camp were especially vulnerable."

Banbury paused to pour a glass of water, took a sip, and continued, "At the Farge camp, prisoners were organized to work on the bunker in two twelve-hour shifts starting at 7 a.m. each day. Initially, the prisoners were marched from the camp through the village to the bunker. Eventually a railway line was built connecting the camp to the bunker. Presumably this was more efficient, and they used the railway line to transport prisoners back and forth instead of marching them. But no local resident could legitimately claim ignorance about what went on there. It was all there in plain sight for anyone and everyone to see."

Banbury stepped over to the table and grabbed a stack of photographs that he passed around the table. The photos documented the deplorable living conditions at the Farge camp.

"The majority of the prisoners were housed in an empty naval fuel storage tank," he said as he passed around photographs of the camp's living quarters. "As you can see from these photographs, prisoners lived in the most primitive conditions. The privies were anything but. The men had to use these fifty-five-gallon drums until they were full. There were only two showers, and these long tables," he said, pointing them out on another photograph, "presumably were used for washing. The racks of bunks here," he said, pointing to another photograph, "were organized into what we believe were five prisoner blocks. Prisoners were generally segregated by nationality. Overall, the tank had a circumference of about fifty meters. It was roughly seven meters high on the inside, and it housed at least two thousand prisoners, likely more. Unfortunately, the mortality rate within the camp was so high that it is difficult to ascertain the total camp population." He paused to let this statement sink in before continuing and took another sip of water.

"This wasn't a death camp, right?" asked Lehman. The photos reminded him of what he saw at camps like Dachau, with two notable exceptions: there were no gas chambers or ovens. "Why was the death rate so high?

"It was not a death camp as we have come to know them, such as Auschwitz, Bergen-Belsen, or the other camps whose sole purpose was extermination," Banbury replied, knowing full well Lehman's experiences at the Dachau camp. "At Farge, the prisoners were grist for the mill, and they were subjected to all manner of abuse. They were malnourished, they were beaten, one camp commandant was alleged to have drowned a prisoner in the human waste from one of the camp latrines. The prisoners were deprived of sleep and lacked proper medical supplies and medical care. Disease was rampant—there was at least one outbreak of cholera, and there was typhus, dysentery, you name it. Ultimately, prisoners at Farge were simply ground down by the labor itself. They were worked to death building the Valentin Bunker. That's why the death rate was so high."

Banbury pulled out more photographs to illustrate his point. The photos, taken by the German journalists who were given access during construction, showed how Farge prisoners performed the heaviest labor and most difficult construction tasks by hand. He showed them photographs of prisoners covered in concrete dust from lifting and mixing enormous bags of cement, which was then poured to form the floors, walls, and ceilings of the bunker, which in some places measured more than five meters thick. "You can see very clearly on these photos how thick the concrete was," he said, pointing to annotated features on a photo he passed around. "We have heard prisoner testimony that in the cases where workers died on the spot, concrete was simply poured around them and over them, and they were encased in the bunker floors, walls, and ceilings. Construction never stopped."

"The worst work, however," he said, pulling out even more photographs, "was carried out by the ominously named *Eisenkommandos*, or iron detachments. These men had to move enormous iron and steel girders into place. We interviewed a French survivor who said a better name for iron detachments would have been *Himmelfahrtskommandos*, or suicide squads, because if you were assigned this work, life expectancy dropped dramatically."

Banbury continued to provide details of prisoner life, and by the time he finally finished, it was after 1600 hours and the table around which they sat was filled with hundreds of photos taken from each of the sites. The three Americans in the room continued to look through the pile of photographs in silence, each of them trying to comprehend the magnitude of the atrocities documented before them. Lehman sat for several minutes holding up one photograph taken just after the Farge camp had been liberated. It revealed a group of prisoners wearing ill-fitting striped uniforms, their faces gaunt, their bodies thin as rails, their heads shaved, looking at the photographer with blank, hopeless stares. *What were they thinking? What was the photographer thinking?*

"Excuse me, Major," Lehman said, finally breaking the silence. "It seems like you know everything there is to know about what went on at these two facilities. What are we supposed to do? What's our role? Is there a mission in this?"

Banbury was about to answer, but Haas suddenly interrupted him.

"I can answer that for you, Captain Lehman," she said, finally breaking her silence. "The man responsible for disrupting our agent networks in Poland and capturing my husband was assigned to the Valentin Bunker. He was the head of security there. We believe he is still here in Bremen, and we want him."

The eyes of every man in the room were now on Haas, and finally it was her chance to be heard.

Chapter Ten

"*Stahl*," she said to Lehman in German. Although he understood the meaning of the word, he didn't understand what she meant and shook his head and stared at her with a puzzled look.

"'Steel,'" she repeated to Lehman, this time in English, "was what prisoners called the Gestapo officer who rolled up our networks in Poland in 1944. He is directly responsible for the death of at least twenty of our agents, and probably more. His real name is Dettmer. Heinz Ulrich Dettmer, Oberleutnant, and he ran counterinsurgency and counterintelligence operations in and around Warsaw. After the Red Army recaptured the city, he retreated with the rest of the German army. He eventually became the head of security at Valentin."

"Why "Steel"?" Lehman asked.

"The inmates at Pawiak prison gave him that name," Haas replied, "because he had an affinity for beating prisoners with a thin steel rod he had fashioned into a type of quirt. At the end of the rod, there were four or five loose leather thongs that were tipped with razor-sharp steel barbs that he used to flay the flesh off prisoners during interrogation. He was known for being cruel and brutal, but unlike many of the thugs who were in the rank-and-file of the Abwehr, he was also very smart. He made a name for himself by running operations in Poland that compromised more than a dozen SOE cells, including that of my husband. My husband was among those he captured, interrogated, and eventually sent to Farge, along with several hundred Polish Home Army fighters. That was just the tip of the iceberg, as you say, as thousands of Poles were eventually shipped there to die at Farge. Dettmer was an exceptionally cruel man among an army of cruel men. We want him, and we want to know who worked with him. We believe we were betrayed by one of our own, by somebody close to us. Dettmer couldn't have done it without inside help, and we want to know who that person was."

"Look, I don't want to get too far ahead of ourselves here," Banbury said, trying to refocus the discussion to keep everyone's emotions in check. "There is a reason we've gone into such detail here today. We want you all to fully understand what you're signing up for, what you're committing to."

"Signing up for what, committing to what?" Lehman asked as he looked over to Richardson, who sat patiently while the conversation played out before he chimed in. "Our mission here in Bremen is to screen refugees, debrief ex-POWs, hand out ration cards, and send everybody on their merry way to a DP camp or back to wherever they're supposed to go. What are you talking about?"

"We're throwing our hats in with our British friends here. That's what we're signing up for," Richardson said with more than a hint of irritation in his voice. "Cap, I have a letter here signed by General Eisenhower that will explain everything." He pulled a letter out of his coat pocket, opened it, and slid it across the table to give Lehman a few minutes to read it over. He knew Lehman would immediately grasp the letter's weight and meaning.

So this is what Richardson meant when he said this came from the very top, Lehman thought to himself. He continued to read as Richardson spoke.

"You can read that Ike gave me a chance to decline his request if I didn't think we could accomplish the mission. I don't want to do that because I think we can do this. I want to go ahead, but I need your support on this too. You have to be completely on board, because, ultimately you're the one who's going to be responsible for pulling this off."

"So, what's the long and the short of it, sir?" Lehman asked impatiently. He figured he had nothing to lose by being direct and impertinent, even if it took him to the point of insubordination.

"The long and the short of it is this. Flight Officer Haas here, Luba, is being assigned to your unit as a counterintelligence agent. She'll be billeted here at the hotel, so you do not have to worry about housing for her. Major Banbury has taken care of all of that. She'll also take her meals here, but I want her to have a meal card so she can dine in the officer's mess. There's no reason she shouldn't see how the other half lives while she is working with us." Richardson was taking a stab at humor, but the only reaction was a weak smile from Haas.

"She'll be a fully credentialed agent in the U.S. Army Counterintelligence Corps. I have her credentials here," he said, sliding an accordion-type file folder filled with the documents Haas would use to identify her as a CIC agent.

"She'll carry the badge as you all do, and she'll assume the same duties and responsibilities that everyone else in this unit has. That means she'll pull her shifts as duty watch officer just like you do. Over the next week or so, I want you to take her around and introduce her to all of the commanders of the units garrisoned here. I expect them to support her the same way they support you, and if they give either of you any grief," he said, looking at Lehman and then at Haas, "I want to know about it immediately. I also want her briefed on all of your current case files. There is nothing she cannot know, there is nothing she won't have access to. Oh, and get her on the pistol range and qualified. I want her carrying a sidearm. Any problems with all that, Cap?" he asked before turning to Haas. "Luba, are you good with this?

Haas nodded. Richardson looked back at Lehman.

"No, sir, no problem with any of that. But what does that have to do with the Valentin Bunker and with Farge and all of this?" he asked, pointing to the mound of photographs lying on the table.

"The official story of why Luba is here is that she's on loan from British intelligence to help us identify those responsible for working thousands of POWs to death at the bunker. She's the technical expert. But it's just a cover story. A ruse, if you will. What this is really all about is we're going to help our British friends here find Dettmer, suck him dry of information, and find out who worked with him to compromise their networks in Poland. And when we find that sonofa-bitch or sonsofbitches, whichever it is, we're going to turn them and run a double-cross."

"What if they have nothing to give us? What if they're all dead already? Or, I don't know, there are a million possibilities," Lehman said, looking around the room, searching for flaws in their logic.

"May I call you Cap?" Banbury asked, sitting down at the table directly in front of Lehman so that he could get closer to him and up into his face.

"Sure, everyone else does."

"Cap, you're right. This is the classic intelligence conundrum. It's not like assembling a child's jigsaw puzzle where all the pieces come wrapped neatly in a box, and we know what the puzzle is supposed to look like when we put it together. In this case, it is still a puzzle, we don't know what pieces we have or what it is supposed to look like, and we won't know until we capture Dettmer and find out what he knows and who worked with him. We have ideas about who might have worked with him, but we still have to find out. We have to put the pieces of the puzzle together to reveal whatever picture is there for us."

"Why would anyone be inclined to work with us? Why do you think we could turn him, or them?"

"We have leverage. I'm sure that if they are still alive, whoever worked with Dettmer wouldn't relish the thought of being turned over to the Polish authorities, who would love to make an example of a traitor who was responsible for the death of their countrymen. It's our best shot, Cap. And we can do it under the guise of bringing those responsible for the atrocities at Valentin and Farge to justice, for the military personnel at least. As for civilians, honestly, I am not as optimistic. We've had preliminary conversations with the German prosecutors here and in Hamburg. They're tired of it all. They say, 'You have your trials at Nuremburg, now leave us alone.' I think the German appetite for prosecuting war criminals is waning. They aren't inclined to pursue these specific cases because they don't think there is sufficient evidence—at least when it comes to pursuing civilians. Most of the victims who were worked to death at the bunker or met their demise through other means inside of Farge were Poles and Russians, and nobody loves the Russians. Regardless, they're dead, and they cannot give testimony. So, since there is no one who can step forward and make a case, the Germans want to move on. Their view is that we can't put everyone in jail. There'd be no one left to run the country."

Lehman thought this over for a few minutes, then turned to Lefkowicz and asked, "You've been awfully quiet. What do you think?"

"Cap, we've known each other for a long time, and we've been through it all together, but you're asking the wrong guy. My family came from Poland, and unless they got out when I did, as far as I know they're all gone now. When we were humping our asses across Africa, Italy, France, and now here, you always used to say that 'at least we have something worth fighting for.' You were right. And we still have something to fight for. You saw what they did at Dachau," he said pointedly, and Lehman's eyes closed briefly as he recalled the horrible events there. "So, if we can find this guy and make him talk, I think it is worth it. It's worth taking a shot. Hell, you and I used to do this all the time in New York, and we used the same kind of leverage we have here. We always could turn a guy who was afraid of some other guy. We know how to do this, Cap. You always say, 'No unnatural acts' and this is as natural to us as it gets. It's second nature," he said, then turned his attention to Banbury. "What did you say, Major, you said this was a chance to avenge the death of thousands? How about millions? I'm in, Cap. All the way."

The room became still as Lehman mulled over everything that had been said. Finally, it was Banbury who broke the silence.

"There is one more thing that we need to mention, Cap. There is another important aspect of this, but I need to make sure you are in, isn't that right, Colonel? You want to make sure everyone is on board with this."

"He's on board, they're on board. We all are," Richardson said impatiently.

"Yes, sir, of course I am," Lehman said with resignation.

"Go ahead and tell him."

"The disaster of the Polish uprising finally convinced us that we couldn't trust the Russians. It was clear they were going to present significant problems for the remainder of the war and afterwards. Of course, some people," he said looking at Haas, "understood this long before our leadership did. Knowing that it was just a matter of time until the war ended, some of us took steps and made a contingency plan that could continue to give us eyes and ears, and possibly more within the Soviet zones of influence."

"What contingencies?" asked Lehman. "What do you mean?"

Banbury leaned across the table and in a voice barely above a whisper laid out the final piece of the puzzle.

"We still have assets in Poland, and in the Russian zone in Germany, 'stay-behinds.' They're still there, and they're ready. Luba put them in place, and they are awaiting orders from us. It is called Operation Nightfall."

Chapter Eleven

Their meeting broke up at just after 1800 hours. Lehman hadn't eaten since breakfast, he was hungry and tired, and although he had gone through nearly an entire pack during the meeting, this was a moment when he desperately needed another cigarette.

"Major," Richardson said, "can you please give Cap and me a minute? I want to discuss a few things with him privately." It was now Banbury's turn to be sent off like a schoolboy.

"Of course. Captain Lehman, it's been a pleasure. I look forward to working with you," Banbury replied. Turning to Richardson, he said, "I shall wait for you out by the car, Colonel," Banbury revolved smartly on his heel and left. Lehman looked at Haas and Lefkowicz.

"Walt, can you please show the lieutenant around? Give her the dime tour, please. I'll meet up with you both in my office in . . . how long, Colonel?"

"Shouldn't be more than five minutes," Richardson replied.

"In that case, make it the nickel tour," Lehman quipped. "I'll see you both in about five minutes."

Haas quietly stood up from the table and looked at Lefkowicz, who simply said, "Just follow me, ma'am, and I'll show you around," and they filed out of the room together.

Richardson waited for them to close the door before he began. "You have doubts."

"Sir, I know we'll find this guy as long as he's still in Bremen," Lehman said. "And even if he's not here, we can still get him. It's just a matter of time. And I'm also sure that once we capture him, we'll be able to get whatever information he has. It could take a long time to vet that information, though. So we'll just have to see. As for the rest of it, I just don't know."

"You've run CI operations before. You did that all the way across France. And in Italy."

"Yes, but that was during the war. This is peacetime. Or it's supposed to be, anyway. We had clear rules of engagement that we understood., and so did the enemy."

"That's the lawyer in you talking. It's not like the Nazis ever played by the rules."

"That's true. But at least *we* had rules. And *we* followed them. Or tried to, most of the time. What about running an operation in Poland? That's a sovereign nation. And as for the Soviet zone in the eastern part of Germany, I don't know. Each side is on tenterhooks as it is. If we get caught, it could all blow up. Somebody could get hurt with all of that. Or worse."

Lehman was tired, he felt a migraine coming on, and his stomach was in knots. He just wanted this day to end.

"Something still doesn't add up for me, Colonel."

"What is it?"

"Why do the Brits need us? They have the assets in place. What do we bring to the party?"

"I'm listening."

"I think what we bring to the party is plausible denial. They want someone to blame if and when it all hits the fan."

"Come again, Cap?"

"Look, if this operation goes south, they can claim they had no real knowledge of it. It was just some half-baked scheme led by a disaffected and disgruntled ex-SOE operative. It gives them cover, and we have to take the heat and the consequences."

"That's not it at all," Richardson protested. "We're the only unit that has even a tinker's chance of being successful. This is our chance to be the pointy end of the spear and get into the next battle. The president disbanded the OSS at the end of the war. He was scared by the idea of creating an American Gestapo. Well, that's exactly what we need to fight the communists."

"An American gestapo?"

"No, of course not," Richardson said impatiently. "You know exactly what I mean. The CIC can run this operation. If it goes right, we will have access that we don't have today. As Banbury said, we'll have eyes and ears in places that are off limits to us. We'll be right in the Russians' backyard. And we'll have a chance to beat the Russians at their own game. We're going to need this to prevent the next war or fight one if we have to."

"Maybe, sir. We'll see. That's definitely looking at the glass and seeing it half full."

"Captain, do you know why you are here?" Richardson asked.

Lehman stared at Richardson and offered no answer, but he knew he would hear one.

"You're here because I wanted you. I specifically requested that you be assigned to this command. I wanted you because you have an impressive record for getting results. That's why you're here. There are a lot of men out there who wanted this job, but none have your experience."

Who'd want this job? Lehman thought. *In this backwater town? Berlin, yes. Munich, maybe. Even Bonn. But Bremen? Hardly.*

"I know you've had a tough go of it, you've been through a lot since the very beginning of the war. I know it cost you your marriage. And then there was the incident at Dachau," Richardson said, pausing because he knew he was treading on very sensitive turf.

Leave my wife out of this. And if I hadn't threatened to kill the sonofabitch, he'd have murdered those guards after they surrendered, Lehman thought, his face turning a bright red.

"Look, I know you can handle this," Richardson continued. "I also know you're smart enough to play this game. I know that if you don't know the rules, you'll be able to figure them out or make up your own. Through it all, you always get results. And that's what I expect now."

Richardson hesitated for a moment and then made his pitch to close the deal.

"Remember, the reason you are here is because I asked for you specifically. No one else. I wanted you here. Just get results. Understand?"

When someone said yes or agreed too quickly, Lehman's nature was to doubt. His cynicism was like thick calluses on a laborer's hands. "They aren't being truthful," he would say. "They're lying. They're just telling us what we want to hear." Or "They're hiding something. There's something they're not telling us."

Why was Richardson pressing so hard? What's in this for him? Something didn't add up in Lehman's mind, and he didn't like it. But despite his doubts, despite every alarm going off in his mind, every red flag raised, despite every instinct screaming at him to run away from this as fast as he could. Lehman didn't think twice before immediately answering, shocking himself as the words came out of his mouth.

"Yes, sir, I understand."

Now in the back of his mind, he wondered if he would pass his own test for truthfulness, and he was afraid that he knew the answer.

"So, what am I supposed to do with Haas? Is she working for me, for us, or for them?"

"She's working directly for you. I want you to watch her like a hawk. Banbury says she's brilliant and fearless. But she can also be reckless and careless. And she's a loner. So you're in charge, it's your operation. Use her knowledge, use her contacts, use her in whatever way you want, but she does nothing on her own. Keep on top of her at all times, is that clear?"

"Perfectly clear, sir."

"Good. And nobody outside of this room today gets briefed on Operation Nightfall. Stick to the cover story about finding Dettmer. Is that also clear?"

"Yes, sir. Loud and clear, sir."

"All right, I'm going to get out of your hair now, Cap. I need to get back to Frankfurt before the weather socks us in here for the night. You don't want or need me as an overnight guest. Get with Luba and work it out. I want your plan in the next forty-eight hours. And after that, I expect weekly briefings. Call me at any time if anything comes up. And as I said earlier, if you get grief from anybody, you let me know. I'll make sure you have air cover."

He waited to see if Lehman had anything else to say. Nothing.

"All right, I'm out," and with that Richardson pushed his chair back from the table. "Good luck, Cap."

"We'll do our best."

"I know you will."

***

Lehman looked at the stack of intelligence reports, surveillance photos, and charts from Banbury's briefing strewn across the conference room table. He began to organize them into neat piles when Lefkowicz and Haas stuck their heads through the door.

"We saw the colonel and Major Banbury leave," said Haas. "We know you said to meet in your office, but we thought you could use some help with all of this."

"Thanks. Let's store this in the large safe in my office, away from the other files. This is for our eyes only, at least for now."

Chapter Twelve

They each grabbed a stack of the files, documents, and photographs from the table and made their way back down the hallway to Lehman's office, where they dumped everything on his desk. Lehman walked over to a tall black safe that stood against the wall. He dialed the combination, heard the click, pulled open a drawer, and Haas and Lefkowicz handed each piece of material to him one by one as he stuffed them into place. He had to wiggle, pull, and tug on the file folders to make sure they would all fit, but eventually he managed to secure all the documents inside. He shut the drawer and spun the dial. Their secrets were now locked away safely, at least for tonight.

As Haas waited to see what would happen next, she looked over at what she presumed was Lehman's desk. It was as neat as a whistle, with a clean white blotter in the center, two file trays, one for incoming correspondence, the other for outgoing on either side of the blotter. There was nothing in the incoming box, but a stack of forms and documents in the outgoing. *It seems he keeps up with his correspondence. He's organized. That's good,* she thought. A black fountain pen with a white, rounded-star logo on the cap lay to the right side of the blotter. *He is most likely right-handed,* she thought. She looked carefully at the fountain pen. *A Montblanc? A Montblanc Meisterstück fountain pen? How would he have come into this?* She resisted the urge to pick it up, to feel its balance and weight in her hand. But it reminded her of her grandfather. In an instant she was transported back to a time when she was a teenager, and she was sitting in her grandfather's study. Her legs were curled underneath her as she sat reading in the wingback leather chair across from his massive oak desk. That was the place where they would retire every evening after dinner and while he wrote in his diary, she would pick out a selection from the wall of books that stood floor to ceiling across from his desk. Now, she closed her eyes, and she could hear the scratch from the pen as it moved across the pages of her grandfather's journal. In the past, she would have thought that only a man like her grandfather would have written with such a pen, but her experiences during the war demonstrated that men were not always what they appeared to be. *Surely he hasn't carried this with him throughout the war? He looks ordinary and common, but he writes with an extraordinary and uncommon instrument. There is more than meets the eye with him. I will have to ask him how he came to possess this. I have much to discover about him,* she thought to herself and continued on with her observations.

A single photograph in a gold frame adorned the desk, and it was the only other personal item on display. *A woman.* Haas pondered, *Was this his girlfriend, his wife? It's a young woman,* she thought and as she strained to get a better look at the photo, she saw the woman's clothing was from at least twenty years ago. *His mother,* she decided. *She is very young in the photograph. She had to have married young. She must have been a teenager when this photo was taken.*

Lehman interrupted her train of thought and said, "So, let's start over from the beginning now that it's just the three of us. I'm not sure what Banbury and Richardson were trying to put over on us today. But from now on, it all falls on us. We're the ones who have to make it all work. So, I want to start at the very beginning, from square one. I guess that means welcome to the 323rd," he said, offering Haas his hand.

"Thank you, Cap," Haas replied, shaking his hand. "I'm just happy to be out of London. And I'm very happy to be here," she quickly added.

"Is it okay if we call you Luba?"

"That's my name. It's actually Ludmilla, but my friends call me Luba."

"Ludmilla is a Russian name."

"Yes, I'm named after my great-grandmother. She was from St. Petersburg, Leningrad now. My great-grandfather was a ship's captain who sailed out of Danzig and regularly made calls to the Great Port at St. Petersburg. The story was that he met my great-grandmother at a dinner hosted by her parents. My great-great-grandfather ran an import-export business, and I suppose he was doing business with this ship's captain. Anyway, the story goes that he was immediately smitten upon seeing my great-grandmother. It was love at first sight and apparently it was mutual. But the family didn't see it the same way because, you see, the captain wasn't Jewish. They objected to the relationship, and I think that actually drove my great-grandmother away. So she returned with him to Danzig, and they were married. That's the story anyway."

"That is a good story," Lehman replied.

"My mother says that's where I get my stubbornness. And impulsiveness. I don't know what she means, of course."

"Is that how you wound up with the SOE? Was it an impulse? I know I can read all of the details in your file, but I'd rather hear your version," Lehman said.

"I was engaged just prior to the war to a Polish foreign service officer. I was to meet him in London where we were going to be married."

"Now that sounds impulsive."

"A little, yes," she replied with a laugh. Lehman noted how her eyes lit up when she laughed or smiled.

"We had planned to get married and then sail to Cairo where he was assigned. But the Germans decided to invade Poland on my wedding day. You could say that our marriage was overtaken by events. Gregor, that was his name, was immediately called back to Cairo. I spent the next few months in London, trying to volunteer my services as well. Nobody was interested in what I could offer except the SOE. I speak multiple languages, and they seemed to think that women might be less conspicuous, since all the able-bodied men should be off fighting, and if they weren't, they had to be up to no good, right? That's when I met James Banbury. He was my handler, so we've known each other for a long time. A lifetime. And, yes, now that I retell the story, going to London to marry Gregor was a highly impulsive act."

Lehman fumbled in his shirt pocket for his cigarettes, pulled out three, and as he once again searched for his lighter, he asked, "Do you smoke? Cigarette, Luba?"

"Yes, I'm dying for one," she replied as he handed her and Lefkowicz a Lucky Strike, unfiltered. He lit their cigarettes, then extinguished the flame and waited a few seconds before lighting his own, observing the "three on a match" superstition. There was no need to take unnecessary risks, he thought, and they stood smoking for several minutes, savoring a quiet moment.

"Ah, American," she said approvingly as she deeply inhaled the smoke.

"It's what we get here at the PX," said Lefkowicz. "You can buy all of Bremen with the cigarettes and booze we sell. Your ID card will give you access to the commissary, too. They're located near Camp Grohn, and we'll show you where all of that is."

"Thank you, Walt," she said her face lighting up with another smile.

"It obviously never worked out," she said to Lehman before he could ask the question.

"What's that?"

"Marrying Gregor. We decided to call it off, because, well, it just seemed like the right thing to do at the time. After he left London, I never saw him again. By the time I dropped into Egypt, he was gone."

"And then you met someone else."

"Yes, and he was the passion of my life."

"You're lucky. Most people marry for convenience or opportunity," Lehman replied. "What was his name? Your husband."

"Hmm, I think there must be a story in that, Cap," Haas replied. "His name is Wojchiech. Wojchiech Dabrowski. I never took his name. Neither of us thought we'd survive the war, so it seemed unnecessarily complicated. Do you know what his name means in Polish?"

"No."

"It means, 'He who fights battles in oak forests,'" Haas replied. "It was a prophetic name, given how he chose to live his life."

"I don't think he had much of a choice, given the circumstances."

They continued smoking and then fell back into silence.

"So, Luba, I'm not sure where to begin with this mission. We have to plan it all out. Richardson is expecting the details in the next forty-eight hours, and I'm sure your people are, too. But I'm too tired to think about it tonight, so I'm going to just start off with the same spiel I give everyone who's assigned to this unit. You up for that?"

"Of course."

"Okay. So, it's definitely not the Army way, but we treat everybody as an equal in this unit. That's the way Walt and I have been running things for over five years now, and that's what we'll continue to do. We got a lot of smart guys in the outfit, too smart for their own good sometimes. Everybody here speaks at least three languages, I think, so you have to watch what you say. Don't cuss out somebody under your breath in Basque, Hindi, or whatever obscure language you might know, because I guarantee that somebody will be able to understand you. We got guys here with PhDs. and every other sort of degree you can imagine from schools like Harvard, Yale, you name it, we got it. I've got a physicist, an M.D., the company clerk is a Princeton grad with a degree in linguistics. if you can believe that. They're smart as hell. Smarter than me, that's for sure. Hell, I'm just a kraut lawyer from Louisville who had to work his way through college. Do you know anything about Louisville, Luba?"

"Not a thing," she replied. But at least now she knew where Lehman's accent was from. She'd never heard anything like it before.

"Helluva town. Everybody knows about Churchill Downs and the Kentucky Derby. You've heard of that? It's the big horse track and race?"

Haas just shrugged her shoulders and shook her head no.

"Not a racing fan, I gather. No matter. Louisville is also the home of some of the finest jazz music you'll ever hear anywhere. I'll tell you all about it over a beer someday. No," he corrected himself, "we'll make it a bourbon. Anyway, my German family—on my dad's side, that is—

comes from right here in Bremen. I don't have a clue if they are still here, if they're still alive, or what's happened to them. At some point, I'll get around to finding out, but it will have to wait." He took a pause to inhale from his cigarette.

"Now, Walt here," he said pointing to Lefkowicz who had been standing on the other side of the room listening to their conversation, "Walt's an ex-cop from New York, but his family's really from Wroclaw. I know you know where both those places are. He came to the States with his family when he was about thirteen, isn't that right, Walt?"

"Yep. Straight off the boat and to the Bronx," he said.

"Walt actually runs things around here, so if there is anything you need, he's the person to ask. As a courtesy, please address him as First Sergeant when you're around the rest of the men. It makes him feel better."

"Go to hell, Cap," Lefkowicz replied with a laugh.

"Seriously," Lehman said laughing. "Seriously, he is the only reason this unit keeps running. So, he's First Sergeant in front of the men, otherwise, he's Walt."

"Yes, First Sergeant. I understand," replied Haas, clearly enjoying the banter between the two of them.

Turning back to Haas, Lehman became serious. "Look, you and I both know what you're *supposed* to be doing here. You're here to help us with this special assignment that's been dropped into our lap. We know what you're *supposed* to do, but I want to know *why* you're here. Is there something you want to tell me now that Banbury and Richardson are gone? Something he left out of his briefing today? Something he forgot to mention? Is there anything you need to add? Now's your chance." This line of questioning was straight from the "Tell us everything you know, and it'll go a lot easier for you" section of the Army field manual of interrogation.

Where is this coming from? she thought as she tried to make sense of his question. She was trying to see it from Lehman's perspective.

Well, he obviously does not trust me, she thought. *I can understand that. The entire mission has been dumped on him. That's not a problem.*

We'll have time to work through all of that. He certainly wasn't shy about expressing his feelings during the briefing. I can imagine what he said to Richardson when they were alone together. But there's no hidden agenda, not that I'm aware of, anyway. I've taken this mission at face value. But what does he see? I've worked with Banbury long enough, and I trust him. Lehman doesn't know him or me. Does he see something that I don't see? Did all that time with those prissy schoolboys at headquarters dull my senses, my instincts? Is there something I've missed? What did Richardson and Banbury talk about? Is this all one big set-up? No, Banbury would have told me. He always told me everything, she thought. *I know what's at stake and what we can gain. Lehman may have his doubts, but I don't.*

"Cap," she replied, "my orders are simple. Bring Dettmer in. Nobody has told me to do anything different. I'm here to get Dettmer and find out what he knows and who worked with him. And then, we'll see if we can restart Nightfall. That's it. Beyond that, I do have a personal agenda in all of this. I want to find out what happened to my husband. I want to know for certain if he's alive or dead, and if he's dead, how did he die and where is he buried? That's all. If there is anything else going on, I don't know what it is, and I'm in the dark about it just as you are. If I find out that there is anything else going on, you'll be the first person to know. But I don't think there is, so you'll just have to find a way to trust me."

Lehman stubbed out his cigarette and quickly pulled out another, lit it, and said, "Fair enough. I believe you, and we'll leave it at that for now," he said. He paused and then remembered something that Richardson said.

"You'll still need to sit on watch desk duty just like everyone does in this unit. Hell, Walt and I do it, so you'll pull the duty. too. It will help you fit in and get used to the routine. Once we put the word out that we're looking for Dettmer, we're going to get a shitload of leads on his whereabouts from all over Germany. Most of them will be dead ends. There's a whole cottage industry that's sprung up finding ex-Nazis and turning them in, and there are a lot of crackpots out there. But one or two leads will come in that will help us run him to ground."

He waited for a reaction from Haas, but she said nothing, betrayed no emotion, and sat patiently waiting for him to continue.

"Look, I told Richardson my reservations about this mission. We're not set up to run a CI operation outside of Germany, so we're going to have to figure out how to do that. I understand why British intel wants to know who sabotaged their operations in Poland. That makes sense. I also understand how important it is to you personally. But we're going to do this as a team. I don't want you doing anything on your own. You've got the on-the-ground knowledge, and we'll follow your lead, but I expect you to put together a plan that Walt and I will sign off on.

"Walt and I will question you to death about every detail of your plan. We'll need to understand every little nit about it before we proceed. If we question you, it's not because we doubt your ability. We're going to ask a lot of questions because we don't want anyone to get killed. We've all been through enough of that, and nobody needs to die in peacetime. Even though the shooting has stopped, people can still get killed in our line of work. And I'm not going to let that happen.

"Those crackpots I mentioned, they're the ones that will be taking the shots, and I don't intend for you or me or anybody else in this unit to be caught in their crossfire. And don't get all in an uproar about any of this. We're not treating you any differently. This is how we'd do it with any man and now woman assigned to this unit. You'll be treated just like everyone else here. We're all equals here."

Lehman finished his second cigarette, pulled out a third for himself, and offered one to Haas and Lefkowicz. He searched for his lighter again. *Right pants pocket, that's where you always put it.* He offered a light all around, and they all continued to smoke.

"So, that's what I expect of you. Now here's what you can expect from me and Walt." *All right, that was the stick, now let's offer the carrot, he thought.*

"Walt and I will always have your back. We will always support you, even if you screw up, and from what I know about your record I don't think you screw up too often, but we'll be there for you if you do. That means that even if Banbury or Richardson are running some sort of parallel operation using this as a cover and everything goes south, we're not going to ask you to fall on your sword, swallow a pill, or take a bullet for us. We'll succeed together or fail together. We'll do everything in our power to make sure you accomplish your mission here. Just be honest with us. Always come to us with everything you know, be direct, and don't mince words. From what little I do know about you, I don't think you'll have a problem with that," he said with a smile. "I just ask that you be as respectful as possible if you need to tell us to go to hell. But, if you need to tell us to go to hell, I want you to tell us. Does that all make sense, Luba? Do you read?"

"Loud and perfectly clear, Cap. And since we're opening up ourselves so candidly, may I say something?"

"Have at it."

"This is a fresh start for me. I'll have to tell you all about my time at headquarters with all of those Eton boys prancing around. They can't be trusted. It wouldn't surprise me if they were actually working for the Russians. But that's a whole other matter, and we'll swap stories about it sometime. You can tell me about Louisville and jazz music, and I can tell you about what it's like to work with people who say one thing and mean something completely the opposite or spread lies and innuendos behind your back. I've got nothing to hide, Cap. I'm an open book. If there's anything you want to know, just ask me. Face-to-face, not like an adolescent schoolboy but like a man."

Haas walked over to look at a large map on the wall depicting Germany. It displayed each of the Allied zones of occupation and the western sections of Poland.

"You know, I begged my mother to leave Gdansk," Haas said as she slowly traced her finger along the blue line representing the River Oder, which marked the new Polish border. "I could have gotten her out. I begged her, but she wouldn't leave. She wouldn't leave her home. She said, 'This is where I was born, and this is where I will die.'"

Haas turned and looked directly at Lehman.

"The people that I selected and put in place there, they're good people. The best," she said. "I can't just leave them there."

"That's what I would expect you to say. They're your people, and we'll just have to find out if they are as good as you say."

"I know you're not in love with this mission and with me being here," said Haas. "I know you have doubts." She looked over at Lefkowicz. "Earlier, Walt said that you always felt you had something worth fighting for. Well, this is worth the fight."

She paused to compose herself and collect her thoughts. She was tired, too, and didn't have the strength to play games. "I promise that I will follow your rules. I won't hold anything back from you or from Walt or anyone else here. Just being here makes me feel like I'm part of something again. I need to be a part of something. I burned a lot of bridges back in London. I think I burned them all. I don't have a home anymore, I don't have a country, I don't have a family. So being here among you and your men will have to suffice. This is where I am now, and I am very, very grateful. I will do my very best to fit in and belong."

I wonder if she's tough enough to see this through, Lehman worried. *I know she used to be, but does she still have it? Hell, who am I kidding? That's what they're saying about me at headquarters. Maybe we're both being tested.*

"Well, life was a lot easier when all we had to do was hand out an ID and ration cards, and interview a few refugees along the way," he said. "But we'll figure it out. Together. No solo acts, right?"

"Right."

Lehman took one long, last drag from his cigarette and then extinguished the butt in the metal ashtray on his desk. "I don't know about you guys," he said, "but I could use a drink. The hotel bar is open, so let's go there. Do you drink, Luba?"

"Yes, I'd love a drink, Cap. I'm parched."

"All right. Let's lock this place up and get out of here. All of this will be here in the morning," he replied.

They headed for the door with Lehman in the lead. He held it open for Haas and Lefkowicz and reached back inside to turn off the lights. They stepped out into the dimly lit hallway and were greeted by grinding and screeching chords from an accordion and the off-key and flat notes from a clarinet coming from the other end of the hotel. A bad German band in the bar was starting the first of their five nightly sets.

Here we go. Toss her a lifeline and see what she does with it, Lehman thought.

"Welcome to your new home, Luba."

Chapter Thirteen

If anyone had observed Therese and Dettmer as they walked together, they would have appeared to them as an odd and incompatible
couple. As they crossed the Stephani Bridge, a careful observer would
have noticed a well-dressed woman pushing two children in a pram and
walking alongside a man in ill-fitting and dirty clothing while engaged
in an animated conversation. But nobody on or near the bridge, or on
any street on which they traversed that day, paid them any attention.

The pair had been wandering through the Altstadt district for nearly
an hour when Dettmer motioned for Therese to move the pram to the
edge of the sidewalk to allow people to pass them. He had grown weary
of their arguing back and forth and of Therese's attempts to evade him.

It was late in the afternoon now, and people were leaving their places
of work. The streetcars passing by were full, taking people home, and
the usual hordes of people with no homes to go to walked aimlessly
along the streets. The sidewalks were filled with people headed to wherever they planned to spend the night.

Dettmer turned to Therese and said, "We've been wandering in circles for an hour now. This is getting us nowhere. I know where you live,
Frau Weber. There's no reason for us to walk around in circles. Turn at
this next street on the right and continue walking until you are across
the street from the small park there. Do it. Now!"

Therese swallowed hard but did exactly as he instructed, and they
walked for no more than five minutes when she saw the park across the
street. She was just a few blocks from her flat and the relative safety it
provided if only she could get rid of Dettmer. She stopped pushing the

pram when they stood directly across from the park, and she wondered what would come next. The children were restless and began to fuss and whine. "Why aren't we home yet, Mama? Where are we going?" They didn't understand why they were walking with this stranger for so long, and Therese was wondering the same thing herself.

"Please keep the children quiet. I don't want to draw more attention to us than necessary," Dettmer said calmly.

"Children, please be still. Be quiet while Mommy speaks to Herr Dettmer. We'll be home soon, and then you can play," she said, leaning into the pram and kissing each of them on the forehead.

Dettmer and Therese continued to speak in intense, hushed tones as the late-afternoon crowd passed them by. Therese tried to capture their attention, but only occasionally would someone glance at her and Dettmer before scurrying off. Whatever was going on between this woman pushing a pram and this disheveled man was no concern of theirs. A row between husband and wife? Maybe. A spat between lovers? Not as likely because of the children. Whatever it was, they wanted no part of it.

"Look," she said, returning her attention to Dettmer. "I don't know how I can help you. What is it you want me to do, exactly?"

"It's very simple. You have items in your possession that I need and want. You stole these items. You kept them when we abandoned the bunker. Now I don't know where you have these items hidden, but when we get to the alley, I am going to hold your children and everything you have hidden in your pram until you return with what I want. You know what I am referring to. And, yes, I also know about your little business. I know you are carrying jewelry and very likely gold and diamonds. It's all hidden in your pram. I know this because I watched you conduct your little business earlier today. I will hold your children until you return."

"So you've resorted to kidnapping now?"

"I'm not doing anything more than what you are doing, Frau Weber. But unlike you, I'm not only trying to survive, but I also intend to live long enough to fight another day. There are many more like me. You of all people should understand this. You were a party member. You know what is at stake. If you had done your duty a year ago, you wouldn't be in this predicament today."

As they wandered on the streets, Dettmer told Therese the whole story. He told her how he had escaped first the British and now the Americans. He had taken a soldier's book and identification papers off a dead private, who no doubt valiantly put up resistance against the British. Dettmer was briefly captured and endured the indignities of being confined with lower-ranking soldiers, but he knew that if he could just bide his time, he would eventually be set free. He told Therese how he now was living using an assumed name, right under the Americans' noses, and sharing a small room with a former Kriegsmarine corporal in a seedy boardinghouse near the Port of Bremerhaven.

"I did more than my duty, Herr Dettmer, and I've already contributed enough," Therese said hotly. "I've lost my husband, two brothers, my sister, and her children. I have no intention of giving you anything."

"You have done nothing, Frau Weber. Your husband did his duty and gave everything. Now I expect you to do the same. You will bring to me the items from the bunker that you kept. They do not belong to you, and you have no right to them. And I think perhaps I should also take the items in your pram. What do you have today? I know there is gold and jewelry. It will fetch a good price on the market, I think."

"If you take everything I have, how will I explain it? I can't go back empty-handed to—," She paused, not wanting to reveal Perdue's name.

"To whom? To Sergeant Perdue?"

Therese's eyes widened, and she gasped.

"Yes, I know who he is, and I know all about your little band of thieves, the Bremen Stadtmusikanten you call yourselves, eh? Well, I think that Sergeant Perdue has far greater problems right now than some missing merchandise. In fact, I may be doing him a favor, and you too, by taking all of these items off your hands," Dettmer said.

"What are you talking about? What have you done?"

"What I am talking about is this. We are going to continue to walk down this street and turn right at the corner. There is a small alley on the right-hand side that we will turn into. We'll walk to the end of the alley, and that is where we will stop. There will be a man there waiting for us. I believe you will recognize him. You will open the secret compartment door on the bottom of your pram and give me whatever jewelry, gold, and other items you have, including any food. He and I will then wait for you in the alley. We will hold your children as collateral.

"You will go to fetch the documents I want. We will wait for you to return, but we will not wait for very long. You will have one hour to return with the documents. If you do not return, you will never see your children alive again. Don't think I won't do this, Frau Weber. I've done far, far worse. And if you return, we will release your children and leave you alone. You will not mention my name or tell anyone about what has happened today. *Anyone.* Is that clear? If you follow my instructions, you will never see me again. But if you do not, if you go to the Land-politzei or to the Americans or to the British and tell anyone about me, it will not be pleasant for you, for your children, or for your parents. Your father is an old man now, and it seems that he might be prone to accidents. So that's it. I will get what I want from you. Or else."

"Or else what? What if I just scream bloody murder right now, right here in the middle of the street? What if I tell the whole world that you are nothing more than a cold-blooded murderer? You have blood on your hands."

"Keep your voice down," Dettmer hissed. "It will be your word against mine, Frau Weber. I'm just a lowly ex-soldier, trying to get by. I gave everything to my country during the war. But you. You have far more to lose than I," he said, gazing down at her children, who by now were crying loudly. "You're a common criminal now, exploiting others. They will take them away from you, the children. They will call you unfit. They'll send you to prison for your little black market operation and you'll never see them again. Is that worth it? Are you willing to pay that price? As for blood, Frau Weber, we all have blood on our hands."

Therese began to look at the people passing by on the street, hoping to draw someone's attention, but they all averted her gaze as they scurried off. She wondered if she should just cry out and ask for help. *Think, Therese, think,* she said to herself, trying to remain calm.

Dettmer watched as Therese's eyes darted back and forth scanning for someone to connect with, and he said with emphasis, "They won't help you, Frau Weber. These good Germans don't want to be bothered by the likes of you. They've avoided helping others in need for years now, and they aren't going to start today. Why would anyone stop and help you? These people will just close their eyes and ignore you because that is what they always do. They've been conditioned to do that, and they've had fourteen years of practice doing that, ignoring everything around them, seeing nothing around them, quietly and obediently acquiescing to everything. So you see, Frau Weber, you are all alone."

What should I do? she asked herself. *I have to get away. Should I run? Should I scream? Should I simply fight him here on the street?* Her heart raced as she frantically thought about what her next move would be. And then, as she looked over Dettmer's shoulder onto the street, a solution came to her.

In the corner of her eye, she saw a convoy of American army vehicles moving down the street. At the front of the convoy was a Jeep, followed by a half-dozen large, open-bed trucks. Their canvas tops were removed, and she could see that each of the large vehicles was filled with American soldiers sitting opposite each other. She could see that the jeep held three occupants: the driver, who was a sergeant; a passenger who appeared to be a young officer—she couldn't make out his rank—and a young corporal who manned a fifty-caliber machine gun mounted on the back, She waited as the convoy moved closer and closer.

"I'm waiting for your answer; Frau Weber," Dettmer said. "What shall it be?"

The convoy moved closer, and closer. Now!

With a violent thrust, Therese pushed the pram over the curb and bolted out into the street directly in the path of the jeep and the convoy. Dettmer lunged for Therese and tried to grab at the pram to hold her back, but he was too slow. As she darted into the street, Dettmer fell forward onto his hands and knees screaming, "No!" as the jeep and the convoy of soldiers bore down on Therese and the children.

She looked up and saw the startled look on the face of the young officer as the jeep bore down on her. She stopped in the middle of the street, directly in the jeep's path, then threw herself over the pram in an effort to shield the children from the impending collision. She heard screams and cries from onlookers. She heard the blare of the jeep's horn and the squeal of tires as it careened and skidded toward her. She closed her eyes and prayed as she waited for the blow, waited to be struck and for the pain that she knew was inevitable. She only hoped that she could save the children.

Chapter Fourteen

The scene unfolding in the street awakened the crowd of people who were rushing home from their workday. No longer lost in their own thoughts, the first sound that came from them was a collective gasp. Many wanted to turn away, some averted their eyes to what they thought was inevitable. But others on the sidewalk screamed warnings and continued to look on as the driver of an American army jeep laid on the horn and slammed on the brakes. The jeep's horn blared, and the hard rubber tires screeched, as the jeep began to fishtail and skid toward Therese. The corporal in the rear held onto his machine gun for dear life, and the jeep finally came to a stop, narrowly missing Therese and the pram by a foot.

The deuce-and-a-half truck that had been following lurched to a halt, throwing the soldiers inside off their benches onto the truck's bed, causing an eruption of shouts and profanities. More screams and shouts came from the myriad onlookers on the sidewalks. The jeep's driver, a now highly perturbed sergeant stood up in the jeep and leaned over the windscreen, screaming.

"Lady, what the hell is wrong with you? Are you trying to get yourself killed?" The young officer to his right just sat there, stunned, looking as if he had swallowed his tongue. The young corporal in the rear of the jeep was splayed over his fifty-caliber machine gun, the impact by the near collision having knocked the wind out of him.

A group of Germans rushed into the street to check on Therese and the children, surrounding her and peppering her with questions.

"Are you hurt? Are you alright? What about the children?"

"I'm fine, I'm okay," Therese replied shakily. She turned her attention to the children, who were crying uncontrollably. She reached into the pram and picked them both up, kissing them and holding them tightly, tears of relief streaming down her own cheeks now as well.

"Lady! Lady! Do you speak English? *Sprechen Sie Englisch?*" It was the perturbed sergeant, who was now more concerned about Therese and the growing crowd that was surrounding them.

"Johnson! Johnson," he called to the young corporal, by now standing upright again on the back of the jeep. "Check on the lieutenant. And check on the men in the deuce-and-a-half behind us. Make sure they're all okay. If they are, tell them to remain inside their vehicle. Do not dismount, is that understood?"

The corporal signaled he understood, and the sergeant once again turned his attention to Therese, who was sobbing softly, kneeling beside her children and clutching them tightly..

"Ma'am, are you okay? Do you speak English? *Sprechen Sie Englisch?*" he asked again.

Therese looked at him and finally she replied in a barely audible whisper, "Yes, I do. I speak English. And I'm okay. I'm fine. The children are fine. We've just been through a fright, that's all."

"Well, ma'am, you've given us a helluva fright, too. What were you doing? One minute you were standing on the sidewalk, the next thing I see is that you're right in front of this convoy. You could've been killed!"

Therese wasn't sure how to reply or what she should tell the sergeant, but then they were joined by his young lieutenant, who apparently had not swallowed his tongue and wanted to assert his authority.

"Sergeant, what the hell is going on here? What was this woman doing?"

"I'm trying to figure that out, sir. She's not hurt, thankfully. And neither are her children."

Looking at Therese holding the children, the lieutenant tried to assess the situation for himself. The children were still fussing, and Therese was doing her best to keep them quiet. She looked at the growing crowd of onlookers who had gathered along the street, but she couldn't see Dettmer anywhere. The lieutenant looked at Therese sternly and said, "Ma'am, do you speak English?"

"Yes, she does, sir," answered the sergeant.

"Let her answer for herself, Sergeant," the lieutenant said with an annoyed look.

"Sorry, sir," the sergeant replied.

"Yes, Lieutenant. I speak English," Therese replied.

"Well, then, I have to ask you, what in the world were you thinking? You and your children could have been seriously injured or worse. To make matters worse, you're now holding up a convoy of the United States Army," he noted with an officious air.

"I'm terribly sorry for all the trouble I've caused," Therese replied. "I was trying to get away."

"Get away? Get away from what?"

"A man over there," Therese said pointing to the sidewalk. "He was accosting me and threatening me. And my children."

"Who was this man?" the lieutenant asked. "Point him out. Is he still there?"

Therese looked at the crowd, which was growing larger with people asking each other what had happened and listening to multiple versions from the eyewitnesses offering their first-hand accounts of the incident with the woman and the convoy to anyone who would listen. Dettmer was nowhere in sight.

"He was right there, on the corner," Therese replied, "I'm sorry, Lieutenant, but I do not see him." Therese continued to scan the crowd, desperately trying to find Dettmer. *Where could he have gone? He was just there.*

"You say he threatened you, ma'am," the young lieutenant said. "Why would he threaten you? Did you know this man?"

Therese thought carefully before she replied.

"No, I never saw him before," she lied. "He wanted my purse. And my earrings," she said as she reached up to her ears to show the young lieutenant the two simple gold posts she wore. "They were a gift from my husband," she said, which was the truth. "He's dead—my husband.

He was killed in Yugoslavia, and it's the only thing I have from him. Other than the children, of course."

The lieutenant looked at Therese, wondering if she was telling him the truth, but the growing crowd was more unsettling to him than her story. He decided it was time to beat a hasty retreat and leave the area.

"Do you live around here?" the lieutenant asked Therese.

"I do," she replied. "It is just up this street, five blocks in that direction," she said, pointing to her left. "And then it's a left onto Hollerallee. I live in a house, a flat I share with other families. It's the third house on the left. On Hollerallee." Therese looked at the young lieutenant wondering if he would just let her go when his sergeant spoke up.

"Sir, we should make sure she gets home safely," the sergeant said, looking at Therese. He gave Wilhelm and Anna Karolina a goofy smile, reached into his field jacket pocket, and asked the children, "Do you like chocolate?" as he pulled out a large bar of American milk chocolate.

He began to open the wrapper when the lieutenant snapped, "Sergeant, what are you doing? We're not operating a nursery here."

"Yes, sir, I know, sir," he replied as he handed the children the small pieces he had broken off. "Is it okay for them?" he asked Therese. "Just a little chocolate?"

"Yes, it is okay," Therese replied, finally offering a smile. The children took the chocolate from the sergeant but weren't sure what to do with it.

"Here, like this," he told them as he broke off a small piece for himself and took a bite. The children put the pieces of chocolate to their mouth, not sure what taste they would experience, and then squealed with glee and approving smiles and laughs as they experienced their first taste of American chocolate candy.

"Sergeant, that is enough," the lieutenant said. "Get this convoy moving. Now."

"Yes, sir," he said, handing the remaining chocolate bar to Therese. "Here. Please take this. For you and the children. You can take it and enjoy it later."

Therese could only smile and say repeatedly, "Thank you. That is very kind of you. Thank you very much."

"Sir, I have a suggestion," the sergeant said as he turned to face the lieutenant.

"Now what?"

"Sir, this crowd is getting pretty big, and we have to get back to our barracks. I suggest we have the men dismount, move the crowd back off the street, and the vehicles can move forward. The men can move alongside in column formation and keep people off the street. The woman here—er, what's your name, ma'am?" the sergeant asked Therese.

"Weber, Sergeant. Frau Weber. Therese Weber."

"Thank you." he replied. "Frau Weber and the children can walk alongside the column with the men. We can escort her up to her street, which is just—what, five blocks up ahead? Is that right, Frau Weber?"

"Yes, that's right. The street is Hollerallee. But you don't have to do that. I can make it home by myself," Therese no longer wanted to be the center of attention, but it was too late for that.

"No, we'll make sure that you and the children stay safe," said the lieutenant, now eager to demonstrate that he was in charge. "Sergeant, order each platoon to dismount. Where's that new guy who speaks some German? What's his name?"

"That's Private Gerber, sir. He's in second platoon, in the second vehicle."

"Well, get him up here. Have him tell this crowd of people to clear the street and that we are going to escort this woman and her children up to where she lives."

Within minutes, the full company of infantry soldiers moved the crowd out of the street and onto the sidewalks. The soldiers then formed into columns on either side of the street. The new guy in the company—Private Gerber, tall, lanky, barely eighteen years old, and hailing from Cincinnati, Ohio—relished his opportunity to be of good use. He was the youngest guy in the company and consequently took a lot of ribbing. The son of a German immigrant family, Gerber grew up speaking German at home. Now he would demonstrate that he could be useful to his buddies who constantly picked on him. He could show them that he had skills that no one else in his company had. He shouted out to the crowd in German as the soldiers moved the people back off the street and onto the sidewalk.

"*Achtung an alle!* Attention, everyone! Please move back off the street and onto the sidewalk. This military convoy is moving out and everyone must remain off the street."

Even Therese was amazed at how compliant the crowd was. The soldiers' mere presence prompted the crowd to move onto the sidewalk, where they could watch the spectacle that unfolded before them. Therese placed the children back into the pram. They were completely occupied with their treats, their faces smeared with chocolate. "Children, we'll be home soon," she said as the Americans lined up in two columns, flanking the two-and-a-half-ton vehicles.

"All right, Sergeant. Let's move out," the lieutenant said decisively. "You and Johnson walk with her. I'll drive the jeep. When we get to the street where she lives, I want you two to escort her down to her house. We'll hold in place on the corner until you return, and then we'll get the hell out of here and return to the barracks."

"Yes, sir," said the sergeant as he moved to stand next to Therese.

Johnson ran up and joined the sergeant and Therese. "We'll make sure you get home safely, ma'am."

"Move out," shouted the lieutenant as the column slowly lurched forward.

Therese was aware that everyone's eyes were now on her, wondering, "Who is this woman?" Some in the neighborhood recognized her immediately. "Is that Frau Weber? Yes, why, yes it is!" And one of them called out to her, "Frau Weber, Frau Weber, you've done something even the Führer couldn't do! You're marching with the Americans!"

Therese blushed with embarrassment and tried to ignore the calls. She walked with her eyes straight ahead for what seemed like an eternity as she and the soldiers traversed the five blocks to Hollerallee. When they finally reached the street corner, she quickly turned, and the sergeant and Johnson followed her up the street. At last she stood in front of her house.

"This is it," said Therese. "This is where I live. Thank you very much for your help today. You are very kind. I hope the lieutenant isn't too angry."

The sergeant looked at the house. It was huge, bigger than any house he had ever seen back in the States.

"This place is huge," he said. "Do you live here alone?"

"Oh, heavens, no," cried Therese. "Two other families are living here with us. Plus, our landlady. A total of eleven of us live here. It looks bigger than it really is," She was impatient for him to just leave. She was sure her neighbors and housemates were peeking from behind drawn window coverings trying to ascertain why Therese was speaking with two American soldiers.

Just then, the sergeant noticed a jeep parked on the street, several houses down.

"Well, it seems the U.S. Army is already here," he said jokingly, pointing to the jeep parked on the street.

At first Therese didn't understand what he meant, but upon seeing the jeep parked nearby, she replied, "There usually are no Americans in this area. I can't imagine why a jeep would be parked on this street."

The sergeant nodded and then said, "All right, Corporal Johnson here and I will leave once you are inside. Do you need any help with the carriage or getting the children inside?"

"No, Sergeant. I can manage on my own," replied Therese. "Thank you very much for all of your help today. And for the chocolate, too." She turned and quickly pushed the pram up the walkway to the front door of the house. When she reached the stoop, she held onto the pram with her right hand while using her left to open the front door. Thankfully, it was not locked. She turned to look at the sergeant and the corporal one last time, gave them a weak wave, and entered the house, closing the door behind her. Once inside, she leaned back against the wall of the entry alcove, closed her eyes, and let out a long sigh of relief. But her relief would be short-lived.

"Therese, Therese," said the landlady, startling her. "There is someone here looking for you."

"Omigod, you frightened me," Therese replied.

"There is someone here for you," the landlady repeated, this time with greater urgency. "An American."

Now what, she thought? Who could this be?

But before she could answer herself, a figure emerged from the adjacent room and stood behind the landlady. It was Perdue.

"What are you doing here? You shouldn't be here," Therese insisted.

"I need to talk to you," Perdue replied.

There was a moment of awkward silence, as no one was quite sure what to do next. Finally Therese said to the landlady, "Can you give us a moment, please?"

The landlady looked at Therese, then back at Perdue, wondering whether or not she should go when Therese said, "It is okay. Everything is fine. This will only take a minute."

The landlady gave Therese a worried look, but said to her in German, "I'll be in the next room if you need me." The landlady gave Perdue a disapproving look and then left the room.

Therese waited until the landlady was gone, knowing all too well that she would be listening to everything they said.

"What is it? What are you doing here?" she whispered to Perdue.

"It's Karla. She's been arrested."

"Dettmer!" Therese spat his name out with rage and venom. *Two can play this game, Oberleutnant Dettmer*, she thought. Therese knew what she had to do next, and she immediately began formulating her plan. She was furious, but she was not out of control. Once again, Therese Weber would prove herself to be a woman of action.

Chapter Fifteen

Lehman arrived at his office early the next morning and was hard at work organizing the piles of intelligence reports and photographs that Banbury had left behind. His office was not set up as the situation room, so he constructed an evidence board, where the key pieces of evidence, suspects, assumptions, and motives would be pinned to a wall, a technique that would make it easier to identify relationships, all relevant facts, dates, and, ultimately, would develop the clues that would enable them to find and capture Dettmer. It would also help make the case for the military prosecutor once Dettmer was captured.

Lefkowicz popped his head into the doorway and said, "You're here early," looking at the wall clock displaying 0615 hours.

Lehman continued to work and, without looking up, said, "I wanted to get a head start." He walked to a small table at the far end of his office. It held a collection of field manuals and training circulars, as well as a stack of local German newspapers that he read each day to keep up with the goings-on in and around Bremen. He transferred the items to the floor and said, "I'll find a place for these later. Can you give me a hand? I want to move this table to right in front of my desk. This is where I want Haas to sit."

"Keeping your eye on her all the time, huh?"

"Exactly."

They lifted the table and placed it in front of Lehman's desk. It wasn't particularly heavy, but it was too bulky for one person to handle alone. Lehman then grabbed the chair that sat next to his desk and placed it at the table so that anyone sitting there would be directly in front of him.

"There," Lehman said, looking at the new arrangement feeling satisfied with his handiwork. He reached into his shirt pocket, grabbed a cigarette, immediately found his lighter, and lit up.

"What time did you tell Haas to show up?" he asked Lefkowicz as he surveyed the new layout in his office.

"I told her to be here for Detachment formation at 0730."

"Good. That's perfect, in fact. Hey, can you spare one of those bulletin boards that you have in your office? I want to set up an evidence board here so we can methodically look at everything."

"Yeah, I can move it over here this morning."

"That'll work. Here's what I want to do. I want you and Haas to organize all of these reports. We don't need everything they gave us, at least not now. Our first job is to find this Dettmer guy, and we don't even know what he looks like. So I want you two to go through everything and see if we can get a description. As soon as we have a description, send a TWX to all commands, to the Brits, the French, and even to the Russians, and indicate that he is to be apprehended immediately.

"I also want to find out who else worked with him at the bunker. Do we have anything on them? Have they been interviewed? Let's locate anyone who knew him and might be able to give us a line on where he is now. My guess is that he's gone underground and is using false papers. He would have been high enough on the pecking order for the Brits to have grabbed him, so he's probably impersonating somebody. That's why we have to get a description out there. He's in the country somewhere. In fact, I think he's still here. He wouldn't want to go to the Russian zone. It's possible that he's in Bavaria somewhere or even Austria, trying to get out through the ratline."

Routes of escape called "ratlines" sprang up before the end of the war and provided a way for Nazis and Fascists to escape and flee Europe. There were two primary routes. The first ran from Germany to Spain and the second from Germany and Austria into Genoa, Italy. Both of these routes would eventually lead to safe havens located mainly in

Latin America, but the United States and Canada were also potential destinations. Even the CIC used ratlines as an operational tool. High-ranking officers, German scientists, and other Nazi officials were offered the means to escape to freedom in exchange for their cooperation or for information if CIC agents felt it would help ensure success of their own operations. It was a dirty business.

"Make sure we check all of our CIC contacts, especially down at the 430thin Austria," Lehman said. "Those bastards are knee-deep in Nazis. We need to make sure he's not on somebody's list. But unless he's getting help, he's still here. It's expensive to book passage for that trip, and it's not like he can travel in steerage on the *Queen Mary*."

"I'll bet a dollar to donuts that he's trying to get to Spain," said Lefkowicz. "From there he could get anywhere in South America. That would make sense since he's ex-Gestapo. He could easily make it to Spain from Hamburg or Bremerhaven. Once he's there, we can kiss his ass goodbye."

"If we find out he's out of country, that's going to change things entirely. But I think the Brits believe he's still here, too. Otherwise, they wouldn't be pressing us for help. So let's go on that assumption until we find out otherwise."

Lehman stubbed out his cigarette in the ashtray on his desk. "Haas needs to weigh in on our little theory, too. She knows this stuff better than we do, so I'm sure she has an opinion. Let's find out what she knows and thinks."

Lefkowicz nodded in agreement.

"Have you had chow?" Lehman asked, checking his watch, which read 0650. "We have time to grab something quick before formation."

"Nope. I just came over here when I saw the lights on."

"All right let's go. We'll have to make it quick."

***

The detachment's morning formation was normally a routine, re-petitive event. In fact, it wasn't really a formation, at least not the way other units in the U.S. Army ran formation. First, the men of the 323rd didn't line up outside "in formation" for roll call like every other U.S.

Army unit did each morning. Second, they didn't take a roll call, where a company clerk or first sergeant would call out each man's name and listen for a reply such as, "Here," or "Yo!," or occasionally, "Present," to indicate the person they called was indeed physically present and ready for duty.

Instead, the men of the 323rd met in a large debriefing room, the very room that Lehman and Lefkowicz used the day before for their meeting with Banbury and Richardson. Per routine, Lefkowicz checked off each man's name from his roster as they entered the room.

With only thirteen men assigned to the 323rd, it seemed more efficient to do it this way. Both he and Lehman also felt their way of running formation helped to make a group of highly educated men feel comfortable and part of a team. Their job was to make sure the mission got done, and neither of them was so gung-ho about doing it the Army way of following form to interfere with efficient function. Also, they had secrets to discuss, and those types of discussions were best kept inside away from prying ears and eyes.

But on this morning, their normal routine was disrupted. Upon entering the room, the first thing the men of the 323rd noticed were the curtains, they couldn't help seeing the enormous table and the chairs that now dominated the room, and finally the flowers sitting on top of the table. Finally, they saw Luba Haas standing next to Lehman, engaged in a quiet conversation. Normally, there would be chatter among the men, in at least four different languages. But today, when they saw Haas, the men immediately fell silent. They looked at Lehman and then at Lefkowicz in disbelief.

"All right, you guys," said Lefkowicz. "Let's get in here so we can get started. I know you've all seen a woman before."

Haas stood next to Lehman, and she gave each man who entered the room a "do not mess with me" look. Her presence was striking. Her hair was down, framing her face and giving her a soft look that was a stark contrast to the rest of her appearance. Instead of the flight officer's uniform she wore the day before, Haas was dressed in utility fatigues, immaculately pressed and starched. She wore brown combat boots that were bloused, her trouser legs tucked neatly into her boots, and around her waist was a leather belt and holster bearing a Webley MK IV-38 revolver. But the cherry on the sundae—or perhaps more appropriately the coup de grace, the death blow of certainty that left no doubt Haas was all business—was the long sheath strapped around her left leg that housed her weapon of choice, her Shanghai knife with a nine-inch-long blade. Even Lehman had been startled by her appearance when she walked into his office shortly after he and Lefkowicz returned from chow. Lefkowicz could only mumble a "What the hell?" when he saw her, while Lehman's response was simply, "Good morning, Luba. Sleep okay?"

Haas knew that she had disrupted the usual ritual. That was her intention. She sought such a disruption because it was powerful, and whenever she could throw her adversaries off their game, it helped her establish control. Above all else, Haas liked to be in control.

Lefkowicz continued to call roll, calling out each name from his list indicating their presence until he had checked off all thirteen names, including his and Lehman's. When he finished, he turned to Lehman and said, "All present, sir."

Lehman stepped forward to address the now very curious group of men in front of him.

"All right, listen up, everyone. We have new orders that will become your number one priority in addition to all of your other number one priorities. This woman here," he said pointing to Haas, "is Flight Officer Ludmilla Haas. She's an officer in the Royal Air Force, and she's been assigned to our unit. She's also a member of the British Intelligence, and she served in Poland, North Africa, France, and Lord knows where else during the war. She's here to help us carry out those orders. So listen up gentlemen and get ready. This mission may be the most important thing you'll ever do in your life."

Chapter Sixteen

Therese looked at Perdue. He was nervous, scared, and she asked, "Are the MPs looking for you?"

"Yeah, they are," Perdue replied. "I was over at Karla's apartment while she was out delivering booze and cigarettes, but she never came home. I had the jeep and drove around her neighborhood looking for her, that's where she was supposed to be. But I couldn't find her anywhere and got scared that something must have happened. When I got back to her place, her landlady came out screaming and yelling at me, saying a couple of plainclothes CID guys had just been there looking for me. They told her that Karla had been arrested for dealing on the black market, and they wanted to know where I was. She told them I had been there, but that I must have gone back to my barracks. I begged her to let me in, and she did, she said I could stay the night, but that I had to leave in the morning. So that's when I came over here. I figured you could help. Now I'm AWOL, I didn't show up. I didn't open up the newsstand, and—oh, man—this is just a mess," he said, holding his face and sobbing. "I don't know what to do. You've got to help me figure out what to do."

Therese thought for a few moments in silence, processing what Perdue had just told her and pondering what the next steps should be.

"Now you listen to me and listen to me very carefully. Here's what we're going to do. You have to turn yourself in. Every minute, every hour you are AWOL, you make it worse. So, you're going to turn yourself in to the MPs."

"What? Are you crazy? That's nuts! I can't do that! They'll throw me in the stockade, I'll get busted."

"Maybe you will, but what choice do you have? You can't stay here, and you can't make believe you're a German citizen. You don't have papers, you don't have a ration card, you have no way of supporting yourself. Thinking you can hide and not face the consequences, that's crazy thinking. You should be grateful there is no longer a war going on. Otherwise, they would shoot you as a deserter. No, you'll turn yourself in, and I will help you."

"How? What can you do?"

"I have something they want. I have information they need, and if they want that information, I will give it to them. But they'll have to release Karla, and I'll make you part of the deal, too. That's the deal, as you would say."

"What are you talking about? What kind of information would you have? You're just a *hausfrau*."

"Hausfrau? You think that's all I was? I was a party member and proud of it. My husband was an SS officer, and I was proud of that, too. I did important work for my country. I had a job, a responsible position. I kept track of the books and accounts at a submarine factory that was being built not far from here. It would have changed the war. No, Lanny. I wasn't just some hausfrau. I have always been much more than that."

Perdue looked at Therese in confusion and asked, "So, what information do you have that could be of use to them?"

"There is a man I worked with. His name is Dettmer, Oberleutnant Heinz Ullrich Dettmer. He was a Gestapo officer and head of security at the bunker, and he did many terrible things. I saw him do something terrible. I saw him do many terrible things. War crimes, that's what I saw. But he was never captured and arrested for his crimes, and he is still in Bremen. I know where he is, or at least how to find him, and I will use that information to get them to release Karla."

"I don't get it. How does this help me? I don't see how this helps me at all."

"Don't you see? We can go to the American authorities together. If they agree to drop any charges against you and Karla, I will help them find Dettmer, and I'll testify against him at any trial."

"What about your crimes? If what you are telling me is true, you were there. I've heard about these places. The camps and everything. You were involved in all of that stuff, too, right? Jesus, I can't believe this."

"No," she replied adamantly. "I never killed anyone. I was not responsible for any of the deaths. It was the guards, the Kapos, and men like Dettmer. They did it, they are responsible. Not me. Not me."

Perdue simply looked at Therese and shook his head.

"Yeah, that's what every German says. It wasn't me, it was them. It was some other guy, but not me." Perdue let out a laugh and said, "Yeah, every German always says, 'Oh, I never fought against you, I love Americans. I fought in the East against the Russians.' Hell, if I had a buck for every German who told me that, I'd be rich." Perdue walked over to the front door and pulled back the curtains to look outside to see if anyone was searching for him. He observed a few Germans on the street walking by, but no military vehicles, no soldiers, no MPs.

"Look, Therese, time is on their side. They got all the time in the world. And they'll eventually find this Dettmer guy whether you help them or not."

"No. You don't understand. Dettmer plans to be on a boat next week that will take him to Spain. He told me about it, but he needs something from me. It's something I kept from the bunker, and he wants it. He also tried to force me to give up everything I collected today, all of the gold and jewelry. He'll escape unless I help them."

"How do you know that?"

"Because I just saw him. I spent over an hour with him. He was at my parents' house earlier this morning, and then he tried to follow me home. He's responsible for Karla's arrest. He told me he was arranging a demonstration. He threatened my children and said I would never see them again if I didn't help him. But I wouldn't give in to him. So

I ran. I escaped with the children by running in front of an American convoy. They almost ran us down. The soldiers who escorted me home, they were part of that convoy. I tried to point out Dettmer to them, but he disappeared. He's working with someone else. Someone that I am supposed to know."

"They'll never buy it, Therese. I'm done. They're gonna lock me up. And they'll do the same to you too."

"Lanny stop. Get ahold of yourself. Listen to what I am saying. They won't lock you up. I will tell them it was my idea. That I made you and Karla do it. I'll tell them that you only were trying to help us and help our families survive. That's why you got into the black market. And that's true Lanny. You are a good man. That's what I'll tell them. That you are a good man and got caught up doing something wrong. But we never hurt anyone. We were just trying to survive. I'll tell them that. I will," she said earnestly.

Perdue continued to look outside, knowing that it was inevitable, they would find him eventually. There was only one place he could go. So he turned around and walked back to where Therese was standing.

"All right. I'll do it. I'll turn myself in. But you have to help me like you said. I'll do it with you. You'll do that, right?"

Therese walked up to Perdue, stood in front of him, and lifted her hands to gently cradle his face. She tried her best to console him, wondering at the same time how the Allies were ever able to win a war with soldiers like Perdue in their ranks. She genuinely felt sorry for him, but then anger swelled inside her. She became angry for allowing herself to become mixed up in all of this in the first place. She knew she had to find a way out, and as she held Perdue's face in her effort to comfort him, she replied, "Yes, Lanny. I'll help you. I'll help you because it has to be done. And I know it is the right thing to do."

***

In less than a week, Haas had won over nearly every man in the 323rd. She impressed them with her willingness to roll up her sleeves and work. She fit in perfectly with a group of men who were more intellectual than physical. She especially enjoyed speaking to Lefkowicz and the men who spoke Polish, her native tongue. She helped them screen the continuous stream of refugees that arrived in Bremen. She sat in as Lehman's men interviewed persons of interest, helping them translate, asking follow-up questions, and identifying those who needed additional screening and interrogation. On her fourth day in the unit, she volunteered for watch officer and pulled a twenty-four-hour shift alongside a young Jewish corporal named Falkowski. She regaled him with stories of her childhood in Gdansk. When prodded, she shared some of her war experiences in Poland, France, and the Middle East, and the young corporal on his first assignment was spellbound. She never came across as being boastful. It wasn't bragging, she was simply giving testimony to what she had experienced and witnessed during the war.

Even Lehman noticed how the men had taken to her. It wasn't just that she was a woman. In just a few short days, her no-nonsense, mission-first attitude caused the men to see her as just another soldier. She jumped in, rolled up her sleeves, and worked. No task was too small, nothing was beneath her.

One of the first things Haas accomplished was to compile an updated description of Dettmer based on photographs, first-hand accounts, and testimony from prisoners contained in the MI6 files. The detailed description had gone out via radio-teletype to all Allied commands throughout Europe, along with orders that Dettmer was to be immediately apprehended. He was a wanted man now, and everyone in the world knew what he looked like and the crimes he was alleged to have committed.

In London, the men at MI6 headquarters had viewed her with suspicion. Her experience intimidated them. But the men in the 323rd valued her experiences and treated her with respect. Haas responded by returning that respect, and none of the clashes, the jealousy, the rivalry that she experienced in London, seemed to follow her to Bremen. Haas kept hearing Lehman's words from the first night—"Welcome home, Luba"—and for the first time in years, she felt that she had a home.

Hass's sense of being welcomed and feeling at home changed when she returned to her room that evening. She had just completed a twelve-hour-plus day compiling all the leads on Dettmer that had been coming in from all over Germany.

She climbed the three flights of stairs and walked down the dark narrow corridor to her room, pulled out her key, and unlocked the door. When she entered the room and flicked on the light, she immediately saw the signal. A single yellow rose stood in a small vase on the table just inside her door. It was a meeting request from her handler. The color was significant. Yellow meant it was a routine request. Red meant that there was an emergency.

She looked around the room. It appeared empty, but she knew she could take no chances. She slowly closed the door and stood with her back pressed against it. *What is happening?* she thought. *Why the need for a meeting so soon after arriving in Bremen?* She felt a knot in the pit of her stomach and knew she had to make sure the room was clear, that nobody else was in the room with her, that she and the operation hadn't been compromised.

Still standing against the door, Haas unholstered her Webley and released the weapon's safety. She assumed a combat position, holding the pistol out in front of her with a two-handed grip, knees slightly bent, then stepped forward and moved into the room toward her bedroom door, which was closed. *The door opens to the left,* she thought, *and the wardrobe is on the right,* so that meant she would clear the room from left to right.

She silently walked to the bedroom door and, using her left hand, reached down and slowly turned the door handle. She could hear the click of the handle as it released. She gently pushed the door to let it swing open naturally and then quickly entered the room, turning to her left, she and her weapon ready to engage with anyone, and then to the right. Still silent, she walked over to the wardrobe and, with her left hand, opened the door. She saw nothing but her clothes and personal items inside. *Clear,* she thought, and sighed in relief.

Satisfied that the room was empty, Haas set about responding to the meeting request. She walked back to the table where the vase was, picked it up, and carried it to the window that looked out over the street below. She carefully raised the blinds, first all the way to the top, and then lowered until they hung halfway. She placed the vase with the yellow rose on the narrow window ledge, and the signal was now in place. The request for a meeting was set and acknowledged. She and her handler would meet, and she only needed to find out exactly where and when. Standard procedure dictated she would receive the meeting details within the next twenty-four hours.

***

Haas entered a small bakery on Albertstrasse at just after 2 p.m. It was a small shop with a counter in the front and an area off to the right where patrons could sit down and enjoy their pastry along with a cup of coffee—ersatz, as coffee was still heavily rationed. She told Lehman and Lefkowicz that she just needed to go out for a walk.

"I need to go out for a walk to clear my head," she said to Lehman. "I'm going blind reading all these reports."

"Sure. You okay? Do you want some company?"

"No," she replied. "If you don't mind, I just need a short break."

"Okay. We'll see you when you get back."

And that's all it took. In a little more than a week, she had developed a good rapport and sense of trust with Lehman and all of his men. She felt a little bit guilty about having to deceive him, especially since she considered it unnecessary to put the relationship at risk by conducting a clandestine meeting.

But despite her feelings, Haas nevertheless made sure she wasn't being followed. Her handler would wait for no more than ninety minutes. If she hadn't arrived by then, the meeting would be aborted, and they would attempt to set up another date and time.

The meeting location was less than a fifteen-minute walk from headquarters, but Haas allowed herself forty-five minutes to get there. She wanted to ensure she wasn't under surveillance and that nobody was following her. To a casual observer, it might appear that she was just on a random stroll about town, crossing streets, even backtracking so she could stop in front of several shop windows where she could use the reflection in the glass to see if she could identify anyone who might be following her. By her estimate, she was less than three minutes away from her destination when she was satisfied that she was alone. Nobody had followed her.

She walked quickly, but not so quickly as to arouse suspicion or give any notice, to a small bakery and café, the Backerei & Konditorei Schmidt. As she entered the bakery, James Banbury was already seated at a table at the far corner of the dining area, next to the window that looked out over the street. He had watched Haas approach and was relieved that she would be on time.

Haas picked out a pastry and ordered a small pot of coffee from the young girl behind the counter. She paid and told her, "I'm joining the gentleman sitting in the far corner," pointing to Banbury.

"Yes, madam," the girl replied. "I'll bring your order over to you as soon as it is ready. It shouldn't be but a moment."

"Thank you very much."

Haas moved to the table to join Banbury. He appeared to be distracted by reading a German newspaper, but Haas knew that it was a ruse; his German wasn't that good. He could order a meal and get around a city in taxicabs or other public conveyances, but he didn't possess the fluency to read a newspaper, especially the *Süddeutsche Zeitung*, a center-left paper published in Bavaria, purportedly on the same printing presses used to print Hitler's *Mein Kampf*. It was the first paper licensed by the American army after the end of the war. *He must have picked it up at the train station. It's a leftist paper, he'd never read it anyway. If his German were adequate, he'd no doubt read* Die Welt, Haas thought as she pulled out the chair in front of him and sat down.

"How are you getting on, Luba?" Banbury said as he looked up smiling from his newspaper,

"Bremen suits me," she replied, somewhat curtly. "The work suits me, and my new colleagues actually know the difference between their ass and their elbow, which is more than I can say about my old friends back in London."

"It's good to see you haven't changed, Luba. I'll make sure to pass along your best wishes to the team."

"Please do. And tell them I miss them very much."

"Quite."

They sat for several minutes in silence. The counter girl approached carrying a tray holding a small container of coffee, cream but no sugar, and the small torte Haas had ordered. She placed the items on the table in front of Haas.

"Thank you, Fraulein."

"You're welcome, madam. Will there be anything else?"

"No, thank you. This will be all."

The girl replied, "Guten Apetit!", gave a nod of acknowledgment, and walked back to her position behind the counter. Haas poured a bit of cream into the coffee and stirred it for a few seconds, waiting for Banbury to speak. It was, after all, his meeting. He had called it.

"Were you followed?"

"Of course I wasn't followed. And you know, we can actually avoid all of this clandestine nonsense, don't you think? Everyone here knows that I work for you at MI6. They know that I'm on a temporary assignment here, and they would understand that you have every reason to want to meet with me privately from time to time. There is no point in going through all of the cloak-and-dagger nonsense. It's only going to arouse suspicion. For God's sake we could even meet back at Lehman's office. He wouldn't mind, I'm sure of it."

"I don't want you to get out of practice. And I want you to be careful. And I want you to know that no matter how close you think you are to these men, no matter how much rapport you think you can build between you and them, you are still, and will always remain, an outsider."

"I'm not so sure about that."

"Just be mindful of your surroundings at all times. Watch yourself. There's nobody else here to watch your back. That's all I'm trying to say to you."

"I'm always careful." Haas turned her attention to the pastry in front of her and discovered she had lost her appetite.

"And how's that going, by the way?" Banbury asked.

"How's what going?

"The search for Dettmer. Anything new? Any breakthroughs?"

"It is going as Lehman predicted. You know what we have done, since you've received all of our outbound communiqués. Just as he said, we're getting leads from every crackpot in Germany, and we're methodically running them down. I have to say, Lehman is putting together quite a case against Dettmer. Did you know he is, or was, a solicitor?"

"Yes, we did know that about him."

"Well, he's very thorough, methodical, and organized. I believe that we will find our man."

Banbury took his last sip of coffee. "I'll be off now, Luba. Good to see you."

"What are you doing here, James? What is it you want?"

"I just wanted to make sure you are well. That's all."

"I'll just take you at your word then, James. Have a safe flight back to London if that's where you're going."

Banbury stood up from the table, straightened his tie, and buttoned his jacket, ever fastidious.

"Stay alert at all times, Luba," he said. He picked up his newspaper, tucked it under his arm, and headed for the door.

***

The next morning, Haas arrived at the office early, ahead of Lehman, which was unusual. *Lehman must live at the office,* Haas thought. *He must hardly sleep because he's always here.* She immediately got down to work at her table in front of Lehman's desk, scouring the files and reports for more information about Dettmer that she would place on the evidence board. Using an evidence board was a new experience for Haas, and she loved Lehman's ability to organize disparate bits of information into a coherent set of assumptions and facts about what they knew and didn't know. Twice each day, once in the morning and then again at the end of the day, he would call Haas and Lefkowicz over to the board and say to them, "What do we have so far?" Together they would review all of the information they had on Dettmer and reach a consensus on any gaps of information and what they would need to do to fill those gaps.

Haas had been working for nearly an hour, painstakingly adding information to the board when Lehman finally arrived. She could hear Lefkowicz's voice from one of the other rooms, and several other men could be heard talking in the hallway outside the office.

"You're here early," Lehman said to Haas. "I'm going to make some coffee, would you like some?"

Haas stopped working to look up at him. "I got up early and decided to get a head start. And, yes, I'd love a coffee."

Lehman puttered about as he prepared the coffee. He had an electric hot plate in his office, and he used it to make coffee each morning. Somehow he had been able to acquire a Silex double-bubble, vacuum percolator. Every morning, he would grind fresh coffee, and he and Walt, and now Haas, would enjoy a cup before they started their day. Like every other morning, he ground the coffee, prepared the percolator and got it started.

He looked up and took note of the evidence board and the new information it contained. As he walked over to give it a closer look, Lefkowicz burst into the room.

"Cap! Luba," Lefkowicz yelled excitedly, "you're not going to believe this!"

"What is it?" a startled Lehman asked.

"It's almost too good to be true but it's true. A blue bird of paradise has just shit all over us."

"What? What does that mean?" Haas asked, not understanding the coarse idiom.

"We found him," Lehman shouted excitedly. "Dettmer. At least I think so. We have a line on him. We have a way to get him."

"Where, how?" Lehman asked.

"I don't know how, but there's a woman sitting over at CID headquarters right now with some American supply sergeant. She says she wants to talk, that she has information about a Gestapo officer who worked with her at a secret bunker. She says he's been hiding and she knows where he is. It's gotta be Dettmer, right? I just know it."

"That's incredible," exclaimed Haas. "What do we do now? When can we talk to her?"

"Yeah, incredible," said Lehman with a skeptical look. "It seems too good to be true. I wonder what the catch is? How would she know that we were even looking for him?"

"I don't know. She may not have a clue. Or maybe she got word through the jungle grapevine that we were looking for Dettmer. Word travels fast. But no matter how she found out, she wants to make some sort of deal. Remember that tip we gave to CID about a woman running a black market operation? And they picked up a woman a couple of days ago in the Altstadt? Well, that woman is this woman's best friend. CID says the two of them and this supply sergeant they nabbed have been running a black market operation out of the *Stars and Stripes* on Camp Grohn. Can you believe that? This woman, the one that just walked in, she says that she's got info about a guy who was a Gestapo officer at the Valentin Bunker. Now, how many guys fit that description? I wonder who that could be? It's gotta be Dettmer. I can just feel it. I'll take luck any day, Cap. But we need to get over there ASAP and take a crack at her before the CID guys screw it up. This isn't their show now."

Lehman sat at his desk and rubbed his forehead. He hoped he didn't have another migraine coming on. They had only sent out Dettmer's description the day before. "It seems too pat. It's too easy. I don't like it," he said to Lefkowicz.

"Yeah, I know you're Mister Cautious, and maybe you're right. But maybe it's easy because we just got lucky. So from my point of view, it looks to me like a big fat gift that just fell right out of the sky into our lap, right?"

"We'll see," Lehman replied. "But I don't believe in miracles, Walt. I stopped believing in that crap a long time ago. I guess there is only one way to find out, though. Luba, do you know enough about Dettmer's background to determine if this woman is blowing smoke up our butt?"

"If that means, will I know if she's telling the truth, of course I will," Haas replied. "Plus, we do have this one photograph of him. It's not very clear, it's grainy, but we could bring it along and show it to her. This was taken when the Germans invited a crew to document how wonderful the conditions were at the bunker and at the Farge camp."

"Bring along all of those, right there," he said pointing to a stack of photographs on her table. "Take the ones with the soldiers in them. Let's see if our girl can pick him out. It's the closest thing we have for a lineup or a mug shot book. Walt, grab a courier pouch for Luba, and we'll hand carry the photos with us."

"What do you think?" Lehman asked Haas.

"Let's assume for the moment that this woman knows Dettmer and where he is. The question is how? What's her tie to him? Is she related? Was he a friend, a neighbor, a lover?" Haas curled her lips and nose in disgust when she uttered the word "lover" as if she smelled a bad odor. "But it doesn't surprise me that Dettmer is still here. His last assignment was here, and he most likely was unable to escape when the British liberated the city. He's smart, and he used the confusion to get away. It wouldn't surprise me if he used fake papers to avoid capture. He wouldn't be the first."

Lehman nodded in agreement. "Did he have any ties to Bremen? Any other reasons for him to stick around?" he asked.

"Not that I, or we, know of. But he was born in Lübeck, and that's not far from here. It's less than fifty miles from Bremen, if I'm not mistaken. And remaining here would make it easy for him to try to escape through Hamburg or Bremerhaven. If that's his goal. Don't forget, we captured and convicted his boss for war crimes. Dettmer certainly wouldn't want to stick around for that. He has to know his time is running out."

"Somehow he's been hiding. He may be getting help from somebody around here. We have a lot of questions, but no answers. But that's usually the way it is."

Lefkowicz returned to the room with a brown canvas courier bag with a zippered lock across the top and the key inserted in the lock.

"Here you are, Luba," he said as he turned the key to unlock the bag. He unzipped the bag and handed Haas the key. "Just drop whatever you want to take with you inside."

Haas smiled, thinking *I'm not an idiot you know. I do know how to operate a zipper,* but she kept her thoughts to herself. There was no sense in arguing, especially now that Dettmer may actually be within their grasp.

Lehman stood up, grabbed his service cap, and headed for the door.

"C'mon, Luba, let's go see what this woman and her sergeant friend have to say for themselves. You're going to scare them shitless anyway when you walk in with a revolver and knife strapped to your leg," he quipped. "One look at you, and they'll be telling us their whole life history." He stopped and turned back to Lefkowicz. "Walt, call CID and tell them we're on our way. And tell them to just hold onto them. Just let them cool their heels for a while until we get there. I don't want CID asking them anymore questions until after we've had our chance. Once we get what we need, then they can do whatever they want to nail the two of them for selling Spam, booze, or whatever they were pushing."

Haas finished placing the handful of photographs in the courier bag, zipped it closed and locked it. She removed the key and smiled at Lefkowicz as she held the key up in her hand to show him. *See,* she thought? *I know how to zipper up a bag!* Lefkowicz just gave her a goofy smile. He was simply in a good mood because they may have received a big break in their hunt for Dettmer.

Lehman looked back at the wall where they had set up the evidence board. They had built a case against Dettmer that the military prosecutors could use. It detailed at least a dozen examples of war crimes Dettmer could have committed at the Valentin Bunker. But they still had no information about Luba's husband and what happened to him. *Let's catch him, and we'll put him through the wringer. We'll squeeze the bastard dry and get what we need to know out of him,* he thought.

"I'm ready," Haas replied as she followed Lehman to the door. "So tell me. What's this about a bird that shits all over you?"

Lehman laughed and said, "C'mon, let's get over there. I'll tell you all about bluebirds of paradise on the drive over."

Chapter Seventeen

Dettmer had been nursing a beer in a small tavern just a short walk from the docks in Bremerhaven. It was a favorite hangout for the port workers, and on this night, like most, the room was filled with sailors, stevedores, and other frequent patrons with dubious pedigrees. The room was shrouded in cigarette smoke, a blue-gray fog hung near the ceiling, and the unmistakable acrid scent of Sulima cigarettes wafted throughout the room. Four men at a table next to the long bar to the left of the entrance were playing a loud card game and the barman and barmaid were arguing because she had been stiffed of the tab by a patron who just got up and left when her back was turned. Over in the far corner on the right, the darkest in the room, a couple were passionately kissing and groping, the man's hand shoved up the woman's dress. But nobody was paying any attention to them.

Hanging on the tavern walls were cheap prints of scenes from the Northern German coastal plains and beaches. The tavern's original owners, now long gone, thought they would add a level of charm to the room. The prints depicted the sand dunes, coastal tide pools, tall beach grasses, and blue waves that were common along Germany's North Sea coastline. There were also a few prints of bathers wading in the sea, playing in the surf, and lounging on the sand. The prints were obviously made long before the war, because missing were scenes of the Atlantic Wall, the system of coastal defenses that included enormous coastal fixed-gun positions, bunkers, and other fortifications for mortar, artillery, anti-tank guns, and machine guns. Sand dunes where lovers once could sneak off for romance in the grasses that hid them from view were replaced by dragon's-teeth anti-tank obstacles. It would be years before the North Sea coastline would once again return to a more natural state. Man would have to pitch in and help with this effort and remove whatever nature couldn't do on her own.

Dettmer sat at a table along the back wall. There was a hallway immediately to his right that led out to the back entrance just in case he needed to make a quick exit. He had been waiting for nearly an hour when he saw the Spaniard enter.

The Spaniard seated himself on the other side of Dettmer's table.

"Good evening, Herr Dettmer," the Spaniard said in German with a surprisingly good Hochdeutsch accent. "Do you have something for me?"

Dettmer looked nervously around the room before answering.

"No. Not yet. There was a problem. But I will have it for you soon. I just need a few more days."

The Spaniard looked at Dettmer coolly and didn't respond. He shouted over to the barmaid, "Miss, a beer please. And two Schnaps. One for me and my friend."

The barmaid looked at him and nodded her head. The Spaniard then turned his attention back to Dettmer.

"Ach, Herr Dettmer, this presents a bit of a problem, I'm afraid. Our friend in Berlin is very anxious to receive the merchandise. He has made it perfectly clear to me that he is willing to go to great lengths to acquire it. He feels a loyalty to you, but as you know, loyalty has limits."

Dettmer glared at the Spaniard. *There was a time, Spaniard, and there will come a time . . .,* and then he held his thoughts, for now was not that time. He needed the Spaniard, and he could not afford to take risks and ruin his best chance at escape from Germany. So he held his tongue.

"I only need two or three more days. That's all. I will have the merchandise in three days," Dettmer repeated emphatically.

The Spaniard waited to reply as he saw the barmaid approach with their drinks. She placed them on the table, pulled out a stubby pencil stuck in her hair, made two tick marks on the cheap cardboard *bierdeckel* for the schnapps and one mark for the beer, then looked over to the other side of the room and shouted at the couple making out in the corner.

"Hey, get out of here if you're going to do that. This is a respectable place. If you're going to act like dogs in heat, take it outside!"

The man abruptly stood up, indignant at the public rebuke, and in so doing, the woman on his lap fell on the floor, where she sprawled out and was displayed in a very unladylike fashion. The two erupted into a torrent of curses, first directed at each other and then at the barmaid, and then at anyone who dared to look at them and laugh. This drew the attention of the barman, who moved out from behind his station at the bar, truncheon at hand, ready to act.

"Get out! Get out now, you filthy swine," the barman bellowed.

The man muttered more curses under his breath but decided that now was not the time to take on the barman. So he reached into his pocket, found a roll of Reichsmarks, and threw the notes onto the table to pay for his beer.

"There, take it all. It's worthless anyway," he shouted. "We're leaving. Satisfied?" he yelled, glaring at the barman and barmaid. He reached down to grab the hand of his paramour, who was still splayed out on the floor beneath his feet. "Come on. Get up," he yelled at her. "Let's get out of here." With a mighty pull, he hoisted the woman back onto her feet. She pulled down her skirt and dusted herself off to the sound of catcalls and lewd comments from the tavern's patrons.

The Spaniard took a sip of his beer as he watched the fracas. The man and woman slowly made their way to leave, but at the last minute they stopped at the door. The man whispered into the woman's ear. She smiled and let out a throaty laugh. The pair turned to face everyone in the room and gave a bow as the patrons hooted and laughed. The couple then abruptly turned one more time, with their back to the room. Suddenly, the man dropped his trousers and the woman lifted her skirt, and the couple displayed their ample bottoms, mooning the tavern's patrons and causing even more laughter, yelling, and shouting.

"Get out, get out now," screamed the barman as he raised his truncheon and ran toward them. The couple quickly pulled up their clothing and made a hasty exit through the door, just before the barman reached them.

"That's right, and don't come back," the barman yelled. "Don't ever come back." With that he turned his attention to everyone in the room and shouted, "All right, now. It's all over. There's nothing more to see." And with that, the tavern's patrons returned to their game of cards, their cigarettes, and to whatever solace they found in their drinks.

The Spaniard once again turned his attention to Dettmer.

"The government really must get the housing situation under control," he said. "People need their privacy, and certainly the public doesn't want to see displays such as that, don't you think?"

"I wouldn't know," replied Dettmer. "I have my own problems and don't concern myself with how others conduct themselves."

The Spaniard stared at Dettmer and took another sip of his beer.

"We have known each other for many years, Herr Dettmer. You and I have had some glorious experiences together fighting the leftists and the communists, haven't we?"

Dettmer didn't reply, but he vividly remembered those days. It was over ten years ago when Dettmer first met the Spaniard. He was just a young recruit, new to the Gestapo, and he was thrilled to be part of something that was bigger than himself. He volunteered for service in Spain and, over time, became one of Germany's point men during the civil war. He started as a messenger and runner, passing messages between the Gestapo, the Abwehr, and Franco's forces. Eventually, he worked his way up to a position where he coordinated intelligence between the Gestapo and the Spanish secret service. It was during his time in Spain that Dettmer learned the limits of how much pain a human could endure under severe interrogation. He was able to observe it first-hand and developed quite an appetite for delivering it.

"We are old friends, Herr Dettmer," the Spaniard continued. "There is a ship leaving from Hamburg to Valencia in ten days. That is the earliest date on which I can accommodate you, so I can give you your three days. I can give you a week. For that matter, I can give you all the time you need, but I'm certain you will want to be on this ship, given your current situation. I'm told," he said, then held his thought as he looked directly at Dettmer and paused to take another sip of beer. "I have heard they are looking for you. So I am sure the passage that I can arrange will be the best situation for you. I wish the payment for it didn't have to get in the way of our friendship, but we all have to answer to someone, don't we?"

Dettmer returned the Spaniard's stare and asked, "What have you heard?"

"I am told there is a renewed interest in your whereabouts," the Spaniard said. "It seems now that the Americans are here, they are interested in speaking to you about certain goings-on, things that you were involved with during the war. It's probably nothing, but one cannot be too sure these days. The Allies are still looking to make examples of those who had to make the difficult decisions during the war, no?"

"I will have your payment, the merchandise," Dettmer replied. "I will meet you here one week from tonight. I will need identity papers, passports, exit visas, and so forth. And money. I'll need money from you in exchange for my payment to you."

The Spaniard nodded his head gravely.

"You will have everything you need to safely leave the country and start a new life. The merchandise we seek has great value, and our friend in Berlin is willing to ensure you are adequately compensated for it. Now," he said, sliding the glass of schnapps across the table to Dettmer, "let's drink to our old times together, to our friendship, and to your bright future."

***

When Therese and Perdue walked into the military police and CID headquarters, the young MP on duty, who didn't look to be a day over eighteen, didn't know what to do or make of them. When Perdue explained who he was and that he was turning himself in because he was wanted on suspicion of black market activity, the confused MP just looked at him and said, "Wait right here," assuming that Perdue and whoever this woman was would not have second thoughts about turning themselves in, that they would do as he asked, and they would wait right where they stood and not run away.

The MP returned a few minutes later along with a tall master sergeant named Colgan who was clearly in charge and looked as if he didn't have the patience to be bothered by cranks and crackpots. He looked at Perdue and then stared at Therese by his side.

"Sergeant, can you explain to me what it is you want? It seems that my young private here is a bit confused. He says you want to turn yourself in for selling goods on the black market. And he also says this woman here," pointing to Therese, "has information that she wants to provide about a Gestapo officer? But she'll only give us that information if we let you go. Have I got this straight? Maybe you can explain this to me. What the hell is going on here?"

Once again, Perdue went into the speech that he and Therese had rehearsed earlier.

"Look, uh, Master Sergeant Colgan," Perdue said as he read the MP's name off the name tag on his chest, "my name is Perdue—Staff Sergeant Lanny Perdue—and this woman here is Therese Weber, and she works with me at the *Stars and Stripes* over on Camp Grohn. A couple of days ago, the Landpolitzei arrested my girlfriend for black marketing, and she spilled the beans about me. We've been selling stuff for a while now, and a couple of CID guys were looking for me over at her apartment. I'm ready to turn myself in, but Therese here—Frau Weber, that is— has some important information about a Gestapo officer who is still on the loose. But she won't give you that information unless the charges against me are dropped and against Karla, too. Karla, that's my girl-friend. You know? The one the Germans got the other day?"

The master sergeant looked incredulously at Perdue and Therese. Finally he said, "Wait here. Don't move." He then turned to the MP private and said, "You! Watch them. Don't let them out of your sight, and do not let them leave. Understand?"

"Yes, sergeant," the private replied with a feeling of satisfaction in his voice and redemption in his soul for having his version of the story confirmed by Perdue.

A few minutes later, the master sergeant returned, this time with a plainclothes CID agent in tow.

"You're Perdue?" the agent asked.

"Yes, sir. That's me."

The agent looked at Therese. "Do you speak English, ma'am?"

"I do," she replied. "Yes I do."

"All right, I want you both to come inside with me. Private, please take Sergeant Perdue here over to Processing and then place him in room 2. Ma'am, I want you to please come with me."

"You can't arrest him," Therese shouted. "If he is arrested, I won't give you any information. Do you understand?"

"Ma'am, please calm down. It seems that Sergeant Perdue here is wanted on suspicion of black market activity. So we have to take him in. All we're going to do right now is process him in, because those are the rules, and we go out of our way to follow the rules here. While he's doing that, you and I are going to have a little talk. And then we'll see about what happens next." He waited while Therese and Perdue stood there in silence.

Perdue had a pained look on his face, and Therese was thinking *This is not going as I had planned.*

"Look, ma'am. Let's go inside, and I'll give you a chance to explain your side of the story. It's the only way this is going to work," the CID agent said pointedly.

"Very well," Therese replied. *It looks like we have no other choice. At least for now,* she thought. So they followed the agent into the MP headquarters, and the private escorted Perdue to the left while the CID agent escorted Therese to the right, to a room down a long hallway. As the pair split, Therese called out, "Don't worry, Lanny. I'll get you out of here. Don't worry!"

"Oh, Jesus Christ," Perdue mumbled, "what the hell have I done? What have I gotten myself into?" he said, shaking his head as he was led off down the corridor for processing and detention.

***

Therese sat at a table in a windowless room painted a light brown. The MP headquarters was located on a Kaserne used by a Wehrmacht artillery battalion during the war. The walls of the room, and of the entire building, for that matter, were all painted in the same brown used on every army building in Germany. Hanging from the ceiling were six light fixtures with naked bulbs, each shining brightly, creating a harsh and uncomfortable glare.

After she was brought in and told to sit down, the CID agent listened patiently as she told her story, just the way she and Perdue had rehearsed it. He took notes throughout, jotting down the details, listening carefully to everything she had to say, asking her the same questions in different ways, which required Therese to repeat her answers as he jotted down more notes. When she finished, he looked at her, closed his notebook, and said, "I need you to wait here, ma'am. Would you like some water, or do you need to use the facilities? The restroom, the WC?"

"No, I'm fine. Thank you," she replied.

He looked at her again and replied simply, "Please wait here. I need to make a telephone call. I'll have someone look in on you, and I'll be back as soon as I can."

So she waited. She had already been sitting there for nearly two hours.

She tried to remain calm, but she could feel her heart racing. She got up and walked to the long wall on the other side of the table. She thought it odd that such a large mirror would be on the wall. She stared at her reflection in the mirror, turning her head back and forth, and almost didn't recognize the woman in the mirror. Her green eyes were bloodshot, sunken deeply into her face with dark circles underneath. Her skin, normally pale anyway, had a gray pallor. Normally, she would be wearing makeup, but it was hard to come by these days, even with her connections on the black market. Besides, food for her family always took priority. She noticed lines at the corners of her eyes. *When did I get these?* Her strawberry-blonde hair hung limply. She recalled when she would regularly go to the salon to have her hair styled in the latest fashion. *Is that a gray hair?* And then she wondered whether her husband, if he were still alive, would find her attractive anymore. She pinched her cheeks to try to rouse some color to her face. She still had the high cheekbones that were common among the women in her family. She thought that was her most attractive feature. She fluffed up her hair in an effort to make it look fuller. She wondered if she had overplayed her hand. *Why didn't I just give Dettmer what he wanted? No, then I wouldn't have anything to bargain with. I did the right thing,* she thought, trying to convince herself. As she continued to fuss with her hair, she couldn't help but notice. *There is something odd about this mirror.*

***

Lehman and Haas were standing in a small room lit only by a red light about the entrance. It was the kind of light photographers use in their darkrooms, and it provided just enough illumination for them to see each other—but just enough. They were listening to the CID agent recount his interrogation of the subject sitting in the next room. They stood in front of the two-way mirror that gave them an unobstructed view of the room next door.

"She gave us her name as Therese Weber, and I checked her ID papers. Her papers check out," he said. "She lives in Bremen on Hollerallee 96. That's in the Altstadt district. She has two kids, and she works as a stock keeper and cashier at the *Stars and Stripes* over there on Camp Grohn."

As the CID agent listed the details as he understood them, Lehman and Haas watched through the two-way mirror as Therese stood up and walked slowly over to the other side of the mirror. She appeared to be gazing at the mirror, tilting her head back and forth.

"You sure she can't see us?" Lehman asked.

"Huh, what?" asked the CID agent. He looked up at the two-way mirror and finally noticed Therese standing there barely two feet away from them.

"Oh. Nah. She can't see through the glass. As long as we keep this room dark, it just looks like a mirror on that side of the room.

"She's very pretty," commented Haas absentmindedly, noticing Therese's high cheekbones and strawberry blonde hair. "What else did she say?"

"Huh, oh, yeah, I guess so. Um, let me see, she basically said she was the special assistant to the project manager on a construction project. They were building a bunker, a pretty big facility, from what I gather. She called it Valentin or Valentine, something like that. Anyway, she said that she had information on the whereabouts of a former Gestapo officer who worked at the bunker as the head of security there. But she won't give us any information about him unless we agree to cut a deal and release her along with this other guy we're holding. Oh, and this guy has a girlfriend. And we gotta let her go, too. But it sounded like the Gestapo officer is the guy you are looking for. So, after I heard that, I gave Walt a call."

"Thanks, we really appreciate it," said Lehman. "That's pretty heads-up of you to pick up on that. It's really good work."

"We just got a copy of your TWX, and I read the damn thing a few days ago, so it was top of mind, I guess. But here's the deal. We can't hold her. We have no jurisdiction. We're supposed to turn over civilians like her to the Germans, and they'll deal with her. They got her friend now, she's just sitting in jail. So I thought you'd like to have a crack at her first. But I don't know about cutting any deals and letting them go, Cap. The AG's got a real hard-on for going after GIs who are selling stuff on the black market. Oh, um, beg your pardon, ma'am," he said, looking sheepishly at Haas, who just smiled at him in return. He turned back to Lehman and continued.

"So, Cap, if that's what you're thinking, you're going to have to go pretty high up on the chain of command to pull that off, if you know what I mean. The adjutant isn't just going to let our sergeant friend go. No, sir. He's going to get busted down to private, he'll do some time, and he'll probably get a dishonorable discharge. I'm telling you, the AG has one serious hard-on about cases like this. Oh, I'm sorry, ma'am. Beg pardon."

"Think nothing of it," Haas replied. "I've heard worse, and besides, how hard can it be?" Haas gave the CID agent a wry smile as his eyes opened wide, not knowing how to answer the question.

Lehman just ignored the exchange and said, "We'll cross that bridge if and when we need to. In the meantime, what's going to happen to this sergeant? What's his name?"

"His name is Perdue, Cap, Staff Sergeant Lanny Perdue. He's a supply sergeant, and he is running the Stars and Stripes newsstand. Jesus, it's always the supply guys."

"Yeah, so it seems. Too much temptation, maybe," Lehman said as he continued to stare through the glass at Therese on the other side. "So, normal procedure is to release him back to his unit until the AG decides what charges to bring. Isn't that right?"

"Yep, that's right. I think we got everything we need from him. Once we brought him in, he spilled his guts. He knows he's in deep shit."

"Do you have a report of his interview, the investigation report, or whatever you call it? A copy we can have for our files?"

"Yeah, the guys are working on that now."

"Good," Lehman replied. "Please just send us a copy of the report at your earliest convenience, okay?"

"Yeah, not a problem, Cap. I can get it over to you later this evening."

"That sounds perfect. I really appreciate all your help here."

"Hey, we're all in the same army, right? Is there anything else you need from me now?"

"No, I think we're good for now," Lehman replied. "Depending on how our conversation goes, we'll let you know if you can release her or if she's coming back with us. Give us about thirty minutes. If we don't get what we need, you can let her go. And hold off on sending the sergeant back to his unit until we finish up with the woman here, okay?"

"Sure, Cap. Just let me know how you want to play this."

The CID agent walked over to the door. The room was connected to an anteroom that was also dark. He held the door open for a moment and said, "The light switch is here on the right-hand side," he said pointing to it. "But make sure you close this door before you turn the light on. Otherwise, they'll be able to see in here from the other room. Understand?"

"Yep, got it," Lehman replied. The CID agent nodded his head and closed the door behind him.

He turned to Haas and said, "You ready for showtime?"

"Yes, just like we talked about on the drive over. I'll show her the photographs and see if she can identify Dettmer from them. After that, we'll just have to listen to what she says and if she's willing to cooperate with us."

"Perfect, do it just like you did the other day during the screening at the Bahnhof. You're a natural at this interrogation business. Okay, let's see if this woman can lead us to Dettmer."

Both Lehman and Haas looked back into the room once more through the two-way mirror. They watched as Therese brushed the sleeves of her blouse and smoothed her skirt. She took one last look into the mirror and slowly walked back to the table where she grabbed her purse and opened it, presumably looking for something inside.

"Let's go in," said Lehman.

"Right behind you," Haas replied.

Lehman opened the door and entered the small anteroom with Haas following. He shut the door, and the room became pitch black, their eyes unable to see anything in the darkness. Fortunately, Lehman already had his hand on the light switch, and he turned it on. A dim bulb illuminated the room just enough for them to make out the exit door. They moved through the exit into the bright hallway, where they had to shield their eyes from the glare of the overhead light. They waited until their eyes adjusted.

They walked the four short steps to the interrogation room on the left-hand side. Lehman opened the door to the room, and once again Haas followed closely behind.

When the door opened, Therese looked up, and the sight of Lehman startled her. He was about to identify himself to Therese when she saw

Haas standing there next to him. She froze in place, her mouth agape with a stifled scream, and her eyes opened wide as if she had seen a ghost. She was so startled that she dropped her purse, and its contents spilled out as it hit the concrete floor.

"What? You!" Therese cried out in shock and disbelief.

Chapter Eighteen

Kriegsmarine Corporal Ernst Becker was not your typical corporal. At forty-six years old, he could have been the father to nearly all of the men who served with him. He was a giant man, standing over six feet six inches and weighing more than three hundred pounds. He also wasn't the brightest of men. Picked on as a child because of his size and abused by his father, Becker left home and school when he was just sixteen. He bounced around the docks in Hamburg and Bremerhaven supporting himself as a stevedore, where his size and strength made him useful. An uncle, his mother's brother who owned a small bakery, took pity on him and gave him a place to live. His uncle also ran a boardinghouse where many of his employees lived, and Becker received room and board in exchange for performing various odd jobs around the house.

In 1939, just weeks before the German invasion of Poland, Becker enlisted in the German Navy and was assigned to a naval infantry unit. He would see action in Norway and was stationed for a brief time in Denmark. After the SS troops left and the German Navy assumed responsibility for guarding the bunker and its prisoner laborers, Becker was assigned as one of the Kriegsmarine guards.

Despite his intimidating size, Becker was actually soft-spoken, introverted, and shy. He had a trusting nature and could be easily manipulated. It was while serving at the Valentin bunker that Becker came to know Dettmer, the facility's head of security. Dettmer refused to be intimidated by Becker's size and physical strength. Strong of body but pliable of mind, Dettmer thought Becker would be a useful tool for enforcing discipline and order.

"Look at you," Dettmer said when he first set eyes on Becker at his guard post. "You're as big as a house! You'll be very useful to me, Corporal."

Whenever he saw Becker at Valentin, Dettmer would randomly pick out a prisoner. He would then give Becker an order to hold him in place while he administered physical punishment. Becker had no choice but to comply. He had to follow orders, so he decided on his own to avoid Dettmer whenever it was possible. Despite their difference in size and strength—Becker could have snapped the much smaller Dettmer in two with his bare hands—he was intimidated and feared the Gestapo lieutenant. Becker may have been slow-witted, but he fully understood the cruelty Dettmer was capable of. He'd seen it too many times, first-hand. Avoidance was the best course of action.

In late May 1945, at a temporary Allied camp built to house hundreds of German soldiers taken captive at the end of the war, Becker—now a prisoner— noticed a man who looked very familiar, standing alone among the hundreds of soldiers interred there. He didn't place him at first because the man wasn't wearing the uniform of the Gestapo. Instead, he was dressed as a lowly army corporal, the same rank Becker held, and this didn't make sense to him. He spent more than ten minutes staring at the man who looked so familiar, and finally when he was convinced he knew him, he managed enough courage to walk up to him.

The man was standing alone, looking out toward the tall barbed-wire fence topped with a tangle of rolled concertina wire. He stood watching the activities of the British soldiers on the other side. Vehicles moved back and forth, soldiers walked in formation, and he could even see a group of men off in the distance playing football. He appeared lost in thought as Becker walked up to just a few feet behind him, a man he recognized. The man standing there watching the activity on the outside of the fence was none other than Oberleutnant Dettmer.

"*Herr Leutnant*?" he said, "Lieutenant, is that you?"

The moment he heard the voice behind him, Dettmer whirled around to confront the speaker. He squinted as he looked up, and he saw an enormous man standing there. His mind raced, he looked for signs of recognition, and then finally realized that it was Becker, the corporal, one of his charges from Valentin.

"Quiet," he whispered as he looked around to see if anyone was listening and paying attention to them. "Quiet," he repeated as he walked up to within inches of Becker. He fumbled for a cigarette and said, "Do you have a light? Give me a match."

Becker reached into his trouser pocket and pulled out a small box of matches. He handed it to Dettmer, who quickly pulled a match out, struck it, and lit a cigarette, passing it to Becker.

"Here," he said as he handed the cigarette to Becker. "Have a cigarette with me. You do smoke, don't you?" Becker took the lit cigarette and nervously began to smoke it. He was not a regular smoker, and the cigarette smoke made him cough uncontrollably.

"Yes, they taste like shit, don't they, Corporal," Dettmer said as he pulled out a second cigarette and, using the same match, lit it for himself. He put the stubby brown butt into his mouth and inhaled deeply, his face contorting from the bitter, acrid taste. "Maybe we can find a way to get some British cigarettes while we're here. Do you think we could manage that?"

Becker didn't know how he should reply, and the two men stood together in silence, eyeing each other warily.

Finally Dettmer said to the big man, "I just arrived here yesterday. I was picked up by a British patrol as I walked on the main road towards Lübeck." He paused to look around at the hundreds of other German prisoners milling around the camp. "How long have you been here?"

"I'm not sure," Becker replied. "It has been maybe a month, I think, but I can't keep track of time easily." He appeared confused as he looked down at Dettmer wearing the Wehrmacht corporal uniform. "I don't understand, what happened to your uniform, Herr Leutnant?"

"Quiet, dammit. And don't call me that," Dettmer replied angrily. "While we are here, please address me as Corporal Bohlmann. Do you understand? I took this uniform because I am trying to escape. Do you understand?"

"Yes, Herr Leutnant, I mean, yes, Corporal Bohlmann. Who is Bohlmann? What happened to him?"

"He's dead, and he didn't need his uniform anymore, so I took it from him along with his soldier's book," he said referring to the identification papers carried by every German soldier. "Thankfully, we're about the same size. And nobody here needs to know that I was an officer. So, this is our secret, do you understand, Becker? You can keep a secret, can't you? And you still know how to follow orders, do you not?"

"Yes, of course," he replied.

"So, what's my name?" Dettmer asked. "Say it. What's my name now?"

"It's Bohlmann. Corporal Bohlmann," Becker replied, speaking the name slowly, the words coming unnaturally.

"That's very good, Becker. Very good."

The two continued to smoke, and Becker wasn't quite sure what else to say or what he should do next when Dettmer spoke again.

"You come from here, you're from Bremen, aren't you, Corporal?" Dettmer asked.

"Yes, I still have family here. A few people anyway. My uncle runs a boardinghouse in Bremerhaven. I used to work on the docks before the war. I hope my uncle is still around and will be able to take me in after they let us go. I want to go back to work on the docks there. That's what I did before the war. I worked on the docks and lived in my uncle's boardinghouse. They will let us go, don't you think?"

"I think we'll be here for a while," Dettmer replied. "At least until they figure out what to do with us. If they're smart, they'll put us to work. They need to give these men something to do, or they'll have a riot on their hands."

And that is exactly what happened. It wasn't until the end of 1948 that the British and Americans were finally able to release the majority of German soldiers held captive. They were not even considered POWs. Instead they were designated as disarmed enemy soldiers, which helped the Allies skirt around numerous technicalities and comply with the Geneva Convention.

But in late 1946, the demand for labor was great. The country needed to be rebuilt, crops had to be harvested, and work had to be done. So Becker and Dettmer, now aka Corporal Bohlmann, were released on condition they report for work at the docks in Bremerhaven. At first, they were put to work on a construction crew, the irony of which was not lost on Dettmer. But they eventually were able to obtain employment helping to unload the ships delivering the supplies needed by the occupying powers. Working on the docks wasn't a walk in the park by any means, but it was better than the backbreaking work required to rebuild the port facilities of Bremerhaven and Hamburg.

The two became unlikely companions. They were hardly friends, but Dettmer, now masquerading as Bohlmann, had once again manipulated Becker to get what he wanted.

"We served together," Dettmer said to Becker. "You can't deny a former comrade in arms the help that he needs, can you?

And that is how they came to share a dingy room in the dingy boardinghouse near the loading docks in Bremerhaven operated by Becker's uncle. Normally, a man like Dettmer wouldn't even consider associating with the likes of Ernst Becker, but this was a relationship built on opportunity and necessity.

Becker was used to Dettmer's temper and mood swings. He had experienced both first-hand when he served with him at the bunker. But this time Dettmer's mood was especially foul. He was livid that Therese had been able to escape and that he had to negotiate with the Spaniard for the additional time he needed to acquire the merchandise that would secure him passage to Spain. As he watched Dettmer pace back and forth across their tiny room, Becker knew the best course of action was to simply sit, listen, and wait it out, which he was content to do.

He sat in silence and thought about what had transpired earlier in the day. He had followed his instructions from Dettmer to the letter. *Just wait here*, he told himself over and over. *Don't leave. Wait for me. That is what he said I was supposed to do.* He did as he was told, and for several hours he waited for Becker to appear in the alley with the woman, Frau Weber. That was how he always addressed her. That was the name by which he knew her.

"Do not leave the alley until I get there with the woman. Do you understand?"

"Yes, I won't leave until you get there with Frau Weber," he replied. So, he waited and waited until he completely lost track of time. Finally saw Dettmer, aka Bohlmann, enter the alley from the street ahead and slowly walk toward him. When he finally reached Becker, he looked around the alley to make sure they were alone.

All he could say was, "She got away, dammit. I cannot believe it, but she got away."

Hours later, back in their room, Dettmer had finally calmed down and he looked over at the big man sitting across the room from him.

"I'm going to tell you exactly what I want you to do. Do you understand?"

Dettmer ended nearly every conversation with Becker with the phrase, "Do you understand?"

Becker nodded his head in affirmation but said nothing. Dettmer pulled the room's single wooden chair in front of Becker and sat down. He leaned forward with his elbows on his knees and stared intently into Becker's face and said, "We need to borrow your uncle's delivery truck for a few hours. We have some items to pick up. Now listen to me very carefully. This is what you are to do."

Chapter Nineteen

Lehman and Haas watched Therese as she bent down to retrieve the items from her handbag.

"I'm very sorry," Lehman said, "We didn't mean to startle you. Are you all right? Do you need anything?"

Therese looked across the room and couldn't believe what she saw. *Are my eyes playing tricks?* she wondered.

"Are you all right? Can we get you anything?" Lehmann repeated. "Perhaps something to drink, a glass of water?"

Therese could only stare at Lehman. He spoke in an accent that was identical to hers. *An American, speaking flawless German,* she thought. *Who is this man?* she wondered. *And the woman? How did she . . . What is this?*

Lehman motioned to Haas that they should move forward, and they approached Therese.

"Frau Weber, that is your name, is that correct?" Lehman asked.

"Yes," she replied softly, her voice barely a whisper.

They now stood just a few feet in front of Therese. Lehman stepped forward, extended his hand, and indicated that she should sit down. "Frau Weber, we're from U.S. Army Counterintelligence, and we'd like to ask you some questions. Would that be all right? Do you mind answering a few questions for us?"

Therese couldn't take her eyes off of Haas and didn't respond.

"Frau Weber?"

"Yes. Yes, that will be fine," she said as she moved to the other side of the table. She placed her purse on the floor next to the chair and sat down. Lehman and Haas each took a seat directly opposite her, Haas on the right, Lehman on the left.

"So, Frau Weber," Lehman began. "We understand that you have information about a man that we are looking for. Oberleutnant Heinz-Ulrich Dettmer. Do you know this man?"

Therese was tired, and as she looked across the table she wondered how much longer this would go on. *This is what they do*, she thought. *They keep asking you the same questions over and over to wear you down. I can do this. I can play their game.*

"Yes, I know him," she replied, not giving any more information than she had to give. *Make them work a little*, she said to herself.

Lehman looked at Haas and nodded his head. Haas opened the zippered bag she had been carrying and pulled out six black-and-white photos and neatly laid them out onto the table in front of Therese.

"Can you point him out to us, Frau Weber?" Haas asked. "Which of these men pictured in the photographs here is Dettmer?

So that is what her voice sounds like. She's a Pole, too, thought Therese. Therese looked at the photographs. They were taken when the Waffen SS guarded the facility, before the Kriegsmarine took over the assignment. She looked over the photographs carefully and placed two fingers on the single photograph that contained Dettmer's image. She turned the photograph around and oriented it so that it faced Haas. There were two SS guards in the photograph standing next to Dettmer, who stood on the far left.

"This is him, right here," she said, placing her finger on Dettmer's image. She looked at Lehman to make sure he could see that she had identified Dettmer. "This photograph was taken approximately fifteen months after construction began on the bunker. If I recall correctly, it was in the early autumn of 1944."

"When was the last time you spoke to Dettmer? Have you been in contact with him, Frau Weber?" Lehman asked.

"Yes, I saw him just two days ago. He accosted me on the street. I was walking home with my children. We had spent the afternoon with my mother and father, the children's grandparents. He was even snooping around their house, asking for me. It was on my way home that he confronted me on the street."

"What did he want?"

"He wanted my help. He wanted me to give him the . . .," Therese paused and looked down at her hands. "He wanted me to give him the merchandise I was carrying. He was planning to sell it himself to raise money. He needs money to secure passage out of the country."

"Did he threaten you?"

"Yes, he did. He threatened my children and parents. He said I'd never see my children alive if I didn't cooperate with him. He also implied that he was responsible for Karla's arrest. I don't know how he could have arranged that, but somehow he provided a tip to the Landpolitzei about Karla. That's how she was arrested three days ago."

Lehman's mind raced upon hearing this information. *How could this be? It was our guys who provided the tip to the German police. They had picked up information during their routine screening interviews.* Lehman wondered, *Has Dettmer somehow infiltrated our operation?*

"He also said that the next time we met, our conversation would not be as pleasant. And he implied he could hurt my children. And my parents. That is why I ran from him."

Therese took in a deep breath and sat back in her chair.

"And how is that you know Dettmer?" Haas asked. "What is your connection to him?"

"I gave the nice CID agent much of this information already," Therese replied. "I worked as the special assistant to the construction project manager at the Valentin Bunker. I kept the books. I did all of the project accounting and kept track of all the expenses. I knew Dettmer because he was assigned to the bunker as the head of security there. All of the guards reported to him. That is how I know him. I have known him since October 1944. That was when he was assigned to the bunker. He came to us from Poland, and he personally oversaw the transport of a large number of Polish prisoners. I know this because I had to account for all the prisoners who worked on the project. That is how I know Oberleutnant Dettmer."

Therese's words stunned Haas. *She can actually link Dettmer to his activities in Poland,* she thought. She tried to contain her excitement about hearing this information but wasn't sure if she was successful.

"So, Frau Weber, you've been in contact with Oberleutnant Dettmer. Or perhaps it is more accurate to say, he's been in contact with you," Lehman said. "Do you know where he is now?"

"At this very minute, no, I do not know," she replied.

"Please don't play games, Frau Weber," said Haas, "You were doing so well. Don't get cute with us now." Lehman gave her a sideways glance and shook his head, indicating she should back off. Haas took a long, slow, deep breath and leaned back into her chair, trying to cool down and control her anger. *Just give me five minutes alone with this woman,* she thought. *She'll tell me everything she knows.*

"I was about to say that I do not know where Herr Dettmer is at this very minute," Therese said, feeling that she had won a small victory, "because I've been here for several hours. But I can tell you that he is still in Bremen. At least for now. However, he will not be in Bremen much longer, and I can help you to find him and capture him. I can help you, but only if you help me, and you help my friends."

"Frau Weber, you have admitted engaging in black market activity," Lehman said, "and a friend of yours has already been arrested by the police. Your co-worker, Staff Sergeant Perdue has also admitted to his involvement, and he is facing serious charges. It will be easier for you if you simply cooperate with us. If you cooperate, we can speak favorably to the local authorities, and we can possibly recommend you be charged with a lesser crime. But if you don't cooperate," Lehman said, "I'm afraid we cannot help you."

This is it, Therese thought. *I will play the cards I have, and I will not give in.*

"Captain," she said, noting Lehman's rank. "I know exactly what I have done, and it doesn't give me pride. I was a member of," she paused for a second, not wanting to finish her thought and then continued, "I was an officer's wife, and I know right from wrong. But I also know this. I know Dettmer plans to leave Germany very soon. I do not know precisely when, but I know it will be very soon. I know how he plans to get to his destination and know what his destination is. So it should be very simple for you to put the pieces all together. But to do so, you will need my help." Therese paused for a moment and then asked, "Do you have a cigarette? I'd like to smoke, please."

Lehman said nothing, but he reached into his top pocket for his cigarette case. He opened it, pulled out a cigarette, and handed it to Therese. He reached into his right pocket for his lighter and lit her cigarette.

Therese took two quick puffs on the cigarette and exhaled.

"So the question I put to you both is this. How badly do you want to find Dettmer? How important is he to you? And to you?" Therese said, looking directly at Haas, who could only glare back at her. "Dettmer's time in Bremen is counting down. You do not have weeks or months to find him. You only have hours or days. He will not be in Germany much longer, and if he leaves, the chances are very good that you will never catch him. I know that he is a terrible man. He has done many terrible things. I've witnessed some of those things personally. I know what he has done, but do you? I can help you. So I ask you again, how important is Dettmer to you. Is he important enough for you to give me and my friends a few small considerations? I know you can make these things happen because you, after all, are the victors. You are the military rulers of my country. You are the conquerors, and now you are the occupiers. You can make it happen, and I can help you. But time is running out for you. I have all the time in the world, you see. I live here. You two? You two are merely visitors. No matter what you decide to do today, eventually you will leave. But I will still be here. In my country."

Therese paused for a moment and stared across the table at Lehman and Haas.

"I want my friends released," she continued. "I want all charges dropped against them and against me. In exchange for this consideration, you will have my complete cooperation. I will help you find Dettmer before he leaves the country, and you will be able to bring him to justice or whatever it is you want to do with him. That, as you Americans say, is the deal. So, Captain," she said, inhaling on her cigarette one last time, "do we have a deal?

Lehman sat quietly for a minute and considered Therese's words and the offer she had just made. He looked at Haas once again, and she appeared to be ready to explode with anger. *I'd better get her out of here*, he thought. He turned his attention once more to Therese.

"Give us a minute to confer," he said softly. Turning to Haas, he simply said, "We need to talk," He pushed his chair back, stood up, and said again to Therese, "Just give us a minute. We'll be right back."

"I'm not going anywhere," Therese replied.

Lehman and Haas got up together to leave. When they got to the door, Therese called out.

"Captain?"

"Yes?"

"What did you say your name was?"

"I didn't," he replied. He had one hand on the door handle and was about to open it but thought for a moment, and finally he said to Therese, "It's Lehman."

"Lehman?" Therese replied. "What a strange coincidence. That's so interesting. My father's name is Lehman. Karl Josef. Lehman is my maiden name."

Lehman sucked in a deep breath before replying, "That is interesting, and it is a remarkable coincidence."

Chapter Twenty

Lehman and Haas stood in the hallway outside of the interrogation room.

"Are you okay?" Lehman asked.

"Yes, I'm fine. I sometimes get impatient, that's all. I'm sorry I lost my temper."

"It's not important now. It was strange, though. When she first saw you, it looked as if she saw a ghost. You've never met her before, right?"

"No, of course not. I've never been to Bremen in my life until a week ago."

"Hmm. Well, I guess we'll just file that for future questioning," Lehman said, nervously tugging on his ear. "So. What do you think? Is she the real deal? Or is she just trying to get out of the black market charges?"

"She's obviously trying to stay out of prison and keep her friends out as well," Haas replied. "But I believe she is the real deal, as you say. The details she mentioned about Dettmer, about his being in Poland and personally escorting Polish prisoners back to Germany, to Farge. We hadn't known that before. It's a detail that she didn't need to mention, but it gives her instant credibility."

"Yeah, and the bit about Dettmer providing the tip to the German police. It was our guys who gave them that tip last week. Dettmer would have had to pass that information on to someone we screened. That's pretty damned disturbing. It's not impossible, but it's damned disturbing. Walt's gonna have a shit fit when he hears about that one."

"Frau Weber is definitely giving us just enough information in the hopes that we'll believe she's credible, that she's telling the truth."

"Do you believe her?"

"I do," Haas answered without hesitation.

"Yeah. So do I." Lehman pulled out his cigarette case and said, "Smoke?"

"Yes, please. I was quite miffed you didn't offer me one inside," she said with a smile.

Lehman reached into his trouser pocket and pulled out his lighter. He found it on his first try. *Right pocket. I remembered.* Haas noticed, too.

"Your memory is improving, Cap," she said, still smiling.

Lehman let out a little chuckle. Haas was beginning to grow on him. He could see why she was such a hit with the men. He really liked her easy-going manner, and although she was a very serious person, she wasn't full of herself. *She's gone out of her way to fit in,* he thought. *Whatever happened in the past seems to have remained in the past. It isn't affecting her work here.*

He lit both cigarettes, handed one to Haas, and said, "Feel free to jump in if you have any better ideas, but here's the plan. This is what I think we should do. I'm going to call Richardson. We're going to need him to provide air cover on this one. He's going to have to pull rank on the local AG to spring this Perdue character. We'll also have to jump through some hoops with the locals, but I'm sure we can get her friend out of the tank. The Germans have enough on their hands, and they'll be happy to release her to us. We'll need to get a German judge to sign off on the release.

"But the AG is going to be a problem, and Richardson will have to help us. While I talk to him, I want you to go back to the office and get Walt. I want him to get in touch with our liaison officer with the Landpolitzei and get the ball rolling to release Weber's friend—what's her name? Karla Jung, right? Unfortunately, we can't just waltz into the jail and spring her. A German judge is going to have to authorize the release. You and Walt will have to appear before the judge with our liaison officer. Tell him whatever you need to tell him, but we need to get her out."

"I'll tell him Eisenhower has personally asked for her release. That should get his attention."

Lehman tugged on his ear, while he thought through the entire scenario. "Do you really know Eisenhower?"

"We've met."

"Damn. You'll have to tell me about that someday."

"It's a story that is best shared over a drink. Or two."

"Okay, I'll buy," Lehman replied, bringing out a laugh and a smile from Haas. "All right, it's probably going to take us until tomorrow sometime to get all of this done. Hopefully sometime in the afternoon you, Walt, and Weber can go and pick up the children. We'll put them all up together at the hotel. Walt can arrange that, too. The hotel manager will be happy to accommodate us, I'm sure."

"What about her parents? She said Dettmer threatened them, too. I think we should round them all up together."

"That's a good idea. Get the children first and then the parents. Weber will help us with that. She'll see we're just trying to give her protection while all of this goes down. So don't mention any of this to the Germans. As far as anyone is concerned, Weber and her family are coming voluntarily with us. The Germans are a bit touchy about knocks on the door late at night, or anytime during the day, for that matter."

Haas made a mental note of everything she had to do and said, "What else?"

"I'm going to take Weber back to our place tonight for further questioning. We have no authority to hold her, but I'm going to use all of my Southern charm to convince her we're really on her side and that we're working to get her what she wants. Have Walt arrange for a room that's large enough for her and her children. I want to make sure she and her kids are going to be safe. We can keep her at the hotel and arrange for protection there. We'll put a man in the hallway outside her room. This guy Dettmer is probably getting desperate, and who knows what he'll try next."

"Understand," Haas replied. "One room for Weber and her children and another for her parents. What about her friend? We can bring her to the hotel to show Weber that she's been released. It seems that we'll need to offer some protection for her as well, don't you think?"

"Oh, boy," Lehman sighed. "Richardson's going to have a real hissy fit. But, as he told me, as long as we get results, right? I'm sure we can put her up too. We'll put them all up at the hotel."

"Agree. Okay, I'm off to make this happen. Is there anything else you need from me?"

"No, not that I can think of. I'm going to call Richardson. And then I'll tell the good frau what our plan is. Hopefully, she'll buy into it. We're going to need time to pull it off, because there are a lot of moving parts to this idea."

Haas stubbed out her cigarette on the concrete floor but picked it up. Lehman watched her field strip the butt, just as she would have done when she jumped into Poland or France. She carefully pulled the butt apart, crumbling the remaining tobacco between her fingers and then carefully tearing apart the white cigarette paper. She glanced along the hallway and saw an open office door, walked over to the door, and looked inside. A trash bin, she thought, and she quickly dropped the waste into the bin. Watching Haas take such meticulous care with the cigarette brought a smile to Lehman's face.

She walked back over to him and was about to say something when she noticed him smiling. She looked up at him. "What?"

"It's nothing. Go ahead. Go make all that stuff happen. I'll meet you back at headquarters."

Haas turned to leave but suddenly remembered something she had forgotten to ask him.

"Cap, I almost forgot. I wanted to ask you. What was all that about Weber's name? Her maiden name, I mean. Her father's name is Lehman, and she's a Lehman, too?"

"That's what she says. We'll have to verify it, but I have no reason to doubt her. We have their address, and we can check it out in the local city directory. He should be listed there."

"I guess it's just a strange coincidence, then? Didn't you say you still have family in Bremen?"

"Yeah, I do. But I don't know where they are. I don't even remember them, because my family left Germany when I was three. So I've never seen or spoken to them."

Haas had a puzzled look on her face as if she wasn't really buying what Lehman was selling.

"I mean, what are the odds, right? It's just a coincidence," he said. "Go ahead. We have a lot of work to do."

"Yes, just a coincidence," she repeated. Haas gave Lehman a long look and a chance for him to say something more, but when he said nothing, she merely nodded, turned, and headed off down the hallway.

Coincidence, Lehman thought as he watched Haas retreat down the hallway. *It's a coincidence all right. It's a strange coincidence that I actually happen to have an uncle named Karl Josef Lehman. What are the odds? Jesus Christ, this had better be a coincidence,* he thought. He stubbed out his cigarette and went to look for a phone. He didn't have time to field- strip his cigarette and still needed to call Richardson.

Chapter Twenty-One

"You're welcome to use my phone here, Cap," the CID agent said, pointing to the phone on his desk. "You think you'll be able to get them released into your custody?"

"I'm going to try," Lehman replied. "This assignment comes straight from the top, and I'll call in the big guns if I have to."

"The top, huh," the CID agent replied skeptically. "Well, I wish you luck. We're getting ready to release Perdue back to his unit. Should I hold onto him while you call in your big guns?"

Lehman had already picked up the phone on the CID agent's desk and was asking the operator to put through a call to the G2 in Frankfurt. He put a hand over the mouthpiece and said, "Yes. Just give me a little more time."

"Not a problem. I'll tell the guys to hold onto him until you say he can go."

"I'll tell them when and where he can go," Lehman replied.

"Oh, yeah, I'm sure you will. Here, you can have the office. Do whatever you have to do. I'll arrange everything with the guys, and then I'm heading out for the night. If you need me, you can find me at the BOQ. I have a date with a bottle of Scotch."

Lehman chuckled and nodded, "Thanks for everything. I owe you one."

"I'll remember that. I like Johnnie Walker."

"Do you like bourbon?"

"Nah, it's too sweet for my taste."

"Okay, Johnnie Walker it is, then," Lehman replied and then quickly turned his attention to the person speaking to him on the other end of the phone line,

"Yes? Can you hear me?" He waited a few seconds and then was connected to the G2 office in Frankfurt. He reached the officer on duty, who told Lehman that Colonel Richardson had just left for the evening to return to his quarters.

"I need to speak with him tonight. It's a top priority, Captain," Lehman replied. "The colonel asked to be notified as soon as we had a breakthrough in our search for a suspected Nazi war criminal, a Gestapo officer. Well, we've just had that breakthrough, and I need his assistance in wrapping this all up."

"I understand, Captain Lehman. We are aware of your special assignment, and the colonel has left standing orders to notify him immediately if any new information comes in. So I'm going to do that, but I'll need about 30 minutes. I'm going to send a driver over to the colonel's quarters to fetch him. The colonel will return your call as soon as he returns here to headquarters. Where are you now, Captain? Where can he reach you?"

Well, so far so good, Lehman thought. Lehman explained that he was at the Bremen CID office and he gave the duty officer the number at the desk where he could be reached. Now all he had to do was to wait for Richardson to call back.

The call came in twenty minutes. Lehman answered on the first ring.

"Cap, it's Colonel Richardson. You have news for me?"

It took Lehman less than three minutes to recap the events of the day, the details of his plan to capture Dettmer, and, of course, the big ask—freeing Perdue and Karla Jung and dropping all charges against them and Therese.

"And you are certain this woman is legit?" Richardson asked.

"Completely, sir. She's been in contact with Dettmer. He's using an assumed name, a fake identity. She knows where he's living and what he's planning to do next. He's planning to run, sir. So we have to act pretty quickly. There are daily ships out of Hamburg and Bremerhaven to Spain, Portugal, and South America. That's my bet, sir. He's headed to Argentina."

"What about Haas? What's her take?"

"We're in complete agreement, sir."

"Where is she now? Can I speak with her?"

"Well, as we speak, she's working with Sergeant Lefkowicz and our Landpolitzei liaison to secure the release of the Jung woman. That's Weber's friend and accomplice. But we're all meeting up back at our headquarters as soon as I can get everything sorted out here. I can have her contact you then."

Richardson thought for a moment and said, "No, that won't be necessary. I trust your judgment. Do you need any help with the Germans?"

"No, sir. We have a good relationship with the locals here. But, as I mentioned, Staff Sergeant Perdue is another matter."

"You need me to rein in an aggressive AG, is that it?

"That's it, sir. You told me to ask if I needed any help running interference. That's the help I need now, sir. And I'm asking for it."

"All right, Cap," Richardson replied. "I can do that. But I may have to throw him a bone. I am sure that when I explain how important capturing Dettmer is, he'll cooperate. But he'll probably want a little blood, not a whole pint, but probably a few drops. I'll go in asking him to drop charges, but my fallback will be reduced charges, probably a reduction in grade, forfeiture of some of the sergeant's pay. A slap on the wrist given command's interest in stopping black market activities. What's his name again?"

"Perdue, sir. Staff Sergeant Lanny Perdue."

"Got it. I will tell the AG there that Perdue will be released into your custody until Dettmer is captured. And I'll speak to him about going easy on the young man. Can you work with that?"

"Yes, I can make that work, sir," Lehman said. "Weber doesn't need to know all the intricacies of the military justice system. She'll just be happy to see him and her friend." Lehman closed his eyes and tugged nervously on his ear. *Interesting*, he thought, *no migraine. Okay, is there anything else I'm forgetting? I hope not*, he thought.

"So, with your permission, I'd like to go ahead with our plan."

"Agreed. You are authorized to proceed, Cap. Dammit, I told you I wanted results, and you came through, just like I knew you would."

"We still have to capture Dettmer, sir."

"You will, Cap. You will. Just carry out your orders and keep doing what you're doing. Call me if you need anything else. And call me the minute you find and capture Dettmer. I want to be there when you interrogate the son of a bitch."

"Yes, sir. You'll have a front-row seat."

"Good, Cap. All right, Richardson out."

Lehman placed the receiver down and pulled out his cigarette case. *I need a cigarette*, he thought. *No, I need to get Perdue and Weber out of here.*

***

Therese had fallen asleep in the interrogation room, her head lying on her arms on the table like a kindergartner at recess. The MPs had looked in on her earlier, and she declined their offer of food, but she did take some water. She waited for Lehman to return but grew tired and decided to close her eyes. She fell asleep immediately, but it was a fitful sleep. She dreamt Dettmer was chasing her and the children. She was trying to outrun him, running down an empty street and pushing the pram with the children inside as fast as she could. But no matter how fast she ran, no matter how hard she pushed, she could see Dettmer gaining on her. He was closing in and just about to reach out and grab her. She screamed.

She didn't hear the door open but awoke with Lehman shaking her shoulder.

"Frau Weber? Are you all right?"

She took in a sharp breath and opened her eyes. She lifted her head off the table, realizing that it was just a dream. When she looked up at Lehman, she saw another man standing next to him. She smiled. It was Perdue.

"Frau Weber, I've arranged for Sergeant Perdue's release. And your friend Karla is being released, too."

"What?" Therese was still groggy from sleep and tried to make sense of what was happening. "You did it? Lanny, is that really you?"

"Yeah, it's me, Therese," Perdue replied. "I've been released to Captain Lehman here."

"That's right, Frau Weber," Lehman interjected. "And tonight, you're both coming back with me. Karla is being released, too. We're going to put you all up at the Hotel Zur Post. Do you know where that is?"

Therese nodded her head.

"Good. And in the morning, we're going to pick up your parents and children. They'll stay with you at the hotel, too."

"Are they being arrested?"

"No, of course not," Lehman replied. "I only want to make sure they are protected and safe until we capture Dettmer. We can look after them at the hotel and post a guard for their safety. Look, I'm not going to go into all the details tonight because it's getting late, and I want to get you out of here, but you three are not out of the woods completely. You still have to cooperate with us. Understand? And if you cooperate, I am pretty sure we can get all of the charges dropped. Do you understand me?"

"Therese, just tell the man whatever he wants to know," Perdue pleaded. "Just tell the man, for God's sake."

"So, if I cooperate, you say we will all go free?" Therese asked Lehman, ignoring Perdue's plea.

"Just tell the man, Therese!"

Lehman ignored Perdue and said, "We will do everything we can to make that happen. But only if you cooperate. Is it a deal? You cooperate, and we'll see the charges are dropped?"

Therese, now completely awake, sat upright in her chair, folded her hands, and placed them on the table.

"Well, this has turned out better than I could have imagined," she said.

"Therese," Perdue said, "For God's sake, just tell the man."

Lehman looked at Therese and awaited her answer.

"Yes, Captain. It is a deal."

Lehman looked directly at Therese and said, "Good. Now, please tell me. Where is Dettmer, and how do we find him?"

"If you want to find him, the first thing you must do is search for the right man. He no longer goes by the name of Dettmer. He's been using the name Bohlmann."

Chapter Twenty-Two

It was nearly midnight when Haas and Lefkowicz finally returned to headquarters. They had been able to convince a German judge to release Karla. They brought her back to the detachment headquarters, and she was waiting in the large debriefing room when Therese entered the room. Karla and Therese had a tearful but happy reunion. She had a different reaction when she saw Perdue.

"You got me arrested, you idiot," Karla screamed, running over to him, her hands flailing and slapping at his face. She continued to pummel him with slaps to his head and face as Lefkowicz and Haas moved in to separate the two.

"Aw, baby, it wasn't my fault," cried Perdue, raising his hands to protect his face. "It was a set up! I didn't do anything! I swear!"

"That's enough, you two," shouted Lefkowicz as he and Haas separated the pair. "One more outburst like that, and I'll have you sent back to jail, you understand me?" he said, directing his anger at Karla, who continued to give Perdue a look that said, "If I get my hands on you, I'll wring your neck."

"And you," Lefkowicz said, pointing in Perdue's face, "you sit down over there and shut up. I don't want to hear a word out of either of you. Understand?

The room fell silent just as Lehman walked in.

"What's going on here? Is there a problem, Walt?"

"It's nothing, Cap. Fraulein Jung here was just expressing her displeasure at our man Perdue over there. But we won't have any more of that, right?" He glared at Perdue, Karla, and Therese. "I said, we won't have any more of that, right?"

"No, of course not, right, right," they all replied.

Once again, silence came over the room.

Lefkowicz looked around the room, glaring at the three of them, and even gave Haas and Lehman a look that said, "Don't you mess with me either,' reminiscent of the "Don't make me stop this car!" look that fathers give their children in the back seat of the car when their playfulness gets out of hand.

Lefkowicz took a deep breath, slowly exhaled, and once he was satisfied the room had returned to order, he said triumphantly, "There. That's better. They're all yours, Cap."

"Thank you, Walt," Lehman said, doing everything he could to suppress his laughter. "All right, listen up, everyone. In case you are wondering, we have brought you here for your own protection. We're going to put all of you up in the hotel for a few days. You are not under arrest, because we can't arrest you," he said, looking at Therese and Karla. "Well, you," he said, turning to Perdue, "we can arrest you, but you're not under arrest either.

"But," he said, emphasizing the word, "you cannot leave the hotel."

"I don't understand," Karla interjected. "What are you protecting us from?"

"That's a fair question," Lehman replied. "It seems that your friend here, Frau Weber, knows a very bad man. And until we capture this bad man, you three are going to remain in the hotel. It's for your own protection because this man has already threatened Frau Weber and her family. And he's also the person responsible for your arrest," he said, looking first at Karla and then at Perdue. "We're still trying to sort out all of that. So you don't get a vote in this, you're staying here. But if you don't want to cooperate with us, and if you give us a hard time, we'll just turn you two over to the German authorities and you can go back to jail," he said, looking at Therese and Karla. "And you," he said to Perdue, "we'll turn you back over to the CID. There's a military prosecutor that can't wait to get his hands on you."

"I'm good here, sir," Perdue replied. "I'm happy to stay here as long . . ."

"Shut up, Sergeant," Lefkowicz said, cutting Perdue off in midsentence.

Lehman gave Lefkowicz an appreciative glance and continued.

"So, First Sergeant Lefkowicz here, along with these two fine military policemen," Lehman said, pointing to the two MPs who had just entered the room, "will escort you to your rooms. You'll be on the top floor of the hotel, and these MPs will provide security to make sure you're safe and that none of you take any midnight strolls around Bremen. They will escort you down to breakfast in the morning, which will be at 0700 hours—that's seven a.m. for you civilians. Frau Weber, after breakfast tomorrow, we're going to ask you to accompany us to pick up your children and your parents. It will go more smoothly if you are there with us. We want everyone here until our operation is over and the man we are seeking is in custody."

Therese simply nodded, indicating she understood. She was exhausted from the events of the day and was looking forward to getting a few hours of sleep.

Lehman looked at all three and asked, "Any questions?"

Whatever questions they might have had, each of them reached the conclusion on their own that silence would be a better course of action.

"Good," Lehman said. "Walt, they're all yours."

"Yes, sir," he replied. "All right, I want the three of you to follow me. As we leave the room, grab one of the personal comfort packages on that table over there. The two on the left are for you ladies, and the other on the right is for you," he said to Perdue. "The package contains various toiletries and other items so you can clean up and make yourselves presentable. As you can see, we've spared no expense to ensure your comfort while you're staying as a guest of the United States government. Now, follow me."

Therese and Karla immediately lined up behind Lefkowicz. Perdue walked over slowly to join them and looked at Karla warily. He wasn't sure if he would have to continue to defend himself, but Karla refused to look at him, turning her nose up dramatically as he got close to her. Each of them took their respective package and followed Lefkowicz out and down the hallway, with the MPs bringing up the rear. Karla and Therese whispered to each other, back and forth, as they walked down the hallway and then up the stairwell to their rooms. The last thing that could be heard was Lefkowicz bellowing, "Quiet!" And then there was silence, once and for all.

"Whew! What a day," Lehman said as he collapsed into a chair. He pinched the bridge of his nose and took in a sharp breath. Then he leaned forward and put his head between his knees. He kept breathing deeply in an effort to prevent himself from vomiting, while with his right hand he reached back to rub his neck.

"What's wrong? Are you not feeling well? Are you ill?" Haas asked.

"I feel a headache coming on. They sometimes make me nauseated. Sick to my stomach."

"You should see a doctor. Maybe they can help."

"I have. They gave me pills. They don't work." Lehman continued to sit bent over at the waist and rubbing his neck.

"Here, let me," Haas said. She went to his side, gently moved his hand out of the way, and began to massage the back of his neck.

"You don't have to do that," Lehman said, but not protesting too strongly.

"Shh. I know. Just continue to breathe and try to relax."

After several minutes, Lehman slowly raised his torso and sat upright in the chair with his eyes shut. Haas moved around to stand in front of him and placed her hands on his shoulders, looking for signs of distress.

"How are you now? Any better?" she asked.

"A little. I'm sure I'll live. They always pass. Eventually."

"How long has this been going on?"

"Hmm. A while," he vaguely replied. "The headaches started in '44. It seems I developed an allergy to German artillery. I'm told it's a common allergy. That's when it started—when the Germans attacked us at Bastogne. Stress makes it worse."

"Ah, yes. It's called the Battle of the Bulge, am I right? That's what they called it in all the papers and on the newsreels," Haas said. "You may need to find another line of work."

"Yeah. I don't know what that would be. Life is inherently stressful," Lehman said as he took in several deep breaths and finally opened his eyes. He looked down at Haas's hands on his shoulders, and she slowly moved them away.

"Smoke?" he asked as he reached into his shirt pocket to offer Haas a cigarette.

"Yes, sure," she replied. Lehman lit her cigarette and then did the same for himself. He looked up at Haas and said, "Sit down. Take a load off."

Haas pulled up a chair and sat down with a confused look on her face. "A load off? What does that mean?"

"It's just an expression," Lehman replied. "It means, 'take a load off,'" he said, lifting his feet off the floor and into the air. "You know? It means, sit down. Relax."

"Of course. Clever," Haas replied. "You Americans have many colorful expressions."

"I suppose so," he said, and they sat in silence, continuing to smoke. It was the first time all day they had been able to take a break.

"You did well today," Lehman said. "Getting Weber's friend out of jail was no mean feat. You and Walt both did a great job."

"I once talked a Gestapo officer into releasing two agents who were about to be executed. Of course, two million francs in cash also helped convince him," she said. "Convincing a German judge to release the woman was a lot easier."

"Damn," Lehman replied. "That's another story you'll have to share over drinks."

"I'd do it tonight, but I'm too exhausted."

"Me, too. And we have another busy day ahead of us," he added.

"So," Lehman said slowly, "Walt is going to lead a platoon of men over tomorrow morning to raid the boardinghouse where Dettmer is supposedly living." Once again, crickets. "And you," he said slowly, "will come with me to pick up Weber's children and her parents. We'll have a squad of infantry with us, too, just in case we need them."

"I should be with Walt. I want to be there when they capture Dettmer," Haas protested.

Lehman already had an answer for her.

"Don't worry, you'll get your crack at him. Look, we don't know if he's going to be there. I want you with me and Weber because of the way Therese reacted when she saw you earlier. There's something she's not telling us. I want to see if we—and by 'we' I mean you—can develop a rapport with her so she'll share whatever she's not telling us. We still need her testimony to nail Dettmer. So your helping to keep her kids and parents safe will go a long way toward building that rapport. I want her to tell us everything. Make sense?"

"I suppose so. But I think it is really because you don't trust me. You want to keep your eyes on me all the time. Isn't that what Richardson told you to do? 'Don't let her out of your sight.' I can hear him saying something like that."

"I trust you implicitly," he replied, not wanting to get into an argument while wondering how she could possibly know what Richardson said to him, that keeping her in his sight at all times was precisely what he'd been told to do.

Haas stood up, walked over to the other side of the room, and picked up an ashtray. She put out her cigarette and once again proceeded to field-strip the butt. Old habits are hard to break.

"When did it happen?"

"When did what happen?"

"Your implicit trust in me."

"It's been growing. You make a good impression on people."

"It's your call. You're in charge. I'll be with you tomorrow, and I'll be happy to be there."

"Thanks, Luba. Are you heading out?"

"Yes, it has been, as you say, a long day, and we have many long days ahead of us until we catch Dettmer. We have to keep up our strength.

And you have to take better care of yourself," she added. "Good night, Cap."

Haas started to leave, but when she got to the door, she turned around and said, "Cap, trust works both ways. Remember that." She paused in the doorway, waiting to see if and how he would respond.

"I know it does, Luba. And I will. Good night."

"'Good night," she said as she departed down the hallway, leaving Lehman to sit alone with his thoughts.

Chapter Twenty-Three

The line of jeeps had pulled up outside of the detachment headquarters at the hotel before five a.m. Their day-to-day mission was to guard the port complex at Bremerhaven, but today the job of supporting the raid on the boardinghouse where Dettmer lived fell to a platoon from Alpha Company, 382nd Military Police Service Battalion.

Lehman and Lefkowicz stood on one side of the table in the debriefing room. On the center of the table lay a large city map of Bremen. On the other side stood a platoon leader, who was a second lieutenant straight from West Point, and his platoon sergeant, whose body was slightly twisted to the left, a weathered man who had been serving as an MP since he was called up in 1942. The lieutenant's name was Whitacre, and he had a look of eagerness and optimism as sunny as the cornfields in Ames, Iowa, where he was born. The platoon sergeant's name was Cariota, and he seemed less eager. He was wary and cautious.

"We're ready to carry out the mission today, Captain," Whitacre said eagerly to Lehman. "We're looking forward to seeing some real action, something more than just guard duty." Cariota just stood quietly at his platoon leader's side. He would wait until he heard the details of what the morning's mission entailed before he would express any eagerness.

"Well, hopefully this will all go down without any snafus," Lehman replied. He couldn't help but stare at the scar on Cariota's face, which extended from his left ear all the way down to the corner of his mouth. The scar tissue itself tugged on his mouth to make it appear that he was wearing a perpetual smirk.

"Malmedy, 1944, sir," Cariota said, seeing that both Lehman and Lefkowicz had noticed the scar. It was hard to miss. "Got hit with a piece of German shrapnel in a little dustup that took place there."

"Yeah, I think I heard something about it," Lehman replied, realizing that the weathered platoon sergeant standing in front of him this morning was one of the fortunate survivors of what became known as the Malmedy Massacre, where hundreds of American POWs were summarily executed by their German SS captors in a series of incidents that took place from December 1944 to January 1945. *Some carry their scars on the inside, others on the outside,* Lehman thought.

"Cariota? Where you from?" Lefkowicz asked. "I knew a Cariota from Staten Island back when I was on the force. NYPD. I served with him for a few months back in the thirties."

"That would have been my dad, or my uncle," Cariota replied.

"Sal Cariota?"

"That's my dad. My uncle Ernie also served."

"No kidding!"

"Yep. My dad's still on the force. He made lieutenant now. Vice."

"See?" Lefkowicz said, looking over at Lehman. "See what I'm missing out on? I didn't know your uncle. Is he still on the force, too?"

"He enlisted right after Pearl. Marines. He's still in Okinawa. They're still looking for him."

Their banter suddenly stopped and the room fell silent.

"I'm really sorry to hear that, Cariota," Lefkowicz said softly, taking the platoon sergeant aside. "After this all goes down, let's get together for a beer. On me. I want to hear all about your dad and how he's doing."

Cariota nodded. "Sure, I'd like that," he said.

As Haas made her entrance into the room, it gave Lehman the opportunity to change the subject. The two MPs were taken aback by the presence of a woman. They hadn't been told there was a woman CIC agent, and they were startled to see she was carrying her standard sidearm and knife strapped to her thigh. *Well, she's not from the typing pool*, thought Whitacre.

"All right, let's get started," Lehman said, quickly getting down to the business at hand. "Gentlemen, this is RAF Flight Officer Haas. She's on assignment with us from British intelligence. She's an expert on our subject and will give you the details on the man we are looking for. Luba, it's all yours," Lehman said, turning attention in the room to her. She began by passing out copies of the most recent photograph on file of Dettmer.

"Good morning, everyone," Haas began. "We've made enough copies of the photograph so that every man participating in the operation today will have one. Where is our German police liaison, Lieutenant? Are they here today?" As Haas turned to Whitacre, another uncomfortable silence settled over the room.

"I told them to wait outside, ma'am. I wasn't sure what the protocol would be. I thought we could brief them afterwards."

"We don't stand too much on protocol here, Lieutenant. No, we need them here now because we're searching a civilian establishment. Can you or someone please go fetch them? And make it fast, because the longer we wait, the greater the likelihood of missing our man. Now, please."

Whitacre wasn't sure if he should do as Haas had asked or if he should order Cariota to bring the Germans into the room. He looked at Lehman, who only gave him a blank stare.

"I'll go get them, sir," offered Cariota, immediately taking the attention off his junior superior officer. *I told him they should be here*, he said to himself.

"I'll go with you," Lefkowicz said, giving Lehman the opportunity to deal with the junior lieutenant officer-to-officer.

The two left the room, and another awkward silence fell over the room.

"Sorry, sir," the lieutenant began, looking at Lehman but ignoring Haas.

Lehman shook his head with an admonishing look and said, "No skin off my nose, Lieutenant. And Flight Officer Haas is leading this operation today. So, please address any questions you have to her."

"Sorry, ma'am," he stammered. "I. . . I'm . . . Uh, I'll just hold my questions until you're finished."

"Quite," she replied. Haas strummed her fingers on the table while they waited for Lefkowicz and Cariota to return. Lehman began to gently tug on his ear, feeling another headache coming on.

It took only a few minutes to round up the German police officers. Lefkowicz was the first to return to the briefing room. He was followed by two men, the first a middle-aged man, short and rotund, his hair closely cropped, and he wore a pencil mustache. The second man was taller but gaunt and thin. They both wore surplus U.S. Army–issue fatigues with no insignia of rank. Their only designation was an armband on their sleeves, indicating they were members of the Landpolitzei.

Haas spoke to the Germans as they entered the room.

"I presume you are the German Police liaison officers who will join us today? Thank you for being here," Haas said. "In the interest of time, we'll dispense with introductions. We'll have time for that later. Do you speak English?" she asked the two Germans, who clearly had not been asked for their opinions by an American or Brit any time during the past year. "It will be easier for me to conduct the briefing in English. Will that be acceptable to you?" Haas asked,

"Oh, yes, yes, of course," the rotund liaison officer replied. "Yes, that will be most acceptable, won't it, Willi?" he asked, turning to the man on his right. They both noted Haas's sidearm and scabbard with surprise and awe.

"Yes, yes, certainly," they replied in unison.

"Good. Then let's get started. The man in this photograph," she said, holding up the best photo they had of Dettmer, "is Gestapo Oberleutnant Karl-Ulrich Dettmer. He is using the name Bohlmann now, and he has also probably changed his appearance. But he is the man we are looking for. We do not think he is armed, but he is considered extremely dangerous, and we want to take him alive. So, above all else, let's make sure we do that. He is no good to us if he is dead."

Haas went on to lay out the operation. The bulk of the MPs would accompany Lefkowicz to the boardinghouse. Two squads of MPs were to surround it, blocking off the street and covering the exits to prevent Dettmer or any of the occupants from escaping. Lefkowicz and the German police liaison officers would conduct the search inside, accompanied by the third squad of MPs. Lehman and Lefkowicz had already sent out another TWX with the latest information about Dettmer, aka Bohlmann. CID would place the boardinghouse under surveillance, a job they would turn over to the German police. They would also distribute copies of his photograph around the Port of Bremerhaven. Every ship would be searched, beginning with those bound for Portugal, Spain, and South America, until Dettmer aka Bohlmann was captured.

"If Dettmer is there, he is to be arrested and brought back here for interrogation," Haas said. "We also require a section of your men, Lieutenant," she said, addressing Whitacre, "and one of the liaison officers to accompany me, Captain Lehman, and our contact, Frau Therese Weber. We're going to her flat in the Altstadt district to pick up her children. After that, we'll be picking up her parents, and everyone will return here to CIC headquarters, where they will remain under protective custody for an undetermined amount of time."

"Sir," Cariota said to Whitacre, "I'd like to recommend that we assign Corporal Duddy's section. His guys are pretty new, so this'd be a good way to break them in."

Whitacre thought about it for a few seconds. "Yeah, that's a good idea, Sergeant. Let's go ahead and do that. And you," he said, pointing to the portly German police liaison officer. "You will join Corporal Duddy's team."

By 5:45, Lefkowicz and the MP platoon were ready to roll out to the boardinghouse. Traffic would be light, and they estimated it would take about an hour to reach their destination. They would arrive just at daybreak, which took place at 6:50 that morning. Lehman and Haas would not leave headquarters until after 7:30.

"Lieutenant," Lefkowicz called to Whitacre, "you're welcome to ride with me. We're in the lead vehicle, and I'll drive, but I could use your help keeping us on the map and everyone else in the column behind us."

"Sure, First Sergeant. I can do that," Whitacre replied, finding that his eager nature was now returning.

"Just be careful, Walt," Lehman said as Lefkowicz started the jeep. Whitacre hopped into the front seat and began to unfold a large map. The gaunt German liaison officer jumped into the rear to sit directly behind Lefkowicz. The column of jeeps began to slowly roll away from CIC headquarters. Lehman and Haas stood in front of the building and watched the line of vehicles move down the road, then make a sharp left to head toward the Port of Bremerhaven. They should arrive at the boardinghouse in less than thirty minutes.

Lehman turned and walked over to the three MPs who sat in the remaining jeep. The German liaison officer sat in the back, taking up a fair amount of space. Lehman walked around the vehicle to the corporal, who sat in the front passenger seat.

"Are you Duddy?"

"Yes, sir."

"Did Sergeant Cariota explain what you and your men have to do this morning?"

"He did, sir. To the letter."

"Good. Any questions?"

"No, sir. Well, one question, sir. When are we heading out?"

Lehman looked at his wristwatch and said, "I have 0550 hours on my watch right now. We're not planning to leave here until 0730. Have you men had chow?"

"We just grabbed some K-rations, sir. Mess hall wasn't open before we had to leave."

"Okay, well, you men might as well grab some chow here at the hotel. They have a restaurant inside, and they won't kill you. Just tell them you're with the CIC, and they'll send us the bill. They probably do that with most of the guests here anyway," he quipped. Switching to German, he asked the liaison officer, "If they have any problem, just explain to the restaurant staff that I said it was okay. Tell them Lehman said to charge the meals to CIC, understand?"

"Yes, of course," he said. "I'll be very happy to help. I've heard the food here is very good."

"Yeah," Lehman said, looking at the rotund German. "I'm sure you have. Okay, Corporal. Have your men back here at 0715 hours, and then we'll head out."

"Yes, sir. Thank you, sir."

Duddy and the other MPs, along with the German, dismounted from the jeep and headed inside. Only Lehman and Haas were left standing on the street. Haas walked over to Lehman and asked, "Do you have a cigarette?"

"Sure." He reached for his gold case and pulled two cigarettes out, offering one to Haas. "Here you go." He immediately reached into his right pocket to pull out his lighter and struck it, the bluish-gold flame lighting up the sidewalk.

"How do you feel about the operation this morning?" Lehman asked.

"I don't know. It seems almost too easy, and I don't like it when things seem that way. That's usually a sign of trouble."

"Well, we've had some breaks. I mean, we couldn't have predicted that someone would fall into our lap and offer up Dettmer to us on a plate."

"I suppose." Then she abruptly changed the subject. "I need some coffee. And some breakfast, too. Chow, you call it, right? Join me?"

"Love to."

As they turned away from the street to head inside, Lehman looked at Haas, and he once again understood why the other men in the detachment were so taken by her.

"Hey, about last night," he said.

"What about it?

"I do trust you. Implicitly."

"That's what you said," Haas replied. "Come on, let's get something to eat."

Chapter Twenty-Four

As expected, traffic on the northbound side of the highway to Bremerhaven was light. Most of it was coming out of the port and headed south, a steady stream of lorries bulging with materiel and goods to feed the machine of American and British occupation.

The MP column had been making excellent time and had reached the outskirts of Bremerhaven in about fifty minutes when they ran into a snag near the Bremerhaven-Wulsdorf railway station. A delivery truck, loaded with beer from Union Brauerei, took the sharp turn onto the highway a little too fast, tipping over and spilling its load. Hundreds of bottles and cases were strewn across the highway and along the side of the road. The roadway and median strip were littered with broken glass and foam from the beer bottles that had exploded on contact. Heavy wooden cases, twelve bottles each, were still intact. The cases had been ejected from the truck, and now dozens of Germans, drawn outside by the noise of bottles exploding as they hit the pavement, were scrambling to retrieve a bottle or two of their favorite local brew.

To their credit, some people first helped to extricate the driver from the cab of his vehicle. After determining that he was no worse for wear, the assembled crowd set about to clean up the highway and roadside. It was their natural inclination for order that compelled them as they set about to rescue the hundreds of bottles and the dozens of cases of beer that survived the crash. At least temporarily, the highway was blocked by the growing throng of people, bringing the column to a halt.

"Do you think we can just slowly push our way through?" Whitacre asked Lefkowicz.

"I don't think so, sir. The median is blocked off, too," he said, motioning to a group of four German police vehicles that had arrived. The German officers jumped out of their vehicles and ran at full speed to the crowd of civilians, yelling, "Stop! Drop the beer and leave the roadway!"

"Do you think you can find another route on the map?" Lefkowicz asked.

Whitacre briefly scanned the map. "We'll have to go the wrong way on that ramp right there," he said, pointing to the entrance ramp to the highway. A few vehicles were backed up on the ramp, but there was a narrow shoulder on the right-hand side they could use.

"Let's do it. We need to get someone to direct traffic," Lefkowicz responded.

"Start inching over to the ramp," Whitacre said. "Slowly. I'll hop out and direct traffic. Wait for me at the bottom of the ramp. And go slowly! Make sure all of our guys are following you."

Whitacre jumped out of the jeep and ran over to the line of vehicles on the ramp shouting "Stop! Halt! Stop!" The vehicles on the ramp weren't moving much anyway, they were only inching forward impatiently, but he was able to get the drivers' attention. He then motioned to Lefkowicz, who drove over slowly to the shoulder while Whitacre blocked the traffic from moving forward. Lefkowicz continued down the ramp, headed in the wrong direction until he got to the bottom. He waited for Whitacre to return as the other vehicles in the column lined up behind him. As the last vehicle passed him, Whitacre sprinted down the ramp to the jeep.

"That was a damn fine piece of directing traffic, Lieutenant," Lefkowicz said as Whitacre hopped back into the jeep. "Now, do you think you can get us to that boardinghouse?"

"Not a problem, Top. I was captain of the Orienteering Club back at West Point my senior year. I'll get us there, don't worry. Turn left here and take this road for approximately two clicks. Then we're going to make a left, and it looks like a couple of quick rights. Just head down there, and I'll keep checking the map to make sure we're going in the right direction. And don't lose our guys! Make sure they stay behind us."

"Yes sir, we'll take it nice and easy, and we won't lose anyone!"

Lefkowicz slowly pulled out about fifty meters onto the roadway, and turned around to make sure the other jeeps in the column were following. As they came into line, he drove onto the road.

"All right, sir, just let me know where to turn."

The two sat in silence for a few minutes as they approached the first turn.

"Turn left here," Whitacre said, "Then we'll make a right in about three hundred clicks. So, do you think we should have stopped to help?"

"Nah. Not our jurisdiction, sir. The locals will handle it just fine, and as far as I could tell, the only thing that was broken was some beer bottles and the driver's pride."

The column of jeeps reached the boardinghouse at five past seven.

***

Johanne wasn't sure what caused her to awaken. Was it the sun that was just beginning to rise in the east, or was it the sound coming from a lorry engine that kept getting louder and louder? The engine noise seemed to be coming from the alley behind their house. She lay quietly in bed, listening and wondering why a vehicle would be in the alley. *Nobody should be back there, especially at this time of day*, she thought. She distinctly heard doors being shut, two she counted, and then she heard a man's muffled voice. She could not hear what he was saying. *Why would anyone be in the alley? Maybe I'm dreaming.* She looked over at her husband Karl, lying next to her and sound asleep. She could hear his heavy breathing; it was the sound of a deep sleep.

Johanne would have dismissed it as a dream had she not heard a loud crack coming from the rear of their house. It sounded like wood being broken. Then she heard the rear door open, the door to their kitchen, the door that she had been asking Karl to fix because it made a loud squeak every time it was opened or closed. She heard muffled voices again and thought, *this is no dream. There is someone in the house.*

She bolted upright and shook her husband, trying to rouse him from his deep sleep.

"Karl, Karl! There's someone in the house. They're in the kitchen! I can hear them!"

"What, what," he mumbled. "You're imagining things. Go back to sleep."

"No, no. I heard them breaking in. The door, I heard them open it. Listen! Listen!"

Karl opened his eyes and tried to force himself to wake up. He slid up in the bed, kicking off the duvet cover, and tried to stifle a yawn but was unsuccessful. He listened carefully for several seconds before finally pronouncing, "I don't hear a thing. You must have been dreaming."

"No," Johanne whispered. "I heard a lorry. Out in the alley in back. And then I heard voices, the door squeaking. I've been asking you to fix that for weeks, you know."

"Well, if it hadn't squeaked, you wouldn't have heard these intruders," he said. "Now go back to sleep, it's too early to get up."

"No, I tell you, I heard . . ." and then there was a crash and the sound of glass breaking.

They both sat up in fright.

"Do you believe me now? There is someone in the house. Downstairs."

"Yes, I heard it, too," Karl replied. "Quick. Get dressed. I'm going downstairs to see what it might be."

"Wait! I'm going with you."

Karl quickly pulled out from beneath the bedcovers. His trousers were draped over a chair adjacent to the bedroom door. Johanne slipped on her robe while her husband put on his trousers. He didn't bother with his shoes. As he opened the door, it creaked slightly, and they both winced. They knew they would be heard by anyone downstairs, but they stepped out into the hallway and onto the stairway landing outside their bedroom door. Karl led the way, with Johanne following close behind, down six steps to a second landing where the stairwell turned sharply to the left. They crept slowly down the last five steps and then stood in the narrow corridor that connected the parlor in the front of the house on the left and a small dining room and the door that led to the kitchen on the right. They could hear nothing.

"Perhaps we were just dreaming," Karl said. "I don't hear anything, do you?"

"We weren't dreaming. There's someone or something in the kitchen."

"Is anyone there?" he called out. "Show yourself. Is anyone there?" he repeated.

There were no sounds. There was nothing but silence.

He reached out into the dimly lit room and felt for the light switch on the left-hand side of the wall. He found it and turned it on, and the dim overhead light illuminated the narrow hallway. They looked at each other, nodded, then crept forward, inching their way to the kitchen door. When they reached it, Karl pressed his ear to the door, listening for a sound, anything to help him discern who or what might be on the other side.

Again, silence.

He slowly turned the handle. The door opened in toward the kitchen and to the right. Once open, it would give him an unobstructed view of the entire kitchen. There was no place for an intruder to hide.

"Who's there? Who's in here?" he repeated, slowly opening the door wider and wider.

Suddenly, the shape of a huge man stood before him, and Karl cried out in alarm. The man grabbed Karl's arm and pulled him into the kitchen, hurling him to the floor like a rag doll. Johanne screamed as she was grabbed from behind by another man and felt a knife blade on her throat. The second intruder had her in a choke hold and pushed her into the kitchen, where she fell on top of her husband.

"Quiet, or I'll gut you like a fish right here on your kitchen floor," the second man hissed as he emerged from the doorway into the kitchen. It was Dettmer. The huge Corporal Becker stood over the dazed couple on the floor. Dettmer looked down at them and said to Becker, "Pick up the woman, and put her on the chair by the table."

Becker reached down to grab Johanne's arm, pulled her to her feet, dragged her over to the table, pulled out a chair, and sat her down. He turned back to face Dettmer to await further instructions.

"Leave her alone," Karl cried out, which resulted in a kick to his ribs from Dettmer. The blow knocked the wind out of him, and he gasped for air.

"Don't hurt him," Johanne cried. "Stop!"

Dettmer walked over to Johanne, looking her straight in the eye. He revealed the knife in his hand and brought it to her throat once again. It's amazing what one notices when faced with danger. Johanne saw that he was holding her favorite kitchen knife. It was a lightweight and perfectly balanced knife with stainless steel rivets, a wooden handle, and a six-inch carbon-steel blade— a cross between a full-bladed chef's knife and a small utility knife. It was a gift from her mother and was one of the finest knives Wüsthof ever made.

"Take care of that knife," she said to Dettmer. "It was my mother's, and she gave it to me. She could have given it to my older sister, but she hated to cook, so she gave it to me instead."

Her words startled Dettmer. He looked down at the knife in his hand and slowly withdrew the blade from her throat. He didn't even realize that what he felt for just a brief moment was empathy. It was a new sensation and not something he was used to. In that moment, and just for a moment, he, the persecutor, saw the humanity in this small, frail woman sitting on a chair. It gave him pause, and for just one moment, his anger receded.

"Very well," he said, now admiring the fine workmanship of the knife he held in his hand. "I shall indeed take good care of it for you. And I shall return it to you. If you cooperate. Oh, and I'm sorry about the cup," he said, pointing to a broken teacup on the floor. "I didn't see it on the counter, and I inadvertently knocked it off."

Johanne looked over to where Dettmer was pointing and saw her favorite teacup in shards scattered across the floor. She had left it on the counter the night before. She and Karl usually enjoyed a cup of tea before retiring for the evening. Last night, she drank alone.

"What is it you want?" Karl wheezed, still trying to catch his breath and recover from the vicious kick he had received.

Dettmer slowly turned to Karl and offered his hand.

"Get up, old man. And go back upstairs and put your shoes on. You and I are going on an errand. We have to pick up something very precious and dear."

Karl took Dettmer's hand and slowly got up from the floor.

"What are you talking about?"

"You and I are going to gather your grandchildren, and then we are going to bring them back here to your house. I'm sure they love their Opa, isn't that right? And they love their Oma, too, isn't that right? I said, isn't that right?"

"Yes, yes, of course they love us. What is it you want with them, with us?" Karl asked.

"I want nothing from them or from you. It's something I want from your daughter, and with all of us here together under one roof, I believe we can convince her to give me what I want. Now, go upstairs, grab your jacket and hat, put on your shoes, and be down here in, oh, let's say, two minutes. Can you do all of that and make it back here in two minutes, old man?"

"Yes, yes, of course I can."

"Well, get to it," Dettmer said, waving the knife into the air with a circular motion to indicate that Karl was to move quickly.

"You have two minutes, old man. If you aren't back here in two minutes, I'm going to start breaking your wife's fingers, and we'll move on from there. Do you hear me?" Dettmer shouted.

"Yes, yes, I hear you. I hear you. I'm moving as fast as I can. Don't hurt her. I'm coming," he yelled from the upstairs room, grabbing his shoes, trying to put them on while running back down the stairway to the kitchen.

Dettmer looked at the clock that hung on the kitchen wall. It read 7:25. Karl returned to the kitchen with one shoe on his right foot and the other in his hand, and he struggled to put it on his left.

"If we aren't back here by 9:30, kill her," he said to Becker.

"I will take care of your knife, old woman, don't you worry about it."

Chapter Twenty-Five

The four occupants of the boardinghouse were all lined up outside in front of the house. They were not a happy group of people, as they were beginning to draw the attention of their neighbors walking by on their way to work or to the market to purchase whatever was available and as much as their ration cards would allow. The neighbors shook their heads disapprovingly, not knowing what kind of trouble these people were in, but trouble was trouble, nonetheless.

Two of them were Becker's uncle and aunt, a couple in their late seventies who ran the house along with a bakery on the first floor. The other two were boarders, a German and a refugee from Latvia who worked on construction at the docks. Whitacre and a squad of his men watched the entire group while Lefkowicz, Cariota, and his squad of MPs searched the house for signs of Dettmer. So far, they had found nothing.

As Lefkowicz and Cariota walked out to the street, Whitacre turned to one of his MPs and said, "Just keep an eye on these four and don't let them move." He met with the sergeants on the sidewalk. "So, any sign of him?"

"No," Cariota said. "But it looks like there are two people missing from the house. We know which rooms these people occupy. Dettmer obviously occupied another room. It's empty now. And there's another empty room. Somebody's been living in each room, and they're not here now. It has to be Dettmer and one other person. It's probably that Becker person. They aren't here, so they must be together."

"Yeah. It's like Goldilocks. Who's been sleeping in my bed?" Lefkow-icz cracked. He looked at the forlorn group standing on the sidewalk and said, "Bring the couple over here, the owner and his wife. And where's that liaison officer?"

"He's still inside helping with the search."

"Good, keep him there. Let's talk to this couple and find out how happy their marriage really is."

"Okay, I'll bring them over," said Whitacre. He pulled them out of line and marched them back to Lefkowicz.

Lefkowicz stared at them as he pulled a photograph from his field jacket pocket.

"Listen, you two," he began, addressing them in German. "Do you see this man?" He showed them the photograph of Dettmer. "This man is accused of war crimes, and you've been hiding him. He's been living here, and we know all about it. Do you know what else that means? That means you're going to be charged with war crimes. And do you know what we do with war criminals? We shoot them!" He formed his hand into the shape of a pistol, placed his fingertip on each of their foreheads in turn, and pretended to fire. "Or, if we don't shoot them, we hang them, until they're dead." He pretended to hang a noose over his head, jerked his head up and down, and stuck out his tongue, mimicking the effect of hanging.

"So if you don't want to be shot," he said, brandishing his imaginary pistol and aiming it at their foreheads, "and if you don't want to be hung," again mimicking the effects of hanging, "you will tell me where this man is, right now. Understand? You have thirty seconds to tell me everything you know, or I will haul your sorry, stinking German asses off to a jail, and I'll kill you myself," he screamed as the couple stared back at him in wide-eyed horror.

"Tell them," the woman said, poking her husband in the ribs. "Tell them! I'm not going to be shot because of your stupid nephew."

"He left," she said, turning to Lefkowicz. "He left an hour ago!"

"Quiet," the man shouted.

"Oh, really?" Lefkowicz screamed at the man. "You want to play games? I'll play a little game with you." He turned to Whitacre and Cariota and said, "Take this piece of German shit out behind the house and shoot him." The two looked at Lefkowicz, horrified and not knowing what to do next. "Go ahead, do it," he repeated, giving Cariota and Whitacre a wink, and then, with his imaginary pistol pointed into the air, he fired another imaginary shot.

"Oh, I understand. Yes, First Sergeant, I understand. Come on, sir," Cariota said to Whitacre. "let's go ahead and shoot this guy." He proceeded to drag the man off toward the rear of the boardinghouse, with Whitacre following closely behind. "Just play along, sir. Just follow my lead and play along," he whispered to Whitacre in between the curses he directed at the old man, who now began to protest.

"No, wait, I'll tell you everything! What do you want to know?"

"Too late. You had your chance, but you're too late," Lefkowicz yelled. Cariota and Whitacre dragged the poor man behind the rear of the house, and they disappeared from view. A few seconds later, a shot rang out. And then a second.

"Oh, my God! What have you done? You've killed him," the woman sobbed.

"Yes, and you're going to be next," Lefkowicz yelled, waving Dettmer's photograph in the woman's face. "Now, where is this man? Where is he?"

"He left an hour ago with our nephew. My husband's nephew. He's dumb and useless and good for nothing."

"Your nephew. His name is Becker, right?"

"Yes, yes, that's him!"

"Where did they go?"

"They said they had to pick up something in Bremen."

"In Bremen? How did they get there? That's fifty kilometers from here."

"They borrowed our delivery truck. They said they'd bring it back later this morning so we could make our deliveries. They said they'd be back here by noon at the latest. Oh, my poor husband," she wailed as she saw Cariota and Whitacre approaching them from the back of the house. "What have you done? He was a good man," she sobbed.

Lefkowicz quickly walked over to the approaching men and said, "You didn't really shoot him, right?"

"Nah," Cariota said. "We just fired two shots into the air. He shit his pants after the first shot. He passed out after the second one. He's fine, though. He's coming to out in the back of the house. I told the guys to hold him back there until you gave the okay to let him go."

Meanwhile the German liaison officer came running out from the house and up to the three men. "What is going on? I heard gunshots. Is everyone all right?"

"Yeah, everything's fine," Lefkowicz replied. "Somebody thought they saw Dettmer, but it was just a rat in the back alley."

"Oh, my God! Thank God no one got hurt!"

"Yeah, right," Lefkowicz said. "Look, we do have another problem, though. The old lady said that Dettmer and her nephew left over an hour ago to go to Bremen. They're in a delivery truck. They borrowed it to pick up something in Bremen, she said. I think something is up. We'd better get back to Captain Lehman and Haas.

"Lieutenant," he continued, "we should leave two or three men here in the off chance that Dettmer returns. They can arrest him on sight and bring him back to Bremen, but I don't think that's going to happen. I think he's in Bremen. So we're going to need your navigation skills again. We'll need to split up. One squad needs to go to the Altstadt and the other to Neustadt. Here are the addresses," Lefkowicz said as he pulled out a small notebook from the breast pocket of his field jacket. "Dettmer is going to be at one of these two places, and we'd better get there. Fast."

Lefkowicz turned to head back to the jeep, and Whitacre fell in alongside him. "You know, Top, that wasn't exactly by the book. I think the Geneva Convention has a rule against stuff like that," he said. "But it was pretty damn brilliant."

Lefkowicz stopped in mid-stride and turned to Whitacre. "Well, thankfully, he's a noncombatant, so I don't think that applies. Sometimes you have to bend the rules a little. That's how we got shit done during the war, sir. That's why we won. Now, like I said, we need your map skills. We need the fastest route back to Bremen. You ready to roll, sir?"

Whitacre nodded his head. "I'm ready, let's go!"

"All right sir, I'm ready too. Let's move. On the way back, though, I gotta tell you about the time Cap impersonated a Russian officer. We were interrogating this German SS officer, a real sonofabitch . . .," he said as they walked together back to their jeep, got in, and headed back to Bremen.

***

Lehman, Haas, and Therese piled into his vehicle promptly at 0730 hours and left the hotel, with Corporal Duddy and his MPs following right behind them. Lehman drove with Haas sitting up front next to him. Therese took the seat in back, sitting next to the liaison officer.

They set out on the winding streets just as traffic was beginning to pick up, but it would still take no more than ten minutes to reach Therese's flat, where the children had been staying in the care of her landlady. The plan was to pick up the children and bring them back to the hotel, where Karla would look after them while the three would head out once more to fetch Therese's parents. Lehman hoped that both trips would take no more than an hour. Once Therese and her family were safe at the hotel, they could focus on hunting down Dettmer.

"I've never been in a jeep before," Therese said, the wind whipping through her hair. "It's fun. Little Willi loves motorcars, and he will especially enjoy riding in a jeep."

"After all this settles down, maybe we can arrange for a longer ride than what he'll get today," Lehman replied. "I just want to get everyone into the hotel where you'll be safe."

"Yes," Therese replied, as her worried look returned. "That would be lovely."

As he drove along the streets in the Altstadt, Lehman couldn't help but notice the stately architecture, which despite the aggressive bombing of the war was still visible. Many buildings and houses had been reduced to rubble, but the façade of others had collapsed, peeled away by explosions and revealing the contents of their previous inhabitants. Here and there, other houses and structures remained completely untouched, somehow spared from destruction by the random and capricious nature of aerial bombing.

"It was a beautiful city before the war," Therese said, noticing that Lehman was looking at the buildings as they drove. "This neighborhood was especially lovely. The streets were lined with trees that blossomed each spring. So very beautiful. And now," her voice trailed off as she looked at the destruction around her, "it is not as beautiful. But we still have our memories of the old days."

Therese craned her neck to look out over the jeep's windscreen and saw a familiar landmark. "There is a church coming up on our left," she said, pointing out the tall spire that could be seen just a hundred meters down the road. "It's the church where Wilhelm and I were married." She suddenly became silent, saddened by the memories that were evoked by merely mentioning his name. As they drove past the church, Lehman turned to look and nodded his approval, but Therese couldn't bring herself to cast her eyes on it. Then, suddenly realizing where she was, she said to Lehman, "The next street on the right, turn there. It is a shorter route, and it will let us drive up right to the front of the house. Oh, the children are going to be so excited."

Lehman slowed down to make sure Duddy and his team were still following. He gave a physical hand signal indicating he was turning to the right, and the MPs followed.

"How much farther?" he asked Therese.

"Drive straight for two more blocks, and then turn left. My flat will be the fourth house on the right. We can drive right up in front of it. There are never any vehicles on the street." Lehman slowed down to ensure the MPs could stay right behind him, then gave another hand signal indicating they were turning left. He slowed down to ten miles per hour as he counted off the houses. *There's the first one, two, three, ah, there it is. I see it.*

As he slowed his jeep to pull up in front of the house, Lehman became alarmed as he looked directly ahead. Haas had the same reaction, and she straightened up in her seat so that she could look above the windscreen.

Haas and Lehman simultaneously said to each other, "I think we have a problem."

***

Johanne sat on the chair where Becker had deposited her. At first, she had been terrified. She was frightened by the men who had broken into her house. She was frightened by the man who took her favorite kitchen knife and threatened her with it. And she was especially frightened by the huge man sitting just a few feet away from her. They had been sitting in silence for over twenty minutes, and the longer she sat, the more her fear began to wane, slowly turning into anger. *I'm an old woman*, she thought. *I've lived my life, and it has been a good one. And I am not going to let this man terrorize me. If he kills me, so be it. But I will not be afraid.*

She looked at Becker and said, "So, do you really plan to kill me?"

Becker looked back at her and said nothing.

"Can you speak?" Johanne asked, using a tone that a mother would use to admonish a recalcitrant child.

"Yes, I can speak," he slowly replied.

"Well, you didn't answer me. I asked if you plan to kill me. If my husband and your partner—what is his name?—if they aren't back here by nine-thirty, your partner said you should kill me. Are you going to do it?"

"I don't want to," Becker replied slowly. "I don't want to kill you."

"Well, that's a relief, because I don't want to die today." She looked at Becker, wondering what was going on in his mind. She continued to stare at him, and he began to look uncomfortably around the room.

"Have you eaten? Have you had breakfast?" she asked him.

"No, I haven't."

"Are you hungry? Because I am hungry. Are you?"

"Yes."

"Well, then, I think I shall make us breakfast. If I make it, will you eat?

Becker looked slowly at Johanne, not sure what he should do, but his stomach was growling from hunger.

"Yes. I would like some breakfast, please."

"Good, because I am hungry, and although you said you don't want to kill me, I don't know if I can trust you. You might decide to kill me anyway. And I don't want to die hungry."

"No, I don't want to kill you. I . . .," he began to stammer. "I will not do that. I hope he'll return in time, but I couldn't kill an old woman."

"An old woman, eh? Well, I suppose I should be grateful that I am old. Since you say you will not kill me, then I shall make us breakfast," she said, rising from her chair and going over to the small pantry in the corner of the kitchen. "Let's see. I have some bread, and I have some cheese. I'll start you off with that. Would you like to start with bread and cheese?"

"Yes, please," Becker replied.

"Good, I'll get you started with that. And I have some eggs. When was the last time you had a real egg?" she asked looking back at Becker.

"I can't remember."

"Well, you'll have eggs this morning. And I have some delicious tinned meats. They're American, you know! Our daughter gets them for us. Have you ever had something called Spam?"

Becker shook his head.

"No? I'll make you fried Spam. You'll love it. It's like a sausage, and it's delicious. Oh, and I have coffee too! Also American. Not ersatz but real coffee. I'll make us coffee, too. We'll have a feast."

Johanne began to cook, moving about the kitchen humming softly as she prepared what she thought might very well be the last meal of her life. *But,* she thought, *at least I have bought some time and I won't die hungry.*

***

"What is it?" Therese said, fear rising in her voice. "What is happening?"

Lehman turned to face her, "We need you to wait here. Just wait in the jeep for us. We'll go inside to get the children."

"No, I want to go in with you. What is happening?" she yelled.

"Keep your voice down," Lehman said, bringing his index finger up to his mouth, the universal sign that said "Quiet!"

Haas turned around and spoke directly to Therese. "Frau Weber, this is the situation. Do you see that small lorry in front of your house? Just nod your head."

Therese nodded her head, and her eyes opened wide with a growing sense of fear.

"That vehicle belongs to Corporal Becker's uncle. It's a delivery vehicle, but it definitely shouldn't be here. The only reason it would be here is if Dettmer or Becker drove it here. So we think Dettmer may be inside, or at least in the neighborhood. Now, Captain Lehman and I are going to go inside to make sure the children are safe, and we'll bring them out. We're going to have the MP corporal—what's his name, Cap?"

"Duddy," Lehman replied.

"Corporal Duddy, the MPs, and this German police officer will stay with you. They will protect you."

"I want to go with you. I want to see my children."

"You will see them," Haas said. "But we have to keep you safe. So just let us do our job, and you'll see your children, okay?" Haas reached into the back seat and grabbed both of Therese's hands. "I promise you. They will be fine. Let us go get them. You have to trust us. You have to trust me. I promise you that we will bring them to you safely. Now, do you trust me?"

Therese nodded her head in agreement. Reluctantly, but in agreement.

"Cap, we should position one MP around the back," said Haas. "It looks like this path leads to an alley that is behind the house. Frau Weber, is that correct?"

Again, Therese nodded. She was too frightened to speak. *Oh my God,* she thought. *What have I done? If anything happens to the children, oh my God,* she repeated to herself over and over.

"Agree," Lehman said. "That makes sense. I'll tell Duddy the plan. Wait here. And you," Lehman said speaking directly to the liaison officer, "You stay here with Frau Weber. Don't move until I tell you to move, understand?"

"Oh yes. I understand completely," the officer replied with a sense of relief that he would be out of any line of fire. "I'll make sure Frau Weber stays here and remains safe."

Lehman hopped out of the vehicle and quickly explained their plan to Duddy and the MPs.

"I don't think they'll be going out the back," Lehman explained. "The vehicle they drove is right there, so they'll want to come right out the front door to get to it. But cover the rear exit so we can cover our ass. Understand?"

"Yes sir," Duddy replied. He gave the order to his most senior MP, a private first-class, to move down the path to the rear of the house and stop and hold anyone trying to leave the house.

"You stay here with Frau Weber and our German friend here," Lehman said to Duddy. "And the same goes. If you see anyone but us coming out of the house, stop them."

"Yes, sir, understand."

"All right, Flight Officer Haas and I are going in. If we're not out in ten minutes . . .," he said. "Never mind. We'll be out."

"Um, sir?"

"What is it, Duddy?"

"You're not armed, sir."

Lehman tugged nervously at his ear for a second, now wishing he had chosen to carry his sidearm. He didn't think it would be necessary. *Who needs a sidearm to pick up children?*

"I know. But she is," he said, pointing to Haas.

"All right sir. Just be careful. We'll have the house covered and we'll be ready. Just give us the word."

"I will. Just wait here for now."

With that, Lehman turned to head back to the jeep to rejoin Haas and Therese. He was just about to say something to Haas when the front door to the house opened and out came Therese's father, holding Anna Karolina in his arms, and Dettmer, who held young Wilhelm's hand. Therese was the first to notice them, and she screamed, "Run, Papa. Run, children, run! Run!"

Her scream stopped the two men in their tracks, but not for long. The quiet order of the morning quickly transformed into chaos. Upon seeing his daughter sitting in the back of an American jeep only yards away from him, Therese's father bolted forward, running as hard and as fast as his old legs could take him, with Anna Karolina jostling in his arms. Young Willi tried to run, but Dettmer held on to his hand. Dettmer still wasn't sure what was happening, but he knew he couldn't let the young boy go.

"Run, Papa, run," Therese yelled as she jumped from the back of the jeep onto the sidewalk. Time seemed to slow down for everyone. It was barely twenty feet, but it seemed like the longest distance that Therese's father ever ran. He finally closed the gap and crashed into his daughter with his granddaughter in his arms, and they all fell into a heap on the sidewalk, a tangled mess of arms and legs.

"Anna, Papa! Are you all right? Are you hurt?" Therese cried out, frantically grabbing at her daughter from her father's arms. "Yes, yes, I'm fine! We're fine," came his reply. Anna Karolina's eyes were wide open, first in fear, then in shock, and then she broke into laughter, the kind of laughter that children always erupt into as they are about to say, "Do it again! Do it again!"

A cacophony of shouts erupted from Lehman and the MPs. "Don't shoot, hold your fire! You might hit the child," he yelled as both Duddy and the other MP drew their service weapons. The third MP of Duddy's team, upon hearing the commotion out front, came running from the back of the house to the end of the walkway, about ten yards from where Dettmer stood, now cradling young Willi underneath his arms and covering his face and mouth with his left hand.

The MPs began to slowly move forward with their weapons pointed at Dettmer when he cried out, "Stop! Don't move any closer. I will kill the boy if you take another step!"

"Stop," Lehman yelled out to the MPs, translating Dettmer's demands into English. "He says he'll kill the boy if we get any closer. Don't move. Let me talk to him. Clear?"

"Clear, sir," Duddy replied. "Hold your positions, men, and hold your fire. Don't move."

"Herr Dettmer," Lehman said. "Or should I address you as Oberleutnant?"

Dettmer didn't reply. He continued to hold young Willi, who was beginning to squirm in his arms. "Stop it! Hold still," he yelled, slapping the boy on the side of the head. "Stop it, I said," he yelled as young Willi began to cry.

"No," cried Therese. "Let my boy go!" She got up and began to move toward Dettmer.

"Don't you come any closer either, or I'll kill the boy right in front of you," Dettmer yelled.

"Duddy! Keep her back," Lehman yelled. Duddy moved in front of Therese and gently moved her back to where her father and Anna Karolina stood on the sidewalk.

"Just stay back, ma'am," he said. "He's not going anywhere, and he won't hurt your boy."

"Look, Dettmer," Lehman said. "Nobody needs to get hurt here. Just let the boy go. All we want to do is talk to you."

"Talk? Very well, I'll give you talk. But I will do the talking, and you will listen," Dettmer replied, tightening his grip on Willi. "I'm going to get back into my truck and drive out of here. You will not stop me. You will let me go."

"You need to let the boy go."

"Oh, no, I'm taking him with me. And if you try to stop me or if you follow me, I will kill him."

"And where do you think you're going to go? You'll never get out of Bremen, much less Germany," Lehman replied. "Every Allied soldier in Europe is looking for you. You won't be able to get away."

While all of this was going on, Haas slowly reached down to un-button the snap on the sheath to her dagger. Imperceptibly, she inched forward. She knew she needed to close the gap between herself and Dettmer.

"If you do not allow me to pass, I will kill the boy right in front of you," Dettmer said. He still had hold of Willi off the ground, his left arm under his armpits and wrapped around his chest with his hand covering his face and mouth. The young boy's feet dangled in the air as Dettmer reached into his jacket pocket to pull out the kitchen knife, which he held in his right hand for everyone to see. "Now, let me go, or I will cut this boy's head off."

But young Willi had other ideas. Willi was a biter. If he didn't get his way, he would bite. And that is just what he did to Dettmer. He bit down as hard as he could on the hand and fingers covering his mouth.

"Ahhgggh!" Dettmer screamed out in pain as he shook his arm and hand to try to shake Willi off, his teeth firmly embedded into Dettmer's hand. Finally, Willi had enough. He opened his mouth and immediately dropped to the ground onto his hands and knees. The startled Dettmer continued to shake his hand in pain. Willi had drawn blood.

"Run, Willi, run!" Therese cried out. The boy looked startled but instantly got up and ran for his mother. Dettmer grabbed at him, but he couldn't reach him in time, and in a split second Willi was reunited with Therese.

With Willi free, all three MPs began to shout and move forward, "Drop the knife and get on the ground! Drop the knife!" They contin-ued to advance towards Dettmer.

"Hold it," Lehman screamed. "Nobody move, dammit! Stay back." The MPs held their positions with the service weapons trained on Dettmer.

"That's enough of this," said Haas. She took three full strides and stood just five feet from Dettmer. She slipped her Shanghai knife out of its sheath and held it next to her left leg.

"Luba, what are you doing?" Lehman said, his level of anxiety rising. "This is no time to ad lib. What are you doing? Talk to me, Luba!"

"Drop the knife," the MPs again screamed in unison, which drew another response from Lehman.

"Stand down, dammit," Lehman shouted to the MPs. "Don't fire! And that's a goddammed order."

Lehman turned his attention back to Haas. "Luba? What are you doing? Talk to me, Luba. Tell me what you're doing."

"I'm ending this now," she said in reply. Then to Dettmer she said, "Drop the knife and give yourself up. Or you can die right here, right now. It's your choice."

Dettmer looked incredulously at the woman standing in front of him. He had a six-inch height advantage, and he outweighed Haas by at least sixty pounds.

"You? You think you're going to kill me?" And he lunged forward.

In knife fights, there are almost always three elements, and more often than not, these elements determine how the fight will play out.

First, knife fights usually last about twenty seconds, a few seconds more, a few seconds less, but on average about twenty seconds. They are usually over so quickly because of the second element. In a knife fight, someone always gets cut, and the shock of being stabbed, often repeatedly, brings the fight to closure very quickly. Finally, the third element is that the aggressor, the one who attacks with the knife, usually has the advantage, unless the defender can turn the tables and go from defense to offense. These were the hard truths that were drummed into Haas over and over during her unarmed combat training, but her training also gave her the chance to alter the way these elements played out.

So for the next twenty seconds, give or take, Haas's world went into slow motion, and she and Dettmer began to perform a deadly ballet for the audience assembled in front of Therese's flat.

"Luba! Look out," Lehman yelled. Therese screamed, but Haas could hear nothing. She was completely focused on Dettmer's movements.

Dettmer, the aggressor, played his part perfectly. He had moved into a low crouch with the knife in his right hand, his left foot forward, his right foot back. And then he lunged, not with the knife but with his free hand. This is what aggressors usually do; they grab first and strike second. Using his left hand, he grabbed Haas's shirt and pulled her toward him, meaning to strike her repeatedly with the knife in his right hand, and she needed for him to come close.

Haas, the defender, knew her part. She had been standing with both feet shoulder-width apart, her weight evenly distributed on the balls of her feet. Dettmer had a size advantage, but Haas was quicker.

As Dettmer grabbed at Haas's shirt, her open right hand made a sweeping motion, breaking his grasp. She now had his forearm locked as her hand grasped his upper arm just above his elbow. In a sweeping motion, she moved her left leg to her rear and was no longer directly in front of Dettmer but standing perpendicular to him, and she completely avoided his jabs. Her left hand slashed at Dettmer's knife hand, slicing into the fleshy part of his thumb and taking off the tips of his index and middle fingers. Her knife was double-edged; Dettmer was armed with a kitchen knife of high quality but not suited for the task at hand—it had only a single edge. He started to fall forward, the wound to his hand causing him to drop his knife, and Haas continued a sweeping motion with her left leg, her arm still holding onto Dettmer's elbow with her hand now grasping his shirt. The advantage had shifted. Now she was the aggressor. Dettmer continued his fall, but his left arm remained in Haas's grasp, moving in an unnatural direction. Haas now stood behind Dettmer. He had nearly completed his fall and was about to smash face-first into the concrete pavement. Just as he hit the pavement with a sickening splat, dislodging one of his front teeth, Haas administered the final blow. It was probably unnecessary, because Dettmer was knocked silly from landing on his face, but it was a blow that gave Haas immense satisfaction. With every ounce of strength she had, she drove her right foot through Dettmer's shoulder joint. There was a loud snap as the ball separated from the socket, cartilage ripped, and bone splintered and snapped. Dettmer screamed in agony, and then he passed out.

Haas looked down at Dettmer lying at her feet. She dropped his now useless arm, and it fell to the pavement. She looked at the tip of the nine-inch Shanghai knife, noticed it had Dettmer's blood on it, and knelt down to wipe the blade off on his shirt. She then calmly slipped the knife into her sheath and stood up. She walked over and picked up the kitchen knife, admiring its weight and heft, and slipped it into her belt for safekeeping.

About twenty seconds. That's all it took. For everyone else, it all happened in an instant, but for Haas, it happened in slow motion. She turned around to face Lehman, the MPs, the liaison officers, and Therese with her family, and calmly shrugged her shoulders. They all looked back at her with looks of astonishment. "What?" she asked.

There was a moment of silence. Haas's audience couldn't believe the ballet they had just witnessed. It was Duddy who finally broke the silence with a single word.

"Damn."

"They will never believe this back at headquarters when I tell them what happened," the German liaison officer said, giving Haas a look of admiration.

To which Duddy could only add, "Damn."

***

"I think this man will need first aid," Haas said to Duddy. "Do you have a kit or something in your jeep you can use to patch this poor man up, Corporal?"

"Yes, ma'am. Go get the first aid kit," Duddy said to one of the MPs. Duddy and the other MP walked over to Dettmer, who was beginning to come to, moaning from the pain in his shoulder and bleeding profusely from his hand, his mouth, and his nose. The fall to the pavement probably broke his nose, too. The MPs rolled him over onto his back, and he screamed out in agony. His shoulder wanted to stay where it was and didn't want to move with him.

"We'll need to get him to a hospital," Lehman said. "The British hospital isn't far from here. We can take him there."

"I can go with the MPs to take him there," Haas said. "We'll need to have a guard posted on him until he's released back to us for interrogation."

"Yeah, about that," Lehman started to say when a column of jeeps began to roll up. It was Lefkowicz and Whitacre with two squads of MPs.

Lefkowicz watched as the MPs did their best to bandage up Dettmer. One of them had wrapped his arm tightly against the front of his body, while the other wiped the blood from his mouth. He was still groggy and obviously in pain.

"I see we're just in time. Is everyone all right?" Lefkowicz asked, and then he looked down at Dettmer. "Apart from him, I mean?"

"Yeah, we're fine," Lehman started to say, but was interrupted once again, this time by Therese and her father, each with a child in their arms, running up to him and shouting.

"Captain!" Therese exclaimed. "We have to get to my parents' house! My mother is being held there by the man who's been helping Dettmer. It's Corporal Becker, and he's supposed to kill my mother if Dettmer doesn't return by nine o'clock. You have to help! We have to hurry!"

Chapter Twenty-Six

Lehman came up with a simple plan. Whitacre and a squad of MPs loaded up Dettmer and transported him to the nearby British hospital. Whitacre would ensure that Dettmer remained under guard until he could be moved and taken into custody. Lehman, Lefkowicz, and Haas would take a squad of MPs to Therese's parents' house, where they would free Therese's mother and capture Becker. Duddy and his two MPs would take Therese, her father, and the two children back to the hotel and wait there. Lehman also asked the liaison officer to go back to the hotel.

"You can get a preliminary statement from him," Lehman said to the officer. "Just get his version of what happened and I'll coordinate with you when we return, understand? You can ride back with the MPs."

"Oh yes," the liaison officer replied. "Yes, of course. I will be happy to get a statement from the gentleman," he added. His uniform was drenched in sweat from the excitement of the morning and he was relieved that he would not have to take part in any more confrontations.

But Therese and Karl objected to Lehman's plan.

"We need to come with you," Therese protested.

Lehman started to respond, but Haas cut him off.

"Frau Weber," Haas said. "I understand. I lost my mother in the war. But we will bring your mother back to you safely. No harm will come to her. I promise you."

Therese started to reply, she wanted to register her objection but caught herself. She looked Haas directly in the eye.

"You're right. Be careful." She turned around to her father and said, "Let's go. Everything will be all right, Papa." Duddy escorted them back to his jeep. Therese and Karl jumped into the rear as the MPs handed each of them one of the children, who would ride on their laps and were delighted with the idea.

Haas turned to Lehman and Lefkowicz. "How much time do we have?"

"About twenty minutes."

"We'd better hurry."

***

The column of jeeps stopped about a half block away from the house. From there, everyone would dismount and move as quickly and quietly as possible to take up positions at the front and rear of the house. Therese's father had been able to give them a detailed description of the interior. He told them that when he and Dettmer left, Becker was with Therese's mother in the kitchen, where he believed he was holding her. That would be the most likely location.

"I don't think he is armed," he said. "But he's an enormous man. Very strong. He could snap her in two like a twig."

The MPs would take no chances. Once inside the house, they planned to rush Becker to subdue him. Lehman wanted Becker taken alive. He wanted to question him, so the MPs were instructed to use lethal force only if it was absolutely necessary. Two MPs were given the assignment to get to Therese's mother and whisk her out of the room and away from Becker. They wouldn't knock. They wouldn't announce themselves. They would burst into the house and move as quickly as possible.

The MPs at the front of the house were the first to move in. The door was not locked, and they went in quickly through the front parlor and dining room, down the hallway to the kitchen. The second group of MPs threw the kitchen door open and charged in just as the first group entered the kitchen.

"Down, down! Don't move, don't move," they yelled, and two MPs charged at Becker, who was sitting at the kitchen table. He had just broken off a piece of bread, slathered it with American salted butter, and had jammed it in his mouth when two MPs jumped on him, toppling him and the chair he was sitting in.

Two other MPs rushed to Therese's mother. She was standing at the stove with a skillet full of Spam. An MP reached out and grabbed her, planning to whisk her out of the room, but she would have nothing of it. She smacked the MP across the side of his face with her spatula and yelled to him, "Let me go! What's wrong with you? Get out of my kitchen," she screamed at the MPs in German. "Ernst, are you all right?" She turned to the MPs who had tackled Becker and screamed, "Get off of him! What are you doing? We're eating breakfast, for God's sake. Let him go this instant!"

Lehman and Lefkowicz burst into the kitchen from the rear and Haas from the front of the house. The scene in the kitchen was pure chaos. Two MPs were struggling to handcuff Becker and get him to his feet. The other two MPs were trying to restrain Therese's mother, who, between smacking the MPs with her spatula, kept screaming, "Let him go! Don't hurt him! He was just having breakfast with me!"

"Quiet!" Lehman screamed from the top of his voice, and the room went still. He turned to Lefkowicz and said, "See? I learned that from you."

All eyes in the room were now on Lehman. He turned to face Therese's mother and said, "Ma'am, we've captured the man who broke into your house this morning. Your daughter, your husband, and your grandchildren are all safe. They are waiting for us to bring you to them. They are all at the Hotel Zur Post. We will take you there now."

Johanne gave Lehman a stern look and asked, "What about him?" pointing her spatula at Becker. "What about him, are you arresting him, too?"

"You're not being arrested, ma'am. And we need to question him. So we're taking him with us, but I don't think there is anything we can arrest him for. If you want, you can press charges with the German police, and they can arrest him. He held you against your will, and he was ordered to kill you."

Johanne looked at Becker and said, "I want you to go with these men. They won't harm you. Right?" she asked Lehman.

"He won't be hurt as long as he comes with us peacefully. We just want to ask him some questions, that's all. After that, we can probably let him go."

"Very well," she said. "Now, Ernst, I want you to go with these men and answer all of their questions. You will do that for me?

"Yes. I will answer their questions," he replied.

Lehman nodded to the MPs who stood on either side of Becker. Becker's face was covered with bread crumbs and butter. The MPs started to lead Becker out the back door when Johanne called out, "Wait!" She took a napkin from the table, walked over to Becker, and stood on tiptoe as she gently wiped off his face.

"You're a good man, Ernst. Answer their questions, and they will let you go. And if they don't let you go, if they hurt you in any way, there will be hell to pay," she said. "From me!"

Lehman nodded one last time and the MPs escorted Becker out the back door.

"Ma'am, if you'll come with us, we'll take you to your husband and daughter."

"I'm not going anywhere until I get this kitchen cleaned up. Here," she said tossing the towel that hung from her apron to Lehman. "You can help me. And you, too," she said to Haas.

Johanne then noticed Haas's belt. "My knife! You brought back my knife! Thank you very much," she said, walking up to her. Haas pulled the knife from her belt and handed it over to Johanne. "This was a gift from my mother, you know," she told Haas. "It means a lot to me and I thank you very much for returning it. Now, help me clean up this mess."

***

Lehman drove back to the hotel with Haas up front and Johanne in the rear. Throughout the entire ride back, a journey that lasted no more than ten minutes, Johanne vented her feelings about the morning's events.

"I told her that it would come to no good end. I told her," she said over and over. "I told her it was dangerous, that if she were to be caught, she could go to jail. But she wouldn't listen to me. 'Everybody's doing it, Mama.' That's what she said."

As Lehman pulled up in front of the hotel, he said to Haas, "I think you and Walt should head over to the British hospital and check on Dettmer's status. I think you tore him up pretty bad, so I want to know when they think he can be released into our custody so we can interrogate him. If he can't be moved, I want him guarded twenty-four hours until he can."

"Yes, we'll take care of it, Cap."

"And you and I need to talk about . . . ," he paused as if he were trying to control his emotions, as if he were trying to find the right words so that he didn't explode with anger.

"I know what you're going to say, Cap," Haas replied.

"No, I don't think you do. What did I say the first day you were here? We do things as a team, we don't go around like some angry lone wolf. None of this had to happen the way it did. We would be interrogating Dettmer right now if you hadn't taken matters into your own hands. Now he's not really under our control, he's in the British hospital, and we have to hope he doesn't escape."

Haas sighed deeply. "I know, Cap. I'm sorry. I truly am sorry. I lost it. I lost it when I saw him holding the boy and then threatening to kill him. And there were other reasons."

Lehman reached across the seat and put his hand on Haas's, giving it a soft, reassuring squeeze. "I understand. We'll talk about it later, okay?" His hand remained where it was as he looked at her and said, "You're not off the hook. I'm still really mad about this. But I have to say . . . ," he said, his voice softening as he searched for the right words. "I have to say, that I have never in my life seen anything so damn brave. Crazy? Yes. Stupid? Hmm, maybe. But, damn, it was brave. You know, I think

I'm most pissed off about the fact that we could have lost you. Dettmer could easily have killed you."

Haas looked at his hand on hers. She could not remember the last time she had felt the touch of another human being. It was warm, and it felt good.

She looked up at Lehman and said, "That would never have happened." And then she gently moved her hand out from under Lehman's in such a way as to let him know that she didn't object to his touch. That in another time and place it might even be welcome.

"Walt and I will check on Dettmer," she said. "We'll make sure he's under constant guard, and we'll be back as soon as we can."

"Sounds good. Okay," he said, turning around to face Johanne, who sat patiently in the back of the jeep. "Now it's time for me to organize a little family reunion."

***

Therese and her father were pacing back and forth in the large briefing room in the CIC headquarters. Duddy and the MPs told them to wait there for Lehman and Haas to return with Johanne, and they had been waiting for nearly two hours.

"What is taking them so long? I'll never forgive myself if something happened to your mother," Karl asked.

"It will be fine, Papa. They'll bring her here. You saw what the woman did to Dettmer. Mama will be fine. That's what she said. She said she will bring her back to us. She promised."

At that moment, the door to the room opened just slightly, and Lehman poked his head inside to say, "There is someone here to see you." He then opened the door completely to let Johanne pass through into the waiting arms of her husband and daughter. They all cried out in joy and relief that Johanne had been released and appeared to be unharmed.

"Mama," Therese cried. "You're safe! Are you all right? Are you hurt?"

"Oh, Johanne," Karl said, "we were so worried! I don't know what I would have done if he had hurt you, if something had happened to you."

"The children? Where are the children?" Johanne asked. "They are safe?"

"Yes. They're fine. They are here upstairs," Therese replied. "Karla is looking after them now."

"Karla," Johanne scoffed. "She's the one that got you into this mess. If it weren't for her, none of this would have happened."

"Mama, please. Not now. Please."

"Well, take me to see my grandchildren," she replied.

"Everyone! May I have your attention please? Just for a minute," Lehman said as he walked to the far side of the room and took a seat at the interview table. The room became quiet as he spoke. "If everyone could be seated, please. We'll take you upstairs to your room, and you can see the children, but I need to ask you a few questions first. Please take a seat at the table here, and I promise that I will be brief. I know you've been through a lot today."

"Come, Papa, come, Mama. Please sit and listen to what the captain has to say," Therese urged her parents.

"Thank you," Lehman said as the three of them sat down across the table from him. He looked carefully at Karl, noting the color and shape of his eyes, his nose, the shape and size of his ears, even his hairline, which that he noticed was receding with a prominent widow's peak.

"So," Lehman said, turning his attention to Therese's father, "I will keep this very brief. I need to understand what happened today. Tell me, what did the men who broke into your house today want? Why did they break in?"

"He said," Karl replied, "the man you call Dettmer, he said that my daughter had something he needed. That is why he wanted to bring the children back to our home. He wanted to use them as a bargaining chip for Therese to give him what he wanted."

"Did he say what that was? Was it money, or something else?"

"No, he didn't specifically say, and I didn't ask. The big man was holding Johanne, and Dettmer gave him instructions to kill her if we didn't return. That was the only thing I had on my mind. I thought that Therese would gladly exchange whatever he wanted for the freedom of her children and her mother and me. Whatever it was, money, or whatever it was. That's what I thought," he said looking over to Therese, who sat in silence.

"What could you possibly have that would drive him to such lengths?" Lehman asked Therese. "It seems like such a desperate act—holding your mother, threatening to kill her, taking and threatening the children. Surely it had to be more than money?"

"I have nothing more to say, Captain. I've told you everything I know. I've given you everything you need to know to arrest Dettmer and bring him to justice. You can put him on trial just as you have with the others in Nuremburg."

Lehman stared coldly at Therese, trying to determine if she was telling him the truth. All of his instincts were screaming at him that there was something she was holding back. There had to be something more. Something just didn't add up.

"Hmm," he replied. "All right, that's enough for now. I'll take you all upstairs to the children. I know that we have Herr Dettmer and his accomplice in custody, but once again I'm asking you all to remain at the hotel. You are not under arrest. But we need to make sure there aren't other accomplices. I want to make sure you remain safe, and that there is no one else out there who intends to harm you. So I hope you will understand and enjoy the evening here as our guests, courtesy of the United States government. I'm sure you'll be able to go home very soon. Possibly tomorrow, and definitely in the next few days."

"Thank you, Captain," Therese replied. "We will stay here, and we will not give you any trouble, I assure you. We are very grateful for your assistance."

Lehman simply nodded and then turned one more time to Karl and said, "Wait a minute. Don't go yet. I do have one more question that I need to ask you. Have you always lived in Bremen?"

"Why, yes," he replied. "I was born here. I've lived here all of my life, except for when I served in the first war."

"So you have other family here, then?"

"My parents died years ago. I had a number of aunts, uncles, and cousins on both my father and mother's side of the family. Those that survived the war are still here. And of course, we had our children. Therese is the only one to survive, I'm afraid. And the grandchildren of course, thank God. My two sons, my other daughter and her children, they are all gone now."

"I'm very sorry. Truly sorry. That is an unimaginable loss."

"Yes, well, that is what war usually brings. Loss and suffering, no?"

"Yes, that's very true. One last question. Did you have any siblings?

Karl paused for a moment and said, "Yes, I had a brother. But he left with his family for America before the first war. He had a wonderful family, a wife, three beautiful daughters, and a son. They left, oh my, I think it was in 1912? Could it have been so long ago? Yes, I think that is so. It was before the first war."

"What was his name? Your brother."

"His name was August. August Josef Lehman."

"Hmm," was the only sound that Lehman could get out. All the other words seemed to be stuck in his throat.

"By the way, Captain. I've noticed that you speak German very well. Impeccably," Karl said as he sat in the chair directly in front of Lehman. "Did you study German in university?"

"Yes, I did. But I actually grew up speaking German at home because I was born here. In Osterholz."

"Osterholz? That is barely twenty kilometers from here," Karl replied.

"Yes, and my father was born right here in Bremen. He left, though. To come to the States. Before the first war. He left with his family."

"What is your name, Captain? Tell me your name."

"Papa," Therese said, "the captain's name is the same as yours. The same as ours. It's Lehman, too."

"And what was your mother's name? Was it Cecelia? And did you have three older sisters, Rosalie, Eleonora, and Else?" Karl asked as the memory of his brother's family flashed in his mind's eye. He could see what they wore on the day they left for America. He remembered waving goodbye from the dock at Hamburg, watching the ship slowly pull away and his brother, August, his wife, Cecelia, and their three daughters all waving goodbye. Cecelia held her son in her arms. It was a very young Caspar Lehman, and she was waving his little hand goodbye to his uncle Karl, who remained behind because it was his duty as the elder son to look after his parents.

There was a long silence as it became obvious to everyone in the room that a remarkable twist of fate had just occurred. What are the odds of reconnecting with family members who had been separated for over forty years?

"It can't be," Karl said. "Is it possible? August left here with his family so many years ago. He took his whole family, his wife, three daughters, and his one son to America. He said he wanted a better life, a place where he could work hard and build a future for himself and for his family."

"Where did he go after he left here?" Lehman asked. "Do you know where he went?"

"He went to New York, of course, but that is not where he settled. He told me there were many Germans in America and that he would be able to live among them in a place named Louisville." Karl leaned across the table and looked closely at Lehman's face. Now it was his turn to notice the color and shape of the eyes, the nose, the ears, and how the hairline had receded and that there was a prominent widow's peak.

"I can tell you that he had a good life there," Lehman said. "It wasn't a long life, but it was a good life. Both he and my mother died when I was young. August Josef, your brother, was my father. I'm Caspar. Caspar Lehman. I'm his son."

"My brother's son. My nephew! You were only a small child when you left."

"I was three."

"How did you come here? Of all the places in the world for you to be, you are here in Bremen," Karl said. "It must have been fate that you should come here to find and help your family."

Lehman looked across the table at Therese, his cousin, and his uncle Karl and Aunt Johanne. "I don't really believe in fate. I do believe in luck, and I think it was just dumb luck that brought me here. That's it."

"No, son. It was something much more than that," Karl insisted.

They all sat at the table in shock, taking in what had just happened.

"I'll take you all upstairs to your rooms, and you can rejoin the children. Your friend Karla and Perdue are still here," he said to Therese.

"Karla," said Johanne, "She's a good for nothing . . . "

"Mama, that's enough."

"I'll take you upstairs. The hotel will bring you your dinner there. It's all been arranged," Lehman said as he pushed back his chair and stood up. He motioned to the door, inviting them to head to the door. "I'll check in with you all in the morning. Hopefully, it will be a quiet evening."

Chapter Twenty-Seven

Lehman was alone in his office, the clock on the wall reading 1755 hours. He had poured himself a stiff drink, then another, and was on his third when Lefkowicz and Haas entered.

"You started without us," Lefkowicz quipped, noticing the bottle and half-empty glass on Lehman's desk.

"How's Dettmer? He'll live, I hope," Lehman replied.

"He's going to be laid up for a few days. Our sweet sister here," Lefkowicz said, looking at Haas and beaming like a proud brother whose sibling just beat up the neighborhood bully, "rearranged his anatomy pretty good. She snapped his shoulder and arm. Broke it in three places. Dettmer had surgery, but he'll be okay and ready to move in a couple of days. And," he added, "I don't know how she did it, but she single-handedly got them to place a twenty-four-hour watch on Dettmer. He won't be able to take a piss without us knowing it."

"I just had a cordial conversation with the officer in charge," said Haas. "I explained the situation, and he most graciously accommodated my request. I can be very persuasive when I need to be."

"Yeah, I saw how persuasive you could be earlier today," Lehman replied. Haas said nothing, just stood there with her arms crossed and a frown on her face.

"So, Therese's parents do not want to bring any charges against Becker. According to her mother, Becker was duped by Dettmer. She said Dettmer told him that he could be accused of war crimes if he didn't go along. Becker was a guard at the Valentin Bunker, and Therese confirmed this. She said she knew him and that he tried to help the laborers there by smuggling in food and medicine, that he was always trying to give workers extra breaks whenever he could.

"So I think what we should do is to simply take a statement from him. That's what I'd like you two to do first thing in the morning. Just question him about what he did at the bunker. Find out why he helped Dettmer. And unless you find out in your interview that he's responsible for the disappearance of Glenn Miller's airplane or something like that, just let him go. Just tell him we'll be watching him all the time, and he'd better keep his nose clean. He's low level, and we'll have his statement and a record on file. We can always go back and pick him up if somebody above our pay grade decides they want to investigate further. Can you two handle that tomorrow?

"Sure, Cap," Lefkowicz replied. "Luba and I can take care of that, right, Luba?"

Haas just stood there, still frowning with her arms crossed.

"We're just going to let him go? Just like that? Because he's too low level?"

Lehman let out a deep sigh, took a gulp of his whiskey, and said, "Walt. Give Luba and me a minute, will you?"

"Sure, Cap. I'll be in my office if you need anything. Luba, I'll check in with you later, okay?"

"Thanks, Walt," she replied. "I'll stop by."

Lehman waited for Walt to leave the office and close the door behind him.

"Sit down, Luba. Have a drink," he said as he poured two fingers of whiskey in another glass and then filled his. Haas unfolded her arms and pulled out the chair at the table that served as her desk directly in front of Lehman's. She reached across, picked up the glass, and downed the whiskey in a single gulp.

"Another?"

"No, maybe later."

They both started speaking at the same time.

"Look, I know. . . "she began.

"Luba, what you did today was. . ." Lehman said.

"What? What I did today was what?"

"I want to make sure you are okay. Are you all right??"

"I'm fine."

"You've been through a lot today. You took a man down, single-handedly, I might add. And then you took part in a potential hostage rescue. That's a pretty good day at the office, Luba."

"I'm fine. It's what I was trained to do. Nothing more," she replied tersely.

"Look, this will be the last time I mention this. You remember what I said on your first day here? I said we work as a team. Today, you went out on your own. And that's not what we do. So, in the future, don't go John Wayne on us. Okay?

"John Wayne, isn't he an actor?"

"Never mind. It's not important."

"Do you know why I did it?"

"Tell me."

"Dettmer was the man responsible for rolling up our operations in Warsaw."

"Allegedly."

"No, he was the man. I was there, and I know what he did. If we had the opportunity to kill him then, we would have done it. I also never had the opportunity to fight in Germany. I was passed over on at least three occasions. A lesser-qualified agent was sent instead. And do you know what happened to them? They all died. Every last one of them. Then I found out that Dettmer was sent back to Germany and that he ran security at Valentin, where Wojchiech was seen. I could have easily killed him, you know? Easily. But I didn't. Because I know what the end game is supposed to be. I'm sorry that I went all Hopalong Cassidy on you."

"John Wayne."

"Whoever! I just wanted to make him suffer just a tiny bit for everything he has done. That's all." Haas let out a sigh and then closed her eyes and her head dropped to her chest. "I will have that drink now, please."

Lehman got up and walked around his desk to Haas's table and poured another whisky for her. This time, it was at least three fingers.

"Are you trying to get me drunk?"

Lehman chuckled and returned to his seat. "I'm trying to get you to talk about it. It's not good to hold things in."

"That's funny coming from you. Walt tells me you've been holding your emotions in for the past four years." She regretted her words almost as quickly as she had uttered them. Lehman replied with a startled, almost hurt look.

"I'm sorry," Haas said. "That . . . that was uncalled for. I'm out of line. I'm very sorry."

"No, as always your honesty is, well . . . brutal, but . . . always on point." Lehman stood up and pulled his desk chair around to the table where Haas sat.

"Not long after I met Walt," he began, "he told me a story about when he was on the force. You know, the NYPD, the New York Police Department? Anyway, he told me about the first time he had to shoot a man. There was a robbery. A man had robbed a grocery store and was trying to come running around the corner. The store owner was yelling, 'He's getting away!' And he was pointing to a man who was running directly at Walt. So Walt does what any good cop does, he does what he was trained to do, he pulls out his service revolver and orders the man to stop. The man sees Walt, he stops, and then he turns and tries to run away in the other direction. Walt yells at him to stop, and then he fired. Three times. He hit the guy in the back and brought him down. Killed him right there on Delancey Street in the Bowery. In broad daylight. The guy was carrying a bag of money he stole. There was about twenty bucks in the bag. That's all. Twenty bucks. They said the shooting was justified. He killed a robber who was fleeing and ignored his order to stop. He said the worst part was when people, other cops, came up to him to congratulate him. He never considered it to be a particularly brave act, and he said he never completely got over taking a man's life. So, I understand how easy it is to lose control. But there is always a price to be paid."

"I've killed a lot of men," Haas said. "Out of necessity. I didn't kill Dettmer, although I thought about it."

"Yeah, and you could have, too, couldn't you?

Haas left the question unanswered.

"So what happened to you at Dachau?" Haas asked. "Walt said you were almost court-martialed."

Lehman looked at his glass and swirled the whiskey inside for several seconds, watching how it coated the sides of the glass.

"I was accompanying an infantry battalion," he said, "and as we approached the camp, we were still about—I don't know, four or five miles out, maybe? Maybe more? But the smell. It was a stench, and we had no idea what it was. It wasn't until later, until after we liberated the camp—if you can call it liberation, because I don't think you can liberate death. Anyway, we realized that the smell was that of burning flesh. I don't know how anybody could stand it, it was foul, and it made you sick to your stomach, and I don't know how anyone living in the villages and towns nearby could claim they didn't know what was going on. It's inconceivable.

"Anyway, when we got close to the camp, the SS guards opened fire on us. And we just let them have it. We just shot them all to hell. Eventually a bunch of guards, there were at least a dozen, I'm not sure how many, but they wanted to surrender. They tried to surrender and they came out with their hands up shouting, 'Don't shoot!' But our guys weren't having it, so they just mowed them down where they stood."

Lehman paused and drained the remaining whiskey in a single gulp. "So I ran out in front and started yelling to our guys, 'Stop shooting! Hold your fire! They're trying to surrender.' I stood in the line of fire knowing that the Germans could pop me any second, but I just didn't care. And the battalion CO was so incensed at what he had seen that day—hell, everybody was—that he ran over waving his .45 in his hand at me and saying that he was going to blow my effin' head off if I didn't get out of the way.

"Well, I just walked up to him, I stopped right in front of him, I got right up into his face, and he stopped dead in his tracks, and I said that if he wanted to blow my head off, he could do it, but I wouldn't let our guys kill anybody who was trying to surrender. You should have seen the look on his face. He turned this incredible shade of red. It was almost purple. Hell, I thought he was going to explode, and then he starts yelling that he's going to bust me down to private, throw me in the stockade, have me shot, court-martialed, and I can't even remember everything he was yelling."

Lehman paused to look at Haas, who was sitting on the edge of her chair, leaning in and taking in every word he was saying.

"It was a very bad day," Lehman continued. "More guards were killed. I remember walking through the camp, and I came upon a group of prisoners, they were emaciated, they were just skeletons, skin on bone, their eyes sunk deep into their skulls, and they all had this lost, distant look on their faces. It was as if they couldn't believe they were now free, but they had nowhere to go. Anyway, I came upon this group of fifteen or twenty camp prisoners. They apparently had killed an SS guard. It looked like they had whacked him over the head with a shovel, and one of them was trying to decapitate the guard with it. He kept whacking away trying to separate this poor SOB's head from his body. They were all just looking on, very nonchalant about it all, as if cutting off someone's head could ever be normal. They had gone through so much, they had seen so much killing, so much death. There were bodies everywhere. Stacked up like cordwood. Bodies in open burial pits, there were enormous mass graves, I'd never seen anything like it. None of us had. So one more dead German didn't matter to this group of prisoners."

Lehman reached into his pocket for a cigarette. He offered one to Haas which she accepted. He reached into his pocket, searching for his lighter. *Right pocket. It's always in the right*, he thought.

"Anyway, I can remember that day and virtually every day that we spent there, for about two weeks. Twelve days, to be exact. Walt and I interviewed hundreds of prisoners—the former inmates, right, because they were no longer prisoners. And we interviewed the guards. They were the new prisoners now. I can remember all of that. The sights, the sounds, the smells. I can even remember the names of the guards we interviewed. But I never can remember which pocket I put my lighter in. It's funny what you remember and what you try to forget. Anyway, the battalion CO wanted to court-martial me, but the division commander interceded. He actually re-lived that battalion CO of his command and replaced him with someone who was more . . . even-tempered."

They sat and smoked together in silence. Lehman pulled out two more cigarettes, and they sat and smoked some more. Finally, Haas reached over to Lehman and placed her hand on his, the hand that was resting on the table.

"I'm tired of all of it, Cap. I just want to go home, but I don't have a home to go to."

"I told you, this is your home now."

"Yes, and I appreciate that. Everyone here in this place has been . . . remarkable. It must be because you're all Americans. You are so different from everybody else. You say funny things, you all have different accents. But you're all so friendly. Even after this terrible war, you all seem to embrace your life."

"We're friendly because that's just the way we are," Lehman said. "Plus it helps that America was never really bombed, except for Pearl, of course. We can go home and we don't have to look back. We don't have destruction all around us to remind us of the war. We can just pick up the pieces of our lives and begin again. Most people can, anyway. I didn't feel I had a home to go to either. My wife left me during the war, and I never expected that. It left a big hole in me. So that's why I'm here. At least for now, this is my home. And it's yours, too, for as long as you want it."

"That is a lovely thought, Cap," Haas said as she leaned over to kiss Lehman on the cheek.

"What's that for?"

"It's just to let you know how much I appreciate you. And, Cap, I don't really want to be alone tonight. I'm tired of being alone. And I don't think you should be alone either."

Lehman looked down at Haas's hand on his, feeling its warmth and softness.

"You have no idea how tempting that is, Luba. No idea. And there is a part of me . . ."

"But?"

"But I think it would make things very complicated. We'd wake up in the morning, and we'd regret it. I don't want to do something that I know we'd both regret. I'm a mess, Luba, and you don't need that in your life. You deserve better than that."

"I understand the complications and the risks. But I think you should let me decide what I need and what I might regret."

"I know, I get it. But I'd like to think this through a bit. I don't want to rush into anything and make a mistake. I know I can't speak for you, but I don't want to do anything rash. But know what I would like to do."

"Go ahead, tell me. What is it you'd like to do?"

"I want us to finish this assignment together. You, me, and Walt, too. I want us to bring Dettmer back here and question him. We need to find out how he compromised your networks in Poland. I want to find out who he's working with here. How was he planning to escape and who was helping him? I want to suck every bit of information he has out of his head. I want us to try to track down survivors from the Farge camp and from the bunker who can pick out Dettmer in a courtroom and testify to the crimes he committed. And after a tribunal or whatever is convened, deliberates, and convicts him, I want to see him hanged."

"Becker was there, too. That's why I don't think we should just release him," Haas said.

"Okay, then ask him what he knows, and if you and Walt think he should be held, you go ahead and make that decision. Again, we'll sort it out. Together. Right? Together."

"Thanks. I think that's the right decision."

"I do, too. See, working together has a lot of benefits, right?"

"Right. So, I want those things, too, Cap. But I was also thinking about you and me. And the possibilities."

"Well, dear Luba, after we see this through to the end, I'd really like an opportunity to get to know you. I mean really know you."

"That's what I think I just offered, but you declined," Haas replied, her eyes flashing as she gave Lehman's hand a squeeze.

"You know what I mean. I want to take you out and have a proper dinner with wine and music, and not some crappy oompah band in a hotel. I want to go to the theater with you, maybe run up to the beaches on the North Sea for the weekend. I want to listen to jazz with you and share my love of music. Luba, I just want to do it . . . properly."

"I think I hear the whiskey talking now."

"No, I'm serious. There's something about you that makes me want to try again. Look, you could have any man in the world . . ."

"Are you saying you want to court me?"

Lehman's expression turned completely serious, his brow furrowed, his eyes squinted as he looked at Haas replied, "Well, yes. That's exactly what I'm saying."

"And you thought I was brave."

Chapter Twenty-Eight

Haas and Lefkowicz left CIC headquarters early to question Becker, who was being held at the MP facility nearby. Lehman decided to leave it up to them as to whether or not Becker should be released.

"I don't think he's going to run," Lehman told them. "I don't think he's going anywhere, and we can always pick him up if and when we need to. But you two decide, got it? I'm going to spend some time with Frau Weber. There's something I still don't understand, and I want to try to clear it up. We can circle back later in the day and compare notes. You two have any questions? Concerns?"

"Nope, not from me, Cap," Lefkowicz replied.

"Perfectly clear, Cap," Haas said, beaming a smile that Lefkowicz noticed immediately.

"What's going on?" he asked.

"Nothing," Lehman replied, trying to shake off Haas's look. "You two get going. We'll catch up later."

Lehman could hear Lefkowicz talking as he and Haas left the office. "What's going on? You two are acting kind of squirrelly."

"You're imagining things, Walt.

"I don't think so."

"Yes, you are. It's all your imagination."

It was just before eleven o'clock when Lehman knocked on the door to Therese's hotel room. As he stood in the hallway waiting for her to answer, he could hear the children playing inside. Their squeals of laughter brought him a smile. *Children*, he thought. *If only we could remain as children and never grow up.*

Therese opened the door and, upon seeing Lehman, embraced him and said, "Come in, please. I was just talking to Mama and Papa about you."

As Lehman entered the room, he saw Therese's father, his uncle Karl, on the floor with the children. They were sitting on his back, riding him like a horse and having the time of their lives. The idea they were all his family was something Lehman was struggling to accept.

"You two are going to be the death of this old horse. You're so heavy," he said, and then mimicked a horse's bray, lifting himself upright on his knees, which caused the children to tumble off his back and onto the floor with howls of laughter.

"Shh, quiet, children. There are other guests here in the hotel. We have to be quiet," Therese said.

"What kind of hotel allows horses as guests?" her father said to the children as they tried to clamber aboard his back for one more ride.

"Papa, Mama, please take the children to your room for a bit," Therese begged. "I need to speak to Captain Lehman."

"All right, children," her father said. "Listen to your mother and come with us while she talks to the captain. We'll see if we can find some nice hay for the horse in our room, what do you say?"

Lehman watched his uncle and aunt each pick up a squealing child and carry them to their room across the hallway. The sounds of their laughter echoed down the hallway.

"Well, I just wanted to check in on you to make sure you were okay," Lehman said. "The children seem no worse for wear."

"Thank you. And, yes, they're fine. We got up very early. Papa wants to go home, though. He says it wouldn't be good for him to get used to living in a hotel. He says it is too fancy and that he'd become very spoiled."

Lehman smiled and said, "I think everyone should be able to go back home soon. Maybe tomorrow. But I would like to do a final debrief with you today. Can you come down to our offices? Say, in a half hour?"

"Yes, of course. How long do you think it will take? I just need to tell Papa and Mama to look after the children."

"I don't think it will take more than an hour. Will that be all right with you?"

"Yes, yes, of course," Therese replied.

"Just come downstairs at say, eleven-thirty," he said looking down at his watch.

"Thank you. And Cap," she said smiling, "it's a strange nickname, you know. I can't get used to it. Oh, never mind, I just want to thank you for yesterday. I want to thank you for everything you've done to help me, to help all of us."

"It's okay. We couldn't have found Dettmer without your help. So I should be the one expressing thanks."

"I think it is one small step on a long journey back toward atonement," Therese replied.

Atonement. That seems like a very tall order, he thought. "Okay, we'll expect to see you in a half-hour."

"I'll be there," Therese replied.

***

She was already seated at the table in the debriefing room when Lehman entered. He pulled the chair out from across the table and sat down.

"Thanks for coming down, Therese. There are just a few details that I want to iron out, just a few questions, and then you'll be free to go. All of you will be able to go. Perdue, too. He's going to get a reprimand, and I think he's going to be reassigned to a unit where he has fewer temptations. But he'll be free, too."

"A slap on the wrist," Therese said.

"Yep. That's it," Lehman replied. He looked at Therese and asked, "Cigarette?" He reached into his pocket for the familiar gold case and pulled out two cigarettes, offering one to her. He lit hers first, then his, and then pulled over a large glass ashtray for the two of them to share.

"So, Therese, there's something I just don't understand," Lehman said. "Dettmer would have had other means to obtain the funds necessary for him to book passage. He didn't need black market merchandise from you. Did he?" He looked Therese directly in the eye. "You had something else he wanted, didn't you? What was it?"

Therese thought for a moment as to how – and if – she should answer the question. Lehman continued to press her.

"Come on, Therese. We've given you everything you asked for. Now tell me. What was it that Dettmer really wanted? Look, you have to give me something. As soon as he's healthy enough to talk, we're going to interrogate him, and we'll get it out of him. But it just doesn't add up. He didn't need money from you. He wanted something else. What was it?"

Therese cleared her throat and said in a voice so soft it was barely a whisper, "I kept my ledgers."

"Your ledgers? What ledgers? What does that mean?"

"The ledgers contain a tally of all the prisoners who worked at Bunker Valentin. They have a complete accounting of how much we were paid to build the bunker. The profits, the losses, and the cash flow. They show all the money that came in and the money that went out. The ledgers contain a record of every company and business that received payment and how much they received. But the firms we did business with were not the only ones to receive payment. There were others. Well, one other. He was getting rich off of it."

"He? He who? Who's he?"

"In addition to the companies that supplied services or the building materials necessary for construction, the ledgers contain the name of one man, Maximillian Scholz. He was the senior project administrator at Organisation Todt. He reported directly to Speer. He was connected to the highest levels of the Reich. He was a party member, and he cooked up a scheme to profit off the war. I suppose I am guilty, too. And so was my direct superior. His name was Richard Schmidt. We, I . . ." she said looking down as her voice trailed off. "We are just as guilty as Scholz. We both looked the other way."

"Why would he do this? Why would Scholz incriminate himself in such a way?"

"Because there must be a proper accounting," Therese replied, as if there could be no other answer. "Everything must be properly tallied, and the record must correctly reflect who was paid, every firm and every individual who received payment. There are no exceptions."

"Hmm. That's amazing."

"I don't see what is amazing about it. I kept meticulous records. I took great pride in it."

"I see," Lehman replied, still astonished by Therese's statement and her simple candor. "Did he offer you anything for your compliance? For your participation in all of this?"

"Herr Schmidt promised that I would be taken care of. He said I would not be forgotten. He said he would not forget my dedication to duty and to the Reich."

Lehman leaned back into his chair and let out a long sigh. He tugged nervously at his ear, fumbled for another cigarette, and lit up. "Smoke?" he asked Therese. She shook her head no. "Scholz and everyone within Organisation Todt are known to us," he said. "We know who worked there. What does the ledger prove?"

"Yes, you know who they are and what they did. They were just following orders, right? Isn't that the line everyone keeps repeating? Well, there is more to it than that. There is blood on their hands, and they know it. If the ledgers got out, it would show people just how much they actually profited. It's blood money. That's why Dettmer wants them. He's acting on behalf of Scholz. Scholz is a very well-connected man. Herr Schmidt just went along because he had no other choice. He is still working here as an engineer in Bremen, you know. He oversees several construction projects for the Allies. He's in charge of construction at the Port of Bremerhaven. Scholz is still in Berlin, supposedly in the Russian zone, and I'm sure he's working on reconstruction projects just as Herr Schmidt is. Scholz is an engineer, too, and his experience would be valued, even if it comes with certain baggage."

"Well, I think that is all in the past now," Lehman said. "Organisation Todt was given a blanket amnesty when the war ended. With an amnesty in place, no German prosecutor would touch this. They'd say, 'You had your chance.' Now, let's move on.'"

"The money is still there."

"What money? Where?"

"I regularly transferred the money to an account in Switzerland. I transferred over seventy million Reichsmarks to the account."

Lehman thought this over carefully, then replied, "I'm sorry, Therese, but so what? The Reichsmark is virtually worthless. Nobody wants Reichsmarks these days."

"No, but they would want dollars," she said. Lehman stared back at her, still not understanding. "Don't you see? The Swiss account doesn't hold Reichsmarks. Herr Schmidt had to sign off on the transfers, and then I purchased and we deposited American dollars into the account. I purchased dollars as part of every transaction when I deposited the funds. So today, if I have calculated correctly, the account holds close to twenty-five million American dollars. Scholz's plan was to eventually access the money years from now when the war was nothing more than a distant memory. He didn't want anyone to know about the funds. And that, my dear cousin, is what is being hidden. The money is accruing interest, Scholz is still profiting, and my ledgers can show that. And there's one more thing.... "

"One more thing? There's more? What in heaven's name could that be?"

"I have the account number and access identification code for the Swiss bank account. I managed the account, and I alone possessed the account access codes. When we were evacuating Valentin, I was supposed to ship the ledgers along with the account codes to Scholz at Organisation Todt in Berlin. But I never did it. I kept the ledgers because I didn't think it was right that he should profit off the deaths of thousands."

"How did he find out you still had the ledgers?"

"It wasn't hard, I suppose. First, he never received them. As far as I know, all of the other files were received. Everything except for the ledgers. So it was just a process of elimination. When we evacuated, I told Schmidt that I sent everything to Berlin. I even asked him if he wanted to take possession of the Swiss bank account information, but he said no. He insisted that everything be sent to Berlin. He said he didn't want anything to do with it."

"Did Scholz or Dettmer contact Schmidt to try to pressure you?"

"He always told me that he never wanted anything to do with the money. But, like the rest of us, he is complicit. And now all he wants to do is forget. All he wants is to appear clean. He always was concerned about his reputation and legacy as an engineer and as a design architect. He always said that he wanted to build great objects. He told me that many times."

"Has he been in contact with Scholz?"

"Yes. He regularly travels to Berlin for meetings with the Allies on various reconstruction projects. That's where he ran into Scholz, who pressed him to help obtain the ledgers and the bank information."

"So, the bottom line is this," Lehman said. "Schmidt sees Dettmer working on the docks. He knows Dettmer has certain skills that can help him. So he approaches Dettmer and says, 'I can make your life a lot easier if you'll do a little job for a former colleague of ours.' Does that sum it up?"

"Yes, pretty much. He thought Dettmer would take care of everything, his reputation would remain intact, and he would be able to go on and create the great objects that he is so driven to build. He wanted to wash his hands of it and be done with it."

"Why didn't you try to take the money?"

"And what would I do with it?"

"You could take it and go anywhere. You could do anything. You could hide forever."

"That doesn't sound like much of a life," she said. "No, I have already done too many things that I regret. People suffered and died because of what I did and what I didn't do. I've had enough of that. I'm not a good person, but I can work toward becoming one."

Lehman let out a deep sigh. "Why didn't you tell me this before?"

"It was—how do you say it?—It was my ace in the hole? Is that the right expression? I think it is, right?" Lehman nodded yes. "I had to hold something back just in case. I'm sure you understand."

"Yeah," Lehman slowly replied. "I do understand. But do you understand that you're still in danger? They're not going to stop until they get the ledgers and the account codes."

"I know."

"Where are they?"

"I have them hidden."

"Take me to them. Show me where they're hidden, and turn them over to me. That will take you out of danger."

"Yes. I will show you where they are, and you can have them. But first, I need to talk to the woman."

"Haas?"

"Yes, Haas."

"Why do you need to speak to her?"

"There is something I need to say to her. Personally. I have something to tell her. I have something to show her that she must see."

"Okay. She's out at the moment, and I expect her to return shortly. I can send her in as soon as she gets back here to headquarters. But first, I have an idea I want to run by you. A sort of proposition for you."

"The last time I listened to a proposition from an American, it got me here. So I'm not so sure I want to hear more propositions.

"Well, I think you'll want to hear this one. This idea I have, I think it will keep you and your family safe after you turn over the ledgers to us."

Therese sat there until the meaning of his words finally sank in. "Go ahead. I'm listening."

***

"I'm not sure what she wants to say to you," Lehman said to Haas in response to her question "Why?" "She just said she wanted to speak to you. Alone. I've just spent an hour with her, and I'm done for now, so I thought I'd give you a chance. She dropped a real bombshell on me. I'll bring you and Walt up to speed after you finish your chat with Therese, okay?"

"What do you think she wants to talk about?"

"I don't really know. I suspect it has something to do with yesterday and you taking down Dettmer and saving her children."

"You were there, too. We did it together."

"Yes, that's true. But, your action was pretty . . .," Lehman searched for the right word before finally saying, "assertive. You broke his arm in two and you carved him up like a Christmas goose."

"It could have been worse. I'm glad you were there. I might have killed him otherwise."

"I'm glad you didn't. We still have to interrogate him once he is healed up enough, which will hopefully be in the next few days. She's waiting for you now in debriefing room 2."

"Okay, I will listen to what she has to say."

***

Haas entered the small debriefing room, where Therese sat in her now familiar position, at a table with her back against the room's far wall.

"Good morning, Frau Weber," Haas said. "Captain Lehman said you wanted to speak to me."

"Yes, thank you so much for agreeing to speak to me. First, I wanted to thank you for saving the lives of my children. You were incredibly brave. I couldn't imagine doing what you did."

"Men like Dettmer don't scare me," Haas said. "He's a bully and a coward, and I'm not frightened by bullies and cowards. The only thing that frightens me is the people who empower men like Dettmer by not standing up to them. Your children deserve to live in a world where there are no Dettmers, although I suppose that is too much to expect. I'm not sure people will ever evolve that far."

Therese sat in silence. She wasn't sure how she wanted to begin what she had to say, so Haas solved that conundrum by asking, "So, what's the second thing?"

"Pardon?"

"You said, first, you wanted to thank me for saving your children. What is the second thing? Did you have something else you wanted to say to me?"

Therese cleared her throat and said, "When I first saw you here, when you came into the room to interrogate me, you startled me. I was in shock when you walked into the room. Do you remember?"

"Yes, I recall you dropped your purse. But I just assumed it was because you were frightened by your surroundings. Or maybe we just startled you. You weren't expecting us. We just barged into the room, after all, and it caught you off guard. Was there something more?"

"Yes, it was more than that," Therese said. "When you walked into the room, I realized I had seen you before."

"I think you must be mistaken," Haas responded. "I don't think that's possible, Frau Weber. I've never met you before in my life until we met two days ago. And it's been barely two weeks since I returned to Germany. I haven't been in Germany in years, and I've never been to Bremen. I think you're mistaken. There is no way we could have met or known each other."

"We haven't met, but I know you. And I'm being truthful about that. I'm not mistaken."

"I don't understand what you mean. How could that be possible?"

"When I was working at the bunker, I saw a man whom I believe you knew," Therese said to Haas. "I was in one of the bays under construction, and he was assigned to a work party. He was on the crew that mixed and poured the concrete for the submarine bays, the walls, the ceilings, and roof. For everything."

"Who was this man? What are you talking about?"

Therese reached into her purse and pulled out a small, badly creased, cracked, and faded photograph. In the photo, Haas and the man that she knew as Wojchiech Dabrowski, her husband, could clearly be seen. The two were sitting together underneath a tree, their arms around each other, smiling at the camera and at whoever it was that took the photograph. The photo captured a happy moment. Therese slid the photograph over to Haas, who looked at it, stunned by the image in front of her. *What? How can this be,* she thought?

"How did you get this?"

"I don't know how he did it, but somehow this man was able to keep this photograph with him, to smuggle it into the camp. He obviously carried it with him all the way from Poland, he carried it with him for all that time. It must have meant a great deal to him. It must have been very dear to him."

As Haas scrutinized the photo, a wave of memories washed over her. She remembered the day she first met Wojchiech, the first time they went out together, the day they married, the first time they made love, and the day he left to parachute back into Poland. Haas said nothing, mesmerized by the photograph. She looked at the now faded image of her beloved Wojchiech, and a single tear ran down her cheek. She stifled a cry, not wanting to show any more emotion than she already had.

"He was your husband, wasn't he?"

Haas just nodded. "We were told that my husband was evacuated from the Farge camp, just before the British liberated it. So you must be lying. How did you get this photograph?"

"I am not lying. Whoever told you that was . . . mistaken, or they had other reasons for saying what they did. But I absolutely know, I know for certain, that your husband was not evacuated."

"Go on."

"Your husband was in charge of a work party. Once a week, he would report to me and tell me the actual number of workers who were on the shift. I would get the numbers from all of the work party leaders and then tally them up. That was my job. I kept the books. I counted up the number of workers so that I could send the bill to the government for payment. We were paid based on the number of workers. Your husband seemed like a decent man. All of the workers under him looked up to him. It drove Dettmer mad. I was there on the day your husband died. It was in the early evening, actually, on the second shift, just about an hour after the shift changed at around 8 p.m. I saw Dettmer kill him."

"He would have been just another slave laborer to you," Haas said. "A Pole and a prisoner of war. What did you call us, *Untermensch*? Subhuman?"

Therese just sat in silence.

Haas leaned back in her chair to consider what Therese was telling her. She sat for several minutes, staring into Therese's eyes, trying to hold back her rage. *What is the truth here?* she wondered.

"How did it happen? Tell me everything."

"I was only there to count the number of workers. That was my job. I was merely trying to finish my work. The corporal, Becker, the man who held your mother captive, was there, too. And he can corroborate my story. He was escorting me when your husband came up to me to give me the number for the evening. He started talking to me. He said, "*Guten abend, Fraulein*," and I responded that I was not a Fraulein, that I was married and had children. He apologized for his mistake, saying that I looked too young to be married and have children, and then he smiled at me, and that is when Dettmer saw him talking to me.

"All he was supposed to do was give me the number of workers present that evening. That's all. Saying anything else was forbidden. Talking to me was forbidden. He was only to respond to me with the number, and it was something we had done each week, but Dettmer saw your husband talking to me, and I know I should have just walked away, but he saw your husband look at me and speak to me. That sent him into a rage. Dettmer was in an especially cruel mood that evening."

"Go on."

"Dettmer yelled, 'Don't you look at her! Don't ever look at a German woman, do you understand?' Your husband just turned around, gave Dettmer a look, and walked away to get back to work pouring the cement. But Dettmer continued to scream at him. 'Stop,' he yelled. Don't walk away while I am talking to you.' So your husband stopped and turned to face Dettmer. Even though he was weak and exhausted —they all were—he refused to cower in front of Dettmer. Dettmer ordered the Kapos to grab his arms and hold him in place. He pulled out the steel rod that he always carried with him, and he repeatedly stuck your husband across the face. He hit him so hard that his cap flew off and onto the concrete floor. The beating tore up his face badly, but your husband refused to cave in. Dettmer was so enraged that he pulled out his pistol and fired two shots into your husband, into his belly. Your husband was shocked when this happened, and then he looked at Dettmer and began to laugh. Then Dettmer struck your husband with the butt end of his pistol, which caused him to fall back into a trench where they had been pouring concrete. Dettmer just calmly said, 'Bury him! Bury him alive.'"

Therese paused to look at Haas, whose eyes were now closed as she envisioned the scene of the last moments of her husband's life.

"Your husband fell back into the wet concrete and just cried out into the night as they continued to pour the concrete all around him. I don't think it was a cry of pain or fear. It was as if he was releasing his anger. It was a howl of a man's anger and frustration, a cry of defiance into the night. Dettmer just stood there watching it all. At first the prisoners stopped working, but he ordered them to continue, to keep pouring concrete, he said that he'd kill them all if they didn't obey. Your husband looked up at me as the wet concrete began to rise around him. He didn't look frightened, he was calm, and it was as if there was a look of relief in his eyes. The concrete kept rising higher and higher until it eventually enveloped him, first covering his body and then his face and mouth. His hand raised up for a brief moment, and then it dropped into the wet concrete and sank until he was completely submerged. It was the last time I saw him. It was the last time anyone would ever see him, and I will never forget his cry, the wail of a grown man crying out into the night. But it wasn't a cry of anger or despair. It was a cry of release, a cry of freedom."

The two of them remained still for several minutes. The only sound in the room came from the clock on the wall as it continued its inexorable tick, tick, tick.

"I just stood there, in shock," Therese continued, finally breaking the silence in the room. "I had seen death before. Death was all around us. It was everywhere. You couldn't walk down the street and not see people dead and dying everywhere. But I had never seen a man so deliberately murdered, murdered in cold blood. I didn't know what to do. I just stared at the pool of wet concrete that was now a tomb for this man, your husband. The only thing left of him was his cap lying on the floor of the submarine bay and that's when I noticed something tucked inside the hatband," she said, looking at the photo Haas now held in her hand. "It was just tucked inside his cap on the floor, that's where he hid it. Your husband must have kept it there all this time, close to him. It is a miracle that he was able to carry it at all and keep it for so long.

"When I saw it, I didn't know what it was at first, so I walked over to his cap and stood on top of it, trying to cover it up. Then I looked down, and I could see it was a photograph. It was folded in two, but I could clearly see the image of a young couple, a man and a woman in the photograph, and I knew it didn't belong there, and I didn't want Dettmer to pick it up and destroy it. So I just stood there for a few minutes, pretending to be working, completing my report, tallying up my count of the number of workers on the job. I couldn't decide if I should subtract your husband from the total, but I decided to keep him in my tally for the day."

Haas opened her eyes and looked across the table at Therese. "They were just numbers to you, weren't they? They weren't people to you at all, were they? You didn't know him, you didn't even see who he was. I can tell you, though. He was a Pole and a soldier, and he was proud of it. But to you, he would have been just another slave laborer to you. Another number in your ledger book."

Therese dropped her head, feeling pangs of shame for her complicity and guilt. *I was just doing my job. I was just trying to do whatever I could to survive, just like everyone else,* she thought.

"Yes, they were just numbers to me," she replied, looking straight at Haas. "They were just numbers to me because it was the only way I could get through the day. I couldn't think of them in any other way and look at myself in the mirror. Until that night. That was the first time I began to see them as something other than a number, something more than a figure in my ledger."

"And what changed for you that night?" Haas demanded. "What made you embrace your humanity on this, of all nights? How long had you worked at the bunker? You worked there for how long, for three years? It took you three years to realize your guilt and shame? And it took the murder of my husband for you to finally realize these were human beings, not numbers? They were flesh, and bone, and blood, just like you. I'm sorry, Frau Weber. I don't think I can offer you any forgiveness and understanding."

Therese looked up at Haas and shook her head.

"I'm not asking for that. I understand. I don't expect that from you or from anyone. But I saw this photograph lying inside of a man's cap. A man whom I had just watched being murdered. It was on the floor of the bunker. I didn't know what it was at first. Dettmer was watching me the whole time, but Corporal Becker came over and stood next to me—the giant corporal who everyone thought was dumb and slow. He knew what it was. He stood between me and Dettmer and blocked his view. So when Dettmer turned his attention away from us and began to scream at some of the laborers, I quickly reached down and picked it up. I left the cap there on the floor, but I grabbed the photograph. Corporal Becker prevented Dettmer from seeing me pick up the photograph. And then he accompanied me out of the bay and went back to my office with me. Dettmer was still in the bay, but I just pushed past him and rushed back to my office. When I got there, I thanked Becker for accompanying me and not saying anything.

"Then I entered my office, closed the door behind me, and looked at what I held in my hand. I assumed it was a photograph of a wife or lover. He looked happy, you both looked very happy, and I saw that you had a life together, and that it had meaning and purpose. And that's when I realized that he was much more than a figure in my ledger. From that moment on, every laborer became more than a number to me. They evolved from being a ledger entry to being human, and I could no longer look at my work in the same way. Your husband's cry into the night, along with this photo, made him human to me. And when I saw you, I knew that I was right to pick up the photograph that night. Because one day I hoped the story about him would come out. And when I saw you, I knew I had to tell you about him and how he died and how brave he was until the very end."

Once again, the room was enveloped in a silence that fell over the two women like a cloak as they sat there together. But the cloak was not warm, and it provided little comfort.

"There is nothing I can do or say that will assuage your guilt or whatever it is you are feeling," Haas said softly. "I'm sorry, but I don't want you to feel better. You are guilty. Your entire nation is guilty. You all stood by in silence and allowed evil men to grab power. Their power came from your silence. They came to power because nobody stood up to them. They came to power because they told lies, and they blamed all of Germany's problems on everyone else, on the Jews, on the Poles, on everyone but themselves. I'm sorry, Frau Weber, but no matter how long I live, I don't think I can ever find it in my heart to forgive you or your people for what you have done. I'm sorry, but I'm not that strong."

"You know, we're not that different," Therese said, drawing her arms out wide as if she were taking in the entire world. "In fact, we are quite the same, we're all just trying to live, to survive. They asked us, they told us, we had to commit to total war in order to survive. Well, that's all we're trying to do now. Simply survive. If the situation were reversed, you would have done exactly what I did. You would have scraped, clawed, and cowered, just as I did, just as we all did, and you would do whatever was necessary to survive."

"No, we're not the same at all," Haas countered. "We stood up to the evil. Your people just submitted to it. You gave in because it was easy. I have to ask you one question. Do you have regrets? Did you ever wonder what happened to your neighbors when they disappeared in the middle of the night? Did you ever think about them and question how they could simply vanish without a trace?"

"Yes, and I thought that I was glad it wasn't me," Therese said. "It could have been me instead of them."

They continued to sit in silence and Therese finally spoke out and said, "Maybe God will forgive me, then. Forgive us all,"

"I don't believe in God anymore," Haas replied. "You see, that's the problem with believing in God. People think that God forgives everything. You do something bad, no problem! God will give you a pass, and all can be forgiven at the end of your life. You believe that God is always working for good. Well, I have news for you. God's not working on anything here on Earth. And some things can't be forgiven. Man's responsible for everything that happens on Earth. And man has to own it. God has nothing to do with it."

Haas stopped her rant as she fought to maintain her composure. "Why did you keep it? You could have destroyed it. Burned it. Torn it into a thousand little pieces. But you kept it with you. Why would you do that?"

"I kept it because I knew that somewhere, someone would be grieving his loss. But I knew there wouldn't be a way for them to obtain closure because they didn't know what happened to him, they didn't know how he died and how brave he was all the way until the very end. They would always wonder what happened to him and the unanswered questions would gnaw at them forever. I kept it because I wanted to remember him. I never wanted to forget his cry into the night. I wanted to keep him in my thoughts and in my heart and to act as a kind of surrogate for the woman in this photograph."

Haas sat there, considering Therese's words. "You know that I cannot find it in my heart to forgive you. And it is not just you. It's every German who sat by silently and did nothing. You all are complicit. You all own a share of the collective guilt," Haas said, searching for the right words. "But I also want to say that I am very grateful for this," she said, holding the tattered photograph in her hands. "It is the only memento I have of him. Memories have a way of fading over time. This photograph will fade, but as I grow older I only hope it won't fade faster than my memory and I'll have this to remember him. So, thank you for keeping it and for not destroying it. That I can do. That was . . .," she said, her voice trailing off as she struggled for the right words and finally saying, "That was kind. I do recognize that. You'll get no forgiveness from me, but I am grateful that you were able to muster up the strength within yourself for a single act of kindness."

Therese paused, looked directly at Haas, and said, "Your husband is buried in the concrete pier at Bay Thirteen. It's the last bay that was built. That's where he is today, and that is where he will be for eternity."

***

The three of them sat in Lehman's office, comparing notes and talking about what they had learned from Becker and Therese's revelations about the existence of the ledger and the photograph of Haas and her husband. Lehman had opened his best bottle of bourbon. He had been saving it for a special occasion, but after Haas showed him the photograph and told them how Therese came to have it, he decided that they all could use a good belt. Or two.

"Luba and I didn't realize it at the time," Lefkowicz said, "but Becker told us that he saw Dettmer kill a man in cold blood and then ordered the laborers to just bury him in concrete."

"But you decided to let him go anyway?" Lehman asked. "What made you decide to do that?"

"We talked it over," Haas said, "and we came to the same conclusion that you did earlier. He's not going anywhere, and if we need him for the case against Dettmer, he said he'd talk. He said he wasn't afraid of him anymore."

"Why did he help him in the first place?" asked Lehman.

"Two things," Lefkowicz said. "Dettmer told him he'd be convicted of war crimes because he was a guard, which is kind of technically true, should we try to press a case. He is definitely at risk of prosecution. He was there. Even though Becker showed leniency and was kind, it still doesn't clear him. He was still part of the apparatus that ran the camps and kept the German war machine going. He may not have pulled the trigger personally, but men died while he was there."

"And the second reason," Haas chimed in, "was that Dettmer threatened Becker's uncle. He told Becker he could make his uncle disappear if he didn't go along with him. Becker has a real soft spot for his uncle because he was the only one who took him in after his parents kicked him out of their house. Becker isn't the next Einstein. He's pretty easy to manipulate."

"Yeah, hearing that made me feel bad for pulling that stunt on his uncle the other day."

"What stunt? Is this something I should know about?" Lehman said.

"Oh, not really. I don't think so. It's nothing you and I wouldn't have done," Lefkowicz replied.

"Wonderful. That makes me feel a lot better knowing that."

Suddenly, their conversation was interrupted by two shrill rings from the phone on Lehman's desk, making him jump.

"Damn, I'll never get used to that ring," he said, picking up the receiver. "Captain Lehman speaking."

Lehman sat for several minutes listening to the caller. His face turned from disinterest to concern, then the pallor of his skin went ashen. He interjected an "uh-huh," a "when did this happen," and "who found him," and the clincher that got the attention of both Haas and Lefkowicz, a definitive "and when was he pronounced dead?" Finally he said, "Thank you. We'll be over in thirty minutes," and hung up the phone.

"What is it?" Lefkowicz exclaimed. "Who died?"

"We won't need to interrogate Dettmer. He's dead," Lehman replied, eliciting audible gasps from both Haas and Lefkowicz. "They found him hanged in his hospital room. It seems the guard stepped away for a few minutes to use the can, and when he came back to check on Dettmer, that's how he found him."

"When did they find him?" Lefkowicz asked.

Lehman looked down at his watch, which now read 1813 hours. "A little more than an hour ago. The guard entered his room at approximately 1705 hours. He claims he wasn't gone for more than five minutes, so I think we have a pretty good idea as to the time of death. He said there was an orderly on the floor, cleaning up, and he told the orderly that he'd be right back. When he returned, the orderly was nowhere to be found, and that's when the guard discovered Dettmer hanging from his sheets in his room. At first they thought it was a suicide, but the doctor in charge says there is no way Dettmer could have strung up his sheets and hung himself with only one good arm. Plus, he had been sedated for the pain he was in. So, they've got their CID people searching and trying to nail down the crime scene, but it appears that our friend Dettmer was murdered."

"Sonofabitch," cursed Lefkowicz.

"Cap, I'm really sorry. This is my fault. If I hadn't . . . "

"Forget it, Luba," Lehman said interrupting her, "that's in the past now. What's done is done. He was supposedly under guard. He was supposed to have been watched constantly. There's nothing we could have done. But I'll tell you one thing. Therese and her family are still in danger. Walt, I want you to put on your NYPD hat and go to the hospital. Meet with the Brit investigators, and go over the crime scene here with a fine-tooth comb. Oh, and Walt, I need to get into our armory to sign for my sidearm and ammo. I don't want to take any chances. I'll also tell the guards upstairs watching Therese and her family to be extra watchful. Nobody enters or leaves that floor except for the three of us. The hotel can deliver the food to the guards, and they can bring it to their room."

"What about me?" Haas asked. "What do you want me to do?"

"You and I are going to take Therese and her dad back to his house. That's where she said the ledger is hidden. We have to get it tonight before anything else happens. And there's one more thing I need to tell you both."

"Well, this should be good after everything that's happened today," Lefkowicz said.

"Yeah, well, don't stand up. You'll want to keep sitting for this. The man we have upstairs, Therese Weber's father, is my uncle, Karl Lehman. His wife, Johanne, is my aunt. He was my dad's older brother. He encouraged my dad to leave just before the first war. He was the eldest son, and I guess he felt it was his duty to stay behind and take care of the rest of the family. He somehow had the prescience to know that a terrible war was coming, and he didn't want his kid brother fighting in it. I have no memory of him. Maybe some vague recollections and images. I don't know, I was only three when we left. But that's the story."

"So, that makes Therese Weber your," Haas started to say.

"My first cousin. And her kids are my cousins, too. Therese Weber, nee Lehman, is my cousin, and I want to keep her alive."

"Sonofabitch," cursed Lefkowicz.

Chapter Twenty-Nine

The guard had untied the sheets Dettmer had been hanging from, dropping his body to the floor with a heavy thump. The sheets had been wrapped around the steam heating line that ran across the room's ceiling, then tied in a knot around his neck. The guard rolled Dettmer's body on his back and shouted for help. That is what the investigator from the Royal Military Police told Lefkowicz and the American CID agent accompanying him.

"Naturally, the first thought was that he had somehow hanged himself. It would be a natural conclusion to reach, given how he was found," the investigator said. "But the doctor in charge didn't think it would have been possible for the subject to have been able to do that, given his medical condition. And then we found this," he said, pointing to a small puncture mark on Dettmer's neck. He knelt down alongside Dettmer's body to point out a small drop of congealed blood that had dripped down onto his neck. "We won't know for certain until we conduct a post-mortem, but it appears he may have been injected with something. Cyanide would be my guess, but we'll have to see."

"You'll be conducting an autopsy?" Lefkowicz asked.

"Oh, yes. I've been instructed to investigate this completely. We will look at everything to determine not only how he died, but at whose hands. I'm aware of the subject's background and status and why he was here in hospital. The case has the attention of the highest levels of British command as well as that of headquarters in London. I'm to leave no stone unturned, as they say."

"What about the guard? Did you get a full statement from him yet?"

"We've spoken to him briefly, but the poor chap was badly shaken. He's a young bloke, and he knows he made a bit of a cock-up tonight by leaving his post. He's sitting in a room down the hall, if you'd like to have a go at him."

"We're not here to interfere, but I do have some questions, so if you don't mind, I'd like that very much," Lefkowicz said.

"Surely, just follow me."

They left the room and turned to the left. Lefkowicz noticed a mop and bucket near the stairwell directly ahead of them at the far end of the hallway.

"Was the orderly mopping the floor?" he asked.

"Yes, he entered this corridor from the main hallway, which is behind us and to our right. According to the guard, he was cleaning the floor, and when he got to the subject's room, the guard gave him permission to enter. That's when the guard said he'd return shortly after he used the latrine."

The men entered an otherwise empty hospital room to find a young British Army private sitting on a wooden chair. He was holding his head in his hands and breathing heavily, muttering to himself incoherently.

"Private. This gentleman is with American Counterintelligence and he'd like to ask you a few questions." The soldier didn't respond. "Private," the investigator repeated, until the young man looked up. His face was a splotchy red, and it looked as if he'd been crying. "Buck up, young man," the investigator said. "He just has a few questions for you."

"I wasn't gone more than five minutes, I swear," he said, then dropped his head into his hands and began to sob softly.

Lefkowicz knelt down in front of the soldier and said, "Look, son." The private refused to look up and continued sobbing. "Son, look at me. Look at me," he repeated insistently, and the private finally lifted his head. "Son, I just have a few questions. Can you answer a couple of questions for me? It's very important, so you can do that, right?" The private sniveled and nodded his head.

"So, the man who was cleaning the floors, did you get a good look at him?"

"Yes, sir, I did."

"Can you tell us what he looked like?"

"Well, he was dressed in the hospital uniform, the white uniform, you know? He was average height, maybe five feet seven or eight, I reckon. He had dark hair, black hair, I'm not sure what color his eyes were."

"Was he thin, heavy? What else can you remember?"

"He was rather thin, I should say. Kind of a wiry bloke. Yes, that's how I would describe him. He also had a darker complexion."

"Was he a black man?"

"Oh, no, sir. No, it looked like he was out in the sun a lot. I'm really not sure."

"And what did he say to you?"

"He said he was cleaning the floor and asked if it was all right if he tidied up the room I was guarding."

"Is that how he said it? He wanted to know if he could 'tidy up' the room?"

"Yes, that's what he said."

"Was he British?"

"Oh, no, sir. He did speak with an accent, though."

"What kind of accent?

"I'm really not certain, sir. I'm from Essex, and everyone sounds a bit off to me when they talk."

"Did he sound German to you?"

"No, sir, I don't think it was that. He sounded like he maybe was Italian?"

"Italian? Hmm, anything else?"

"Well, he also spoke kind of funny."

"Besides the accent? What do you mean he spoke 'funny'?"

"When he spoke, he couldn't pronounce the letter 'S.' It sounded like he was saying 'th' instead. He said, 'I have to mop all the floorth.'

"Wonderful, an Italian with a lisp," the police inspector quipped.

Lefkowicz stood up and thought for a moment. "No, I think he might have been Spanish."

"Spanish? How do you figure?"

"Yeah, Spanish," Lefkowicz replied. "It's just a hunch. But the Gestapo had deep connections with the Spanish secret police. They worked together during the civil war in the 1930s. That would explain the funny way in which he spoke. In Castilian Spanish, the "s" sound is pronounced as "th""

"Sir?"

A pair of Royal Military Police officers stood in the doorway to the room. One of them held a large paper bag with the word "Evidence" stenciled on the side.

"Take a look at this, sir," he said as he entered the room with the bag open. Inside was a set of hospital whites, a top and bottom. And resting on the clothing was a syringe.

"We found this in the large bin in the alley. The stairwell at the end of the hallway leads straight down to it. Most likely, sir, that was how the killer made his escape. He just walked out, discarded all of this in the bin, and disappeared into the evening."

Lefkowicz peered inside, turned to the investigator, and said, "I think you may have found our murder weapon."

***

Lehman was behind the wheel of the jeep with Haas at his side and his uncle and Therese in back. There were a few buses and trolleys picking up and dropping off passengers, and a few other military vehicles, but otherwise the streets were empty. Lehman pulled up his jeep in front of his uncle's house. It was completely dark inside, the only light from a street lamp in the front.

"I want you two to stay close to us. Don't go wandering off alone, you understand?"

"Yes, Caspar," his uncle replied. "I have the key to the front door. Just follow me."

"All right. Hold on a minute," Lehman said as he reached under the seat and pulled out two U.S. Army flashlights, the TL-22 models with the bulb assembly that jutted out from the top at a ninety-degree angle. They were designed to slip into a soldier's web gear, the system of belts, harnesses, cartridge pouches, and pistol belts that held the equipment the soldiers needed to carry into combat. When held by hand, they had to be in an upright position. He handed one to Haas and said, "Here's one for you. You bring up the rear, I'll lead the way." He pulled out his service pistol and said, "You should do the same, Luba. Okay, Uncle Karl, Therese, let's go. Follow me."

The four of them got out of the jeep and made their way down the short walkway leading to the front door. Lehman held the flashlight so his uncle could open the door. Haas had her back to it, facing out to the front, watching for anyone who might be approaching. She had her revolver drawn, her finger on the trigger. As the door swung open, Lehman shone the flashlight beam inside. Something didn't look right to him. He was the first to enter and said, "Is there a light switch?"

"Yes, just inside the door on the right-hand side," Karl replied. "It is about halfway up the wall." Lehman found the switch and flicked it on, and a dim overhead light illuminated the narrow hallway. He shone the flashlight into the parlor to their left. His uncle and Therese both let out a gasp when they saw the state of the room. It had been ransacked, and all of the wall cabinet drawers had been pulled out, their contents spilled across the floor.

"Oh, my goodness. Mama is going to hit the ceiling when she sees this mess," Karl said. "What have they done?"

"Luba, get in here," Lehman yelled, and Haas immediately came into the house, her revolver at the ready. "We need to make sure that whoever did this is no longer here. I'll check the kitchen, can you check upstairs? You two," he said to his uncle and Therese, "wait here for me."

"Yes," Haas replied as she slowly moved up the narrow staircase. Lehman proceeded cautiously down the hallway. He pointed his pistol straight ahead and was ready to fire at the slightest movement. As he passed the dining room, he saw that a large china cabinet had been overturned, its contents lay smashed on the floor. He made his way into the dark kitchen, his hand fumbling along the wall searching for a light switch. He finally found it, switched it on, and the light revealed the same destruction they had witnessed in the other rooms of the house. Every cabinet door was open, kitchen drawers were completely pulled out, and their entire contents had been strewn on the floor. But there was nobody there. He quickly walked back to the front of the house where Therese and his uncle nervously waited. Lehman stood on the first step of the stairway leading upstairs and shouted, "Luba, are you okay?"

"Yes, it's all clear up here," she replied. "I'm coming back down." She rejoined Lehman at the bottom and said, "It's a mess up there, too. The entire house has been ransacked."

Lehman turned to Therese and his uncle and said, "Look, there's nothing we can do about this mess right now. Let's get what we came for and get the hell out of here. Where are the ledgers, Therese?"

"In the kitchen," she replied.

"Lead the way."

They all walked quickly down the narrow hallway—the hallway where just a few days ago Karl and Johanne had crept to confront Dettmer and Becker. Looking at the mess that was made, Karl kept repeating to himself, "Oh, my God, Mama is going to be so very mad when she sees this mess. Oh my, oh my God," he repeated over and over.

When they finally reached the kitchen, Lehman swept aside the debris on the floor with his boot and stood in the very center of the room.

"All right, Therese. Where are they?"

"You're standing on them."

"I'll get my tools," Karl said.

***

Karl knelt on the wooden kitchen floor with a small mallet in one hand and a wood chisel in the other, tapping along the seam of one of the floorboards. When the board was loose, he took a small crowbar and carefully pulled it up. He did this a total of four times, finally exposing a small crawl space underneath.

"You probably do not remember, Caspar, but you used to crawl upon this floor when you were a small child," Karl told Lehman "You would all come over for dinner on Sunday, and you would play in the kitchen. You'd pull out Mama's pots and pans and bang on them like you were playing the drums. We always thought you'd become a musician."

"No, I'm afraid I don't remember that."

"That must have been quite a sight," Haas said, stifling a laugh.

"Not just a sight, but, oh, what a racket he would make!"

"Please hurry, Uncle," Lehman said.

"I'm hurrying. But this has to be done carefully, because I want to be able to put the boards back into place properly. I built this house with my own two hands, you know. Your father helped, of course. He helped me install the floor that you are standing on. Our father, your grandfather, was a master carpenter and cabinet maker. He taught us everything."

Lehman thought back to his father, recalling how he would make wooden toys for him and his sisters. It had been over twenty years since his father died. He could barely remember his face and certainly couldn't remember his voice. But he remembered the toys and other handmade gifts that he made for his children and how they all cried out in delight on Christmas morning.

Karl tapped out and carefully lifted one last board. "Therese, give me a hand, please. Reach down below, and pull out the case."

Therese knelt down onto the floor and reached into the dark space below. "Cap, can you please shine the light here?"

Lehman knelt down next to her and pointed his flashlight into the dark crawl space. He could see what appeared to be a dull metal object. Therese reached down with both hands, pulled a tin case up, and laid it on the kitchen floor.

"There," she said, looking at Lehman. "There they are. There are three ledgers inside this case, one for each year of bunker construction. And the account number and access information. It's everything you will need."

"Let's get out of here," he said, "and get you and these ledgers to safety."

***

They rode in silence back to the hotel. When Karl returned to his room, Johanne was there waiting for him. She cried softly as he told her about how their home had been violated, ransacked. "My mother's china and crystal," she said, weeping softly.

"They're just things, Johanne."

"They're not just things. They're memories," she said as he held her in his arms.

Lehman, Haas, and Therese stood in Lehman's office. Therese had placed the tin case on a table, and Lehman and Haas watched as she opened the twist-lock clasp. She lifted the top to reveal three large ledgers, bound in blue leather. She pulled out the top ledger and laid it before Lehman and Haas.

"I can tell you how to read the ledgers," she said. "This one is from 1943, the year we started the construction. Here," she said, pointing to an envelope taped onto the inside cover, "are the numbers and access codes to the Swiss account. You'll be able to see the running total in each ledger, the amount of Reichsmarks deposited and how much was converted to dollars. As I said earlier, the total is now more than twenty-five million U.S. dollars."

"Thanks, Therese," Lehman said. "It's late, so let's go over it tomorrow. You can explain it all in detail so that we have a complete understanding of the information contained here. Now go back upstairs to be with your children."

Therese nodded and turned to leave, when Haas reached out and grabbed her by the arm. "Wait," she said. Therese looked at her, confused at first, wondering if she had done something wrong.

"I think I was a bit harsh with you earlier today. I'm told that my temper is one of my worst traits. I just wanted to say," Haas looked down at the ledgers and then back at Therese, "this . . . this is remarkable. I didn't give you enough credit. To do this . . . you are very brave, too."

"It would have been brave had I done this years ago. It would have been brave if I hadn't joined the mob that ruled this country. But I believed everything they said. No, I'm not brave. But I am sorry. I cannot undo for what was done. But I am truly sorry for everything I did. I know that is not enough, but it is a start."

"It takes courage to say you're sorry," Haas replied. She slowly let go of Therese's arm and said, "Good night, Therese."

"Good night, Luba."

Lehman watched Therese leave the office, then picked up the ledger, and returned it to the tin case. He ran his fingers over the embossed lettering on the cover.

Organisation Todt, Bunker Valentin, 1943

He closed the lid to the case and twisted the latch shut, walked over to his safe and placed it inside, closing the heavy drawer and spinning the combination dial to lock the contents inside.

"You should get some rest," he said to her. "Why don't you call it a night, and we'll catch up in the morning. I'm going to wait for Walt, but there's no reason why you have to."

Haas stood there for a moment, then walked up to Lehman and reached up to kiss him on the cheek. It was a sweet, tender kiss, and her lips were so soft that Lehman had to catch his breath.

"What? What was that for?"

"You have a remarkable instinct for people."

"Hmm. I suppose I got that from my father. He always saw the good in people. I think he learned it from people like his brother, and probably from his father, too, I'm sure."

"Well, it's something that I would like to learn, too. Maybe you can teach me about the good in people."

"I'd like the chance to try."

"Good night, Cap. I'll see you in the morning."
***

Haas opened the door to her room and switched on the light. She immediately saw the rose, this time a single red rose in a crystal vase. She picked it up and carried it to the window, where she raised the shade all the way to the top and then pulled it halfway down. She placed the vase on the windowsill so that it could be seen from the street below.

It was an emergency, and she would meet Banbury in their designated location tomorrow between 5 and 6 p.m. She would have to make an excuse for her absence, which would undoubtedly cause problems, but she decided that she could feign illness, a headache perhaps, and that would provide the cover she needed so they could meet.

Chapter Thirty

It was in the middle of the afternoon on the next day when Haas told Lehman she needed a "lie down" and would meet him later for a drink if he were so inclined.

"Are you okay?" he asked.

"Yes, I'm just tired, and I didn't sleep well last night. Do you mind?"

"No, of course not. I can call on you later if you wish?"

"No, I'll just meet you back here. Let's say, 1900? How does that suit you?"

"That suits me just fine," he replied. "Are you sure you are all right?"

"Yes, absolutely sure," she said as she walked behind the desk where Lehman was sitting, looked around to make sure nobody could see them, and placed her hands on his face and kissed him. It was the sweetest kiss, and as they lingered for a moment, his arms reached up to pull her to him. "I just need to close my eyes for a bit," she said as she slowly pulled away from him. "I'll be back later and then we can . . . we can talk."

Haas had created a bit of a stir in the office when she reported for duty earlier that morning. Instead of wearing her usual utility uniform with sidearm and her Shanghai knife strapped to her thigh, she had chosen civilian clothing, a black short-sleeved knit top, a light-blue wool skirt, and blue leather espadrilles with a two-inch heel. She wore her hair down, not pulled back as she had for her entire time in Bremen.

"Whoa," exclaimed Lefkowicz when he saw Haas enter the office. "Who is this person?"

"What, can't a woman dress up around here?" she replied, flipping her hair and making a quick twirl on the way to her station in Lehman's office. In the short period she had known Lefkowicz, this was the first time he seemed to be at a loss for words.

When Lehman walked into his office, coffee in one hand, cigarette in the other, he stopped dead in his tracks. "I like the new look," he said. "It's very becoming. You look lovely, if you don't mind my saying so."

"I don't mind, and thank you. I thought I'd try something different today," was her reply, and then she set about her work.

Her selection of clothing was by design. Although her dress might attract stares from the men in the office, out on the street where she wanted to blend in, her civilian attire would draw less attention than if she were the only woman on the street sporting a sidearm with a knife strapped to her leg. She still carried the knife, though; it was strapped to her thigh underneath her skirt, and in her large handbag she carried not her normal Webley revolver, but a .32 caliber Welrod. It was lighter than her Webley and also an extremely "quiet" weapon due to its built-in suppressor. She had no reason to be armed, but she had become accustomed to accessorizing with weapons the same way other women might wear a particular brooch, a scarf, or a bracelet. Haas would not have felt she was properly dressed if she were not carrying some form of armament.

Although the area was heavily damaged by air raids in 1944, the emergency meeting location was a small sweets shop and café on the Böttcherstrasse. The street itself was only a little more than three hundred feet long, but the area's unique buildings, most of which were built in the 1920s and early '30s, had evolved into a Bremen cultural landmark.

Haas took the back stairs of the hotel and went out into a rear alley. As usual, she took her time reaching the meeting point. She zigzagged across streets, looking in shop windows, pretending to be interested in the items for sale or on display while looking for the reflection of anyone who might have ventured too close. It was five minutes to six when she finally arrived, satisfied that she had not been followed. She saw

Banbury seated at a small table outside the café. He glanced down at his watch, noting the time as he saw her approach, and she joined him at his table.

"Good evening, James."

"Luba," he nodded. "Were you followed?"

She just stared back at him and refused to answer.

"You know I have to ask."

"No. It's just me."

He nodded and slid a cup and saucer over to Haas. "I've taken the liberty of ordering coffee." He poured into her cup, filling it nearly to the brim. "Sugar? They actually have sugar, can you believe it?"

"Why the emergency, James? Every time you call for these meetings, it does nothing but arouse suspicion. You know bloody well you could just walk into the front door and speak to me in private."

"I know. We've been through this before. But this time there is a true emergency."

"What is it?" Haas asked as she took a sip of her coffee.

"Did you kill Dettmer?"

"What?" Haas replied, nearly spitting out her coffee across the table at Banbury. "Are you insane? Where did that idea come from? Oh wait. Don't tell me. It's the Eaton boys, right? They're back in London spreading rumors about me once again."

"There has been talk, and it's nothing but talk, Luba. But you know how it is. I was asked to come here to Bremen to investigate the situation first-hand. And by "asked," I mean I didn't have a choice. But I know you didn't do it, of course."

"Well, I hope you defended me. You did, didn't you?"

Banbury sat quietly and sipped his coffee.

"Oh, James, you bastard. After all we've been through."

"Look, I know you didn't kill Dettmer. At least I don't think you did. But I have to ask."

"You're damn right I didn't. What earthly reason would I have to kill him? He's the man who compromised our agents in Poland. He would have told us who, if anyone, was working with him, feeding him information about our agents. I had every reason to want to see him hanged, but I certainly wouldn't kill him."

"There are some who think the person who brought down our agents in Poland was you. Either wittingly or through carelessness."

"That comment doesn't deserve a response, James. Go to hell."

"I heard you roughed him up quite a bit. That's what got back to London. And that is what has prompted my trip here."

"He was threatening to kill a child. I only subdued him. Look, James, did you come here to accuse me or to find ways to defend me?"

"As I said, I know you didn't kill Dettmer. If I believed you had been involved, I wouldn't be here today. You would have been invited back to London on some pretext, and we would have taken care of the matter there."

Haas's jaw dropped in disbelief. "James, I don't even know how to respond to that. You would have 'taken care of the matter.' What does that mean? If you're trying to help me here, you're doing a shitty job. But on the other hand, if you're trying to piss me off, you're excelling at the moment."

"Look, Luba, with Dettmer dead, I'm under increasing pressure to bring you back. We'll never know who helped him in Poland. He took that with him. So that means we'll never launch Nightfall. Not in the way it was originally intended, at any rate. We're back to square one and we'll have to start over."

"We know Dettmer rolled up our SOE agents," Haas said. "But the other agents I recruited, those specifically recruited for Nightfall, are still in place. You don't know if they've been compromised."

"No, I don't. But nobody is going to take that chance, Luba. The Russians are in firm control of Poland, for now and for the foreseeable future. Nobody intends to risk another war over this."

Haas sat there fuming. She could feel her temper rising but called on every ounce of willpower she could muster to contain herself. *Exploding in anger will accomplish nothing*, she thought. *Smacking him across his smug face might make me feel better, but it will only make matters worse. "Taken care of the matter"! What the hell?*

"Well, I have a theory, James, and you can take it back to London and you can spread this around. Spread it far and wide. I think you're living in a rotten house. It's infested with vermin. And mark my words, James, the vermin that reside within your house are responsible for Poland. They need to be surveilled. They need to be watched, and a case needs to be made against them. And unless they're shown the door or, better yet, thrown into a cell, they are going to continue to compromise operations in the future. They've been turned, James, I can feel it, I can smell it."

"You are referring to your three colleagues from Eton? Do you have proof?"

"No."

"Luba, what do you expect me to do? I can't accuse them without proof. It's just idle gossip otherwise."

"You don't seem to have a problem listening to idle gossip. At a minimum, they need to be watched. Observed."

Banbury finished his coffee and set his cup and saucer on the table. He absentmindedly continued to stir the empty cup with his spoon, making a scraping noise as he slowly ran the spoon across the bottom of the cup. He abruptly stopped, and the spoon fell out of the cup onto the table with a clatter.

"Luba, I can give you thirty days to wrap everything up here in Bremen, and then I need to call you back. The operation is over. Wrap things up with the Americans, and return to London."

"I'm not coming back to London, James. There is nothing for me there. I won't return."

"And what will you do? Where will you go?"

Haas thought for a second, and then everything became clear to her. She knew exactly what she had to do. "I'm staying here. This is my home now. At least for now. I want to stay on working with the Americans."

"I could prevent that from happening. I could stop it."

Haas looked across the table at Banbury. She slid her hands across the table and grasped Banbury's hands. She held them tight and said softly, but firmly, "Don't do that James. Please. And do not make me beg. But no. Do not do that. Do not stop me. I'm staying here. I'm staying here because this is where I belong now."

The look on her face and tone of her voice left no doubt in Banbury's mind what she meant and what she would do if she were denied.

Banbury looked down at her hands as they clutched his, getting tighter and tighter.

"Very well, Luba. Stay here. I can give you thirty days for you to work something out with the Americans. If it works out, good for you. If not, you're on your own."

Haas loosened her grasp and slid her hands back across the table, her palms resting flat on the surface.

"Thank you, James."

"Thirty days," he repeated.

"I know." They sat there looking at each other, and in their minds' eyes, the memories of the past six years together flashed in front of them. "Can you do one last favor for me?"

"What is it?" And then he softened and said, "Yes. Of course."

"There are a few things left in my flat. Can you have them crated and sent to me here? You can send them to the hotel. I'll have to find a new flat here, but that may take some time."

"Yes, I can arrange that."

Haas stood up from the table. She extended her hand to Banbury, "Goodbye, James. Thank you. For everything."

Banbury looked across the table at her hand, his gaze drifted upward to her face, and he reached out and accepted her final handshake.

"It's the Eton boys, James, and you know it. All three of them," Haas said. Banbury remained silent. Not another word was spoken between them. They shook hands, and Haas turned and walked away to start her life over one more time.

***

Their conversation was polite, at least initially. They spoke using oblique terms, never expressing themselves explicitly, beating around the bush, but the conversation quickly turned, and there would be no doubt what would happen if he didn't cooperate.

Richard Schmidt, the engineer responsible for building the Valentin Bunker, the man who supervised its construction, ensuring that it was built according to his exacting specifications, sat at a desk in his cramped office less than a mile from the docks at Bremerhaven. Engineering drawings of the port complex were pasted on the walls, marked up with blue pencil to indicate where changes had to be made. Lehman and Haas sat across the desk from him.

"I never wanted to be a part of it," Schmidt said. "I thought it was wrong. That bureaucrat Scholz, the administrator from Organisation Todt, he talked me into it. He said that moving money outside of Germany would actually help the war effort. Can you believe that?"

"I'd like to believe you. But you see there is this problem we have," Lehman said. "Your name appears in the ledgers. It shows that you personally signed off on the transfer of millions of Reichsmarks. And then you authorized the purchase of American dollars. That's a bit of a problem. You are clearly implicated."

"And there is the issue of a Swiss account," Haas added. "And there are now millions of dollars in that account. More than $25 million, if we calculate correctly."

"I only wanted to work. That's all I ever wanted. So I went along. My wife and children, you see. I didn't want any harm to come to them," he said as he looked down at the frame on his desk. The photo showed a young woman and two children at the beach, most likely somewhere on the North Sea. They were smiling, laughing, and showing off a sandcastle they had just completed. Lehman noted the photograph, as did Haas. and each made a mental note to put surveillance on his home to ensure his family didn't run. They all needed to be kept inside their cage.

"And what about all the deaths?" Lehman asked. "Was that part of your work? Or were the deaths considered occupational hazards?"

"I had no control over the workers. I had no control over where they were housed, how much they were fed, how long they worked. No control whatsoever," he said emphatically. "None. I was ordered to build the bunker. That was my job. And I did it. I built it, and your bombs could not destroy it."

That point was indeed true. In late March 1945, the RAF and U.S. 8th Air Force attacked the bunker, first with the ten-ton "Grand Slam" bombs and then with two-ton "Disney" bombs that were assisted with rockets to increase penetration. The Grand Slams were able to penetrate about halfway through the fifteen-foot-thick concrete and brought down about a thousand tons of concrete and steel. Only one of the Disney bombs hit the bunker, and there was very little damage. The bunker still stood despite the best efforts of the Allies to bring it down.

Lehman and Haas, having rehearsed their respective roles earlier, sat stone-faced, in silence, revealing nothing to Schmidt.

"Did you have Dettmer killed?"

"What? Of course not! I had nothing to do with that."

"You were the one who got Dettmer involved. You wanted him to acquire the ledgers," Lehman said. "You recognized him when he was working on the docks. You saw him, and you thought he could do your dirty work for you, isn't that right."

"I only got him involved after I met with Scholz. He was the one who wanted the ledgers, not me. I told him I wanted no part. No part, you understand! None. But I told Scholz that Dettmer was working as a laborer. It was Scholz who suggested Dettmer. He said that he would be able to convince Frau Weber to relinquish the ledgers. 'One way or another,' he said."

"And you took that to mean, what, exactly."

"I took it to mean that Dettmer would take this problem off my hands. I meant no harm to Frau Weber or to anyone else. I only want to forget all about this."

Haas took out a photograph and laid it on the desk in front of Schmidt. It depicted a tall man with dark complexion and jet-black hair. He was wearing a light-colored suit and standing in front of the Palace of El Pardo, the private residence of General Francisco Franco. "Do you recognize this man?"

Schmidt looked down at the photograph. "No. I do not. Should I know this man?"

"He's been seen here in Bremerhaven," Haas replied. "His name is Gonzalo Moreno-Alvarez. He's a member of the Spanish secret police. He was seen with Dettmer at a local pub not far from here, just a few days before Herr Dettmer met his unfortunate demise. He has ties to the ODESSA. Do you know of this organization? The Organisation Der Ehemaligen SS-angehörigen? The organization of former SS officers? They help former SS and Gestapo officers avoid arrest and escape."

"I have never heard of that organization, and I swear I have never seen this man in my life."

"Well, you may want to take a close look at him," Haas said. "If you happen to see him, I wouldn't get too close to him. He's dangerous. We think he is the man who killed Dettmer. It seems that someone wants to eliminate people with knowledge of the ledgers. You could be next."

"What? You think I'm in danger?"

"I'm only saying you should be careful. Cautious, that's all. One can never be too careful these days, right, Herr Schmidt?"

"I swear I had nothing to do with this."

"We understand. You know, Herr Schmidt," Lehman said. "We can make your life easier. We can help you if you would consider helping us. The ledgers, the Swiss account, no one has to know of your involvement. It never has to see the light of day if you'll agree to help us."

"How do I know I can trust you? How do I know you won't just use me to get what you want," Schmidt replied?

Lehman leaned forward in his chair and looked Schmidt directly in his eyes and said, "If you help us, we will protect you and your family for the rest of your life. We will make sure you and they are safe. We will do everything we can to ensure that you have a productive life."

Lehman continued to look directly at Schmidt as he slowly slid back into his chair, his words hanging in the air. Schmidt returned Lehman's gaze, staring directly at him, trying to get a measure of the man.

"How can I help you?" Schmidt said breaking his silence. "What is it you want me to do?"

"You're an influential man, Herr Schmidt," Haas said. "An important man doing important work. And we understand your work now requires that you make regular trips to the East, to the Russian Zone of Occupation. And you travel to Berlin? And to be more precise, you have a reason to travel to the town of Zossen?" Haas was probing to confirm what she and Lehman already knew. They just wanted to hear Schmidt admit it.

"Yes, that's correct. I travel there from time to time. That is where I ran into Scholz. He's managing a small machine tool company there that supplies replacement parts for some of our equipment. It's all very hard to come by these days, as you can imagine. The Russians are ripping out all of the manufacturing equipment in the East and sending it back to Russia. But I'm able to secure parts that we need. Scholz has been very helpful. I give him money and other items. On the side."

"And when will you travel there next?" Lehman asked, once again already knowing the answer but wanting to hear the words from Schmidt's mouth.

"In two weeks, just before the end of May."

"And during that trip, the trip to visit the machine tool company, you plan to meet with Herr Scholz?"

"Yes. I hate the man, but, yes, I will meet with him. Unfortunately, I have no choice. It's either work with him or we don't receive the parts that we need for our construction work."

"So, you're just doing what is necessary then? Is that it?" Haas asked.

"Yes. I don't like it, but we all have had to do things we don't like. Scholz is a dark man, a very ruthless man. He's former military, you know? Abwehr. And he and Dettmer were as thick as thieves. Thieves. Ironic, isn't it?"

"He and Dettmer were close, you say?" Lehman asked.

"Oh, yes. They served together. In Spain."

Haas and Lehman both made mental notes about the Spanish connection to both Dettmer and Scholz.

"We think Scholz will be very happy to meet with you," said Haas.

"Oh, and why is that?"

"We think he will be eager to meet with you after you tell him you have some very good news from Switzerland," said Lehman. "That is what you will say in the letter you will write to him. You'll say you want to convey this information to him in person. You'll say the details are too sensitive to convey in a letter, but you'll be able to pass the information along to him at your next meeting. Oh, and you will also be traveling to this meeting with your assistant."

"An assistant? I do not have an assistant," Schmidt replied.

"You do now. That would be me," said Haas. "I will be traveling as your assistant, Herr Schmidt. I will be there to ensure that everything goes smoothly and that your meeting goes well."

"You? That's out of the question."

"Herr Schmidt, I assure you that if you assist us with this small task, the contents of the ledger will never be released," Lehman said. "The record of your involvement with the financial transactions will disappear. We have the original ledgers, and there are no copies. They are in our possession, and they will remain that way unless you give us reason to do otherwise."

"Do you plan to give Scholz access to the Swiss accounts? To the money?" Schmidt asked. "That's what he wants. He is very persuasive and persistent."

"No, Herr Schmidt," Haas said. "We have no intention of doing that. We just want to have a conversation with him about the Swiss accounts. We want to see if he would be as willing as you are to help us. It's just a conversation between friends. It's all here in the letter that we've taken the liberty to write for you."

Haas slid a sheet of paper across the desk to Schmidt. "We've taken the liberty of writing it on your letterhead. All you have to do is sign it. We will post it for you, and we will be waiting for the reply from Herr Scholz."

"This is crazy. I don't know, I don't think I can do this."

"Herr Schmidt, part of the help we can provide, in exchange for your cooperation, of course," Lehman said, "is to promote your design firm. While we can't make final decisions as to which companies will receive construction contracts, we can strongly recommend that your firm be hired. We can put in a good mention, say good words about you. If you'll agree to help us, that is," Lehman added.

"Think of the good you'll be able to do, Herr Schmidt," said Haas. "You'll be instrumental in rebuilding Germany. We'll help you achieve your dream of creating great monuments and buildings. It will be a lasting legacy."

"You can do that? In exchange for setting up this meeting?"

"Oh, yes. And we will."

"Will I be able to continue my work? And you will help my business?"

"Oh, yes, we can be very appreciative, Herr Schmidt," Lehman replied. "If your business goes well, our business goes well. We have a mutual interest in seeing a strong and free Germany."

Schmidt's eyes darted back and forth, looking at Lehman and Haas sitting across the table. *All I want is to do my work. I only want to create,* he thought. "All right then. I'll do it. I will help you. Yes, yes. I agree."

"That is wonderful news, Herr Schmidt," Lehman said. "You will not regret your decision."

"Herr Schmidt," Haas said, "if you would be so kind as to read the letter and then sign it for me. I would like to post it so that it can go out in the afternoon mail."

***

For someone with five-and-a-half years of service in the United States Army, an organization designed to travel and fight battles on land, Lehman had spent an inordinate amount of time at sea, on the open water. He shipped out to North Africa on a troop ship. He sailed to Italy on another troop ship. He returned to England on a troop ship, and then for the D-Day landings, he crossed the English Channel on a troop ship.

Lehman detested being on the water. He hated being cooped up inside with no windows, and the constant motion of the waves, the rocking back and forth, made him claustrophobic and seasick. But as much as he detested sailing, it paled in comparison to the feeling he now had about flying. Until he and Haas took off in the morning of June 8, 1946, for the short flight to Frankfurt, Lehman had never flown on an airplane.

He was strapped into his seat, secured in place with a multipoint harness, but that gave him no comfort. His eyes were closed, and his hands tightly clutched the arm rests on his seat. Haas sat next to him and, being a veteran of many flights as well as having considerable experience jumping from perfectly functioning airplanes, tried to soothe and comfort Lehman, while trying unsuccessfully to stifle her laughter at his plight.

"Just take in a deep breath, Cap. Breathe and you'll be fine," she said, and at just that moment, the aircraft hit a mild pocket of turbulence that lasted for several seconds.

Lehman had just opened his eyes, and when the turbulence hit, all he could do was mutter, "No. This is wrong. I hate this. How much longer do we have?"

"We just took off, Cap, so it will take us about ninety minutes," she said. "Now come on, you've been through worse. It will be okay."

"It's not natural."

"It's very natural," Haas replied. "Birds do it all the time."

"I'm not a bird," he said, "and I think I'm going to be sick."

"Here, use this," she replied as she tried to hand him an air sickness bag. Lehman refused to release his grip on the seat. "Cap, just hold this."

He shook his head no.

"Are you going to be sick?"

Again, he shook his head no. "I can't breathe," he said as he started to hyperventilate.

"Here," Haas replied as she opened the bag and placed it against his mouth and nose. "Breathe deeply into the bag. Just take deep breaths into the bag, and you'll feel better."

And so it went for ninety minutes. He finally relaxed his grip on his seat when the Beechcraft touched down at Frankfurt/Rhein-Main

Airfield and began to taxi to the arrival hangar, where Lehman and Haas would be met and transported to Richardson's office. "We're taking the train back," he said to Haas.

"Cap, that will take us hours."

"I don't care."

Haas smiled, shook her head, and placed her hand on his. "Okay, we'll take the train."

***

"I know it's all in your report, but I'd like to hear it from you first-hand. Tell me about the meeting with Scholz," Richardson said.

"It went according to plan," Haas replied. "He was aloof at first, and then he became hostile when I suggested he had something to do with Dettmer's death."

"What did he say?"

"He denied any involvement, of course. He threatened to kick us out of his office. And then I asked if he knew the Spaniard, Moreno-Alvarez. I showed him the photo, and then he calmed down a bit. The three of them, Scholz, Dettmer, and Moreno Alvarez, all worked together in Spain. He said that Alvarez had been kicked out of the secret police, that he was too mentally unbalanced even for that organization. They got rid of him because he liked killing people a little too much. All of this happened before the war, and Scholz said he hadn't seen or heard from Alvarez since the mid-1930s."

"So, what was Dettmer's connection to the Spaniard?"

"We can only speculate at this point, sir," Lehman interjected.

"Go ahead, speculate! What does your gut tell you?"

"Our working theory is that Moreno-Alvarez is working as a free agent. For whom, we don't know. We do know he had been helping ODESSA exfiltrate SS and Gestapo officers. He has been seen at the ports of Hamburg and Bremerhaven. So we're working off the theory that Dettmer put the word out that he wanted out of Germany, and the Spaniard answered the call."

Richardson nodded, indicating he understood, but he didn't look satisfied with Lehman's answer. "I want you to keep on this. We need to find this guy."

"We will, sir," Lehman replied.

"So, Luba? What else? Is Scholz going to continue to cooperate with us?"

"Well, I casually mentioned that it would be in his best interest. The Russians would be very interested to know his culpability in the death of thousands of their POWs who were worked to death at Valentin. And I also said that while he wouldn't be able to touch any of the funds held in the Swiss accounts, we could reach a suitable compensation agreement with him."

"And did he take the bait?"

"Oh, yes," Haas replied. "The gold helped to seal our arrangement. I said it was merely a down payment and there would be more to come."

"And tell me again where we got the gold coins?"

Haas nodded toward Lehman. "It came from the Weber woman. She received the coins in the last set of black market transactions she conducted before their operation was broken up."

"I hope she didn't object to our using her payment."

"No. I think she feels it is part of her penance."

"Hmm," mused Richardson. "So, when is your next meeting with Scholz?"

"In two weeks," Haas replied. "But this time, it will be in the American zone. It's safer there, and as long as the Russians don't restrict movement back and forth, we will be able to pull it off."

"Good. Do you think we can trust him?"

"He's very motivated by money sir," Lehman replied. "As far is trust is concerned, building trust is going to take time. I believe he views our relationship as transactional. As long as we pay him, he'll perform. The problem is that he could always go to the highest bidder. We have to find out what makes him tick, aside from money. So, we'll have to work to gain his trust and he'll have to do the same with us."

Richardson frowned and nodded his head in agreement and said, "Well, let's keep him on a very short leash."

"We'll start with simple assignments," Haas said. "He definitely has access and a special relationship with the Russians. That's what has kept him from being arrested and sent to one of the Soviet de-Nazification camps. But, if we can tap into his access, that will help us gain insight into Russian troop movements, basing plans, and military construction projects. That's the hope anyway. We'll just have to see."

"The next time we see him, I want to put him on the box," Richardson said.

"The box, sir? What's that?" Lehman asked.

"The polygraph. A lie detector machine. We're just starting to experiment with them back in the States. I want to see if we should use them here. It might help us weed out bad apples. It could be a great interrogation tool. In fact, we have a team coming over from Washington next week. I want you and Luba to fly down here, and you can see it firsthand. How does that sound?"

"It sounds great, sir," Lehman said as his face went pale at the prospect of another flight on a small airplane.

"I'm looking forward to flying down here, sir," Haas said as she brought her hand to her mouth to stifle a laugh. "That should be a very interesting demonstration, don't you think so, Cap?"

"Very good," Richardson replied. "I will send you both the details."

"That's great, sir, just great," Lehman replied.

"You know, Luba," Richardson said earnestly to Haas, "you've done a remarkable job here. We're very fortunate that you have agreed to work with us full time."

"Thank you, sir. I really appreciate the opportunity. I won't let you . . .," she said, turning to face Lehman, "I won't let you or Captain Lehman down."

"I know you won't. MI6's loss is definitely our gain," Richardson replied. "By the way, I got a call from Banbury. Just yesterday, in fact."

"Oh?" Haas replied.

"Yes, he said many complimentary things about you. He said he was personally very sad to see you leave the organization, but he understood your reasons completely. He wishes you great success. Oh, and he said something odd, but he wanted me to pass it along to you."

"Odd, sir? What would that be?" Haas replied.

"He said he believed you and agreed with your assessment. Do you know what that could mean?"

"Yes, I think I do?"

"What is it?"

"Oh, it's just an old argument, sir. Something we've been butting heads about for years. It's nothing. Nothing at all, sir."

"Good, good. Well, as long as it makes sense to you. As I said, we're pretty damned fortunate to have you working with us, right, Cap?"

"Right sir," Lehman replied. "We are very lucky indeed. "Sir," Lehman said, fumbling for the right words. "What's going to happen with the funds? The money in the Swiss account?"

Richardson expelled a long breath. He leaned back in his chair and said, "I think we need to keep that to ourselves. That information is only known by the three of us in this room, and I'd like to keep it that way. At least for now. I think we could definitely find some good uses for it. We can use it to fund operations in the Soviet zone, maybe even in Poland," he said, looking at Haas. "We have some latitude and there's a window of opportunity for us. But I don't know how long we'll be able to run the show by ourselves and I want to make sure we're in a position of strength. As you know, the president formed the Central Intelligence Group earlier this year. And I'm hearing that Congress plans to overhaul the War Department. And they're thinking about creating a new successor organization to the OSS. The State Department and others are pitching a fit over that. Nobody wants to share their rice bowl, you know what I mean?"

"Yes, sir. We'll obviously keep a lid on it."

"Good, good. We're going to need to develop more assets in the Russian zone of influence. It's going to be a messy business. We're going to have to consort with all sorts of unsavory characters. I'm afraid we're going to have to get chummy with a lot of men like Scholz and even worse. That's the nature of our business, though. It's pretty unsavory. But the money will be necessary. So, let's keep a lid on it."

"Yes, sir. Understand completely," Lehman replied.

"Good, good. Anything else for me?

"Just one last thing sir," Lehman said.

"What is it?

"It's about the Weber woman. I need your help with something."

"Fire away."

***

Lehman and Haas stood outside the headquarters building waiting for the car to pick them up.

"So, are we really going to take the train?" Haas asked.

"No. Let's fly. You're right. It will take too long to get back."

"Are you sure? I don't mind. It might be fun being on a long train ride with you," she said, smiling.

"It's tempting, of course. But we need to get back. There's something very important we need to do."

Chapter Thirty-One

Lehman, Haas, and Lefkowicz stood in silence by the wire fence that bordered the Valentin Bunker, awestruck by its sheer size. It was one thing to look at a reconnaissance photo taken from two thousand feet above, or even the photographs taken up close from the ground. But it was a completely different experience to stand directly in front of the bunker, when its shadow fell over you and cast you into darkness even though there wasn't a cloud in the sky. It was only then that one could appreciate the magnitude of the construction. If buildings had a soul, this building's soul would have been evil. If buildings possessed the power of memory, this building would have held onto the names of everyone who toiled there. If buildings had a voice, its voice would be the sound of grown men crying out at night.

"Do you think there is anyone inside?" Haas asked no one in particular as she stared at the structure.

"I wouldn't be surprised," Lefkowicz answered. "It's likely that the fence has been breached somewhere. And there is still access from the canal on the north end. There's no way to fence that off. If anyone is inside, they're either just trying to find shelter or they're up to no good."

"Yeah, we have to be ready. I don't want to hurt anyone, but we're going to protect ourselves," said Lehman, unholstering his .45 caliber pistol. Haas followed suit and pulled out her sidearm. "So our rules of engagement are not to fire unless we're attacked. We return fire if we are fired upon. Understood?"

"Yes, Cap," Haas and Lefkowicz replied in unison.

Lefkowicz looked at the gate in front of them. It was secured by a heavy chain with a lock that was wrapped around both sides of the gate. He stepped forward and examined the lock as he holstered his weapon. He then removed the backpack he had been carrying, reached inside, and pulled out a pair of heavy bolt cutters.

Lehman gave him a look of surprise and said, "Well, I'm glad one of us thought ahead."

"Weren't you a Boy Scout?" Lefkowicz quipped as he stepped to the gate and, in one quick motion, snapped the chain. "Always prepared. That's their motto, isn't it?" he said, smiling as he pushed the gate, which swung wide open to them. "Age before beauty," he said to Lehman, and with a sweep of his arm, he indicated that the two of them should enter. "I'll bring up the rear."

They walked for about twenty-five meters to the rail line and then walked along the tracks and entered the bunker. Lehman had a hand-drawn map of the bunker. It was a schematic drawing depicting its bays and layout. They struggled to read the map in the darkness and had to stop several times to get their bearings. It was pitch black inside, and the only light came from their flashlights.

Finally, after about ten minutes of walking in the darkness, Lehman said, "This is it. This should be bay thirteen."

"Bay thirteen. This is where Therese said he'd be," Haas replied.

Bay thirteen was intended to be a dry dock, and at twenty-six meters, it was the tallest bay in the bunker. The beams from their flashlights lit up the interior, and the only sound that could be heard was the echo of the constant drip of water from the ceiling into a shallow pool below.

"I wish I could say that I could feel his presence," Haas said. "I wish I could hear him calling out to me from this place, telling me that everything was all right, and that everything will return to the way it was. That's what he would say if he could. He was always so optimistic. He always believed the world was a good place and that this whole war was just an aberration. He wanted the war to end so that we could be together, live our lives out, raise a family. He wanted children, lots of them."

Haas panned her flashlight across the darkness of the bay, its beam casting a conical sphere of light in one area before moving on and leaving the area in the blackness of the bunker.

"I wish I could feel him. But I feel nothing," Haas said. "There's nothing."

She stood there for a moment with the flashlight in her hand, and Lefkowicz walked over to stand at her side. He raised his massive arm and put it around her shoulder. She looked at him briefly and then allowed herself to lean into his stocky frame. He held onto her tightly and tried to offer her some form of solace and comfort, Even Lefkowicz, a man who had seen death many times, could only offer her the words, which he spoke in Polish, "Dear sister. I'm so sorry."

Lehman moved to her other side, wrapped his arms around them, and they all melted into an embrace within the darkness of the bunker.

"He died for nothing," she said. "They all did. For nothing."

"I don't know, Luba," Lehman said. "He died fighting for his home-land, and he never gave up. And we know who he is and where he fell. That's more than we can say about everyone else who died here. We don't know how many there were. We don't know where they all went. Most just disappeared. We don't even know their names. But we know his name. Wojchiech Dabrowski. He died here and we can say his name." At the top of his lungs with all his might, Lehman yelled, "Wojchiech Dabrowski," and the sound of his name reverberated over and over throughout the cavernous bunker.

As they stood there together in a tight embrace and surveyed the dark bunker, its expanse seemed endless. Their flashlights created eerie shadows on the dark walls. Finally it was Haas who broke the embrace and softly said to them, "I've seen enough. Let's go."

Chapter Thirty-Two

It was late in the afternoon on a blustery October day. Gusts of wind swirled around the docks, kicking up dust and debris. The sun hung low in the sky and daylight was already giving way to nighttime. Lehman walked with Therese, her children in hand, to the ship's gangplank where they would board. They paused together as she looked up at the ship.

"Is this our boat, Mommy?" asked Willi.

"Yes, my love. It is."

"And we're going to America?

"Yes, eventually. We're going to America. To a city called Louisville. But first we're going to Canada."

Lehman looked down at his young cousins and smiled. They were dressed in matching overcoats, a gift from his sister. "My sister, Rose, and her husband, Walter, will meet you in Ontario. They'll be able to help you with your entrance and work visas. I know she's really looking forward to meeting you and the children. You'll have a job, and you'll be able to start a new life. My sister really needs a good bookkeeper. You'll be a big help to her and Walter." Lehman looked at the passports in Therese's hand. "You have your passport and your new identity. Just stick to the story that we worked out, and everything will be fine."

Therese looked at the documents she held. They were the best that money could buy. Technically, they were forged, but even an expert would find them to be perfect. Next to her photograph on her passport was the name Katharina Eger, the name of Therese's sister who had perished in the battle of Berlin. Her entry visa to Canada also bore that name, along with the fact that she was a widow. Katharina, like Therese, had lost her husband. He had fallen not in Bosnia as Therese's husband had, but in Crete. Her sister, just a year younger than Therese, also had two children who perished in Berlin. Now, young Willi and Anna Karolina would take their places on the new identity papers she possessed, all of which were created by master document forgers in the employ of the CIC.

"My sister never wanted anything to do with the Nazis," Therese said. "She said 'no good would ever come from it.' She was so right about that. She's the one who should be going to America."

"We can't undo the past," Lehman said. "All we can do is try to make the future better. You'll have that chance now, and so will the children."

Therese stepped up to Lehman and threw her arms around his neck, stifling an urge to cry. "Make sure you look in on Mama and Papa. I wish they were coming with us, but Papa wouldn't even think about it. He's so stubborn sometimes."

"It runs in the family," Lehman replied, and Therese smiled.

"Watch over them, please?"

"I will. Luba and I are going over for dinner on Sunday. Just as you always did. We're both looking forward to it. The things your mother can do with Spam. It's delicious," bringing a hearty laugh from Therese. Then she turned serious.

"Take care of Luba, too. She's a woman of remarkable courage. You have found someone very special. Don't screw it up," she added.

Lehman laughed. "I know. She reminds me every day. Don't worry, I'll take care of her and Uncle Karl and Aunt Johanne. They'll be looked after. I'll make sure of it."

"Will you come visit us in Louisville? Will we see you there? I'm sure your sisters miss you terribly."

"I will. Soon. I promise. I have to take care of some things here first. But hopefully in the New Year."

"Good. I want the children to know their cousin, the American army captain. I want them to know what he did to help us."

"I promise. Luba's been bugging me about it, too. She says I've talked to her so much about Louisville that she wants to live there. That'd be something, don't you think?"

"Hmm. I think that would be wonderful." Therese started to say something else, but her words were drowned out by a long blast from the ship's horn. The children squealed and covered their ears.

"I think we had better board now," Therese said as the sound from the ship's horn died down.

"Yes." Lehman knelt on one knee to speak to the children. "You'll both be good children and obey your mother, right? I will visit you as soon as I can, okay?"

Therese took the children's hands and walked slowly up the ship's gangplank, and then she stopped midway and turned around to face Lehman.

"Goodbye, Cap."

"Goodbye ... Katharina."

She looked at Lehman one last time and felt her emotions rise, realizing that she was finally free. She turned her back to him and took a tentative step, and she and the children began to slowly climb up the gangplank, steps that would take them away from the only life they had ever known.

Lehman watched as they reached the top of the gangplank, where she showed their tickets and passports to a purser. He checked her passport photo carefully as he looked at her, then he smiled and gave her the perfunctory "Welcome aboard, and welcome aboard, children" as he waved them through. She turned one last time and looked down at Lehman.

"*Auf Wiedersehen,*" Lehman whispered from the dock below. He watched as a woman now known as Katharina Eger and the children turned and disappeared among the passengers on the crowded deck. He reached for a cigarette and fumbled as usual for his lighter, but he quickly remembered the right pocket. He lit his cigarette, inhaled, and then watched the smoke as it curled up into the early evening sky.

From the shadows behind him a figure approached. It was Haas.

"Are you following me?" Lehman asked without looking at her but staring up at the ship. Haas walked over and stood next to him, then slipped her arm around his waist.

"So, she and the children will begin their new life. She's lucky. Lucky to have you looking out for her. It could have turned out far worse for her."

"It was part of the deal. It was always part of the deal. She gave us Dettmer. And a whole lot more."

"So. Will you take me to Louisville someday?"

"Yes, I will."

"Good. I want that very much. I want to meet your sisters."

Lehman took one last, deep draw on his cigarette and dropped the butt to the ground, where he crushed it with the tip of his shoe.

"Do you remember what Banbury said during his briefing? On the day we met?"

She shook her head. "No, not really."

"He said that we couldn't put them all in jail. There'd be nobody left to run the country. I didn't agree with him at the time, but now that I've thought about it, I think he was probably right. At some point, we have to give them back their country and see if they can rise up and do the right thing."

"If that happens, it will be the first time in this century."

Lehman gave her a very serious look, then burst out in laughter.

"There's always a first time, right?"

"What is the saying? I'm not going to hold my breath."

"Yeah. Well, maybe you're right. So, fancy a drink?" he asked.

"I'd love one. I'm parched."

Lehman extended his arm to Haas. She looked surprised and then amused as she took his arm and they walked away, arm-in-arm down the dock.

"What are we going to do now?" she asked.

Lehman paused and looked into Haas's eyes. "After our drink? I don't have a clue. But we'll think of something. Let's go," he said, and then they turned and continued to walk off, arm in arm together, into the crisp autumn night.

ACKNOWLEDGEMENTS

The act of writing is a solitary process, but it is not a lonely one. While the writer must commit to the act and art of the craft, there are more often than not, many individuals who have supported the writer's effort along the way. This is definitely the case for me. This novel would never have been completed without the encouragement and support of many people, and for that I am extremely grateful.

I offer sincere thanks to my dear friends Donna and Steve Shea, Ned and Sandy Criscimagna, Yvonne and Ed Willits, Debra Kushnick, Cathy Pannunzio, and Barbara Luna, who acted as alpha and beta readers. They patiently read the early, less than perfect drafts, they offered superb suggestions, and words of encouragement.

The editing process can be traumatic for a writer. My editor, Susan Burke was a delight. She tightened phrases, helped me clarify thoughts, and eliminate passages that didn't serve to move the story line forward. She made this a better novel. The aforementioned Donna Shea, in concert with my wife Jody meticulously proofread the work, helping to eliminate those annoying extra spaces and other typos that serve only to distract readers.

If you are reading this book in paperback or on your favorite eReader, that is because my wife Jody, to whom I have dedicated this book, did the digital typesetting and formatting. She also designed and launched my author website, karlwegener.com. She is my life partner in so many ways. And while I may have written the words, nobody would be able to read them without her effort.

Karl Wegener is a former intelligence analyst and Russian linguist who served in the United States Army during the Cold War. He currently resides on the East coast of the United States with his wife and two dogs. Grown Men Cry Out at Night is his first novel. www.karlwegener.com.